Into the Vines

JON ENGLUND

1

The first 45 minutes of the bus trip out of Santiago was relatively flat. The city blended into suburbs and then countryside. I saw small farms that didn't appear that different from those I was used to seeing in Wisconsin, minus the animals. While there were some cattle, I saw mostly sheep and goat, even some llamas. With the prairie now brown in the dead of winter, the scrawny animals appeared hungry.

The foothills were a mixture of brown and white, but looking out the front of the bus I could see that it was the last brown I was going to see for some time. While there appeared to be a handful of private homes set amongst the hills, I continued to see mostly farms. They were scattered about haphazardly, some appearing to lack any level ground at all. And they sat fully exposed, the land devoid of trees. I was surprised by the lack of vegetation at such a low altitude. With Santiago at less than two thousand feet above sea level, we couldn't have been at more than five thousand feet by now.

It was eleven a.m. on a beautiful sunny day. I'd selected a mid-morning bus departure to assure the entirety of my trip would take place during daylight. This had been one thing Fernando had been insistent upon when offering advice for my trip. He'd often referred to the drive from Santiago to Mendoza as the most spectacular route he'd ever taken. In fact he was so moved by the 'spiritual experience', as he liked to call it, that when he visited home he rarely flew into Mendoza. Even for shorter stays, he often sacrificed the efficiency of a 45 minute flight for the scenic trans-Andean bus ride. The only exception was weather; Fernando had mentioned the pass would sometimes close for days at a time in winter after big storms.

One hour into the drive, the grade of the two lane highway escalated. I felt pressure in my ears as we started our ascent for the summit. We passed one final village, and then the valley narrowed. For the next 30 minutes the bus climbed, with no outside signs of civilization. No gas stations, no restaurants, no exits. I was taken aback by the remoteness of the route. I'd read there were only a handful of passes across the Andes along the 3000 mile border between Chile and Argentina. And I knew the route from Santiago to Mendoza was by far the most traveled. Yet with the exception of light highway traffic, we were otherwise surrounded by a barren land-scape. I looked south out the window, wondering how far I could travel without seeing a single person.

I was also surprised by the morphology of the mountains. Now immersed in the heart of the Andes, the peaks were sharp, often jagged, creating a sense of hostility. They were covered by irregular snow drifts, further emphasizing the nakedness of the terrain. And no two mountains appeared to have the same shape, with each peak offering a slightly different degree of slope.

I felt the bus working hard to climb now, the gears grinding, and the smell of diesel intensifying. We'd slowed to no more than 20 miles per hour. And as the bus made a sharp left turn forcing me against the window, the challenge ahead became explicit: I approximated no fewer than 20 consecutive 180 degree switchbacks, each perched directly upon the next. Each level of road was slightly shorter than the one below, funneling the highway into a narrow gap between two towering peaks. As we inched toward the summit, I could see skiers making their way down the open face of the majestic peak which abutted the north side of the highway. With the mountains hugging the road, it created the appearance that the people were skiing amongst the vehicles that had become bunched up by the steep ascent.

I reached into my backpack to pull out my camera. I confirmed from the man sitting in front of me that the ski area was Portillo. Fernando had raved of the area, and I remembered from my reading that it was located just on the Chilean side of the border. But I'd never imagined the mountain this isolated. Shifting to an open seat across the aisle to get a better view, I saw only a single large building at the base, presumably a hotel. Otherwise there was nothing; just a stand-alone ski area in the middle of the Andes Mountains.

As we passed by Portillo the road leveled out and I saw signs indicating we were approaching the border. We entered a long tunnel, then slowed upon emerging as traffic bottlenecked. We arrived to two single story aluminum buildings I presumed to be the border control. Fernando had told me the duration of the trip from Santiago to Mendoza could be quite variable depending upon the line at customs. On a busy summer weekend, the process could take hours. I hoped that on a Tuesday in the middle of winter it would be much quicker. I followed the others as they gathered their belongings and headed toward the larger building.

Off the bus, in the shadows of the adjacent mountains, I was immediately cold. Able to see my breath, it couldn't have been more than 30 degrees. I reached into my backpack and pulled out a jacket. Across the parking lot there was a large Argentine flag next to a sign which read 'Bienvenidos a Argentina. Paso de los Libertadores. Altura 3500 metros.' I did the math, realizing we were above 11,000 feet. Recognizing a good photo opportunity, I started toward the sign, but was deterred by a military officer brandishing a semi-automatic who steered me back with the others.

Inside the building I was relieved to find relatively few people. I stepped into the 'foreigner' line behind a well-dressed man eager to talk. He was in route to Mendoza to visit his daughter. She'd moved to Mendoza more than a decade before to find work. There she'd married an Argentine and started a family, and he'd been coming to visit every six months since. But now with the Chilean economy surging, and political uncertainty in Argentina, they were thinking of moving back to Santiago. He thought this might be his last regular trip to Mendoza.

Despite a few awkward stumbles, I was proud of myself for maintaining a conversation in Spanish, albeit primarily in a passive role. This was now my third day in South America and it was by far my longest conversation to date. And I felt for the most part I'd held my own. I wanted to ask what the man meant about 'political uncertainty', but decided the answer might challenge my conversational skills.

The interaction also marked the first time I realized the pronunciation of my name would be different during my stay in South America. The man tried two different times to pronounce "Jake" during our conversation. The first time it sounded like 'yake', while on the second occasion I thought he pronounced it closer to 'shake'. After so many years I'd forgotten how difficult the name had been for Fernando's family during our gatherings.

Within 30 minutes I was through customs and back on the bus. The process had been smooth, albeit inconsistent. While they'd stamped my passport without a single question, the customs agent had insisted upon going through each item in my luggage. But I wasn't complaining. I was in Argentina now, that much closer to settling in my home for the next four months.

The descent on the Argentine side was of lower grade, allowing a less serpentine route for the highway. And there was much less snow on this side of the pass. Where snowdrifts had risen to seven or eight feet at the margins of the road on the Chilean side, they were now no more than three feet. I saw a clear stream tumbling out of the valley to the north and looked unsuccessfully for a sign indicating its name or our approximate location. I pictured myself back there with my fly rod in a few months when the weather permitted.

Within minutes of our restart, I heard murmuring from other passengers and saw them pointing out the windows on the north side. I again shifted back across the aisle, and immediately saw what the excitement was about. Towering over the smaller peaks in the foreground, exposed under a brilliant blue sky, was a single dominant mountain I knew had to be Aconcagua. I recognized it from pictures I'd seen at Fernando's uncle's home in Madison. It had two distinct peaks, one slightly taller than the other, with a shallow dip in between. It gave the appearance of a condor with its wings spread. It was spectacular.

I felt embarrassed for not having been watching for it. It was a source of great pride for a boy growing up in Mendoza and I'd heard countless stories from Fernando. At almost 23,000 feet, it was the highest mountain in the Americas. It was one of the seven summits of the world, and therefore an important tourist attraction for Mendoza. I knew technically it was considered an easier climb, although one would have thought otherwise after hearing Fernando's stories.

Fernando had grown up hearing tales about the magical powers of the great Aconcagua. Although he was more of a fisher/skier than a hiker, his intrigue with the mountain had always fueled a desire to make it to the summit. He made his first trip to base camp with a group of scouts at age 12. And while they had no intention of going higher, stories shared from climbers on their way out had strengthened his desire. At 16 he made his first attempt to reach the summit with a friend and his father. But after two nights at base camp in the middle of summer, just before the first stage of their ascent, it snowed a foot and they were forced to abandon. A year later, back again with the same climbing party, his dreams were again dashed when the father took an awkward step around 18,000 feet and ruptured his achilles.

Undaunted by these failures, Fernando returned for one final attempt the January before he moved to Wisconsin. This time accompanied by three childhood friends, the group cruised to the Colera camp, their last planned night before their push to the summit. But that night, Fernando and one of his friends developed a headache and shortness of breath and the group was forced to descend. Fernando had often voiced regret in not taking another night at a midlevel camp, knowing an additional night of acclimatization may have allowed him to fulfill his dream.

I again whipped out my camera, attempting to capture the immensity of the mountain. While I had no intention to summit during my stay, I hoped to hike to base camp. In part for the views it promised to offer, but also for what it would mean to my friend.

Further down the valley we passed Penitentes ski resort, every bit as isolated as Portillo with but a few buildings at the base. I was surprised by how full the parking lot was on a weekday, even though August marked the heart of the ski season. Smaller than Portillo, I was again struck by its openness. There wasn't a single tree on the mountain. The majority of the terrain consisted of several large bowls separated by deep rocky crevasses. It would be vastly different from skiing I'd done in the Rockies.

Seeing the ski area made me think about Sara. Her visit was still six weeks away, but that hadn't deterred me from starting to plan for our time together. While there were many things I hoped to pack in during her short stay, skiing was at the top of the list. She was an accomplished skier, and couldn't wait to experience skiing in South America. While Penitentes didn't offer the acreage or snowfall of Mendoza province's prized resort of Las Leñas, it was half the distance from Mendoza city. I thought it might make a nice day trip if time didn't allow a trip to Las Leñas.

Continuing our gradual descent, we passed the city of Upspallata, where rows of tall Poplar trees were more attention grabbing than the small city itself. I realized it was the first vegetation I'd seen in over two hours. And later as we passed the city of Potrerillos, with the 20,000 foot giants now replaced by humbler peaks, I caught my first glimpse of the plain that awaited us below. The brown, flat terrain stood in stark contrast to the still white, mountainous scene from which we were emerging. The Rio Mendoza, which had started as a small, clear river near the top of the pass, was now swollen and brown, having taken on the color of the rock which surrounded it.

I shivered at the realization of how close I was now. After so many years locked up by the diligent pursuit of career, and with the ordinariness of my first job awaiting my return, my trip was finally becoming reality. Now was my time to break from routine and seek the adventure that had evaded me for so long. And to provide a long overdue alternative experience that would help confirm all my hard work had been done with proper purpose.

Yet as spectacular as the first four hours of the trip had been for its unparalleled beauty, it was a brief, surprising interaction that occurred shortly after Potrerillos that would prove the most memorable aspect of my trans-Andean journey. Lost in thought about the motive for my journey, I was startled from my trance by the sudden realization that someone had sat down beside me. I sat up and turned to meet the smiling face of my most unexpected seatmate.

"Pretty spectacular views, aren't they?" she said in annunciated Spanish.

It was a young woman, about my age, with dark brown hair, dark eyes, and olive colored skin. I assumed she must have been sitting somewhere toward the back. I couldn't believe I hadn't noticed her at some point during the customs process.

"Amazing," I responded, shaking my head as much in surprise by her approach as in affirmation of my answer.

She smiled reassuringly. "Are you from the United States?"

"Yes," I answered, still somewhat rattled by the conversation. "I've visiting Mendoza for the next few months."

"A few months?" she said raising her eyebrows. "That's a long stay. What do you have planned during your time here?"

"Improve my Spanish," I said returning the smile. "And just take in the city and the culture. I'm starting a new job soon and wanted to take advantage of some time off to experience something new." I impressed myself with my smooth Spanish delivery, especially given the somewhat uncomfortable situation.

"Well you've made a great choice. Mendoza is my home and I think you'll find it a most welcoming city."

"Great," I said. "I have a friend from Mendoza back home whose been telling me about the city for years. This is a trip I've wanted to take for a long time. Any suggestions for my stay?"

She measured the question, clearly intent on providing a thoughtful answer. "Well there's really so much. The downtown is beautiful. You'll end up spending much of your time there. And the mountains are so close. Hiking, climbing, rafting, there are outdoor opportunities everywhere."

"Sounds fantastic," I responded, admiring how comfortable she was in conversation.

She continued. "But I suppose the two things I'd say you have to experience are the tango and our vineyards. The tango is a symbol of Argentina. While it's not as plentiful in Mendoza as in Buenos Aires, there are still good options. And the vineyards are the soul of our province. Take time to visit as many as you can to enjoy our beautiful wines."

I nodded. "Good suggestions. I'll add them to my list."

She smiled. But then, as abruptly as she'd arrived, she stood up from her seat.

"Well I didn't mean to bother you," she said. "I'm always interested in talking with foreigners and hearing their stories. I hope you have a wonderful time and accomplish your goals."

"Thank you. It was nice to meet you," I said, struggling to comprehend the brevity of the conversation.

She gave a subtle wave, turned, and walked toward the back. I leaned out, just in time to watch her take her seat in the second to last row. She smiled again as our eyes met briefly before she slid over next to the window out of sight.

I tried to analyze what had just transpired. A sudden, direct approach; a brief, pleasant conversation; and a quick, almost awkward departure. I never even had the chance to ask her name. What was the intent behind this visit? Was she indeed intrigued by my international background? Was she just trying to be friendly to a foreigner? Or was there more to it? And if so, was her rapid retreat an indication of her disappointment with our interaction? It was all very odd.

I coaxed myself into returning my focus to the tapering foothills; and I redirected my thoughts to Sara.

Sometime later we arrived to the small city of Cacheuta. There I saw a beautiful old hotel at the river's edge and a suspension footbridge across the river. And minutes later, following a few harrowing turns, I started to see buildings which marked the transition into the city of Mendoza. With daylight waning, lights were popping on and the city was coming alive.

As Fernando had promised, it had indeed been a spectacular ride. As we began our entry into the city proper, and my pulse began to quicken, I thought about all I'd seen during a full day of travel: the steep winding route, the grandeur of Aconcagua, and the astounding harshness and isolation of the Andes.

But what I couldn't appreciate at the time was just how profound of an effect the bus ride would prove to have. Not just on my stay in Mendoza, but on the direction of the life plan I'd been meticulously sculpting for many years. At that moment I had no idea that the unforeseen three minute interaction I'd struggled to decipher would prove the first of a dramatic series of events that would change my life forever, in a way I'd never have considered a remote possibility during the long build-up to my trip.

2

The origin of my travel to Argentina is both complex and remote. I've given it a lot of thought, and I believe it was rooted in my upbringing and spurned on by experiences I had, or maybe didn't have, throughout my college and post-graduate years.

Living less than 10 miles away from us, just north of Madison, my maternal grandparents spent a lot of time with my immediate family throughout my childhood. My grandfather Robert had been a professor at the University of Wisconsin and was a strong influence on me. Raised on a farm south of Madison, he transported his dairy farmer work ethic to the classroom and became a no-nonsense academic. He dedicated 40 years to the university and took tremendous pride in his work. To this day I have vivid memories of being awoken before sunrise to prepare for elementary spelling tests when my parents were away.

His work ethic and fervor for academics were surpassed only by that of his daughter Jill. My mother devoted much of her adult life to elementary education, and surely no second grader ever forgot her. She preached ambition, hard-work, and diligence as the recipe to success in all matters of life. And academics came first before everything but family.

So with an impassioned academic support team guiding me every step of the way, a scholarly career path was never in doubt. By my senior year in high school I'd decided on a career in medicine. And while the inspiration for academic success came from my mother's side of the family, it was my father's side that steered me toward my choice of career. It was a popular, albeit somewhat predictable decision.

My paternal grandfather had been an internist, having returned to school after a short enlistment in the Navy during World War 2. Grandpa Bill had cared for the whole family. I can still remember watching grandpa stitch up my brother John when he went over the handle bars during a sprint down our grandparent's driveway. And I remember countless visits to grandpa's office for my frequent sinus problems created by a lengthy list of environmental allergies.

My father Eric followed his father into medicine, choosing orthopedic surgery and settling into a small semi-rural practice 25 miles west of Madison. I often had the opportunity to round with him on weekends as a child, and sometimes even watch from the corner of the operating room for emergency calls. I always admired my father's calming demeanor and methodical approach to medicine. He effortlessly garnered his patient's trust with his compassion, and always seemed in complete control.

By my senior year of high school I'd acquired more exposure to medicine than most first year medical students. And with math and science always easy, my mind was made up. And if my intentions ever strayed for a moment, I needed only to talk with my two older brothers who were forging ahead with careers in medicine of their own. Ben, who was five years older than me, had followed grandpa's legacy to John Hopkins. John, three years my senior, had stayed close to home and was enrolled in a pre-med curriculum at the University of Wisconsin (although he would later change course and pursue a business degree).

After surviving my mother's arduous college admission process, which started a year earlier than for most, I ultimately settled on Wisconsin too. It allowed me to stay near John, with whom I was much closer. And it swayed me away from Macalester, my mom's alma mater, and my initial inclination I might be more comfortable in a small liberal arts environment.

Despite a few early struggles, which my family ascribed to typical freshman distractions, I soon buckled down and fell back in line. I quickly rediscovered and refocused on the plan created for me by my mother and maternal grandfather, which I've always referred to as the Schmidt master plan. By my second year at Madison, things had fallen into place academically. While biochemistry was a natural choice as a major with a long list of pre-medicine coursework to fulfill, my decision to minor in Spanish came as a surprise to all, myself included.

I was mostly an A student in high school, with one glaring exception. Unlike my brothers who had excelled in language, I struggled with Spanish throughout school. While its Latin derivation made reading and writing simple enough, I was what my mom termed 'phonetically challenged.' I labored with my teacher's native accent, and became so self-conscious with my own speaking that I participated only when obligated. My C grade as a freshman improved to B grades during my sophomore and junior years before I gladly dropped the subject as a senior.

Yet the opportunity to acquire a modest number of retro-credits, along with a not so gentle nudge from mom, convinced me to give it one more try in college. And surprisingly I found it more enjoyable this time around. My first two Spanish professors were American, each speaking with an accent easier to understand. And to my amazement there were many students who spoke an even more Americanized version of Spanish than I did. This provided a less intimidating environment for me to participate in.

So with two classes under my belt after my freshman year, I decided to stick with Spanish and declare it as a minor. I envisioned it a useful skill in my future medical practice. After some encouragement from a favorite professor, I went a step further and decided to spend the spring semester of my junior year in Spain. In good shape with my science requirements, I thought it would offer a nice break from routine.

But fate never allowed the trip to occur. On New Year's Day, 1989, four days before my scheduled departure, my dad had a heart attack. He underwent emergent surgery and spent two weeks in intensive care. I was overwhelmed by the sight of my father in his ICU bed. He'd always been a model of health, and I never imagined seeing him like this. When he stabilized, my parents tried to convince me to fly over late. But I'd lost my desire to travel. I knew dad had a long road of rehabilitation ahead and I wanted to be there. So I enrolled in classes in Madison, and moved home for the semester.

Despite missing out on my abroad experience, by the start of my senior year I'd still managed to complete my Spanish courses and needed only three science classes per semester to finish my pre-med requirements. During that fall semester, in an otherwise unremarkable biochemistry seminar, I had the chance to meet Fernando, who'd come to Madison from Mendoza. His uncle was a professor at Wisconsin, and had convinced Fernando to come live with his family and enroll at the university. Fernando had chosen a soil science major, and although he'd been there three years, he maintained a strong accent and struggled to communicate with other students in a very interactive class.

I developed an immediate friendship with Fernando, based partly on language, but mostly upon a shared interest in two hobbies I'd developed years earlier. During the summer after my freshman year in college, I'd lived in Vail and worked at a luxurious golf resort as a greens keeper. And while the work was monotonous, and the early mornings dreadful, I'd gotten a taste of a lifestyle I became convinced I wanted to live. After work I stuck around and played golf alongside members, many of whom counted Vail as just one of several country club memberships. On the weekends I found summer snow, backcountry skiing with other golf club employees. And when the snow ran out in mid-July, I hiked to high mountain lakes and streams for spectacular fly-fishing. Those three months in Vail had shaped my vision for the future.

Before coming to Madison, Fernando had spent three years working at Las Leñas resort in southern Mendoza province. There he spent winter months working as a ski patrol and the rest of the year working as a cook at the one restaurant that remained open year round. Although he disliked his work in the kitchen, the late afternoon/evening work schedule provided the flexibility to spend long hours fly-fishing the area's many rivers.

Since my summer in Vail two years prior, I'd only been back on my skis once. And although I'd heard there was good fly-fishing in western Wisconsin, I'd never gotten up the momentum to explore. But it didn't take long for Fernando to rekindle my passion for skiing and fishing.

Over spring break Fernando joined me for a week at Vail. Fernando had skied a small area outside of Madison during his first winter in Wisconsin and been so disappointed he hadn't skied since. But Vail quickly reshaped his impression of skiing in the United States. We enjoyed several days of fresh powder at the resort before finishing the trip in the backcountry where I'd learned to become a decent skier. Then on the first Saturday of April, opening day of the fly-fishing season in Wisconsin, Fernando had me out on Black Earth Creek west of Madison, struggling to throw my fly through sleet and 20 mile per hour winds. It was an easy friendship for both of us that grew stronger throughout our senior year.

Meeting Fernando also gave me chances to employ my much improved Spanish. He often invited me to his family's house for Sunday afternoon meals, scheduled around Argentine soccer games the family never missed.

While I wasn't overly entertained by the games, I loved to listen to the family ramble in Spanish. I quickly realized the Argentine accent was quite distinct from others I'd encountered during my studies, yet surprisingly easy to understand. And while Fernando took great pleasure highlighting my difficulties with the language, the rest of the family was patient and supportive and I soon became comfortable in their presence. My days of finding the language intimidating faded away.

About the only thing Fernando and I couldn't bring ourselves to do together was study. In that arena we were as different as two students could be.

I inherited my work ethic from my mother. I was incomparably regimented in my studies. Starting my freshman year of college, I divided semesters into four week blocks. On the first day of each block I sat down and printed out a study schedule. I set timelines for each project. I scheduled in study hours for each exam, starting one week out for midterms and two weeks for finals. I'd assign each exam a number between one and ten based on both projected difficulty and importance and then would use this number in a formula to set aside appropriate amounts of study time. I never allowed myself to study after 11 p.m., in large part because my methodical preparation never left me feeling like I had to.

Fernando took a more laid back approach. He didn't believe in study schedules and rarely studied before ten at night. He often pulled all-nighters, believing he did his best work under pressure. We were paired together for a final presentation in our biochemistry class. We divided the work in half and agreed to meet the week before the presentation to integrate our material. Fernando postponed the meeting three times and finally finished his part at three a.m. of the day of the presentation. We were forced to give the presentation without ever reviewing what the other had put together. It was an approach I'd later learn was as much Argentine as it was my friend's.

Fernando went home to Mendoza for the summer before moving to Pennsylvania to pursue graduate work. He tried to convince me to travel with him to Mendoza and enjoy the Argentine ski season. But I'd committed months before to a summer internship my father had arranged. And with medical school starting in mid-August, it didn't leave enough time. It was another near miss fueling my desire for the international adventure that was still years away.

3

I turned up the intensity another notch as medical school got underway. My study schedule was more rigorous than ever. With the exception of a couple hours per week when I'd run on the treadmill, my weekdays all pretty much looked the same: class until late afternoon, home for dinner, and then off to the library until ten at night. I did most of my studying alone, feeling that studying with classmates interfered with maintenance of my strict routine.

I was a little more generous to myself on weekends. I went out for drinks most Friday nights with classmates. I played pick-up basketball at the gym Saturday afternoons. And I made it a routine to eat Sunday dinner with my parents, who enjoyed having one of their sons close by. But in between, I spent most of my time with my head buried in my books. That was, after all, the core tenet of the Schmidt master plan.

Although Fernando was now away, I continued to spend time with his family. I had an open invitation to Sunday gatherings, and initially attended at least once per month. But as correspondence between Fernando and me waned, so did my Sunday appearances. By the time I transitioned from the classroom to clinical rotations during the third year of medical school, my communication with Fernando and his family was limited to infrequent phone conversations.

My study routine allowed little time for dating. Or at least that was my excuse. I went on a few dates with a classmate during spring of our first year, but it didn't last long. I took her to a jazz bar on our third date and she talked throughout the entire show. I enjoyed the music more than our conversation and found myself tuning her out during the show's second set. We didn't go out again. And although the relationship was short-lived, it counted as my third longest to date.

During my junior year in high school, I dated a girl named Melissa, the daughter of one of my mother's friends. Melissa was an excellent student, and an even better athlete. She was a state champion tennis player by her sophomore year and a standout on the high school soccer team. And in the eyes of my mom, she was the perfect girlfriend.

My mother had started to worry about me by my junior year. My brothers had both been extremely social, each having several girlfriends during high school. But I was awkward when it came to the opposite sex. While my physical appearance was not a deterrent, 6'0 by my junior year with greenish blue eyes and curly blonde hair, I lacked the social confidence of my brothers. When I hadn't sniffed a relationship by that fall, my mother took matters into her own hands. She invited Melissa's family for dinner, had me rent a movie, and all but locked the two of us in the basement together. Melissa had just come out of a bad relationship so her mother was thrilled to oblige with the arrangement.

Their scheme was a success and Melissa and I were boyfriend and girlfriend within weeks. She was smart and sweet, and I was smitten. We studied together on weeknights and watched movies on weekends. With neither of us comfortable in the party scene, we spent most of our free time alone together. I attended all of her sporting events, although I struggled with her successes in the athletic arena. I was an average cross country runner, and lacked the hand-eye coordination to be good in any ball sports. Although we were equals in the classroom, I slowly developed a feeling of inadequacy around her. She seemed to sense this and our relationship staled.

It took three years before I found myself in a relationship again. This time it was me who took the initiative, finally mustering the courage to ask out a girl with whom I'd shared science classes for two semesters. Erin was a beautiful girl from a Chicago suburb, and I'd been drawn to her from the first time I'd seen her. She too was planning a future in medicine, so our course schedules were similar. But while she was studious by nature, the college lifestyle was shifting her focus away from academics. She'd rushed a sorority that year, and her sisterly duties soon dominated her calendar.

Although uncomfortable at first, I gradually began to enjoy the numerous functions to which I was invited. Within weeks of our first date Erin had secured me a fake ID, and bars and fraternity parties became an almost every Friday and Saturday night occurrence. Her striking beauty was good for my social artlessness. Having Erin at my side helped me overcome the intimidation of being in the type of social environments that soon dominated my weekends. While it wasn't my strongest academic semester, it was a time I'd remember fondly for years to come.

Gradually however, I came to realize Erin's struggles with self-esteem. She became clingy to the point of suffocation, and after six months together I needed out. This time the end came with a sense of relief. Although the fun was undeniable, I'd lost my sense of independence. And I'd gotten away from the order and routine upon which I'd always thrived. Away from Erin, and away from the fraternity parties, I redirected my focus back to my studies. I knew that was where it needed to be.

4

My third year of medical school was an exciting time. Having been around medicine my whole life, the transition from classroom to clinicals was a welcomed change. And unlike many classmates who struggled to choose the type of medicine they wanted to pursue, by midway through the year my mind was made up.

By the end of my summer internship following my senior year of college, I'd narrowed my choice to two. Orthopedic surgery was a natural fit. My dad was proud of his field, and often joked with my brothers and me about joining his practice and ushering him into retirement. I enjoyed orthopedics, especially the subspecialty of sports medicine, which allowed the surgeon to cover sporting events and seemed to provide a less demanding work schedule.

The other field of medicine to which I had a natural affinity was radiology. I'd always enjoyed it when dad would bring home films to show my brothers and me. And I'd spent most of a summer working as an assistant radiology technician in my father's office following a sudden employee departure. Then during my two week summer internship, I realized my methodical problem solving approach was a good fit for radiology. The radiologist with whom I worked constantly stressed the importance of working through the entire checklist of structures to be evaluated, rather than jumping to the sometimes obvious abnormality.

By January of my third year, having rotated through both specialties, my decision was made. Surprisingly, I hadn't enjoyed the operating room as I assumed I would. While I'd watched dad operate many times before, I'd always watched from a distance, my role limited to that of a spectator. Now asked to participate, albeit as a second assistant, I struggled with the anxiety of the environment. When things didn't go as planned, I became flustered. I'd never participated in such an intense, high pressure setting, and I found I didn't handle it as well as I'd envisioned.

Disappointed by this realization, I went straight from orthopedics into radiology. And the difference was dramatic from the outset. I was immediately comfortable in the relaxed, low-key environment. I found the dark reading rooms soothing. No one ever raised their voices. And when difficult cases arose, you sauntered over to the next cubicle to confer with a colleague.

The lifestyle also seemed attractive. The radiologists with whom I worked took minimal call. And with the advent of digital radiology, I was assured that in the near future most call would be taken from home. I spent my last week of the rotation paired with a musculoskeletal radiologist, reading MRIs of different joints. With my interest in orthopedics I found this type of imaging particularly fascinating. I knew it was the perfect fit.

I was on cruise control the rest of the year. I completed all of my required rotations, and while I enjoyed the majority, none compared with radiology. My only remaining decision was where to do my residency training.

Wisconsin had a strong program, but after eight years at the University I felt like I needed to leave Madison. So I focused my search on residencies that also offered musculoskeletal fellowships, understanding that completing a residency at such a program would provide a competitive edge when eventually applying for a fellowship. Maintaining my dream of a life in the mountains, I evaluated programs in Denver and Salt Lake City. But both programs had their faults, and I knew I couldn't sacrifice quality for location.

The University of Chicago rose to the top of my list. It had an excellent radiology program along with one of the best musculoskeletal fellowships in the country. And Chicago was a city I knew I'd enjoy. Only two hours from Madison, I'd been there countless times over the years. And with John having stayed in Chicago after finishing business school, I'd have family close by.

By my last semester in school, my communication with Fernando had dwindled to a couple of phone calls per year. But when I realized I could finish in April and have two months off before residency, I tried to convince him to join me on a trip to Argentina in search of the fishing and skiing I'd heard so many stories about. But Fernando was absorbed by his research, beginning to see his PhD work move toward completion. And when he convinced me my timing was off, too late for peak fishing season and early for skiing, I opted instead to spend time down in Naples. My parents had purchased a condo the year before, and I thought a month on the beach would be a relaxing break before starting a demanding residency program.

But my stay didn't go as planned. My social insecurities again caught up with me and I spent much of my time alone at the condo. I struggled with the lack of structure, and was bored within days of arrival. I was briefly rescued from my unhappiness when a classmate popped in for a brief stay on his way home to Miami. But upon his departure, my mood worsened, and for the first time in my life I was overcome by a powerful feeling of loneliness. Several of my classmates were taking advantage of their time off to get married. Others were travelling through Europe in large groups or with significant others. But I was alone in my parents' condo, surrounded by elderly couples.

It was a difficult and humbling time in my life. I found myself questioning the path I'd chosen. I began to wonder if my vigorous pursuit of academics had interfered with my ability to find the balance in life that many around me seemed to be enjoying. And I started to question how and when I'd ever find the right woman to settle down with. I was 26 years old and had really only ever had two girlfriends. And I hadn't been on a real date for almost two years. I limped home from Florida ten days early, ready to move on to Chicago and get a fresh start.

5

I gnoring John's recommendation to find a place near him, I opted for convenience and found a small apartment just blocks from the University of Chicago. Back into a steady work routine, my mood ameliorated. Although intern year meant returning to rotations outside of radiology, I enjoyed the year. I got along well with my class of residents. Unlike some of my medical school classmates, my fellow residents shared my unrelenting work ethic. Everything revolved around our work, an environment in which I'd always thrived.

Yet with memories of my disheartening experience in Florida still fresh, I became committed to finding enjoyment away from medicine. Although I consumed one week of limited vacation time each year with a radiology conference, I did take two non-medical vacations each year throughout residency, something I'd never done. I promised myself I'd make time for fly-fishing and skiing, hobbies that had been overwhelmed by academics during preceding years.

In January of my second year, I finally succeeded in dragging Fernando away from Pennsylvania for four days of skiing at Vail. He'd defended his dissertation the previous summer and opted to stay on as faculty. He was engaged to a woman from Uruguay he'd met at the university. They were already talking children, hoping to be pregnant within months of their marriage. And despite high winds, cold temperatures, and poor snow, we still managed to have a blast. We relived highlights of our senior year, with Fernando continuously chastising me for my rusty Spanish.

Then in June of my second year of residency, I decided to take a long overdue fly-fishing trip to Montana. I recruited John, and one of his friends named Tim, to join me. John had never been fly-fishing before, but Tim was an avid fly-fisherman, and the two of us convinced John to give it a try.

My paternal uncle Steve lived in Missoula, and had always served as a bit of a folk hero for me. Steve was a standout high school student growing up in a Milwaukee suburb. But despite being admitted to top colleges across the country, he eschewed an ivy-league education for the great outdoors and enrolled at the University of Montana. He studied history, and while his grades were good, he discovered his passion for the wilderness exceeded his interest in the classroom. Eventually he met Mary, who worked for the Forest Service and shared his love of the outdoors. They married following Steve's graduation and settled permanently in Montana.

During my childhood I saw my uncle one week every July, when he and Mary traveled east to visit his Wisconsin based family. Yet despite these limited gatherings, he and I spoke often by phone, once or twice per week throughout my high school years. Steve's sense of adventure made a strong impression on me from the beginning. I was drawn to his stories about backpacking expeditions and trout fishing float trips. His stories always made our family trips to the Florida coast seem drab by comparison. It was Steve who had convinced me to spend a summer in Vail, helping find my golf course job through an old college contact.

After a few years working for the Forest Service himself, Steve went back to law school at Montana and became a trial lawyer. And while the backcountry stories eventually slowed, he never lost his sense of adventure and passion for the outdoors. We continued our regular phone conversations throughout my college career. Steve and Mary weren't able to have children of their own, something I always felt contributed to our close bond.

Steve had been lobbying for me to come fish in Montana ever since my summer in Vail. But the invitations had become more frequent since Steve had purchased a cabin on the Blackfoot river east of Missoula. Heeding my promise to myself, and riding the momentum of enthusiasm from John and Tim, I finally took Steve up on his offer.

We flew out in late June following Steve's recommendations, with hopes of catching the legendary Salmon fly hatch. And our timing couldn't have been better. The large flies began to hatch in earnest the day before our arrival, and the fish were rabid. I often thought Steve exaggerated his fishing stories, but I was soon reconsidering my theory. I spent most of the week fishing with my uncle, leaving Tim to provide much of the instruction for John. The fishing was so spectacular that by the third day Steve and I found ourselves spending as much time at the river's edge talking as we did throwing our fly lines.

During one afternoon together, I shared my episodic loneliness and struggles finding a sense of fulfillment. Embarrassed at first, I was soon comforted by Steve's presence. It was the first time I'd opened up to anyone about these negative emotions I'd been battling for some time. Outwardly I'd always appeared a rock to friends and family; but on the inside I'd become fragile. Steve listened intently, and then hugged me. It felt good to finally share these feelings with someone close to me. It was something I could have never done with my parents. Our phone conversations grew even more frequent thereafter.

John and Tim enjoyed the trip as much as I did, and we repeated the trip each summer during my remaining years in Chicago. It became a very important week for my mental health. As much as I enjoyed my work, I found I needed my week in Montana. A week away from medicine. A week of serenity in the mountains. And most importantly, a week with Uncle Steve.

6

It was after six p.m. by the time the bus finally pulled into the Mendoza terminal. What I knew to be just over 200 miles had taken more than six hours. As I waited for the driver to unload my bags from the storage compartment, I watched as other passengers unloaded. I thought I might again encounter the young woman that had approached me on the bus. But to my surprise, she didn't get off. I assumed there was another stop in Mendoza where she and a few others who appeared absent must have been going.

I pulled out my notes to remind myself where I was headed. Fernando had insisted I start with his parents, but I'd graciously declined. First, I had no idea how long it would take to find permanent housing. I didn't want to inconvenience his parents with an extended stay, and also didn't want to force myself into a premature housing decision. But even more importantly, I was determined to create my own adventure. I feared staying with Fernando's parents might somehow make things too easy, providing a layer of shelter that might detract from my experience.

It was dark by the time I stepped outside the terminal. There I found a long line of black taxis with yellow trim, most of which appeared to have been there awhile with engines turned off and drivers congregated on the sidewalk smoking.

"Che flaco, un taxi?" a driver called out.

I smiled. It was the perfect welcome to Argentina. Both 'che' and 'flaco' in the same sentence. I knew 'che' was one of the most common words in the Argentine vocabulary. A slang term unique to Argentina, it was a word I'd heard incessantly on Sunday afternoons with Fernando's family. Used primarily to call out to others as in 'hey' or 'hey you', I'd learned Ernesto

Guevara had been given the name Che during his travels through Latin America due to his constant use of the word.

'Flaco', or 'skinny guy', was just as good. I'd been uncomfortable when I first heard Fernando call his cousin 'gorda' during a dinner together. When I'd later questioned him about calling a family member 'fat girl', he'd informed me that in Argentina, calling someone by their size was a term of endearment. I'd suggested he take care not to employ this usage in English, especially on a college campus.

The cabbie took one final drag of his cigarette, placed my things in the trunk, and we were off. Fernando had recommended I look for a hotel on Juan B Justo Avenue in the downtown area. While he couldn't provide specific names, he knew the area to have a number of clean, economical options, and thought it would be the ideal location from which to begin my exploration.

Quickly identifying me as a 'Yankee' by my clunky destination request, the driver was anxious to talk. He had questions about my background and decision to come to Mendoza. He seemed surprised an American had elected Mendoza as a final destination, and his eagerness to talk suggested little previous interaction with international travelers. But on account of his heavy use of slang, and the car's loud diesel engine, I struggled with communication. I tried to summarize my medical training, but ultimately was content with his understanding that I was a 'medico'. And when he described time he'd spent with relatives in Miami, I missed out on most of the details.

Despite concentrating on maintaining conversation, I did have a limited opportunity to take in my surroundings during our short trip. I noticed that while traffic volume was light, the streets were crowded. We passed through a commercial area with snowflakes and other winter themed lights strung artfully across the boulevard. I also found the traffic pattern somewhat haphazard. There appeared to be a single wide lane on each side of the boulevard, with cars weaving through traffic creating anywhere from one to three cars across. And there was a dearth of traffic assistance at intersections: while major intersections had stoplights, many smaller intersections had no stop sign or traffic light at all. The cabbie navigated this confusion by slowing to 15 miles per hour, blinking his lights to warn of his approach, and then accelerating through to the next intersection. I reached beside me inconspicuously in a failed attempt to find the seatbelt.

The cabbie let me out in front of the Hotel Rex, a small hotel within my desired area. He pointed out additional options across the street, but recommended the Rex, explaining it was owned by a friend's cousin. I paid the driver five pesos, which included a tip for which the cabbie appeared quite grateful. My arrival in Argentina had made the exchange rate much simpler, with the Argentine Peso having been pegged 1:1 with the dollar years earlier to help the country end uncontrollable hyperinflation where supermarket prices would sometimes increase multiple times in a single day.

I entered the narrow lobby and was immediately greeted by the largest toddler I'd ever seen. Looking like he couldn't have been more than three, I estimated the smiling boy was at least 60 pounds. He was running around three pieces of mismatched furniture in pursuit of a similarly sized brown dog desperate to get away. A well-dressed man soon appeared, introducing himself as Jorge and his energetic son as 'Sumo'. Jorge laughed as he crouched forward and extended his arms, mimicking the starting position of a Sumo wrestler. He listened patiently as I explained I was looking for a room for a week or two while I searched for an apartment.

"It would be a pleasure to host you," Jorge said, using a slower-paced Spanish to facilitate my comprehension. "We charge 20 pesos per night for a single, but for an extended stay greater than a week I'll take 15. Sound reasonable?"

"Absolutely," I said. "Do you have a non-smoking room available?"

Jorge shook his head and smiled. "No such thing I'm afraid in Argentina. With that type of regulation we're usually decades behind the United States. But I have a corner room with an extra window that ventilates well. I think you'll be happy there."

"Perfect," I said. "I'll take it."

He led me up a narrow staircase and then down a tile hallway to a room marked "C". He opened the door revealing a full metal-framed bed with a night table, an armoire, a small wooden desk, and two large windows, one bright with the lights of the street below. It was simple but clean, with just a faint odor of smoke. There was no television or telephone, but I didn't mind; I wasn't planning on spending much time in the room anyway.

Jorge opened the bathroom door, and apparently reading my confused look, pointed out the solitary shower head on the wall and the drain in the middle of the floor between the toilet and the bidet. He reached behind the door and grabbed a squeegee, pretending to push water toward the drain. I nodded to convey my understanding, smiling to allay any apprehension I may have inadvertently provoked with my initial disorientation.

Jorge left me in my room, insisting I not hesitate to find him with questions. I sensed in Jorge a great pride in his city and his hotel, and an intense desire for me to find everything to my liking. I organized my belongings in the armoire, and then feeling dirty from a long day of travel, opted for a quick shower. And while it was a little strange soaking all corners of the bathroom, the squeegee worked well. I regretted not having a video camera to capture the moment.

I dressed nicely for my first night out, substituting a pair of slacks and a collared shirt for the sweatshirt and jeans of previous days. I pulled out my map of downtown to organize an evening walk and my first Argentine dinner. I saw that the Plaza de Independencia, the main plaza in the city center, was just ten blocks away. I decided it would be a good place to begin. I looked at addresses of restaurants in my book that I'd highlighted, but decided instead to take Jorge up on his offer and get a local's recommendation. I gathered my wallet and keys, stopped to consult with Jorge, and set off to form a first impression of my new home.

While the blocks west of Peru Street looked quiet with small hotels and a few restaurants scattered amongst residential homes, crossing back east of Peru, with Juan B Justo turning into Las Heras Street, I entered the commercial center of the city. Each block was lined with two or three story buildings, most with a busy storefront at ground level and an office space or apartment above. The tile sidewalks were wide, two to three times the width of the standard sidewalk at home. This allowed for easy transit, even with surprisingly high pedestrian volume. At busier intersections there were green kiosks at the edge of the sidewalk, offering primarily periodicals, candy, and cigarettes.

The 'Mendocinos' themselves dressed as if prepared for a Wisconsin winter, with heavy coats, hats, and mittens, despite what I considered a comfortable evening with a temperature in the mid-40s. Yet despite their bulky clothing, I was able to appreciate a fashionable sophistication to their dress. Many men wore single tone three-quarter length overcoats, adorned with colorful, tightly wrapped winter scarves. Most wore well-polished leather shoes. And while there was more variability within the female attire, I noticed a number of common themes. First, it was evident women preferred tight-fitting lower-extremity clothing. Whether it was a knee-high skirt with leggings, or slacks, women seemed determined to show off their legs. Second, knee high leather boots were in style. Mendoza was known for its leather, and a significant portion appeared to go to footwear. And finally, regardless of dress, the women walked with a style and confidence worthy of a runway. While I wasn't sure whether it was natural or contrived, women walked with purpose.

But what was most striking about the streets, was that they all seemed to be lined with 50 foot trees receiving nourishment from an intricate irrigation channel located between street and sidewalk. I remembered reading about the 'asequias', but hadn't envisioned them so exposed and extensive. I peered down into the three foot deep stone channel, void of moisture in the middle of winter, and imagined water racing through during the spring run-off. Looking closer at the trees themselves, I identified many as Elm, mixed with a second type I didn't recognize. There were a few brown leaves left on the trees, similar to how it might look in late fall at home. As I turned the corner onto Chile Street, I could see the trees also extended down this street as far as I could see.

Five blocks later I arrived at the corner of a well-lit plaza. I continued along its western edge, passing a large theater before arriving at the steps of the magnificent Park Hotel. A large, white stone building of classical style, the hotel entrance was elevated above street level, separated from the sidewalk below by an ornate staircase leading up to an outdoor patio. The hotel was lined with flags and decorated tastefully with massive potted plants. Beautifully lit at night, I was able to see into the hotel. On the second floor, above the lobby, I saw a restaurant with massive windows looking out over the plaza. I thought about Sara. It would merit consideration for a special night out upon her arrival.

I turned left and walked into the heart of the plaza. The plaza was a two block by two block square. The center was marked by a large semi-circular fountain with its flat edge set flush against a stone wall. The fountain was surrounded by a tiled area of a similar surface area, which offered ten or twelve benches at its perimeter. As I'd seen often during my brief two day tour of Santiago, I saw multiple couples amorously engaged amongst the shadows of the plaza's boundaries. But I also saw families. Young children played chase along the edge of the fountain while parents watched from nearby benches. And a group of older children kicked a soccer ball around an open space.

Now standing in the center of the plaza, I could see there were tiled paths in all directions which reached out like fingers, connecting the fountain area to the plaza's perimeter. These paths were well lit and provided benches of their own. In between these paths were green areas of varying sizes, empty this night, but presumably full on warm days. I heard kids playfully screaming from one corner of the plaza and looked to see what appeared to be a playground. Looking west toward the mountains, I saw red lights hovering over the city. Studying them further, I suspected they were radio towers built into the foothills. While I couldn't make out the mountains at night, I imagined they provided a spectacular backdrop by day. I sat on a bench for 15 minutes, taking in the sights and sounds. It was a nice night to spectate: generally quiet and peaceful, with just enough activity to keep my interest. Then, spurred on by both an increasing chill and a sudden hunger, I followed a path through the north end of the plaza and headed back toward the hotel in search of dinner.

Blocks from my hotel, having been given precise directions from Jorge, I easily found Rincon de Los Andes. Having requested an authentic Argentine steak dinner, Jorge hadn't just recommended a restaurant, but had even sent me with specific instructions to order the 'parillada', or mixed grill. He was adamant it was the best in town. I'd been excited by the suggestion, remembering fondly the 'asados' I'd enjoyed with Fernando's family, replete with its different sausages and cuts of steak.

It was after eight when I entered, and just two of the 15 or so tables were occupied. I was approached by a portly middle-aged waiter dressed neatly in a white shirt, black vest, and bow-tie. He offered me a table by the window and I was seated. The restaurant was narrow, but deep, with no more than three tables across at its widest point. The lights were low, allowing the lit candles at the occupied tables to provide the majority of the light. The tables were covered by a white tablecloth, and surrounded by high-backed upholstered chairs. The walls were decorated with photographs of the city, mountains, and vineyards. Quiet instrumental tango music played in the background.

The waiter retuned with the menu, and clearly identifying me as a tourist, took time to describe in detail many of his favorites. I listened patiently, and then explained I might not be allowed back into my hotel if I didn't order the parillada. The waiter smiled, congratulated me on my choice, and was off in search of my glass of wine.

The initial offerings were very good. The Malbec the waiter had recommended was rich and oaky, and was soon followed by another glass. And while the simple dinner salad of lettuce, tomato, and raw onion left something to be desired, it was more than offset by the warm oval-shaped rolls that accompanied it. Tasty enough when dabbed in the table's local olive oil, I found them irresistible when dipped in the green and paprika-colored chimichurri sauce which had presumably been brought out in preparation for the main course.

But neither the quality of the first courses nor my previous experience with the 'asado' could have prepared me for what followed. Demonstrating great pleasure in his presentation, the waiter soon produced an elegant rectangular metal dish, approximately three inches in depth. It was mounted on four sturdy tapered legs, and centered over a Bunsen burner dialed to a low flame. Inside the dish, emerging above and around several arranged lemon slices, was a compilation of sizzling meat products unlike anything I'd ever seen. While I recognized chorizo sausage and at least one cut of steak I'd eaten with Fernando, the familiar was overwhelmed by the unfamiliar. While years removed from my anatomy class, I was pretty confident I identified kidney, small intestine, and possibly the thymus gland amongst the towering pile of meat. I looked up at the server in amazement, both intimidated and uncertain as to even how to begin. He flashed an encouraging smile and left me to my food.

Deciding to begin with the recognizable, I fished out a piece of thin meat similar to flank steak, cut off a piece with my over-sized gaucho style knife, and took a bite. I looked up and caught a glimpse of the waiter standing against the bar, looking my way in anticipation of my initial reaction. I nodded approvingly, smiling as I reached back for another bite. Perfectly salted and cooked to medium rare, it was the most delectable piece of steak I'd ever eaten. While I knew Argentine beef was grass-fed,

I wasn't sure whether it was the quality of the meat, the preparation, or the cultural experience that made it so amazing. I suspected it was multifactorial. Not wanting to fill up on any single component, I nudged the remaining piece to the side and pulled out a thicker piece of steak with the appearance of a sirloin. Slightly more tender then my first piece, it too had amazing flavor. I cut another piece and dipped it into the chimichurri. The tangy, garlicky sauce provided a perfect balance to the richness of the meat. I thought of my late grandfather, the meat science professor who'd been coach of the university meat judging team. I wished he could have been there to share in the experience.

I spent the next 45 minutes methodically sampling everything the bottomless dish had to offer. And while I concluded certain inclusions like the thymus and kidney might require an acquired appreciation, I surprised myself by finding pleasure in the majority of the different components. The tripe, with its crispy exterior, was like a super-charged bacon. And the chorizo had a butteriness to it that made it as good as any sausage I'd ever tried; and this from someone raised in Wisconsin. Finally, feeling giddy from my massive consumption, I was forced to surrender to the still substantial mound of meat. I sat back in my chair, announcing my decision to the waiter, and waited as my remaining food was boxed. While I knew it wouldn't keep in my hotel room, I felt obliged to offer it to Jorge as a small gesture of my gratitude.

I paid my modest bill of less than $20, which included a tip despite my observation that others appeared to be leaving only coins. Now almost ten o'clock, I realized all tables were now full, some even with families with small children. Clearly the Argentines lived by a different schedule than the one I was accustomed to. I put on my jacket, and walked over to shake the waiter's hand in appreciation. Then I stepped outside and made the short walk to the hotel, confident I'd sleep well after a memorable first day.

7

The final year of my residency was a busy time. I'd been selected as chief resident by the faculty, an honor that for me was a source of great pride. It was a recognition that helped justify my dedication to work. And while the extra responsibilities assumed by the chief resident were not substantial, it meant more time committed to work, putting together schedules and working through resident conflict.

I also had to go through the fellowship application process. As chief resident and the only internal candidate within the residency, I was all but guaranteed one of the two fellowship positions. And while I never really intended to leave, my faculty and I agreed it was important to look at other programs. We hoped the visits would confirm my desire to remain in Chicago, as well as provide an opportunity to network with prospective employers in anticipation of beginning my job search the subsequent spring.

So I toured the country for much of September, choosing some programs based on merit, others on location. I saw six programs in all and was pleasantly surprised by what I found. I'd seen the programs in Denver, Salt Lake City, and Boise when interviewing for residencies years before and had discovered the musculoskeletal programs were still in their infancy. Yet upon my return I found the programs had flourished; the addition of new faculty, increased case volume, and technological improvements had amplified educational opportunities. The Denver program was so impressive that I spent the plane ride home thinking seriously about leaving Chicago. But within days of my return, I reconsidered and recommitted to my initial plan. Chicago was considered a top program in the country. I'd be giving up too much to leave. In January I matched into the Chicago program as part of the 1999-2000 class.

Two months later, my routine was again challenged, but this time in a positive way: I finally met a girl. Prior to this point my residency dating history had looked much like that from medical school. During my first year I'd become enamored with a pediatric nurse. After months of anxiety ridden flirting, I summoned the strength to ask her out. We went out three times, but it soon became obvious to both of us we had little in common and the relationship fizzled.

The following year John had intervened by introducing me to Liz, a former classmate. At first I hadn't felt fully comfortable around her. Raised in Chicago, she had an endless number of friends in the area. She was extremely outgoing, and always at ease in a social setting with her peers. During our first dates together, she arranged to meet up with friends. I struggled in this type of group environment. I always felt better suited for a one-on-one setting.

But gradually I became more comfortable around her friends. And after two months of dating, I began to think we might have a future together. This was something new for me. Having not had a girlfriend since college, I'd never before been in a relationship where I found myself imagining what our future might look like together. Unfortunately Liz didn't share these visions. Just as I was gaining confidence in the solidarity of our relationship, she ended it abruptly. She told me the relationship was moving ahead too quickly. I assumed my social awkwardness had again been my undoing.

That spring, again amidst a time when I doubted if it would ever happen, I crossed paths with someone I immediately recognized as special. One of my responsibilities as chief resident was to represent the radiology residency on the residency wellness committee. The committee, which included one resident from each of the 12 university residency programs, convened semi-annually to review general residency issues such as work hours, benefits, and recruitment. I'd attended the fall meeting and thought it an utter waste of time. Each program was very different in its set-up, so much so that it seemed pointless to problem solve as a group.

My disinterest was such that I'd planned to skip the spring meeting. I arranged to do a morning of interventional procedures, covering for a fellow resident on vacation. But when the clinic finished early, I was left without an excuse for my absence and reluctantly made my way to the residency conference rooms.

I entered and took a seat near the door, a location that would facilitate my implementation of the 'fake page and leave' technique if the meeting proved intolerable. I recognized the majority of the residents. While I'd only been to one previous committee meeting, residents from different specialties often interacted in the hospital, often choosing to page each other rather than risk dealing with the occasionally angry or condescending faculty physician.

I was certain, however, I'd never before met the last resident to arrive. She had short blonde hair, black framed glasses, and was the only resident apart from me wearing a physician white coat. While she looked younger than most in the room, her dress and mannerisms provided a sense of professionalism often lacking amongst residents.

She sat down in the only remaining seat, almost directly across from me at the long rectangular table. Like me, she didn't appear interested in the discussion. She spent the majority of her time reviewing something written in a small notebook she carried in her lab coat. This allowed me to be more liberal with my inconspicuous glances, and by midway through the meeting I'd ascertained her name was Dr. Malone, she was an anesthesiology resident, and she wasn't wearing a ring.

My fascination with Dr. Malone made the meeting pass quickly. Before I knew it the meeting adjourned and she was gone. I couldn't have told you a single topic that had been discussed. I walked back to the reading rooms and immediately began my inquiry. I knew that other residents, most much more in tune than I with the resident social scene, would know her story. It was my fellow resident Amy who proved most informative.

Sara Malone was a second year resident who had transferred to Chicago after one year at the University of Colorado. She'd opted to transfer after a disappointing year which included her separation from a longtime boyfriend. Amy and her husband lived in the same apartment complex as Sara and had gotten to know her well. Amy described her as personable and hard-working, and believed we might be a good fit. As the only female resident in our class, Amy was always looking out for her 'guys' as she liked to call us. Knowing me well enough to recognize I was largely incapable of making something happen on my own, she proposed to assume the role of matchmaker. She thought her pre-graduation party the following month would be the perfect opportunity.

The night of the party was the first time I saw Sara since the committee meeting. I was as nervous as I could remember being for a long time. I'd told Amy not to tell Sara I'd asked about her, but I assumed Amy would say something anyway. So I considered it promising when Sara was present upon my arrival.

I knew the majority of the people at the party, and realized Sara would not. I drifted around the apartment making small talk with residents and faculty, all the while waiting for the right opportunity to approach Sara. But I never had to make my move. Stuck in an uncomfortable conversation with a faculty's spouse, I felt a gentle tap on the shoulder and turned to see Amy, with Sara at her side. Amy made a brief introduction, before conspicuously extracting herself from the conversation to attend to the appetizers.

"I think she wanted to leave us alone," Sara said with a confident smile.

"I think you're right," I said, feeling my face flush as I sensed Sara was privy to my crush.

"I've never been around so many radiologists," she said as she glanced around the room. "I have to admit I feel a little out of my element."

"Me too," I answered instinctively. "And I work with the majority of the people here." It was probably more than I needed to reveal about my personality during our first formal encounter.

Sara smiled at me, and I found myself overcome with a sense of calm, a most surprising development given the circumstances. We talked about our respective residencies, always an easy conversation for me. Every time I felt her shifting the conversation away from work, I steered it back, committed to sticking within my comfort zone. After a few attempts at misdirection, she seemed to catch on, and afterwards was content keeping the conversation focused on medicine. She told me about her decision to transfer, detailing her disappointments with her former program while leaving out mention of her ex-boyfriend. She talked about her satisfaction with her new program, lauding the faculty for their commitment to education. I talked a little about my own experience, but more than anything was content just to listen.

The only time I allowed the conversation to shift away from medicine was when Sara explained that her sole disappointment with Chicago was its distance from quality skiing.

"So you're a big skier?" I inquired.

"Absolutely," she responded. "My parents were volunteer ski patrols at Loveland so I got an early start. And I competed for years."

"Really? Like with your high school team?"

"No, mostly with the Vail youth team. Even made it to the US National team for about a year before blowing out my knee." She raised her dress to expose the large scar on the front of the knee. "That pretty much ended my competitive career. Tried to make it back after rehab, but my knee didn't feel the same. And then I became a little tentative, lost my edge."

"That's too bad," I said compassionately. "How old were you at the time?"

"19," she responded. "I graduated high school and moved to Vail for two years. Got hurt in the fall of my second year. A year later I was back in Denver enrolled at CU."

"So you did both undergraduate and medical school at Colorado?"

"Yes," she said. "It was a great experience. And less than two hours from great skiing. I couldn't ski like I did before, but still got out every chance I had."

I smiled. "How much skiing did you get to do during med school?"

"Quite a bit. Really every chance I had depending upon my rotation schedule. I know I skied over 30 days most years."

"Wow," I said, shaking my head. "I'm envious. I love to ski too but it's usually just a long weekend each year. You had something good."

She shrugged. "I did. But I really like Chicago. It's treated me well so far. And I still made it out west twice this winter." She smiled.

We talked for almost an hour before being interrupted by an obnoxious second year resident I'd never liked. I was disappointed our conversation had to end, but relieved it had gone so well. I felt for the most part I'd made a good first impression and I looked forward to getting a performance report from Amy. I said good-bye to Sara, and then fabricated an excuse about having to leave to meet up with my brother.

Things had indeed gone well. So well in fact that I received a congratulatory call from Amy the next morning. Sara had found the conversation 'engaging', and had described my personality as 'intriguing'. She'd even told Amy I was cute. Amy seemed almost as excited as I was as she shared the details. She was anxious to help any way she could, but I declined.

She'd given me the confidence I needed and I was ready to take the next step on my own.

I waited a week and then paged Sara Friday afternoon. I suspected she'd be out of the operating room, finishing up for the day.

"Hello this is Sara Malone, I was paged," she said formally.

"Sara, its Jake calling, Amy's friend, how are you?"

"Oh hi Jake," she responded with a tone of surprise. "What's up?"

"Not much," I responded, unsettled by her reaction. "Just happy to be through a long week. Busy week for you?"

"Uh, not too bad. I had a long call night Monday, but the rest of the week was pretty relaxed."

There was an awkward pause before I returned to medical small talk.

"How often do you guys take call?" I said, aware at this point she was probably on to me.

"Usually once a week as a second year. It's pretty manageable. How about you?"

"It's variable. I'm every fourth right now, but then I won't have any call the next two months."

Again there was a slight pause. I took a deep breath.

"Sara, I was wondering, if you don't have plans, any interest in joining me for dinner tomorrow?"

"Sure," she said without hesitation. "Sounds fun. What'd you have in mind?" I gleaned some excitement in her voice.

"I was thinking Sushi. I know a good place near Wrigleyville. And then maybe some jazz afterwards?"

"Yeah, that sounds nice. What time were you thinking?"

"How about seven? I can pick you up if that works for you."

"Perfect," she said. "I look forward to it. I'll see you tomorrow."

"See you tomorrow," I replied.

I hung up and exhaled forcefully.

She was waiting in the lobby when I arrived the following night, and we made the short drive to the restaurant. Initially our conversation again revolved around academics. She talked about how her experiences with the medical field through her ski injuries had led her into medicine. She too had thought about orthopedics, but had enjoyed anesthesiology and thought the lifestyle might provide a better work/family balance. She talked about how hard she'd worked to get where she was. School hadn't come easy, but her strong work ethic had helped her overcome challenges along the way.

I finally loosened up and allowed the conversation to meander tangentially. I talked about my family and the strong influence they had on me. I shared details of my father's health scare. I told Sara more about my family during that first night together than I'd ever shared with previous girlfriends.

Eventually our conversation returned to the mountains. I told Sara about my summer in Vail. I shared my desire to settle in the mountains after completing my training. She listened intently as I talked. Her smile and gentle affirmations made the conversation flow more smoothly than I was used to, although the wine didn't hurt either. While I'd always enjoyed the taste of wine, I was far from a big drinker. But by the time we finished our meal, almost three hours after it started, we'd been through two bottles of pinot noir. We giggled like schoolchildren and held hands as we walked around the corner to the jazz club.

The club turned out to be disappointing. While the music was excellent, our late arrival left us no choice but to sit in the front row. Our close proximity to the band made it impossible to continue our dialogue. We each had another glass of wine before Sara reached across the table, squeezed my hand gently, and nodded toward the door. With me in no condition to drive, she proposed we cab back to her apartment to find a quieter place to carry on our conversation.

I stayed the night, and then spent the entire next day. And after just 24 hours together, I was convinced my search for the right woman might finally be over. She seemed to possess everything I'd been looking for. She was intelligent, hard-working, and beautiful. She took great pride in her work, yet was committed to finding time to play. We shared many of the same hobbies and had similar plans for our futures. I loved the fact she seemed to know exactly what she wanted.

Within weeks we settled into a comfortable routine. We found time to eat lunch together in the cafeteria once or twice per week. We tried to see each other at least one evening during the week. And on the weekends we were inseparable. We went to museums, movies, lectures, and theater. We methodically worked through a list of our favorite Chicago restaurants. And we drank red wine.

8

By June of that year, my job search was underway. While I still had my fellowship in front of me, I hoped to secure a job early. I wanted my final year of training to be as low stress as possible. I knew there wouldn't be many musculoskeletal radiology positions available in mountain communities and I was committed to finding one. And after just a few weeks of sending out my CV, I caught a break.

Sara had reached out to a former classmate completing a radiology residency in Denver. The resident had heard that a competing Denver program was hoping to start a musculoskeletal fellowship program. I made a phone call to the hospital and was put in touch with Dr. Smith, the residency program director, who confirmed the hospital's intentions and requested a copy of my CV. And within a week of our conversation, Dr. Smith had arranged for me to travel to Denver for an interview.

I couldn't believe it. I'd thought it might take months to find a suitable position, and now in just weeks I was interviewing for what on the surface appeared to be my dream job: an academic position at an excellent hospital in the foothills of the Rockies. I marveled at how close I was to achieving what I'd been working toward for more than a decade.

The interview went as well as I could have hoped. Dr. Smith was finishing the tedious process of submitting paperwork to start a fellowship program. The hospital system was based in a burgeoning area south of Denver. They'd recently acquired a smaller hospital and the system now included three hospitals and a multitude of clinics. They employed 25 radiologists, only one of whom had completed a musculoskeletal fellowship. In order to begin a fellowship they needed a minimum of two musculoskeletal-trained faculty.

The residency program had been started eight years prior and had already grown from two residents per year to four. It had developed a strong reputation, in large part due to its location which attracted both top level faculty and residents. The new musculoskeletal radiologist would oversee the fellowship and be involved with the residency. He would read primarily MRIs, but would be asked to do some general radiology as well. And while there would be some overnight call, this was taken from home and consisted of providing back-up to in hospital senior residents. I couldn't have designed a better position if I'd tried.

I didn't have to wait long to hear back. Two weeks after my return Dr. Smith called with the good news. While they still had to await the official recognition of the fellowship, Dr. Smith felt it was all but a formality. And assuming they were indeed successful, he wanted me to help establish the program.

There were still details that needed ironing out. Dr. Smith didn't have specifics regarding a starting salary, but guaranteed it would be competitive with other academic positions. And they couldn't choose a start date until the program was accepted. He thought they might not be prepared to accept their new fellow until summer of 2001, a full year after my graduation. That meant there might be a three to six month delay after my fellowship before I could start.

I thanked Dr. Smith and we agreed to talk again within the week. I hung up the phone and slumped back on the couch. Having not even begun my subspecialty training year, I was already being offered the opportunity to develop a program of my own. I shook my head in disbelief.

As excited as I was, Sara seemed even more so. While she still had two years left in her training, she too hoped to return to Denver. And as well as things were going between us, she was off and running, planning our future together. While it was too early to apply for jobs, she soon was researching anesthesiology departments at Denver hospitals. And she was advising me on neighborhoods, school systems, and drive times to ski areas.

My parents were ecstatic as well. Especially my mother. She'd always taken great pride in my academic achievements. And a career as a physician in academic medicine was as good as it got for her. My father was excited too, although I gleaned a sense of mild disappointment that I wouldn't be practicing at his hospital. With Ben having opted to stay out east following his training, I'd represented my dad's last chance to have a son practicing with him at his hospital.

In September, the Denver fellowship was accredited and I signed my contract. Sara and I celebrated with dinner at our favorite Japanese restaurant. We were amazed at how things had worked out. My starting salary had exceeded my expectations. And the benefits, non-compete clause, and wording of the contact had been so fair I'd felt comfortable signing and sending it back the next day. While a few other possibilities had surfaced during the previous months, none were in the same league as the Denver job. The opportunity represented the culmination of the vision I'd first had during my summer in Vail more than a decade earlier. And a culmination of the Schmidt master plan.

Really the only minor issue I had with the contract was the start date. As Dr. Smith had speculated, I wasn't able to start until January 1st of 2001, six months after graduation. And while I was hoping to have some time off after training, six months was longer than desired.

But Sara was quick to convince me otherwise. She thought it actually might work out better. I could stay in Chicago for the first few months to minimize our time apart. And then I could go out to Denver a couple months early to begin my house search and acclimatization to my new city. She thought she could do a month rotation in Denver to allow us to look at houses together.

With my contract signed, and everything now seemingly in order, I allowed myself to relax for the first time in a long time. While I continued to work hard, I dialed back the intensity a notch or two. I turned down requests to cover for the other fellow or the residents, something I rarely did during residency. I cut back on my study time, finding more time to hang out with John and his friends. And I increased the time I was spending with Sara. By mid-year we were spending more nights together than apart.

The fellowship itself came without surprises. I'd done several elective MRI months during residency, so I knew what to expect. In fact I'd done so much extra training in preparation for the fellowship that I felt my skills were already pretty strong by the beginning of my year. Yet nonetheless I worked hard to pick up pearls along the way, often reminding myself I'd be teaching well-qualified residents the following year.

But by March, four months before graduation, following a long stretch when everything seemed as good as it could be, I suffered a most unexpected and unsettling development: for the first time in my life I experienced work fatigue. Despite my best efforts to maintain focus, suddenly things at work were different. The environment I'd always found so stimulating began to stale. Reading room days grew progressively longer. I found myself constantly looking at my watch, calculating how many more images I'd have to read before I could go home. And cases which should have excited me to the point of sharing with colleagues became just one more image among a never-ending stream.

I was shocked by the abruptness of the change. I knew I needed to get away and tried to convince Sara to join me for a weekend in Vail. But she was in the midst of a difficult stretch and couldn't get time off. I tried John next, but he wasn't available either, having recently been promoted at work.

I thought about Uncle Steve. Our phone conversations had become less frequent since I'd met Sara. In fact I couldn't remember the last time we'd talked. I decided to give him a call, and was instantly glad I did. It was great to hear his voice again. He always had a way to get me to laugh, and I often found our conversations therapeutic. He had a solution to pick me up. It was time for a Montana ski trip. While I'd visited the previous four summers to fish, I'd never before skied in Montana. Steve had always wanted to guide me around his favorite areas, and I'd often promised I'd make it happen. It was finally time to fulfill that promise.

I changed my schedule at the last minute to allow a Thursday evening departure. Steve met me at the airport and took me to the house where Mary had a late dinner ready. We shared a wonderful meal, catching up on events from a busy year. Steve and Mary talked about their new hobby of winter camping, chronicling several trips they'd taken that winter. I talked about my new job. And we talked about Sara. Steve and Mary couldn't hear enough about her, and I proudly shared the details.

Sometime after midnight, Mary retired for the evening, leaving us to finish off the last of the wine.

"So you found your girl," Steve said, raising his glass to mine.

"I think so," I said nodding, "just as I was beginning to think it might never happen."

"Do we have a proposal on the horizon?" he inquired.

"Still too early to say," I responded. "Our time apart next year will pose some challenges, but if we can endure that…" My voice tapered off.

"Well I couldn't be happier for you," he said. "It's great to see you smiling so much. Maybe she's the last piece of that puzzle you've been meticulously putting together for so long."

"She might be," I agreed. I paused for a few seconds, gathered my thoughts, and then turned back to Steve. "Hey I've always wanted to ask you something. Why did you decide to go back to law school?"

He looked confused. "You mean why did I choose law?"

I shook my head. "No, I mean why did you decide to change careers? You and Mary loved the forest service. You always talk so fondly of your experiences. Why'd you go back to school?"

"I wanted to drink really good wine," he joked.

I smiled, but stayed quiet. I wanted a real answer. While I'd often thought about asking before, I'd for some reason never felt comfortable asking Steve for an explanation.

Steve eventually took my cue. "I guess I don't have a great reason for why I chose law," he began. "I'd always enjoyed the process of formulating an argument. And I thought I could be pretty good at it."

"And your reason for leaving the forest service?" I persisted.

He nodded. "I felt like I'd just gotten to the point in life where I'd settled into a routine that was too comfortable. As exciting as the service could be at times, it just became too easy. I felt like I wasn't being challenged enough, and just knew within it was time for a change." He paused. "Why do you ask? Don't tell me you're having doubts about your career?"

"No, I'm happy. Radiology has been a great fit." I composed myself. "I guess I just feel at times like something is missing. I thought for a long time it was not having somebody to share it with, but now I meet this great girl and still feel I'm not as excited as I should be. Or could be. I mean here I am just finishing my training, haven't even started my first job yet, and for the last month I've felt stuck in a rut."

"I believe they call that senioritis Jake," he said laughing. "It's natural to lose some degree of focus with the end so near. You've been working toward this for a long time."

"Maybe you're right," I acknowledged. "I hope you are. I just feel I've worked so hard, always with a clear endpoint in sight. And, just like everyone I suppose, I've had some doubts along the way. But now I'm almost there, with everything falling into place, and instead of those concerns lessening, they seem to be intensifying. And the most frustrating part is I can't explain why."

Steve smiled at me. "What you need, is a few days in the mountains. Let's go to bed before one of us decides to open another bottle of wine. We're supposed to get snow tonight, so we need to get up early."

I smiled and nodded. I'd already drunk too much, and knew it was going to be a difficult morning. I gave Steve a hug, stumbled into my bedroom, and collapsed into bed.

9

The next morning came early. My head throbbed and I struggled to get out of bed. But two strong cups of coffee later Steve and I were on the road. It had indeed snowed, making our trek to Snowbowl slower than expected. But we were rewarded with excellent skiing. It had snowed a foot at the summit, and we skied fresh tracks all morning. I'd been unlucky with recent ski trips and hadn't skied snow like this for years. And with Steve showing no signs of slowing down despite recently turning 60, I struggled to keep up. By noon my legs were fried and I had to swallow my pride and ask for a lunch break.

While our morning discussion had been for the most part limited to skiing and the great conditions, Steve used our break to resume our conversation from the night before. I sensed his concern about my revelation.

"I was thinking about what you said last night," he started. "About lacking the satisfaction you thought you'd have at this point." He paused. "You think maybe your lack of life experience outside of medicine has interfered with your ability to appreciate what you have?"

"I've thought about that. Maybe some of the doubt comes from lack of perspective. I've only ever known one way of doing things. I've trusted it from the beginning, and never wavered." I took a big gulp of water. "For the most part I'm happy with how everything has worked out. But how do I know there isn't something else out there that would make me happier? I think that's why I asked how you knew you needed something different. You seemed happy, and then suddenly you were off in another direction."

"I don't know if anyone's ever fully certain. I mean I still have days where I find myself wondering. But I think having different experiences through my 20's helped me hone in on what was best for me. Maybe your lack of diversity hasn't provided you with this opportunity."

I listened intently, digesting his words while thinking about my past. I knew he was right.

"Have you thought about what you're going to do with those months after fellowship?" he asked. "Maybe you need to do something different. What about living abroad? How about spending time in Spain like you tried in college?"

I hesitated. "I guess I never considered traveling. Things are going so well with Sara. It'll be hard enough to be apart for six months when I start in Denver."

"You're right," Steve said. "I'm sure she wouldn't be thrilled. But just keep in mind that once you start your job, you may never have another opportunity like this again. Week long vacations will be difficult enough to come by. And you've always talked about being envious of friends who've taken time away from school. Maybe an experience like this is what you need."

"I'll think about it," I mustered in response. I knew he had a good point, but it was hard to imagine leaving Sara behind at this stage in our relationship.

Yet over the next three days, with Steve guiding me through an unremitting snow, I did indeed find myself thinking about it. And the more I did, the more attractive the idea became. Steve was right. This might be my last great chance to do something I'd always wanted. I could finally break the mold and seek out my adventure, and become re-energized in the process.

Sure Sara would be disappointed. But there wasn't that much difference between six and nine months apart. And she would understand my need to experience something new, to break out of my comfort zone. Plus it would be her final year of residency. She would have the flexibility to come visit to minimize our separation.

By the end of my visit, I knew I needed this trip. I even knew where I was going. And I knew just whom to call.

10

ernando couldn't believe it.

"So you're finally going to make it happen?" he said incredulously.

"Yeah, about time, huh?" I replied.

"I'd say. Although I have to admit I'm a little surprised by the timing, with you and Sara doing so well."

"I know," I said. "But as I said I was faced with this void after graduation. I know it'll be difficult for us, but it's something I need right now."

"Sure, I understand. I'm elated for you. You're going to love every minute of it. Just wish I could come down to show you around."

"No chance for even a short visit?"

"No, I'm afraid not. It's just too hard right now with family and work. It's been three years since I was there. It's a lot easier for my parents to come visit us now."

"Makes sense," I said. "I guess I'll have to find someone else to outski and outfish."

He laughed.

"Speaking of that," I said, "you think the timing of my trip will work well?"

"Couldn't be better," he responded. "August and September are both good ski months. October and November are two of the nicest weather months of the year in Mendoza. 80 degrees and sunshine every day. And by mid-November the water table is low enough for dry-fly fishing on a number of rivers."

"Awesome," I replied. "I have goosebumps just thinking about it."

The conversation transitioned to trip specifics. Fernando's natural inclination was to immediately begin to put together an itinerary, but I intervened. This trip was about exploration and discovery. This was me channeling my inner-Steve. A large part of my experience was going to be finding my own way. Of course I wanted Fernando's family's address. And I definitely needed information on ski areas and fly-fishing rivers. But apart from that, I didn't want additional help.

While Fernando was elated with my announcement, Sara was not. Every bit the planner I was, she'd already arranged her fall schedule around maximizing time together. She'd set up three consecutive easy rotations, and even begun to set aside weekends for us to get away. She told me she'd envisioned the fall as an important step for our relationship. I'd planned to move in with her and she'd seen our cohabitation as a trial run for a more permanent relationship in Colorado.

But I was persistent, and eventually Sara capitulated. She'd watched me struggle during the previous months. While our relationship was stronger than ever, she'd commented on several occasions that I didn't seem my normal self. At one point she'd even suggested I consider seeing a psychologist. But now, planning my trip, she told me I seemed reinvigorated. I smiled more, and complained less. Eventually she admitted she knew this trip would be good for me.

We reached a compromise whereby I'd travel for four months. Sara planned to visit for a week in mid-September. This would allow me sufficient time to get settled while still providing Sara the opportunity to ski. And it would get me back by December 1st so we could spend the month together in Denver house hunting.

The rest of the fellowship year went smoothly. My pending trip boosted my attitude. The days went by quicker. My focus improved. And my intensity ramped back up again. The last months arrived accompanied by the frightening realization that I'd soon be reading films without faculty support.

I all but moved in with Sara during June and July. With my trip fast approaching, we were determined to spend as much time together as possible. And despite my looming departure, our relationship continued to flourish. We talked openly about beginning a life together in Colorado. We talked about matching up schedules to allow one day per week to ski or hike. We even talked about children. We each hoped to get started with this endeavor in the relatively near future. We were providing ourselves with a look ahead at our future. And that future seemed bright.

11

That May, weeks after I'd purchased my ticket to Santiago, I agreed to stay on for one month after graduation to work as a staff radiologist. One of our faculty had the opportunity to complete a training in Europe and the department had agreed to his release only if he could arrange coverage in his absence. My decision to stay had been made primarily out of loyalty to the program. They had, after all, provided me with the education to secure my dream job right out of training. The financial incentive, however, had also played a role. I was now financing an unexpected trip, and knew there was a good chance I'd be buying a home upon my return. A month's pay would substantially augment my down payment savings.

Unfortunately, this decision made the days leading up to my departure more chaotic then I would have liked. I'd selected August 2nd as my departure date, thinking it would give me a month to move out of my apartment, study for and take my musculoskeletal board exam, and prepare for my trip. And then there was my desire to spend as much time as possible with Sara. Even without a 40 hour per week job this would have proven an ambitious agenda.

With my decision to work, something had to give. And I soon decided it would be the exam. I'd never before not fully committed to preparation for an examination. But this was different. I knew I could not study at all and still pass. And with my job already secured, my score would have no impact on my career. So for the first time in my life, I decided a passing grade would suffice. I pushed the exam date back to July 31st and spent an hour per night reviewing the musculoskeletal case library I'd assembled over the previous five years.

Moving out of my apartment proved more burdensome than anticipated. Sara's one bedroom apartment was even smaller than mine, and offered minimal space for my things. And while John offered a storage closet in the basement of his building, it wasn't even big enough to fit my bedroom furniture. The hassle of two trips across town in a colleague's Suburban hadn't been worth the minimal square footage acquired. So I turned to my parents for help.

I hadn't talked to them much over the previous months. Neither my parents had understood my decision to go to South America. My mom had met Sara on two occasions and was instantly enamored. She voiced concern that the trip could interfere with the development of our relationship. And my dad didn't understand what I hoped to accomplish. He'd suggested I instead take advantage of the six months to complete an additional radiology training experience.

But when I called to request assistance with storage, my parents had gladly agreed to help. So John and I spent my final Saturday in Chicago packing up a moving truck and together we made the drive to Madison. We spent the night, and the following morning my father supervised while we filled my parents' basement with my belongings. I then said good-bye to my parents, and John and I sped back to Chicago to get me home for an overnight shift at the hospital.

With the board exam and move behind me, I spent my last 48 hours packing. Despite having to pack clothes to bridge me from winter to the hot Mendoza summer, I limited my clothing allowance to a single suitcase. Fernando had convinced me it would be inexpensive to add to my wardrobe in Argentina. He'd even gone so far to suggest I purchase some Argentine clothing upon my arrival to stand out less. I countered that my accent would render my choice of clothing meaningless in any effort to blend in.

I then turned my attention to the more important items: my skiing and fishing equipment. Initially planning to travel with everything, I soon realized the impracticality. I decided the added cost of ski rental would be well worth the reduction of bulk from my luggage. So I decided to be content with traveling just with my skiwear. I was dead set, however, on bringing my fly-fishing equipment. I'd purchased a new five-weight fly rod during my previous trip to Montana and hadn't yet had the pleasure of using it. And Fernando had told me the last time he was in Mendoza the one fly-fishing outfitter had been teetering on the edge of closing.

Then there were miscellaneous items. I chose to travel with a backpack carry-on, knowing it would be perfect for day fishing and hiking expeditions. In it I included a number of essential travel items. Sara had bought me a Frommer's Argentina and Chile travel book for my travel outside of Mendoza, inside of which I tucked away Fernando's contacts and ski and fishing information. I packed the Spanish-English dictionary I'd bought almost a decade earlier in preparation for my trip to Spain. I included a small portable cd player and a limited collection of CDs. And I inserted an obligatory read according to Fernando, a copy of 'El Tunel' by the Argentine author Ernesto Sabato.

My last 24 hours with Sara were more difficult than imagined. After getting over the initial shock of my trip announcement, she'd been very supportive over the previous two months. But as the moment finally arrived, her mood changed. She broke down often, questioning the length of the trip and the impact it would have on our relationship.

I struggled to console her, myself battling a roller coaster of emotions. I too knew I'd miss her tremendously. After years of what often seemed like a hopeless search for companionship, I'd finally found Sara. For the first time in my life I was in love. I fought back tears as I reassured Sara, and myself, that the trip would only strengthen our bond.

Yet deep inside I also felt an overwhelming sensation of excitement. I'd worked so hard for so long, never once deviating from my diligent pursuit of career. And now at age 30, I'd accomplished the goals my parents had helped me set so many years ago. Yet something was still amiss. I yearned for adventure and discovery. I'd waited a long time for this experience. But my wait was over--my trip was underway.

12

After a wonderful first night in Mendoza, I dedicated my first two full days to a general orientation. I made one of my most memorable discoveries the following morning when I stepped out the front door of the Rex and enjoyed my first view of the city in daylight hours. Looking west up the steadily climbing Juan B Justo Avenue, I was awed by the massive snow-capped mountains resting against the edge of the city. With my night time arrival I hadn't appreciated just how close the mountains were to the city.

After several walking tours of the city, I felt I'd acquired a pretty good feeling of its layout. The downtown commercial area encompassed a twelve-block square, with Plaza de Independencia at its center. All streets ran either east-west or north-south, providing an easy grid to maneuver within. The streets were wide, and all were lined by the irrigation channels and large trees I'd noticed the first night. At the perimeter of the square, Las Heras St. to the north, San Martin St. to the east, and Colon St. to the south were the three principal commercial streets. Banks, restaurants, and retail dominated the ground level of these busy streets. The inner layers of the grid offered more of a 50:50 mix of residences and businesses.

I became enamored with the 'peatonal', a four block long tiled street which was a pedestrian only passage. It stretched from San Martin St. to the eastern edge of Plaza de Independencia, and was twice the width of other downtown streets. And while it offered some retail shops and banks, it was lined primarily by cafes and restaurants which took advantage of the wide pedestrian area to set up cordoned off outdoor eating areas. Despite cool daytime temperatures, the street was almost always full of people. Some sat outside with a beer or glass of wine, while others ate a full lunch or dinner. But most seemed to congregate for a cup of coffee and a small pastry. Primarily mid-morning and then again late in the afternoon, the tables were full of people of all ages. Although not a big coffee drinker, I found time each morning to sit outside at one of the cafes, sip my café con leche, and eat a sweet half-moon shaped croissant the Argentines appropriately called a 'media luna'.

While not as spectacular as Plaza de Independencia, I found the other four principal plazas within the downtown zone to be equally pleasant. These quaint squares encircled Independencia in perfect symmetry, all set four blocks away from the corners of the larger plaza. Each named for a different country, they were a quarter the size of the always busier Independencia. But they too offered beautiful fountains, tiled walkways, and inviting park benches. And with fewer people, they did so with a tranquility that could be lost upon Plaza de Independencia at peak hours. While all were beautiful, I found Plaza de España to be my favorite. It had an elegant blue and white tiled fountain, true to the Spanish style for which it was named.

The split work schedule in Mendoza was quite dramatic. Starting slowly at nine a.m., the streets increased steadily in volume, peaking between twelve and one. But with 95% of the stores closing around one p.m., the streets became deserted by early afternoon. I found it almost eerie to be out mid-afternoon with the emptiness providing a stark contrast from the hustle and bustle of the morning. Then almost as if people were anxiously awaiting to again descend upon the city, street volume grew much quicker during the second session of business hours. By 5:30 p.m. the streets were already as busy as they were during anytime in the morning. And peak volume appeared to occur between seven and eight. The nine o'clock closing time appeared flexible, with quieter stores dark right at nine and busier stores still allowing entrants until closer to ten.

While I did most touring by foot, I learned to maneuver upon the city's extensive trolley system. The principal streets of the downtown area were lined with electrical wires some 20 feet off the ground which empowered newer appearing green and white trolley cars. About the same size as a bus, the trolleys offered a quieter, more economical, and environmentally friendly alternative to the black fume emitting diesel buses. Although the trolley had fewer routes extending to the suburbs, it provided comprehensive coverage of the city itself. I took a different ride on the trolley each day, riding the entire loop to see different portions of the city.

Learning to use public transportation afforded me the opportunity to get a better understanding of the greater Mendoza area. I learned that 'Mendoza capital', the city proper, blended inconspicuously into adjacent suburbs. While the population of Mendoza was listed at 200,000 people, Las Heras to the north, Guaymallen to the east, and Godoy Cruz to the south were just the first layers of a large metropolitan area closer to one million. The city of Mendoza itself was divided into six sections. Jorge informed me that Juan B Justo, the street on which the hotel was located, was the dividing line between the fifth and six sections. And while the sixth section was very nice, the fifth section was unquestionably the most affluent area within Mendoza.

With commerce shut down for the afternoon, I walked through the residential areas of the fifth and sixth sections on my second full day. Like downtown, the streets were lined with irrigation channels and mature trees. The sidewalks, with some sections made of concrete and others of a slippery brown tile, were slightly narrower than in the city center. And they were remarkably clean. I saw many residents outside meticulously sweeping and mopping their individual walks, intent upon erasing every last ounce of fine dirt which had settled from the arid environment. The small front yards, some grass and others tile, were immaculate. I interpreted the cleanliness as a sense of pride in ownership.

And while each section offered the same comfortable feel, there were clear differences in residences. While both areas had primarily attached homes, the more modest sixth section had mostly single level homes. The fifth section had more heterogeneity, with a mixture of one and two story homes set amongst a smattering of stately five to ten story apartment buildings. I saw more adobe houses in the sixth section, more brick homes in the fifth. Despite these differences, almost all houses had the same flat clay tiled roof typical of Spanish-style architecture.

Although the two areas were 90% residential, I loved the fact that the 'corner store' concept was still prospering in Mendoza. Every five or six blocks I came across a group of small businesses interspersed amongst private residences. Bakeries, butcher shops, produce stands, and small groceries were equally represented. While they occasionally stood alone, they were often grouped together, offering the shopper the convenience of gathering all of the daily essentials on the same block. There were other businesses as well. Laundromats, salons, and cafes were all scattered throughout the neighborhoods. And it was all done in a very unobtrusive manner. Each store front consumed no more space than the adjacent houses. There were no large or flashing signs, no heavy traffic, and no need for parking lots. I thought it provided a strong sense of community.

After allowing myself two days to play tourist, I planned Friday as a 'work day'. I very much wanted an immersion experience, and part of that goal involved finding daily structure. Not wanting to make too big of a dent in my down payment savings, I planned to find a part-time job. I first considered searching for something in medicine, but realized my language skills presented too large of a barrier. After talking with Fernando, I'd ultimately accepted my best opportunity was to find work as an English teacher.

Initially I'd been reluctant to consider this suggestion, knowing one of the principal goals of my travel was to improve my Spanish. I knew spending time speaking English was not the best way to accomplish this objective. I also had no formal training in teaching of any kind, let alone in English instruction. In fact with the exception of working as a swim instructor during two summers in college, I really had no experience teaching at all. I couldn't see myself putting together a very convincing resume.

But Fernando had assured me that the lack of native English speakers in Mendoza, coupled with a surging number of English institutes, would provide ample opportunity. He recalled having taken an English conversational class at a prestigious institute during his final months in Argentina given by a 19 year-old ski bum from California who arrived to class every morning smelling of marijuana. Fernando was pretty confident my many years of tertiary education would render me overqualified. And when he informed me that teacher compensation was strong relative to the low cost of living, I thought I might get away with working ten hours per week. Surely this minimal English conversation wouldn't hinder my Spanish development too much.

So I headed downtown at nine a.m., having researched the locations of four English institutes Fernando had recommended. Arriving first to the American English Teaching School, hoping my accent might provide an advantage, I soon discovered Fernando had been correct. I was ushered into the office of the director, Graciela, who was excited to learn about my background. I told her about Fernando, whom she claimed to remember, and my desire to teach during my stay. She described the history of the school and its rapid explosion to more than 500 students in just ten years. They'd already had to relocate, having outgrown their initial space. Her English was solid, although not perfect. She spoke with a strong British accent that belied the school's name.

I provided a copy of my resume, which she perused in front of me. Nodding approvingly, she immediately offered two classes. She wanted me to teach both an adolescent and an adult advanced English class. She had ten students signed up for each class, and had been struggling to find the right teacher. I couldn't have arrived at a better time. The classes were starting in two weeks. They were scheduled back to back on Tuesday and Thursday evenings. Graciela promised that the students would already have a strong English base and would be looking to hone their conversational skills. She liked the idea of having a native speaker provide this opportunity.

"So what do you think?" Graciela said with a welcoming smile.

"I think it sounds great," I responded. "It's just what I was hoping to find."

"Okay then," she responded, maintaining her smile. "So how much were you hoping to be paid?"

Caught off guard, I remained silent for several seconds. I hadn't given any thought to this at all. I'd mistakenly assumed I'd be offered a set wage.

"I guess whatever you think would be fair," I said, embarrassed by my inability to even suggest an amount.

"Well most of our teachers are salaried," Graciela informed. "But we pay our substitutes 15 pesos per hour. Does that sound reasonable?"

Quickly realizing my unfamiliarity with the going rate would make it difficult to negotiate, I gladly accepted.

"Super," Graciela said. "Now is it fair to assume you don't have a work visa?"

I felt my face redden. Generally taking pride in my preparation, I'd spent many hours researching in advance of my trip. But somehow I'd never considered the possibility of needing a visa to work.

"Ah, yes, that'd be correct," I responded uncomfortably, attempting to gather myself. "Is that going to present a problem?"

"Not unless you choose to turn it in to one," Graciela reassured with another warm smile. "We're supposed to require a visa. But this is Argentina. As long as it stays under the table, we'll be fine. You can stop by my office the end of each month and I'll pay you cash. Will this arrangement be acceptable?"

"That'll work," I said sheepishly.

I stood and shook Graciela's hand. We arranged for another meeting the following week so she could give me materials other instructors had used in the past. She also hoped to introduce me to other staff. I thanked her for her time and set off for the next school on my list.

With my confidence bolstered by the acquisition of my first job, I had productive discussions at each of the next three schools. Although I wasn't offered additional immediate positions, I left optimistic I could obtain as much work as needed. One of the institutes wanted to open a new section of conversational English, advertising instruction by a native speaker. Another school suggested I might co-teach a high school English class with an Argentine English teacher; she would teach the grammar while I'd focus on conversation. And there were promises of substitute jobs as well.

With English jobs appearing plentiful, it was time to focus on housing. I needed a better idea of my cost of living to determine how much I needed to work. Excited by the notion of being in demand, I had to remind myself I hadn't come to Argentina to work too hard. There was too much good skiing and fly-fishing in the area. Plus there would be a lifetime of opportunity for full work days starting in less than six months. Content with my successful morning, I headed back to the Rex to share my successes with Jorge.

That evening, having resisted the urge to call each of my previous nights in South America as part of a homesickness deterrent strategy, I couldn't hold out any longer. Feeling fairly confident I'd understood Jorge's directions, but less certain about what I was looking for, I was fortunate to stumble upon a telephone kiosk several blocks east of my hotel. I waited in line until the attendant directed me to booth four, which had just become available. By that time I'd figured out the fare was tabulated by an electronic device mounted above each phone, and then paid to the attendant upon completion of the call.

Ten p.m. Mendoza time was seven p.m. in Chicago. I knew I had a decent chance of finding Sara at home. I pulled out my guidebook, found the international dialing instructions, and anxiously dialed her number.

"Hello?" Sara said in a sleepy voice.

"Buenas Noches mi amor, como estás?" I rolled my r for effect.

She laughed. "Better now after hearing your voice. I picked up an extra call last night and couldn't get out of my pain clinic today. I got home an hour ago and crashed on my sofa. But I laid down by my phone hoping you'd call. How's Argentina?"

I detailed the previous days' events chronologically. Sara listened intently, stopping me with just enough questions to show interest, but not so many as to make me lose my rhythm. I smiled the entire time I spoke, happy to hear the voice of the woman I loved.

Sara was exhausted, but seemed happy. She'd picked up the overnight call, and another the following week, to finish clearing her schedule for her visit in September. The conversation turned to her trip and how soon it would be before we were together again.

But then, without warning, Sara pushed the conversation in another direction.

"So have you found what you were looking for yet?" she began.

I paused, caught off guard by the question. "Not yet, but I know she'll surface sooner or later," I joked, opting for a feeble attempt at humor.

"Not the answer I was looking for," she said in a now angry tone.

"Come on Sara, we've talked about this. It's only a short time, and I thought we had an understanding this might be good for us in the long run."

"No I think you had an understanding!" she snapped.

I remained quiet, not wanting our first conversation to escalate into a full blown argument.

"I'm sorry," she said following an awkward silence. "I'm just tired. And I guess it's been hard. Harder than I thought it'd be. I know it's just been a few days, and we've been apart for longer periods, but just the realization that you're gone, and we're barely going to see each other at all until winter. And the uncertainty of being so far away…" Her voice tapered off.

"I know," I mumbled. "I was lonely tonight, wishing desperately you could be here with me. But the time will pass quickly. Before we know it you'll be here to visit."

"You're right. I'm being ridiculous. I don't even know where this is coming from. It must be lack of sleep," she reassured.

"I love you," I responded. "Now go back to bed. I'll call this weekend. We can start to work on our itinerary for when you get here."

"I love you too. Have fun, but not too much," Sara joked, half-crying and half-laughing.

I hung up the phone, paid my almost $20 bill, and headed back to my hotel with my mind spinning.

13

On Sunday afternoon of my fifth day in Mendoza I made the fifteen minute walk to Fernando's parents' house in the sixth section. I'd called them my second night in town, planning to propose we get together for coffee. But once Fernando's mother had gotten over her initial disappointment that I'd waited more than 24 hours to call, she insisted I come to their house Sunday for a traditional Argentine asado. And although I had no intention of declining the invitation after my restaurant experience the night before, Fernando's mother made it clear any attempt to say no would prove futile.

The walk to their home was traumatic. Making the improper assumption the pedestrian had the right of way, I was almost picked off by a small Fiat that had only been slowing to check for oncoming traffic at one of the many unregulated intersections. Hearing the car honk its horn during his approach, I'd thought the driver had been deferring to my crossing. But I later realized that instead of flashing the lights as I'd seen done at night, the driver was honking only to warn other potential cars of his pending intersection arrival. Then, as I was deep in thought about what had transpired minutes before, I was jolted back into the present by the unexpected terrifying yelp of an angry pit-bull. The dog sprung forward against the metal security gate, just inches from my face. I leaped back awkwardly, nearly ending up in the irrigation channel. While it wasn't my first watchdog surprise in Mendoza, it was terrifying nonetheless.

Still shaken from my walk, I arrived at the well-kept single story brick home earlier than planned. Fernando's mother had told me to arrive about one. Having always placed a premium on punctuality, I tried to arrive a few minutes past the hour. But I overestimated the time needed to walk from the Rex, which had included a brief stop to buy a bottle of Malbec.

So at closer to five minutes to one, happy to have arrived to the safety of Fernando's parents' home, I rang the doorbell and waited. And waited. I rang the doorbell again, this time listening closely for the chime to make sure the bell was functional. And while I was certain I heard the bell, there was still no sign of activity inside.

Finally, after more than five minutes, having pulled out my address book to confirm I had the correct address, I heard movement from the house. The door opened slowly, and a woman I assumed to be Maria leaned her head out the door. She had curlers in her hair, and although she tried to maintain her body behind the door, I could tell she was wearing a bathrobe. My face flushed as I suddenly pondered the idea that I'd misunderstood the specifics of the invitation.

"Jake, you're here!" Maria said with equal parts excitement and astonishment. She kissed me on both cheeks, taking care to keep one arm draped across her opposite shoulder in attempt to obscure the sight of her robe.

"I'm sorry if I'm early," I offered meekly. "The walk over didn't take as long as I thought. You did say one, didn't you?"

"Oh don't worry Jake," she responded comfortingly. "It's just that here in Argentina when we say 'around one', people tend to arrive closer to two. Juan is still out gathering a few things for the asado. Would you be comfortable waiting out back while I finish getting ready?"

"Of course," I said. "It's a beautiful afternoon."

I felt terrible. Quite the way to make a first impression. Fernando had been trying to get me to Argentina to meet his family for a decade, and now finally ready to make it happen, I show up more than an hour before they were expecting me. I couldn't wait to tell Fernando. He'd get a good laugh at my expense.

Maria led me out to a rectangular table, neatly centered on a beautiful tile patio. She apologized repeatedly for our cultural misunderstanding, then excused herself. I took a seat at the already set table and looked around the small backyard. The patio occupied almost half the space before giving way to a well-manicured grass yard. A six foot high brick wall enclosed the yard, blocking views of the adjacent homes. And in the corner of the yard, I spotted what I knew from pictures to be the famous Argentine grill, a structure paramount to the preparation of an authentic asado.

I stood up and walked over for a closer look. It was a simple design. The foundation was a large concrete block, roughly five feet wide by two feet deep by three feet high. There was a three foot high concrete border at the back and the sides, with an exposed front edge. The grill itself, which covered the left half of the surface, was suspended by four chains that blended together into a thicker chain which then entered a crank shaft mounted on the left side of the foundation. This clearly provided the grill attendant with the ability to adjust the height of the grill to control the temperature. In the back right corner of the surface there were a number of medium sized pieces of wood leaned neatly against the concrete border. It was clear an asado was imminent.

As I studied the two long handmade skewers that hung off the side of the grill, Juan entered through a small gate connecting the driveway to the yard. He put down the grocery bags and came over to greet me. I started to extend my hand, but Juan was already on the way in for the customary cheek kiss. I'd been slowly getting used to the kiss with introductions to females, but this was my first male to male greeting kiss and it showed with my awkward delivery. Juan placed the heel of his hand on my jaw with his fingers resting on my neck. He patted my cheek as an Italian grandfather would his grandson. I thought I even saw a tear in his eyes.

I helped Juan bring in the groceries, and we returned to the patio. Juan opened the wine I'd brought, and poured two glasses. He had questions for me about my job and family, and he showed patience as I initially fumbled with my Spanish. He asked about my short stay in Chile, joking that I'd tried the hamburger and now moved on to the steak. He asked about whether I'd seen Aconcagua on my trip over to Mendoza, laughing as we recounted Fernando's failed attempts. But more than anything he wanted to hear my impressions of Mendoza. As I detailed my experiences from the previous days, Juan sat back in his chair and smiled, delighted by the impact his city was creating on me.

The conversation then turned to plans for my stay.

"So you're going to do some teaching," he said. "How else are you planning to occupy your time? Have you thought about taking a class at the university?"

I hesitated for a moment, organizing my response in Spanish. "I wanted to spend a little time at the university to see how the system works. And

I thought it would be a good way to meet people. But I never considered taking classes. Do you think it would be possible?"

"I'm sure it would," Juan encouraged. "Our public university system is free, so there wouldn't be tuition issues. And I assume you wouldn't need a university transcript since I can't imagine you'd derive benefit from obtaining credits here. So you'd being sitting in on classes, something we call an 'oyente'. I'm sure professors wouldn't mind. As a former professor, I think most would appreciate having another viewpoint in the classroom."

I liked the idea. I knew it would be great for my Spanish, and it would be nice to learn something during my stay. But I still had doubts about the logistics.

"But haven't classes started already? I've seen students studying at the coffee shops all week."

"Actually your timing is great," Juan reassured. "The second semester just started this past Tuesday. And classes end in early December, about the time you plan to go home."

I considered the possibility. It was looking like the majority of my English teaching would be done in the evenings. If I were able to arrange a morning class schedule, it could provide nice balance to my days.

"I still have colleagues in the history department," Juan said. "If you'd like, I can call them and see if they could help put together a schedule."

I nodded. "That'd be nice. It sounds great."

We continued our meandering conversation, gliding from one topic to the next. I found it easy to communicate with Juan in Spanish. While the wine was clearly helpful, there was more to it. Juan spoke slower than others with whom I'd interacted during my first week, presumably a concession to my struggles with the language. And as a former professor, he employed no slang at all, speaking with a formal vocabulary ripe with English cognates. But what I thought most helpful, was that Juan talked almost as much with his hands as with his mouth. I'd noticed right away upon my arrival that Argentines were quite liberal with use of their hands in conversation. I'd assumed it was a gift from the Italian ancestry I knew common in Argentina. But Juan appeared to have taken the use of extremities to a level that would even impress his fellow Argentines. Almost dance-like at times, I thought I could cover my ears and still have a good understanding as to what he was saying. It was the first effortless conversation I'd enjoyed since my arrival in South America.

Around two o'clock, with Maria still not having reappeared, Juan started the fire. Then at two-thirty, Fernando's sister Marina arrived with her husband and two-year-old daughter. I couldn't help but think this was the time I'd been expected. Finally, at closer to three, Maria appeared, working her way around the table providing greeting kisses for everyone. She again apologized to me, clearly distressed by our uncomfortable introduction.

But she quickly regained her composure and took up her role as hostess. With Marina's help, she filled our wine glasses and then gradually began producing from the kitchen an endless stream of food. Potato salad with carrots and peas, a baked mozzarella dish, a garlicky eggplant spread for the fresh rolls, and the famous Argentine beef empanadas. Oh the empanadas. In Santiago I'd tried the empanadas one night for dinner. And while I'd found the beef filling satisfying, I'd been disappointed to learn that in Chile empanadas were typically fried. These empanadas were different. These were the baked version that had been a staple Sunday afternoons with Fernando, only they tasted even better than I'd remembered. A beautiful light brown color, they had a crispy exterior with a delectable ground beef filling. I tried to show some degree of self-control, but it was a losing battle from the outset.

As the food circled around the table, I enjoyed a conversation with Marina while her husband entertained their daughter on the lawn. Marina had graduated from law school the previous year, and had begun work with a small firm. She asked about my plans for housing, and to my excitement, offered some great suggestions. I'd spent the morning reading through the Sunday classifieds, looking for a short term rental in the fifth or sixth sections, or on the university campus. But to my dismay the options had been few, and I'd struck out with my one telephone inquiry.

Having been to Madison years prior to visit Fernando, Marina informed me the university didn't have a campus similar to what I was used to. She told me the university was isolated from the city center, at the foot of the mountains, and offered limited housing. She thought the fifth and sixth sections were good options, but also suggested the downtown area. While its distance from the university was greater, its more regular bus schedule would make the university equally accessible while putting me closer to my teaching jobs. She recommended I go to the lobbies of the larger schools at the university, promising me the walls would be littered with housing opportunities. She even volunteered to look at places with me to make sure landlords didn't try to take advantage of a 'Yankee'.

As we enjoyed the food and conversation, I kept one eye on the fluid work of the grill attendant. Spending more time at the grill than the table, Juan took great pride in his work. He broke apart the burning wood with a skewer, creating a small mound of ash. He then deftly maneuvered the ash along the foundation to the area beneath the grill, taking time to assure an even distribution. At one point, announcing the fire was too hot, he delicately wound the crank no more than a quarter turn. And despite the grill not appearing to move more than a centimeter above its previous height, Juan seemed confident the subtle tweak had restored order. Finally, after more than sixty minutes of cooking over a low heat, he began the meticulous process of removing the meat, cutting it into small portions, and serving the guests. The tripe came off first, followed shortly thereafter by the chorizo and morcilla sausages. Then, after a ten or fifteen minute delay, other organs and the thinner cuts of steak came next. And finally, as I questioned my fortitude to continue with the meat orgy, Juan delicately sliced the thicker cuts of steak and placed them individually on our plates.

It was almost five o'clock before we finished eating, and I'd hit the wall. A Sunday evening meal with my family lasted no more than thirty minutes. By the time Maria returned from the kitchen with the post-meal coffee, I'd been sitting for four hours. I was exhausted from the concentration required to maintain a conversation in my non-native tongue. Not to mention the contributions from the now substantial afternoon alcohol intake and the excessive caloric consumption. I tried my best to keep up with the conversation that had drifted away to various matters of friends and family. A neighbor girl was getting married. An aunt was recovering from an operation. The details were becoming more and more nebulous, and I knew it was time to go. At six o'clock, with neither the hosts nor Marina's family showing any desire to begin to wrap things up, I announced I had to get going. I thanked Fernando's family for a wonderful afternoon, promised to talk with them later in the week, and set off on a much needed walk back to the hotel.

14

The following morning, inspired by my conversation with Juan, I set out to explore the university. While my plan had been to take the bus, the beautiful blue sky and mountain backdrop lured me into taking on the lengthy distance by foot. I turned right coming out of the hotel and began the steady climb west along Juan B Justo Ave. I crossed the high volume Bolougne Sur Mer Ave., leaving behind the borders of the residential fifth and sixth sections. I continued my gradual ascent through an area devoid of residential properties. On the right there appeared to be a military school. To the left I saw a large sports complex with turf soccer fields and clay tennis courts. As I passed by these buildings, the land opened and the view of the mountains intensified. I was now close enough to make out sparse bushes scattered about the otherwise barren brown foothills. I saw gravel paths winding up the hills, but couldn't make out any roads. I saw the large radio towers I'd seen lit up from the Plaza de Independencia. And towering above it all, I saw the majestic peaks of the Andes, which appeared to have awakened to a fresh covering of snow.

Thirty minutes after I began, my legs heavy from the taxing climb, I arrived to a large sign welcoming me to the National University of Cuyo. With the road veering to the right around a congregation of buildings, I continued straight, passing between the dental and law schools until I reached a clearing. There I came upon a large patio and fountain that appeared to mark the center of the university grounds. I stopped and looked around. There were about a dozen buildings in all which occupied the land with no particular symmetry. They ranged in height from two to six stories, and varied greatly in architectural style. While two of the buildings appeared newer, the rest looked at least 30 years old. Apart from the buildings the land was otherwise barren, with just a few trees sprinkled about the brown and unattractive land.

With the previous night to consider different options, I'd decided to try to find a modern Argentine history class and a political science class. Juan had given me names of the more ebullient professors in the history department. I approached a young woman and asked her for directions to the history building. She pointed out one of the larger buildings still further west that she identified as the school of philosophy and letters. I thanked her and walked approximately two hundred yards to the building, surprised at how empty the campus seemed for ten in the morning.

Stepping into the lobby, I was besieged by a thick cloud of cigarette smoke which wafted through the common area. I walked across the room to the staircase where I found a building directory and then headed up to the third floor. I walked down a long tiled hallway to room 321. I entered to find an elderly woman copying grades into a notebook. I explained that I was a visiting student interested in auditing a class. She introduced herself as Ana, a department assistant, and told me that while she wasn't familiar with other foreign students having done this, she thought it would be possible with professor consent.

She pulled out a binder with the schedule of classes. I paged through it diligently, hoping to find a current Argentine history class taught by one of the professors Juan had recommended. I discovered two such options, but only '20th Century Argentine History' was offered in the morning. I asked Ana about the class. She explained that while students often complained about its difficulty, they enjoyed its content and quality of the lectures. And the majority loved Dr. Martinez. While seen by some as intimidating for his tendency to seek non-volunteered responses, they all respected his knowledge and dedication. I asked if Dr. Martinez was available to receive my proposal, but Ana informed me that most professors spent little time on campus apart from their lecture hours. She said Dr. Martinez was one of many professors who taught at a private university as well. Unfortunately he wouldn't be available until the next class. I thanked her and headed back toward the building entrance.

While making my way through the now even busier lobby, I was approached by a female student.

"Where are you from?" she inquired politely, startling me with the first English I'd heard outside of the English institutes since my arrival in Mendoza.

"Chicago," I responded, going with my now standard answer after my early realization that few Argentines had heard of Wisconsin.

"Have you come here to study?" she said.

I now noticed just a hint of her Argentine accent.

"Not formally," I explained. "I'm here primarily to experience Argentina and improve my Spanish, and I thought sitting in on classes might be a good way to go about it. Are you an English major?"

"Yes, I'm a third year student. My name is Carolina."

"Nice to meet you," I said. "I'm Jake."

I leaned in for the greeting kiss, proud that after a week of awkwardness and uncertainty, I was finally feeling confident in its implementation. I spoke about my desire to take two classes. I explained that I'd chosen a history class and now hoped to find a political science class. She thought my plan sounded feasible, and offered to help me find the political science building and assist in finding a good class. She had friends who studied political science and thought she'd be able to get a recommendation from them.

She led me out of the building still further west toward a newer building at the edge of campus. She talked about her English curriculum and desire to become a teacher. She explained that English students had only rare opportunities to converse with native English speakers. She told me there was a small foreign exchange program from a college in California that spent four weeks at the university each year. But they had their own classes and interacted little with Argentine students during their stay. And apart from these students, it was rare to have a foreign student on campus. She lamented the homogeneity of the student body, explaining they had to rely on television and movies to hear native English. She asked if I'd come to her 11:30 phonetics class to speak with the students. I gladly accepted.

Inside the political science building Carolina found friends hanging out between classes. She introduced them to me, and now back in Spanish, I struggled to keep up with the pace of the dialogue. As comfortable as I'd been talking with Juan the day before, I now found it almost impossible to keep up with the rapid slang-heavy banter amongst students. It was almost as if they were speaking another language altogether. Often requiring

Carolina's assistance with translation, I eventually described my interest in finding a current Argentine politics course. But to my disappointment, the students struggled with suggestions. They informed me that the classes offered this semester were narrow in content and wouldn't provide the overview I was seeking.

As I pondered my next move, a student named Ignacio asked me if I had interest in learning about Mendoza wine. He had a friend in the school of Agronomy who was taking a class entitled "The History of the Wine Industry in Mendoza Province." Ignacio thought it might be an interesting course for me given the local importance of the industry.

As he described the class, I thought about the young woman that had approached me on the bus to Mendoza. That had been one of her suggestions for my time in Mendoza. She'd described wine as the 'soul' of the province.

I thought the class sounded cool. I knew little about wine, but figured Mendoza would be an appropriate place to begin my education. I asked about the class schedule, and while Ignacio wasn't certain, he knew it was a morning class. He gave me his friend's phone number and suggested I call to get the details. I thanked the group for their input and Carolina and I headed back to the 'philosophy and letters' building.

With fifteen minutes to spare before her phonetics class, I asked Carolina if there was a computer lab where I could check my email. I'd been out of the country now for more than a week and hadn't yet checked my mail. While Jorge had told me there were internet cafes downtown with a similar set-up to the telephone 'cabinas', I hadn't yet found one. Carolina led me to the second floor library. There, tucked away in the corner, was a small separate room with three computers that appeared to have been manufactured in the 1980s. Surprisingly, none of the computers were occupied. I sat down and quickly discovered an explanation for their lack of popularity. Devoid of icons to allow simple navigation, Carolina had to show me the cumbersome process of dialing up the internet. By the time I'd finally accessed my email, it was time for the class to begin. I hoped to find a more modern arrangement downtown.

Although I wasn't enthusiastic about the idea of being seen as an opportunity for students to practice their English, I was happy to speak to the class as a favor to Carolina. I told them about my upbringing in Wisconsin.

I spoke about Fernando and my decision to come to Mendoza. I told them about my university experience in the United States.

I learned from the students that the tertiary education system in Argentina was fundamentally different than in the United States. In Argentina, one attended professional degree programs, such as law school or medical school, directly out of high school. There was no need to first obtain an undergraduate degree. And all degree programs required the student to take only coursework specific to their area of study; there were no general studies or non-major requirements to be fulfilled. Therefore it was necessary for students to declare their major upon admission, and a change in interest meant starting over from the beginning.

After class I asked Carolina about housing listings. She guided me back to the lobby to a large poster board covered in hand-written housing opportunities. Marina had been correct about the abundance of listings. Carolina helped me locate rentals in my desired areas and I jotted down the information. I thanked her for her help and we exchanged contact information. I proposed we get together for language exchange, and she agreed. We parted ways and I made my way back to the campus entrance, content I'd found a great way to fill my morning schedule. Tired from a long morning, I found a bus marked 'centro' and made my way back down the hill to the Rex.

15

With my daily schedule taking form, I turned my attention to my last major obstacle in my immersion experience: housing. I spent the afternoon and much of the following day making calls. Not unexpectedly, the short term nature of my housing request proved a deal breaker for most. Yet with persistence, I eventually found three options that would allow me to pay month to month without a longer term commitment. Taking Marina up on her offer, she and I visited each of the places on the second day of my search.

Our first stop was a one bedroom apartment in the heart of downtown. Used primarily as a short term rental for tourists, the owner had been open to my request for a longer term contract. And given we were entering the low-season for tourism in Mendoza, with the high season not starting again until after my departure, the owner was open to negotiating a discounted rate. The building was a six story high rise one block from the Spanish Plaza I'd found so inviting. The apartment was on the fifth floor and was furnished, albeit somewhat outdated. The owner gave us a tour of the small unit, with the total square footage less than 400 feet. The highlight was a small private balcony which provided a partial view of the plaza. At 300 pesos per month, Marina and I agreed it could be a good fit.

From there, we continued on to another apartment complex, this one on the border of the sixth section and the slightly less desirable fourth section. Another high rise, it was one of at least ten apartment buildings within a several block area set against the large 'central park' of Mendoza. Although Marina noted the park could be seedy at night, she liked the area. It was less than a mile from her parents' home. And with the main trolley station just across the street, it would provide easy transportation to both the university and downtown. The apartment itself had attractive features. The two bedroom unit was twice the size of the downtown apartment. And the balcony provided a view of the park. But Marina had reservations. She thought the building might be noisy. And even more alarming, she was concerned about the age of the building. Marina thought from the architectural style that it was likely constructed in the 70's, a decade before a destructive earthquake hit Mendoza in 1986. While the building had survived the quake, she knew its foundation would not be built on the earthquake proof rollers that had become standard with newer construction.

Our final stop provided a unique option. Set in the heart of the sixth section on the tree-lined Cayetano Silva St., the third rental was a single-level attached three bedroom house. The street was quiet, and it was conveniently located two blocks away from one of the small commercial areas I'd discovered during my neighborhood walking tours. The owner was a quiet man, appearing about 30, who introduced himself as Nestor. He lived with his mother in a newer home constructed behind the rental home, separated by a tile patio and a white stucco privacy wall. Nestor explained the house had been vacant for six months since his sister had moved to Buenos Aires on sabbatical. The teaching opportunity had just been extended to a year, and she'd asked him to rent the house until her return.

The house was white, of adobe construction. It had a nice tiled patio in front, with a waist high wrought iron white fence separating the private area from the tiled sidewalk. It had a center entrance, with windows on either side covered by the vertically-oriented theft prevention bars common in Mendoza. The inside was clean, but minimally furnished. In fact the large red-tiled living room at the front of the house was empty, decorated only with a large painting of the Virgin Mary on its back wall. There were single beds in each of the bedrooms, all topped with older mattresses without linens. The modest kitchen was furnished with a simple metal rectangular table with matching chairs. Its walls were covered by a turquoise colored tile providing a 70's feel. It offered basic appliances without the modern conveniences of a dishwasher or garbage disposal.

The house offered more space than I needed. And its dearth of furnishings would require a modest investment. But the price was right at only 250 pesos per month. And although I knew my commute to both work and the university would be less convenient with a more infrequent bus and trolley schedule, this was more than offset by the fact that it just felt right. I loved the tranquility of the street and the feeling of community. And I liked the idea of being close to an Argentine family while still maintaining my independence with my own place. After stepping outside to get Marina's blessing, I returned inside and made a verbal commitment to rent the house.

There was no written contract or security deposit. Marina confirmed this was the norm in Mendoza, at least for a short term rental. Nestor promised to give the house one final cleaning later that day, allowing me to move in the following afternoon. We shook hands and Marina drove me back to the Rex for one final night. While it had been the perfect temporary accommodation, I was excited about the prospect of moving in to my new home.

16

I spent the following two days getting situated. Fernando's family loaned me a couch from Juan's den. They also provided me with linens and basic kitchen supplies. I purchased an end table and a small entertainment stand at a used furniture store. And unable to find a used television, I spent slightly more than I'd hoped on a new 28 inch TV. While it was far from luxurious living, I was quite content with my new abode.

Since it was already Thursday by the time I was settled, I decided it would make more sense to start my university classes the following week. With my now numerous teaching jobs slated to start the subsequent week as well, I decided to take advantage of the following days to take my first ski trip. Marina and her husband had been to Las Leñas the previous weekend and had reported excellent snow conditions.

So following a return visit to Rincon de Los Andes for another spectacular culinary experience, I took the seven hour overnight bus from a ski shop on Las Heras St. to Las Leñas. There I enjoyed two days of fabulous skiing before taking the afternoon bus back to Mendoza on Saturday. During my first chair ride up Friday morning I met a fellow American named Dave. He worked as a ski patrol in Jackson Hole during North American winters and wrote for a ski magazine while skiing throughout Argentina and Chile during his summers. He was part of a 200 person international community from the United States, Canada, and Europe that summered in the remote village of Las Leñas to make skiing a year round activity. Following an eighteen inch powder dump the day before my arrival, he guided me around the spectacular bowl skiing at the top of the mountain that he thought the best in all of South America.

With limited lodging and no good economical options in Las Leñas, I spent my one night at a seasonal hostel an hour away in the sleepy village of

Malargue. With a wide boulevard, lined by buildings which were all either one or two stories, my initial impression was that it had the feel of some rural Montana towns I'd visited with Steve during my summer fly-fishing trips. But then I saw two locals making their way down the middle of the street on horseback, dressed in classic Gaucho style with baggy pants, neck bandanas, and large knives suspended from their belts. Clearly Montana this was not.

I wandered around the village that evening. The streets were modestly crowded with what seemed to be an even mix of locals and tourists. And while the majority of tourists were Argentine, I did hear both a little English and German during my walk. I stopped into a few jewelry stores which all featured a black stone common to the area. I purchased an oval-shaped pendant for Sara, knowing she would appreciate both its uniqueness and authenticity. I also stopped in to a local fly-fishing shop where I met a friendly attendant named Marco who spent over 30 minutes informing me about fly-fishing destinations throughout both Mendoza Province and Northern Patagonia. By the time we were through I'd gone from having no knowledge of fishing in Mendoza to feeling I could almost start my own guiding service.

Following a lazy recovery day back in Mendoza on Sunday, I spent the following weeks transitioning into my new routine. Three mornings per week I took a 20 minute bus ride to the university for my two classes. The other two mornings I either walked or trolleyed downtown to the 'peatonal', where I purchased the local newspaper and enjoyed a cup of coffee and pastry at one of the outdoor cafes. Afterwards I walked back in the direction of the house to an unpretentious sports club where I worked out in the small outdated gym or hopped into a pickup basketball game. From there I walked home, stopping into my neighborhood shops to pick up my food for the day.

My evening schedule was busy too. With teaching requests arising almost daily, I soon finalized my schedule. Monday through Thursday I taught two or three classes each evening. Most evenings I started class at six and finished by nine-thirty. I gave most of my classes at the American English Institute. I also taught two advanced conversation classes at a second private institute. And I filled out my teaching schedule by choosing to give a twice weekly private English class to a local cardiologist. Not wanting to teach more than ten hours per week, I'd considered multiple opportunities before opting for the private class and capping my schedule. Ultimately I chose the private lesson in part as a favor to Graciela, who lived next door to the physician, but also with the assumption it would allow me to understand the health care system in Argentina. Five minutes into my first class I knew I'd made a great decision.

Mariano appeared to be in his late 40's. He was tall and lean, and walked deliberately with the rigid gait of someone with arthritic knees. He dressed immaculately, resting his suit coat on the back of his chair at the start of each class. And he always had a slight smirk on his face, giving the appearance that either he was on the verge of laughter, or knew something those around him didn't. He was married to a beautiful psychologist, who appeared ten years his junior, and they had two teenage children. His parents had immigrated to Buenos Aires from Israel in the 1950's, and had relocated to Mendoza when Mariano was in high school. He'd done his medical training at the University of Cuyo, and had practiced medicine at a private clinic for almost two decades.

He lived in a stately two-level stucco home in the fifth section. The house was surrounded by an eight foot stone wall which obstructed the view of the house from the street. I was greeted at the gate for our first class by the maid, who led me into a private study to wait for Mariano. Graciela had told me that Mariano was an intermediate level speaker who wanted to advance his English primarily to improve comprehension of medical journals. Uncertain of what to expect, I'd prepared for our first class by putting together a list of medical topics to discuss. But after meeting Mariano, it became immediately clear he had no interest in following an agenda.

Mariano's affable demeanor belied his formal appearance. Fascinated with my decision to come to Mendoza, he had an endless number of questions about my family, my studies, and my future. He spoke in truncated English, often having to restart sentences to accurately convey his thoughts. I cautiously intervened, correcting the more glaring mistakes while passing on smaller corrections to maintain flow. Mariano often laughed at his struggles with the language, but sometimes grew frustrated and switched into Spanish. And while I attempted to always speak English, I'd sometimes be lured into Spanish. Mariano was clearly interested in evaluating my Spanish, and seemed to enjoy teaching me Spanish as much as learning English. By the end of our first class the teacher-student relationship was already being replaced by a developing friendship.

I met with Mariano two times per week at his house over the lunch hour. Our bond grew quickly and by the second week I almost felt guilty for accepting payment. We often talked about basketball. Mariano was a huge basketball fan who watched several NBA games per week. He'd traveled to the United States twice and on each occasion had attended a game. And although his days of playing competitive basketball were behind him, he continued to play games at the Jewish sports club. He invited me to visit the club and play with him on Saturday afternoons.

But regardless of the topic on which we began our classes, the talk almost always returned to medicine. I quickly learned a lot about health care in Argentina. Mariano explained that while a public system was available to all Argentines at no cost, the system was both inefficient and inadequate. He described the typical work-up for an individual experiencing chest pain. The patient would wait a month or two to see their primary care physician. The doctor would then order tests which could take weeks or months to complete. The patient would then pick-up the results to take to the primary care physician for review. This physician would then provide a referral to the cardiologist, who would often require additional tests before a diagnosis could be rendered. It wouldn't be unusual for the entire process to take six months.

When the diagnosis was finally made, treatment options were often limited. The technology at most public hospitals was woefully inadequate. And when technology was sufficient, the available public system physicians sometimes lacked the proper training to provide the necessary care. While Argentine medical training was considered strong, the public system physician reimbursement was so poor that the best-trained physicians almost all chose to practice within the more lucrative private system.

This competing system was available exclusively to the more affluent. They either paid cash or purchased private insurance. And while this system was generally recognized as offering better care, it had its own set of challenges. Physician reimbursement was still relatively weak. Mariano told me he received just ten or fifteen pesos for an initial office visit. And the private practice environment in Mendoza was fragmented. There were no multispecialty groups or large physician office buildings. Most physicians started in the public system after completing their training. Then after making a little money, those who developed a good reputation would cautiously venture into private practice, attempting to start a small solo practice on the side. But this process was difficult. The long hours and frequent hospital call created a lifestyle that wasn't always amenable to being the kind of father and husband he strived to be. And with a high start-up cost, practices were forced to build slowly. He and his partner had started into private practice together and couldn't afford their own ultrasound for years. They instead had to rely on an adjacent clinic which created an inconvenience for patients. It had taken five years before their practice was in the black and they could begin to expand their services.

Mariano had a good understanding of how medicine worked in the United States. He'd attended two conferences there and even completed a short training stint in Miami. He marveled at the hospitals in the United States, which he said felt like five star hotels compared with Argentine hospitals. And he knew reimbursement was excellent for physicians. After several classes together, he finally felt comfortable enough to inquire as to the starting salary for a radiologist. He smiled and shook his head when I sheepishly provided the requested information. I again felt guilty for accepting payment for our classes.

I always looked forward to my time with Mariano. And while these classes became the highlight of my teaching, I found my other classes enjoyable as well. I taught two advanced English classes at the American English Institute. I was given a textbook from which to work and did my best to stick to the curriculum. But both the students and I recognized my strength as a teacher was not teaching grammar. My strength was my ability to provide authentic American English conversation. It allowed students to improve their comprehension of the American accent, as well as to pick up expressions and slang not taught in textbooks. So inevitably the classes strayed away from the lesson plan to an array of different conversation topics, many of which centered on differences between American and Argentine culture.

One such discussion led to a memorable experience early on with my adult section. During our first class together the students had gone into great detail explaining the importance of Mate tea in Argentina. I knew a little about the tea from my time with Fernando and his family. I remembered seeing the traditional cups and straws at Fernando's uncle's house, used as adornments due to difficulty in finding the herbal tea in Madison. But I'd never tried it, and hadn't yet seen it consumed in Argentina. The students were shocked I'd spent two weeks in Mendoza without yet being exposed. They explained that while it had a nice flavor, it had a much greater value in the Argentine society. Its consumption was more of an excuse to promote social gathering, with its sharing of a single cup and straw creating a closeness and acceptance they felt represented an endearing feature of the Argentine people.

So as planned, the students brought Mate to the second class for my indoctrination. With fifteen minutes remaining in my last class of the evening, one of the female students announced it was Mate time. She produced an oval shaped wooden bowl from her bag that was taller than it was wide. She filled it about one-third full with a loose tea-leaf that reminded me of another herb I'd seen smoked with great frequency during my college days. She then added two small scoops of sugar before filling the bowl to the rim with hot water she'd brought in a thermos. She added the peculiar metal straw of about four inches in length, pursed on one end like a pipe and flat and rounded on the other with small holes to act as a filter. She passed the initial Mate cup to the student to her left in the circle that had been arranged by the other students.

The first student took four or five sips until producing a slurping sound indicating its consumption. She then passed the cup back to the woman who had brought the supplies, who refilled the cup with water and then passed it to the next person in the circle. When my turn arrived, I began with a small sip to sample the flavor. Despite the sugar, I found it quite bitter. And although the filter kept out the big leaves, the tea still had a graininess to it that made it unique from anything I'd tried before. It was also scorching, with the metal straw providing a well-insulated path for the tea to the roof of my unconditioned mouth. The students watched intently as I took my first sip, and then laughed at my look of uncertainty. They recommended I wait a minute for it to cool, and the student preparing the tea added an additional scoop of sugar for me.

Although not overwhelmed by the taste, I did appreciate the social aspect. Without another class to follow, we continued passing the Mate for another 45 minutes, conversing both in English and Spanish. Every five or six cups, the woman who brought the tea added a small additional quantity of herb and an extra scoop of sugar. We went through three thermoses of water before eventually being coaxed to leave by a janitor needing to clean the room. I went through at least five cups before finally saying 'gracias' as I passed the cup back, the customary way of discharging oneself from the rotation.

What the students failed to educate me about, however, was the high caffeine content in the tea. On the trolley ride home that evening I experienced palpitations for the first time in my life. And when I later lied down for bed, I realized my overstimulated mind had no intention of allowing me to sleep. I tried reading for thirty minutes before finally getting up and opting for a late night walk through my neighborhood. It was five a.m. before I finally fell asleep. From that point forward I was strict about adhering to my self-imposed Mate rules of no more than three cups per sitting and no tea after eight p.m.

My other two classes were marketed as conversation classes, so there was no textbook to follow. I put together a questionnaire for my first classes asking students about their background, hobbies, and career plans. I then used this information as a foundation to lead conversation. I had three basic goals: keep the dialogue flowing, encourage mass participation, and make necessary English corrections. It was easy. Many of the students had never before spoken with a native English speaker, and most had never met anyone from the United States. While they struggled at times with my accent, the majority were eager to participate. During most classes I made it through just a fraction of our planned topics.

I also used the classes selfishly to put together itineraries for my weekends. I shared with the students my desire to ski, fish, and travel; they provided suggestions on where and when to go. Some even went so far as to offer a cabin of a family member or friend. I asked about restaurants and nightlife and received several invitations to show me around the city. They recommended winery tours and other day trips from Mendoza. And within two weeks I had so many invitations for Sunday afternoon gatherings that I generally had to decline.

Yet as smoothly as I'd adapted to my role as a teacher, I found the transition to that of a university student more challenging. I arrived fifteen minutes early to my first Argentine history class to obtain professor approval to take the class. Unfortunately Dr. Martinez arrived five minutes late. This put me in the awkward position of having to introduce myself in front of the entire class with a professor rushing to organize his teaching materials. Dr. Martinez gave his consent, although seemed less than enthused. I made the mistake of introducing myself as an American, rather than being from the United States. He snidely responded that I'd feel comfortable in the class since I'd be surrounded by other Americans, even if they "only hailed from the continent to the south." And I thought Dr. Martinez was only half-joking when he shed light on his own political views by telling the class he hoped my involvement would be less obtrusive than that of the United States in Argentine politics.

The professor took it a step farther midway through the lecture by living up to his reputation of challenging students without warning. When introducing the transition to the government of Juan Peron in the 1940's, the professor asked me to stand and share with the class my impressions of Peronism politics. I could tell from his tone that his motivation was to demonstrate his assertion that citizens of the United States lacked a worldly education. And as much as I wanted to prove him wrong, I could only meekly respond that it was my lack of understanding that had prompted my decision to take his class.

But things did eventually get better. Dr. Martinez stopped me on the way out following my second class in an apparent effort to make peace. He asked about my background and showed interest in my career choice. His nephew was attending medical school and had voiced aspirations of becoming a radiologist. And although the lecture material was nuanced at times, I found the information interesting. I began to appreciate that the complex political history in Argentina played a prominent role in helping shape current day Argentine culture.

My other university class got off to a more auspicious beginning. Dr. Salinas was happy to have me as a student. He'd done some lecturing in California wine country and had an acquaintance in the agriculture school at the University of Wisconsin. And although he lacked the exuberance of Dr. Martinez, I found the material fascinating. I soon realized the wine industry had been fundamental to the development of Mendoza province.

I learned the first vines arrived back in the 1500's. They were Spanish vines brought across the Andes from Chile by early Spanish settlers. Criolla

Chica was one of the first varietals, and became the predominant grape in Mendoza for more than two centuries. It wasn't until the 1800's that the grape stock underwent significant change. Following Argentine independence in 1810, there was a large European immigration. The rapidly growing population included many from the European wine industry looking to escape the Phylloxera insect epidemic which had ravaged vineyards across the continent. This wave of immigration brought a number of new varietals from France and Italy, including the French Malbec.

Production grew slowly through much of the nineteenth century, with development limited due to transportation challenges created by the isolation of western Argentina. Finally in the late 1800's, the Mendoza to Buenos Aires railroad was completed and the boom was underway. Wine making flourished through the early part of the 20th century, mirroring the growth of the Argentine economy which surged to become one of the largest in the world by the 1920's. But the great depression was hard on the wine industry, with production staggering due to both decreased export revenue and foreign investment. The industry temporarily rallied under the Peron administration in the mid-20th century, only to again suffer under the military regime of the 70's and 80's. But with the economic stability and globalization of the 1990's, the Argentine wine industry was changing its focus from one of primarily domestic production to an emphasis on exportation. And with this new model Mendoza wine production was surging. Recent data indicated Mendoza had become the fifth-largest wine producing area in the world, with its provincial production half that of the entire United States.

Dr. Salinas emphasized that Mendoza owed much of its success as a wine-making society to the indigenous Huarpe people, who built a sophisticated irrigation system to disperse the waters of the Mendoza river flowage across the foothills of the Andes. This allowed Spanish settlers to establish vineyards in a climate where the average annual rainfall of eight inches was far less than the usual amount required to support grapevines. In fact Mendoza received just a fraction of annual totals from other renowned wine growing areas such as Napa Valley and Bordeaux, France.

Having overcome this major obstacle, Dr. Salinas explained the Mendoza climate was otherwise ideal. Its 330 days of sunshine per year were great for grape production, as was its warm temperatures during the

October to March growing season. And its wide diurnal temperature variation, with high and low daily temperatures often 40 degrees apart, created a unique grape that was high in both acidity and sugar content. Also, the high altitude of the vineyards, most 2000 to 4000 feet above sea level, in conjunction with the low humidity, meant minimal threat of pestilence including a relative absence of the Phylloxera insect. There was such a low prevalence that many vineyards operated without chemical spraying.

The only major environmental hazard was the regional Zonda wind and hailstorms that could sometimes accompany it. The Zonda was a hot and tumultuous wind that raced down from the Andes, more commonly during the early part of the growing season. The air was often saturated with dust, having lifted up the top layer of soil from the arid landscape. While the Zonda winds provided additional protection against pathogens, more violent storms and hail could be destructive to vines.

I liked the class material from the beginning. And I also enjoyed the other students. Unlike my history class where the majority of students was right out of high school, my wine class offered a greater age diversity. I formed a friendship with a group of three friends taking the class together. Passionate about climbing and trekking, they invited me on the lower altitude hikes they were accustomed to doing in the winter months. And determined to supplement my education about wine in Mendoza, they took me to the Santa Julia vineyard for my first tour.

By early September I couldn't have been happier with how things were working out. My teaching was more enjoyable than expected and had allowed me to meet a myriad of people in a short time. My university experience was providing better depth to my understanding of Argentina, and had been great for my improving Spanish. And my living arrangement couldn't have been more comfortable. My trip was off to the perfect start, and it was about to get better. I was about to have the chance to share my new home with the woman I loved.

17

After a rocky start, Sara and I had enjoyed nothing but positive conversations over the previous weeks. We'd settled into a routine where I called twice per week. I dominated much of the dialogue, excited to detail my new experiences in Mendoza. She listened patiently, needling me at every opportunity for each cultural faux pas. With things in her residency program status quo, she had little to report from Chicago. Now well into her final year of training, she'd switched into auto-pilot mode. And with the interview season for anesthesia positions still months away, her attention was solely focused on her trip to Argentina.

I picked Sara up from the small Mendoza airport at noon on a Saturday. She emerged from the customs area looking exhausted from her long trip, but as beautiful as ever. She ran toward me, and without saying a word, squeezed me as if she hadn't seen me for years. Her eyes welled up as she pulled back to look into my eyes, before pulling me in for another long hug.

"Finally," she whispered as she held me tightly.

I was surprised by my own emotions upon our reunion. While I'd missed Sara tremendously, and had been excited about her visit, I'd been too busy since my arrival in Mendoza to have ever really felt lonely. But now, locked in her embrace, smelling her favorite citrus perfume, I too was overcome by tears of joy.

We took the fifteen minute taxi ride back to my house, and I proudly showed off my new abode. While Sara was somewhat disappointed by the sterility construed by the lack of décor, she loved the charm of the attached adobe construction, the tiled patio, and the quiet tree-lined street. She took me by the hand and led me into the bedroom. I was happy to comply.

Afterwards Sara fell asleep in my arms. I laid with her for over an hour, enjoying the feel of her warmth at my side. Later, taking care not to wake her, I slipped away into the bathroom for a shower. I then dressed and took out the Borges novel I'd checked out from the university library. I read for two hours before Sara finally emerged from her deep sleep.

That evening, as planned for weeks, I took Sara to the Plaza hotel for a romantic dinner. I'd considered cancelling my reservation and taking her to Rincon de Los Andes, but ultimately opted for elegance over tradition and stuck with the original plan. And we were both glad I did. The food was fantastic, each of us selecting the churrasco steak with chimichurri sauce. But the view was even better. We were rewarded for my longstanding reservation with a quiet window table that looked out over the Plaza de Independencia.

After dinner we strolled through the plaza, admiring the bustling activity of a Saturday night. A quick student of local custom, Sara smiled as she placed her hand in my back pocket during our walk. I responded appropriately by draping my arm over her shoulder. We walked six blocks to the popular Aristias Street, lined with bars and restaurants. I showed off the English Institute where I was doing the majority of my work. We enjoyed a glass of wine together on a heated patio before finishing the night with an ice cream cone at the local favorite Perin.

After sleeping late the following morning, I took Sara on a tour of downtown Mendoza. We enjoyed a late breakfast on the peatonal. We sat on a bench in the Spanish Plaza, people-watching and soaking up the warm sunshine that by now seemed an everyday occurrence. We walked through a portion of the fifth section, admiring the classic Spanish architecture. And while not on the top of my list of things to do, we shopped. Sara was awestruck by the volume of boutique clothing, leather, and silver shops. She made purchases for herself, her sister, and her mother. She bought me a handsome suede jacket, insisting it was half what it would cost in Chicago. Finally, with darkness arriving, I convinced Sara we needed to get back to the house to prepare our bags for our overnight trip to Las Leñas.

We spent the following three days at the ski resort. Dave had helped me find a studio apartment rental in Las Leñas, allowing us to forgo the daily commute to Malargue. I'd thought it would make for a more comfortable stay, but I soon regretted having omitted the more culturally rich Malargue from our itinerary. And while the skiing was decent the first day due to light snowfall a day earlier, subsequent days were disappointing. With the powder skied off, and the temperatures unseasonably warm, the skiing suffered. Conditions were icy in the morning and slushy in the afternoon. And without moguls or trees to provide alternative skiing options, we soon tired of the open bowl skiing. We quit early on both the second and third days, preferring a beer on the patio over a full day of suboptimal skiing.

Unfortunately the skiing wasn't the only disappointment. After our first day of skiing, Sara voiced her displeasure with my decision to meet up with Dave. While she found him nice enough, she didn't like sacrificing alone time for us during her short stay. And then when the conditions deteriorated, she announced several times that the skiing hadn't met her expectations. I felt under attack for not providing the experience she'd expected. And when I voiced my frustration with her negativity, the discussion escalated into a full blown argument. We spent much of the bus ride back to Mendoza in silence.

Following a transient return to civility the night of our return, things again soured the following morning with my announcement that I planned to attend my university classes. I explained that missing an entire week of classes during the middle of the semester would make it difficult to keep up.

Sara couldn't believe my words.

"Are you kidding me?" Her face reddened. "I travel six thousand miles to see you, and after four days together you're choosing your classes over me? Who cares if you miss something? It's not like you're getting credit for these classes anyway."

I sighed and shook my head.

"Come on Sara, it's just that…"

She wasn't waiting for my response. "We haven't seen each other in over a month, and won't see each other for another three months. I'm here for all of six days. I'd think you'd want to spend as much time together as possible."

I tried my best to appease her.

"Of course I do Sara. Why don't you come with me? I think you'd like getting a feel for the university. I just don't want to miss an entire week. How would that look to the professors? They've been kind enough to allow me to take their classes, and now after just two weeks I skip out for a week to go skiing? I think that would be pretty unprofessional on my part."

But my words only further enraged her. She was livid now.

"No, you take the week off to spend with your girlfriend who you're planning to move to Colorado with!"

She stormed into the bedroom and slammed the door behind her.

I hadn't explained myself well. I did want to spend time with Sara. I just didn't want to sacrifice the rhythm I had established in Mendoza.

But now I realized this might not be possible. We clearly had different expectations for our time together. She was there on vacation, wanting to see and do as much as possible with her boyfriend. I wasn't interested in playing tourist. I was looking for something more profound, a true immersion experience. And as much as I wanted to be with Sara, I couldn't help but feel her presence in Mendoza was somehow interfering with this goal.

I walked to the bedroom to make peace. I tried the door, but found it was locked.

"Come on Sara. I'm sorry. I won't go to my classes. Let me in so we can talk."

"Just leave me alone Jake." She was crying now. "Maybe we need to be apart for a while. Go to your classes; they are obviously very important to you."

"Please Sara," I insisted. "I don't like seeing you like this."

"Just go away Jake. I don't want to argue anymore. I'm going back to bed. I'll see you when you get back."

I could see this was going nowhere. I knew Sara well enough to know she'd put up a wall that I couldn't maneuver around. She needed to be left alone. The only way to work through our disagreement was to give her time and space. I put on my jacket, gathered my bag, and headed up to the university.

When I returned from my classes Sara had lunch waiting. She'd gone around the corner and made the daily purchases. She smiled at me and pulled me in for a long hug.

"I'm sorry Jake," she said shaking her head. "I shouldn't have attacked you like that."

"It's okay Sara," I responded. "I'm sorry too."

"I was acting selfishly," she clarified. "But I just want to spend as much time together as possible," she said, fighting back tears.

I hugged her again. "I know Sara. I know. I do too. I shouldn't have insisted upon going."

"Let's promise we won't fight for the remainder of the time," she declared.

"It's a deal," I answered.

I cupped her cheeks and gave her a delicate kiss.

And for the most part we were successful. I took her to my English classes that evening. Unlike my university classes, she understood these were mandatory for me and she was happy to go along. My students were excited to meet her, and attacked her with questions much the way they had with me during my first class. I was happy to step aside and have Sara lead the classes.

The following day we packed a lunch and took a short bus ride up to Potrerillos. I took Sara on a three hour hike I'd taken with my university friends. It was a cloudless day and we enjoyed our picnic with a view of Mt. Tupungato in the distance. We then hitchhiked back down to Cacheuta to a recently restored hotel. We treated ourselves to massages and then sat outside in the natural thermal baths. We finished our day with dinner back on Aristias St. in Mendoza.

The following day we enjoyed one last meal together on the peatonal, before I accompanied her to the airport. Emotions were again high as we said our goodbyes. The week had been more challenging than anticipated. What we'd both assumed would be a beautiful week together had proven a rollercoaster ride. But we'd rallied from a midweek crisis to finish on a high note.

I waved goodbye from the small outdoor balcony as Sara walked up the stairs from the tarmac. Her departure was bittersweet. I knew I'd miss her tremendously. And I knew our time apart would create further challenges. But I also knew there was much more I hoped to accomplish in Mendoza. And now I could turn my attention back to achieving those goals.

18

The following days were agonizing. Although I had enough structure with my classes to remain busy most of the day, I spent almost all of my free time thinking about Sara. I knew it was a classic case of wanting what I couldn't have. When she was there, I'd sometimes felt confined, unable to continue the acclimation process that had been going so smoothly. But now that she was gone, I felt alone. I missed her companionship. I missed her intellect, her warm smile, and her soft embrace. The house felt empty without her. I worried I might have inadvertently created doubt in her mind about the strength of our relationship.

But slowly, over the course of the week, I started to feel better. I had an uplifting conversation with Sara on Wednesday where we relived the highlights of our week together while deftly avoiding mention of our negative interactions. She gushed about a Denver house she'd seen listed that she thought could be perfect for us. I promised to look at it as soon as possible.

And my university experience continued to be excellent. On Thursday morning I was disillusioned by Dr. Martinez's introduction of Argentina's 'dirty war'. He explained that the war was born many years before in the late 50's following the coup that overthrew Juan Peron. His support base, which had been eroding during the end of the first term, took a big hit early in his second term with the death of his inspirational and beloved wife Eva to cancer. Following bombings and failed coup attempts in subsequent years, Peron finally succumbed to protestors in 1955 and fled the country. The military-centric weak governments that dominated the next two decades, and the economic decline that accompanied, created a breeding ground for opposition groups from both the right and left. These groups included both Peronist supporters and Marxist-Leninist revolutionaries inspired in part by Che Guevara. While they initially worked separately, they later consolidated in an effort to defeat the partially democratic governments. Tactics included kidnappings, robberies, and bombings, and led to a number of bloody clashes with the military across the country. In 1973 Peron was allowed to return from exile in Spain, and soon after, was re-elected for a third term.

After years away, Peronism ideology had become a ray of hope for many disenchanted groups spanning the political spectrum. Initial supporters included fascists on the far-right, trade unionists in the center, and socialists on the far-left. But following clashes between left and right wing supporters upon his return to power, Peron was forced to choose amongst his diverse factions of supporters. He sided with the right-wing bureaucrats, criticizing the socialists as 'immature idealists'. This soon led to the deposition of a number of leftist Peronist governors and an escalation in warfare between the Argentine government and socialist rebels. By 1974, many outsiders recognized a civil war was underway.

Peron died in office on July 1ˢᵗ of 1974. With his third wife Isabela having assumed power, the military influence increased in an effort to ward off left-wing terrorism. By 1975, Operation Condor, a clandestine agreement to defeat radical opposition, had been officially formed. Right wings dictatorships in Argentina, Chile, Paraguay, Uruguay, and Bolivia, with support of the CIA, unified in their quest to eradicate the leftist opposition by any means necessary. And with Isabel Peron easily brushed aside in a coup in 1976, the military dictatorship of Argentina was prepared to take the lead.

Always a great orator, Dr. Martinez lectured with passion and anger when describing the transition to the dictatorship. I looked around and saw all eyes captivated by the professor. While I'd known from our first meeting Dr. Martinez's ideology lay well to the left, I now wondered if he didn't have a more personal connection to the military regime. I felt my skin break out in goose bumps with the palpable emotion that filled the lecture hall.

After class I walked to the cafeteria for lunch. As I was standing in line, I was approached by Carolina, the English student that had helped me during my first day on campus. I'd since seen her a few times in passing, but we hadn't conversed for any length of time since our initial encounter. We'd hoped to get together for language exchange, but neither of us had yet taken the initiative to make it happen.

We exchanged greeting kisses.

"Can I join you for lunch?" she inquired.

"Absolutely," I said. "If you have a little time maybe we can finally have our first session."

"I do," she said. "Sounds good to me."

We got our food and took a seat at a large empty table.

"So how's your semester going?" I asked in English.

She shook her head. "Not the way I'd hoped," she responded. "One of my professors is out indefinitely with an illness. They couldn't find a substitute so they had to cancel the class."

"Oh no," I said. "That's too bad."

"Yes," she said. "And with limited class offerings each semester, it means another year to finish up my requirements."

"Really?" I said. "Wow. That's disappointing. Hard to believe the university couldn't find someone to teach the class."

"I know," she said. "And things at home are even harder. My younger sister, a junior in high school, just found out she's pregnant. It's been very stressful for the entire family."

"I can imagine," I said supportively. "How's she holding up?"

"Not great. She's fighting with her boyfriend and my parents almost daily. I'm trying to be supportive, but I'm pretty disappointed."

She looked away and sighed.

"How about you?" How are things going here and with your classes?" she said forcing a smile.

"So far so good," I said. "I like my classes. And teaching has been fun too. I've met a lot of great people, and while I'm not always convinced I know exactly what I'm doing, I think the response has been pretty good thus far."

"Another gringo stealing away jobs from my fellow English majors," she joked.

The conversation eventually turned to our respective relationships. Carolina had a boyfriend of five years who had graduated from architecture school the year before. He now worked for a firm in the neighboring community of Maipu. While they'd experienced some difficulties in their relationship, she now felt a proposal was imminent. I told Carolina about Sara. I talked about our intent to move together to Colorado. And I spoke of her recent visit to Mendoza, opting not to mention the difficulties we'd experienced.

Appearing to sense my emotional lability, Carolina had a proposition for me.

"What do you think about joining my friends and me for a movie tonight?"

"I think that sounds great. I could use a night away from my empty house."

"Great," she said. "We haven't picked the movie yet. But we're planning on seeing a later show at the main shopping mall."

"Awesome," I said. "I've been wanting to see this mall everyone is always talking about."

"We're meeting at the southwest corner of the Plaza de Independencia around 9:30. Does that work for you?"

"That's perfect," I said. "I have two English classes tonight, and I'll be done at nine. I'll just head straight over from the Institute."

"Great," she said. "It'll be good for both of us to get out. See you tonight."

She gathered her tray, provided a goodbye kiss, and we went our separate ways.

The rest of the day was uneventful. Following my second class, I took the bus down to the Hotel Rex for afternoon Mate with Jorge. The hotel seemed quieter than ever, but Jorge was his normal cheerful self. He complained about River Plate's poor performance in the Argentine soccer league. Having decided somewhat arbitrarily to support River's arch-rival Boca Juniors, I couldn't provide much sympathy. We agreed to get together to watch the upcoming 'superclasico', the semi-annual match between the country's two most decorated teams.

At quarter after nine that evening, I arrived to the plaza and not unexpectedly found I was first to arrive. Yet within minutes I spotted Carolina across the plaza. I waved and walked over in her direction. She was accompanied by a classmate named Celina. She was a year ahead of Carolina in school, and was already starting to do some substitute teaching. Carolina explained that their other friend Marcela was running late and would meet us at the theater. We walked over to one of many bus stops around the square. The stores were closing for the evening and there were lines of people awaiting transportation home. We boarded a packed bus and made our way to the mall.

We arrived in plenty of time to get seats for the 10:30 showing of Mission Impossible 2. While I was hoping to see an Argentine film, the girls were intent upon seeing Tom Cruise. I was surprised to see it wasn't even the last seating of the night; most movies had a final showing beginning between one and two a.m. Carolina and Celina were excited to show me around the newer mall, but to my disappointment it had the same feeling of any number of malls I'd reluctantly visited over the years. Many of the stores were US based companies, and most were empty. Carolina explained that while the mall was a popular place to window shop, most Mendocinos made the majority of their purchases from the more economical local shops at the city center.

At 10:30, still awaiting the arrival of Marcela, we entered the modestly crowded theater and found our seats. When the movie started, I was quickly humbled. Having been steadily gaining confidence in my Spanish skills, I assumed I wouldn't have difficulty understanding the movie. But the Spanish translation was fast, and clearly not done by an Argentine. I struggled from the outset, often having to ask Carolina for assistance. Finally after twenty minutes I gave up, resigned to the fact I could follow the basic plot despite losing many of the details.

More than 30 minutes into the film, the fourth member of our group finally arrived. She stretched across the seats to provide greeting kisses for all, apologized for her tardiness, and slipped into the seat next to me. I'd assumed before meeting Marcela that I might have seen her or even been introduced to her at some point at the university. Marcela was, after all, probably the most common female name I'd encountered in Mendoza.

But to my great surprise, her instantly recognizable face was not familiar from a previous university encounter. Or even from an interaction I'd experienced during my weeks in Mendoza. To my amazement, I knew without question, that Marcela was the woman from the bus. The woman who had both surprised and confused me with her unexpected approach on the ride over from Chile. The interaction that had been memorable enough that I'd thought about her on more than one occasion over the previous six weeks. I was stunned.

I assumed she would have remembered me given the lack of foreigners in Mendoza, but if she did she gave no indication by her facial expression or actions. While I was initially flustered by our meeting, she appeared just the opposite. She confidently leaned close and asked me for a synopsis of what she'd missed. Further distracted by the pleasant scent of her perfume, I stumbled through an awkward summary, having to twice restart sentences to communicate my answer. She listened patiently, helped me with the words I couldn't find, and then thanked me. I relinquished any hope I'd be able to follow the movie.

When it was over, we made our way out of the theater to the bus stop. The girls gushed about the stunts, the special effects, and the lead actor. With little to contribute, I stayed quiet, enjoying the passion and flow of the conversation among close friends. We made our way aboard another crowded bus back to the Plaza de Independencia from which we would go our separate ways.

Able to make myself less conspicuous amongst the many passengers, and aided by better lighting, I spent much of the trip confirming my initial observations of Marcela. Of average height, she had long brown hair that came forward, covering the front of her shoulders in perfect symmetry. She had dark eyes and a bright smile. And as she turned her head to the side providing a glimpse of her profile, I saw the subtle little bump on the bridge of her nose which gave away her southern European ancestry.

There were other attributes worthy of my admiration. Her light brown skin color was vibrant, one shade lighter than her hair color. She had a slight overbite, which created the sense she was always on the verge of laughter. She had a thin, well-toned build, which unlike many Argentine women I'd met, suggested a genuine interest in exercise. And she carried herself with a sense of calm and confidence I found captivating.

We arrived back to the plaza around one a.m. Despite my desire to remind Marcela of our previous encounter, I remained quiet. Not having said anything initially, I now thought it would be awkward to bring it up. So instead I thanked the group for a fun night and headed off to the trolley stop, unsure as to what time the last trolley ran. I arrived at the stop and was content to see two others waiting as well. I took a seat on the bench and began to reflect on the surprising events of the evening.

Within minutes of my arrival I was startled by an enthusiastic salutation.

"Hola flaco!"

I smiled as Marcela sat down next to me on the bench.

"Where are you headed?" I asked, feeling a rush of nervous energy.

"The fourth section, near the main trolley station," she explained.

I knew the area well. I assumed she lived in one of the high-rise apartments where I'd looked at potential housing.

"How about you? Where are you staying?" she asked.

"I'm renting a house in the sixth section," I responded.

She nodded. "So tell me, how are things going so far? Have you found Mendoza to be as welcoming as I'd suggested it would be?" A smirk appeared on her face.

I smiled. I felt a flush on my neck. "So you do remember me. I thought by your reaction you'd forgotten."

"No, of course I do. If I remember correctly I encouraged you to dance tango and visit our vineyards. Have you taken my advice?"

"One for two," I proclaimed. "I toured the Santa Julia vineyard a few weeks ago and it was great. No tango yet, but I still have time."

"Okay, not a bad start," she encouraged.

I satisfied her curiosity with more details regarding the reasons behind my travel to Mendoza. I went on to summarize the six weeks of my journey, choosing somewhat uncomfortably to withhold the part about Sara's visit the week prior. I then directed the conversation back to her.

"So are you from Mendoza originally?" I asked.

"I am," she said proudly. "I spent the first six years of my life living in the fifth section. But then we had the military coup. And our family moved away for a time to New York City."

"Really?" I responded. "How long were you there for?"

"Seven years," she said, nodding her head for emphasis. "My mom never wanted us to leave Argentina at all, but my father convinced her with the promise we'd return in a few years when things were better. My mother really wanted my brother and me to be raised in Argentina. But we ended up staying longer than anticipated."

"So you moved back after the transition back to a democracy?"

"Yes," she confirmed. "I was in eighth grade at the time. We were so excited to be going home to friends and family. But soon after reality set in. The economy was tough." Her smile was gone. "My dad struggled to get his restaurant off the ground. And after a year he moved back to New York to make money to support the family."

"He went back by himself?" I said.

"Yes. It was just going to be temporary. My mother was convinced Argentina was the best place to raise a family and was dead-set against all of us leaving again. But it didn't work out that way." She paused. "My father did well in New York City, and quite frankly I think he was just happier there. He remained part of our lives for a few years, but eventually he met another woman and gradually distanced himself."

"Wow," I said, suddenly overcome by sadness. "That must have been tough on you and your brother. What is the age difference between you and him?"

"He's three years younger. And it was, especially on him. But my mother was fantastic. She worked hard to make ends meet. Eventually we had to move out of our house and into the apartment where we are now. But we made due. I worked various part time jobs both during high school and after graduation."

I shook my head. "So you still live with your mother and brother?"

"Just my mom. My brother finished high school and saw how hard things were here. So one day he decided to go back to New York City. My father welcomed him and he's been in New York for almost ten years now."

I shook my head again. "And you're a full time student now?"

"Part-time," she corrected. "I took a part-time job as an English teacher five years ago in a small town outside of Mendoza. I don't have my teaching certificate, but the English I learned in New York was good enough in an underserved area. But three years ago, frustrated by my inability to find a full-time job, I enrolled at Cuyo to get my teaching degree. But I had to keep my job. We couldn't afford to give up the income. So it's been a slow process. I'm about half-way through the program now."

"Have you enjoyed going back to school?"

"Yes and no. With several years of teaching experience now, some of the practicum classes seem unnecessary. I'd hoped to get them waved but it didn't happen. And I can't say I feel like the coursework has made me a better teacher yet. But I understand the degree is important for career advancement. And I've met a lot of great people including Carolina and Celina. So it hasn't been all bad."

I smiled. "Good. I'm glad there've been some positives at least."

"Definitely," she said, nodding in approval.

"So what do you remember about your time in New York City?" I said, switching into English to assess her second language skills.

"Muy poco," she responded, her shy smile expressing her apprehension about speaking in English. She continued in Spanish. "They were difficult times. I didn't speak a word of English when we arrived. The school transition was hard and I remember struggling to keep up." She shivered and zipped up her jacket. "When my English did get better, I was forced into the role of interpreter for the whole family. And that was hard. Imagine as a nine year old girl having to go to my brother's teacher's conferences with my parents to translate for them." She shook her head. "It was tough. And since we didn't expect to be there long, we never acclimated. We were just biding time, waiting for things to normalize in Argentina so we could go home."

"Have you been back to New York to see your father and brother since your brother left?" I asked cautiously.

"Not yet," she said, shaking her head. "And I don't see it happening anytime soon. I still have mixed emotions about seeing my dad. Plus it's such an expensive trip. A part-time teacher's salary barely pays the bills, and I'm trying to save a little as well."

I nodded, and for the first time since Marcela had sat down there was a pause in our conversation. I glanced at my watch and saw it was after two. I looked over my shoulder and saw there was no longer anyone else waiting. I looked back toward Marcela, poised to voice my assumption we'd missed the last trolley. But before I could speak, perhaps anticipating what I was going to say, Marcela looked up and grasped my eyes with a penetrating gaze. She held me motionless for several seconds. She then repeated that captivating smile, and asked me about my decision to pursue medicine.

I smiled back, and started in on my story. I spoke about my family and my journey into medicine. I talked about my training, and my decision to become a radiologist. And I did so with a comfort and ease in Spanish I hadn't before experienced. Every time I struggled to find a word or expression, Marcela intervened to maintain flow to our conversation. And as I finished my summary, the conversation continued effortlessly. Our dialogue swayed back and forth like a pendulum, each of us contributing equally to an endless stream of introductory conversation.

Finally, at almost 3:30 a.m., I again looked down at my watch. I looked up at Marcela and shook my head.

"I think we missed the last trolley. Should we share a taxi?"

"Sounds good to me," Marcela agreed. "I know I've taken trolleys after two before, but maybe they only run late on weekends."

I looked across the street and saw two taxis idling at one of the square's entrances. I waved my hand, and one of the drivers flashed his lights in acknowledgement. We got into the taxi and Marcela provided her address. We spent the ten minute ride to her apartment discussing the movie. She did her best to explain parts I'd lost in translation. When we arrived to her building, we said a quick goodbye and exchanged customary cheek kisses. I refused her effort to pay a portion of the ride, and we agreed we would surely cross paths at the university soon.

I slumped back in the cab and sighed. I spent the short ride back to my house analyzing our interaction. I couldn't remember the last time I'd experienced a conversation that engaging. And the fact it was with a young attractive Argentine woman was certainly not lost on me.

This hadn't been part of the plan. Improve my language skills and get to know a new culture? Yes. Self-enlightenment through international travel? Sure. Confirmation of a career path destined to provide happiness? Absolutely. But meeting another woman that stirred up emotions I hadn't experienced in a long time? This had never come up during the planning stages of my trip.

I went inside and lied down on my bed. I thought about Sara. After years of struggling to find companionship, she seemed to possess everything I'd ever hoped to find in a woman. She was smart, driven, and beautiful. We had a countless number of shared interests, including our desire to start medical careers together in Colorado in the very near future. So why then was I feeling this way about Marcela?

I tried to think about it logically. I knew part of it had to be loneliness. It was after all less than a week since Sara had left, and it would be months before I'd see her again. And maybe some of it stemmed from the difficulties we'd experienced during our visit. Despite finishing on a positive note, I was unaccustomed to encountering any negativity in our relationship.

And then there was the cultural piece. I recognized I was becoming infatuated with the Argentine culture which was still fresh and exotic. My feelings for Marcela were likely just an extension of my attraction for the entire Mendoza experience.

I thought about getting up and walking down to the telephone 'cabina' a few blocks away to call Sara. But it was late now and I knew the events of the night had created an emotional turbidity. I'd wait and call tomorrow. And I'd be careful to avoid the English department at the university for a few days. I simply couldn't risk ruining the relationship I'd waited so long to find.

19

I spent the following week staying busy with school work and teaching. I read voraciously for my history class. I read detailed accounts of how in 1982 a faltering Argentine dictatorship tried to rekindle support by attempting to seize the Falkland Islands from the British and reclaim land the Argentine government insisted belonged to its people. I read government news releases that falsely reported the British were retreating and victory was imminent, despite international reports illustrating a one-sided battle always unrealizable for the poorly equipped Argentine army. And I reviewed the aftermath of the three month conflict that left more than 600 young Argentines dead and a country defeated. It was the final blow to a deteriorating dictatorship that was finally replaced by a return to democracy in 1983.

I was just as occupied with my English classes. With several weeks of classes completed, I was running out of topics I could use to stimulate dialogue without preparation. So I spent downtime between the university and my evening classes at the public library, pulling recipes, American music, and American movie scenes I could show to generate conversation. While it required more work on my part, the students remained engaged and I was rewarded with a sense of fulfillment.

And true to my promise to myself, I made extra efforts to stabilize my relationship with Sara. I called her on consecutive days following my night at the movies. I spent an evening at a coffee shop struggling to write her a poem conveying the feelings she'd inspired during our first meeting. And I did everything possible to avoid crossing paths with Marcela. I rode the bus one additional stop at the university to avoid walking near the building where the English classes were taught. I walked to my downtown classes to forgo the trolley route which passed near her building. I even found myself walking with my head down in public, afraid to make eye contact with passersby for fear of the chance encounter.

And yet despite this multitude of tactics, I found myself spending a disproportionate amount of time thinking about Marcela. Her striking confidence that made her so comfortable in conversation. Her continual smile that made it difficult for me to look away. And that look she'd given me during the one pause in our conversation. That inquisitive and mysterious look that I'd interpreted as a desire to get to know me better. I couldn't get her out of my head.

In between my classes the following Tuesday, I made my way to the computer lab to check my email. Although by now I often eschewed the archaic university computers for more modern alternatives in the 'cyber cafes', I knew this might be my only chance to get to a computer on a day that promised to be busy with class preparation and evening classes. As on most occasions, the lab was empty. I took a seat and began the tedious process of logging into my account. Ten minutes later I perused the subjects of the handful of new emails from the previous 48 hours.

While most were junk, one email caught my attention. It was from Dr. Smith, the head of the residency program in Denver. While I'd stayed in regular contact with him throughout my fellowship year, it had been months since our last communication. The subject of the email was 'issue'. I hesitated for a moment, pondering the variety of problems that could warrant such a proclamation. I then clicked on the subject and sat up on the edge of my chair.

Dr. Smith started the email by reassuring me that everything was fine with my future position and that they were looking forward to my arrival. He then outlined the problem. Dr. Minter, the other musculoskeletal radiologist, had unexpectedly resigned to accept a position at Stanford. This had put the Denver program in a difficult situation. We'd been accredited as a fellowship program based on the assumption we'd have at least two musculoskeletal radiologists. Now we were down to one. Dr. Smith was in discussions with the board to see if we'd still be able to offer a fellowship the upcoming year. While he felt confident they would find another qualified physician, he couldn't be certain this would happen prior to the match date for incoming fellows. He felt there was a chance we might have to delay the acceptance of our first fellow.

I sat back in my chair to evaluate the ramifications. As long as the fellowship program was ultimately accredited, a delayed start might prove beneficial. This would give me extra time to get settled in the new system, as well as to acquire additional reading experience. Really the only thing that had worried me about my new position was that my lack of experience might make it difficult to gain the respect of my fellows. But this delay could allow me to be one more year out in front of the trainees. And if indeed there was a delay in the hiring of a musculoskeletal radiologist, I assumed this would increase the amount of time I'd be asked to read musculoskeletal films. While I wasn't averse to general radiology, I preferred musculoskeletal MRI.

But what if they struggled to find a replacement? What if the accreditation had been granted in part based on Dr. Minter's experience? Would the board reconsider the program recognition? While I assumed I'd still have a job, the academic component had been a strong selling point for me. And then there was the disappointment of having lost Dr. Minter. I'd met Bill over lunch during my interview day and we'd hit it off. He was just a few years older than I was and we shared many interests. I'd assumed he would serve as both a mentor and friend upon my arrival.

Deep in thought about these possibilities, and unaware I was no longer alone in the lab, I was startled by a voice from the adjacent computer. And I was even more shocked to see who it was.

"Thought I might find you up her," Marcela said beaming.

"Just trying to get caught up on some emails. What are you doing up here?"

"Killing time before I go out to Tupungato to teach. We don't start until 2:20, and I'm done at the university by noon every day. It doesn't make sense to go home in between. So I usually eat lunch here, get some work done, and then make my hour drive to school."

"Wow, an hour?" I said. "That seems like a long trip for a few hours of teaching. How'd you end up teaching in Tupungato?"

"A couple of reasons," Marcela began. "My grandparents lived there. They passed away many years ago, but I spent a lot of time in Tupungato as a child. When the English job came available, I was contacted by one of the other teachers I knew from childhood. Without a degree, I couldn't afford to be picky. And while I hated the commute at first, I've come to tolerate it because of how much I enjoy the job. I get along well with the other teachers. And I love the families. Both the children and parents are so appreciative of the teachers. I really feel like I belong in the community."

I nodded. "Sounds like a great place. It reminds me of the small town where my father works. I may have to visit at some point."

"That's a great idea," Marcela said. "The children would love it. For most it would be their first opportunity to meet a real live gringo." She flashed the smile that had been reappearing continuously in my head.

I looked back at my computer screen, trying my best to pretend I was able to continue reviewing emails in her presence.

But whether or not she was able to read my bluff, she seemed determined to continue our dialogue. I felt her eyes maintain focus upon me. I now realized she had no intention of using the computer.

"What are you doing Friday night?"

Caught off guard by her bluntness, I hesitated before returning my glance in her direction.

"Uhhh, nothing." I paused to compose myself. "How about you?"

"How about meeting for coffee on the peatonal? I have a girlfriend who waitresses at Bonafide. It's the best coffee in town."

I sat back in my chair, then answered reflexively. "That'd be great."

"Cool," Marcela said nodding. "Nine p.m. I'll meet you there. See you Friday."

She stood up, bid me farewell with the single cheek peck, and slipped out as quickly as she'd appeared.

I turned my chair back toward the computer and closed my eyes. So much for my avoidance strategy. In a matter of days, she'd tracked me down, clearly intent on asking me out. And throwing all logic to the wind, held hostage by that smile, I'd succumbed to her request. And yet rather than regret and apprehension, I was overcome by an overwhelming sense of excitement. I knew I should have declined, but it had just felt right to say yes.

I looked back at my remaining emails and saw there was a message from Sara. The topic was 'another house'. I hovered the cursor over the message for a few seconds, before sliding it to the 'close' icon in the upper right corner. It was getting late. I needed to make my way down to class. And I knew I wasn't in the proper frame of mind to be communicating with Sara anyway. I needed some time to think out my next move.

20

The following few days were tough. I tried to read for my history class, planning to take the midterm on Thursday. But despite my best efforts, attempts to study proved futile. Every few sentences into my reading, my focus shifted away from my material and back to Marcela. And then Sara. And then Marcela again. On several occasions I made up my mind that I needed to call Carolina and get Marcela's number. I could apologize for mistakenly accepting her invitation, explaining that I was involved in a relationship. But each time I talked myself out of it.

After all it was just a cup of coffee. Carolina had surely told her I had a girlfriend. So it wouldn't come as a surprise when Sara came up in conversation. And there wasn't any harm in building another friendship. Sara had many close male friends through the residency program, and I knew she couldn't object to me forming similar relationships in Argentina.

On Thursday morning, after my third consecutive miserable night of sleep, I emailed Dr. Martinez to explain I'd decided not to take the exam because of other commitments. I knew the professor would give me a hard time, but decided the ridicule would be easier to tolerate than the embarrassment generated by a dreadful performance. And I opted out of my wine class as well; it seemed silly to trek up to the university for a single class.

I decided instead to go to the telephone kiosk and call Fernando. I'd only talked to my friend once since my arrival, and I knew it was time to catch up. After two days of self-embattlement, it was time to seek reassurance from a friend. Someone who might understand my emotional confusion, and provide some much needed advice.

I guessed right and caught him at home as he was preparing to head to the lab for the day. He was excited to hear from me and he listened intently as I brought him up to speed on my experiences in Mendoza. He was thrilled to hear I found his city so welcoming, although was somewhat disappointed I'd only been skiing twice.

"I guess I'm kind of surprised as well," I said. "I've just been so busy with things here that I've lacked motivation to explore other ski options."

"You must be," he responded, "because the Jake I know would have definitely spent more days at the mountain skiing than hanging out at the university. I thought this trip was about exploration and discovery? I can't imagine you've encountered anything in the classroom you haven't seen before."

"You'd be surprised," I said. "I think more than anything it's the people. Professors have been great, and I've already made some close friends. It's been just over a month now and I already feel like this a home away from home."

"Hanging out with the kids at the university, huh?" he teased. "Didn't think an old man like you would fit in up there."

"Actually I've met a bunch of different people, many younger but some my age as well. I met a group of friends in my wine class that I've been hiking with. Some English students have become friends. And I met this great girl just this past week."

I stopped there, anxiously awaiting his reaction.

"Excuse me? Care to expand a little on that last one?"

I was ready with my answer. I'd been slowly directing the conversation toward this explanation from the outset. I walked him through the movie night, our subsequent encounter in the computer lab, and our pending gathering at the coffee shop. Again there was silence. Not unexpected, but unnerving nonetheless.

"I don't know Jake," he began. "You need to be careful. It may seem innocent enough to you, but it sure sounds like something that could destroy everything you've developed with Sara. How many times have you told me how lucky you are to have found her? Don't ruin it all over a little crush."

"Yeah, you're probably right Fernando," I said, pausing briefly. "But honestly I don't remember ever feeling with Sara the exhilaration I felt at the trolley stop the other night. Don't I owe it to myself to at least get a cup of coffee with her?"

There was no delay in his response.

"Just remember your adventure will be over in a couple of months, and then it's back to reality. Your job and future are awaiting you in Denver. And I'm pretty certain Sara is a big part of that. While I'm sure an Argentine girlfriend would add another layer of depth to your experience, you need to be rational. Don't get lost in the moment."

I felt the concern in his tone. I'd assumed he would try to talk me out of it, but I thought he might apply a more jovial approach. But there was no jocularity in his words. He was worried for me. And I appreciated his candor.

"Okay," I agreed. "I think it's easy to get lost in the fantasy world down here, especially with all these beautiful women. You always told me Argentine women were the most beautiful in the world, but come on, this is ridiculous."

Fernando laughed, and the tension eased. The conversation transitioned back to his life in Pennsylvania. He was busier than ever, having been asked to teach a second class that fall in addition to his research. And just as the family was adapting to his new schedule, it was time to start over again. They'd just found out they were pregnant with their third child.

We talked for twenty minutes, agreeing to not let as much time pass before we spoke again. He ended our talk with a not so subtle reminder of his earlier words.

"Have an awesome time. Enjoy my country for all its beauty. But be careful. You stand too much to lose."

"Sage advice my friend. Thanks for listening. Un abrazo."

I hung up and walked back to the house. While I was happy to have talked to him, our conversation had certainly not eased my apprehension about my pending gathering with Marcela. He'd told me what I'd expected to hear. The logical decision was clearly to call and cancel, and then refocus my efforts on the teaching and coursework that had brought me so much satisfaction already. Enjoy the experience, but maintain focus on my original intent.

But for the first time in my life, I was prepared to brush logic aside. For the first time ever, I was ready to let feel and desire guide my decision-making. I'd always taken the cerebral approach, always followed every rule to a tee. It was after all, the Schmidt way, handed down from grandfather to mother to son, seemingly stronger with each generation. But something was now different. Whether it was the city, the language, or the culture, I couldn't be sure. But in sharp defiance to the process I'd used to make decisions for the first 30 years of my life, I was succumbing to my emotions. I was not going to call and cancel. I was going ahead with my plan to meet Marcela. And I was excited.

21

eferring to local custom, I dressed for the evening in a pair of dark jeans, a button-down light blue long sleeve shirt, and black leather shoes. I trolleyed downtown and strolled up the peatonal, arriving at Bonafide at ten minutes after nine. After a brief scan revealed I was first to arrive, I settled on an outdoor table on a comfortable night. As always, the peatonal was crowded with locals of all ages. All but two of the outdoor tables were occupied, forcing me to squeeze between people to arrive at a small circular table surrounded by larger tables. While there were a few couples at the smaller tables, they were greatly outnumbered by families and groups of young adults whose boisterous conversation ran together making it difficult to follow any one particular dialogue. After a surprisingly short wait, I was approached by a waitress who provided a menu and asked me if I was ready to order a drink. I deferred, explaining that I was awaiting a friend. I then anxiously glanced at the menu, never allowing my attention to drift away from the many comers and goers for more than a moment.

By 9:30, I was still neither surprised nor concerned. I'd been in this position on countless occasions in Mendoza. Extended waits had become the norm. But by five minutes to ten, I was beginning to lose my patience. This degree of tardiness didn't seem right. She'd extended the invitation, and she'd picked the time. I knew she had a long commute back from Tupungato, with the potential for any number of delays. But we were approaching an hour late. It was starting to be excessive, even by Argentine standards.

By 10:15, it was time to give up. Maybe she'd changed her mind. Maybe she'd spoken with Carolina who had told her about Sara. Or maybe there had been a miscommunication about time or place. I was pretty certain we'd agreed upon this Friday, but it was not yet out of the realm of possibilities that my Spanish had failed me. I stood up from the table, again made my way through the crowds, and walked down the block to the trolley stop. I sat down on the bench amongst a large group of people and waited for the next trolley.

Lost in thought, awaiting my turn to board the trolley, I heard my name. I looked over my shoulder toward the back door of the trolley, and there she was. Her long brown hair alive with curls covering her bare shoulders. A simple white blouse with a black knee high skirt. And that smile again. I laughed as I realized she was getting off the same trolley I was about to get on. I walked toward her.

"Giving up on me already?" she joked, extending her hands up into the air in mock disbelief.

"Still adjusting to the culture I guess," I said sheepishly.

"I'm sorry. I'm infamous amongst my friends for running behind. I should have given you a heads up the other day."

"I'm just glad you made it," I said, my frustration instantly discharged. "It's too nice of a night to be sitting at home watching television."

"It sure is. Come on," she said, putting her hand on my low back to playfully redirect me back toward the coffeehouse. "Let's go find a table."

We walked back up the peatonal and settled on the same table I'd just left behind. The waitress soon appeared and smiled at me.

"Guess you didn't get stood up after all?" she chided.

I blushed. We ordered our coffee, and with neither of us having found time for dinner, we each ordered a croissant. Then without a hitch, our conversation was flowing as it had during our first encounter.

"Long day at school today?" I inquired.

"Yeah crazy, I could've used your help," she responded, shaking her head.

"Oh yeah, how's that?"

"One of my students had a seizure," she explained.

"Oh no, that's scary. What'd you do?"

"Panicked," she said. "It seemed like an eternity, even though it was probably just a minute or two. Afterwards he was out of it, so I decided we needed to get him to the hospital. We called his parents, but the family lives in a rural part of the county, 45 minutes away. I wasn't comfortable waiting that long, so I asked the teacher in the adjacent classroom to watch my kids while I drove him to the hospital myself. And as it turned out that was the easy part."

The smile now gone, I could feel the emotion in her voice.

"When we got to the hospital, we were told the emergency room physician was unavailable. They'd just attended to a patient who had suffered a cardiac arrest, and he was being transported to Mendoza for further care. The patient was unstable and the ER doctor had decided to accompany the patient in case there were complications in route."

"He left the emergency room uncovered?" I said, shaking my head in disbelief.

"Pretty much," Marcela responded.

A tear welled in her eye.

"I mean there was a nurse, and some assistants, but no physician and an overall sense of confusion. And then things got worse. As the nurse was explaining our options, essentially to wait until the physician returned or drive 30 minutes to another town to be seen by a family doctor, the child seized again. And this time it was much more severe."

She paused to gather herself. I felt a sudden desire to reach out and take her hand to console her, but I fought the urge.

"It easily lasted five minutes, and this time he vomited during the seizure. The nurse rolled him on his side, but not before he began to choke. She suctioned out his mouth, but it didn't seem to help. He started laboring to breath, using all of the muscles of his little neck and chest. His lips were blue, and the nurse was shaken. She told one of the assistants to run get the surgeon who was operating in the hospital."

"Oh my god," I said. "How long did it take the surgeon to get there? And what were you doing in the interim?"

"Praying. Holding the boy's hand, rubbing his head, and praying. The nurse put oxygen on his face, but had nothing else she could do. Finally after about five minutes the surgeon ran in with another man, and just as they came in, it stopped."

Her eyes were red now. She looked away, wiping away a tear she could no longer hold back.

"I'm sorry you had to go through that." Again I fought the temptation to take her hand. "How's the boy doing?"

"I think he's okay," she said, forcing a smile. "His breathing improved, but never normalized. They kept him on oxygen. They took a chest x-ray and said it looked a little cloudy. So they started an iv and gave him antibiotics. And the surgeon thought it best that he be transferred. But with Tupungato's only ambulance away with the previous patient, they had to call in another from an adjacent town. And that took forever. Eventually they arrived and transported him to the children's hospital in Mendoza. I spoke with his grandmother by phone just before I left my apartment, and she told me he was better. They were continuing the antibiotics, and were still supporting his breathing, but he was resting comfortably."

"Wow," I said, shaking my head again. "What a traumatic afternoon. I still can't believe the ER physician would leave the emergency room like that."

"Yeah, well it's not shocking to me," she said, smiling again as she fought to overcome her emotion. "Unfortunately it's not the first time I've had issues with the medical care in Tupungato. In fact I've been to the ER three times during the last few years, and none of the encounters have been smooth."

"Really?" I said. "What's the issue?"

She took a deep breath. "They seem to have two major problems. First one is lack of resources. On each of the three visits they ultimately sent us to Mendoza for at least part of the treatment. Second is not having the right kind of doctor available."

"You mean they don't have an emergency room trained physician?" I questioned.

"No, I'm not sure about that. I don't know if they are emergency room trained or not; I guess I assumed they were. The problem is they don't have a permanent physician. Tupungato is not a particularly attractive place for physicians. Rural, limited resources, probably low-pay; it just continues to be an underserved area. To my knowledge there is one general practitioner who lives in the area. The ER physician is always a temporary position filled by recent medical school graduates doing their government required community service before being allowed to pursue their career. They're there 12 months, maybe a little longer if we're lucky, and then they hand off the duties to the next graduate. While they've all been nice enough, they seem to lack the desire to improve the quality of care. There's really no incentive for them, and even if they were motivated, I doubt one year is enough time."

"Yeah, I can see that being a big problem," I said. "Brand new graduates practicing independently without guidance from experienced physicians? That's not optimal. And without any continuity of care, I can't imagine they're tracking results and updating protocols to the extent they should be. Sounds like they're in desperate need of a quality improvement project."

"Yes, they are," Marcela agreed nodding her head. "If only we could find a qualified physician with some free time on his hands to take on the project."

Now the smile was back with all its glory. She raised her eyebrows and tipped her head forward inquisitively.

I smiled back, hesitating for a minute before responding. I'd wanted to gain a better understanding of health care in Argentina. And while I didn't know how much I'd have to offer in the realm of emergency medicine, I did have friends from medical school who had gone on to practice ER medicine. They might be able to provide assistance. And then there was that look from across the table. How could anyone say no to that?

"Well I suppose I could talk with the hospital administrator. Not sure how a US trained radiologist will be received, but I'd be willing to give it a shot."

She nodded approvingly.

"Perfect. I'm pretty sure I can make that happen. I had the administrator's daughter in my classroom two years ago. I know him well. I'll talk with him next week and get you an appointment. And maybe we can coordinate the meeting with a trip to my school to meet my students. Remember you promised a visit."

"Deal," I said.

"Great," she said, with any sign of her previous tribulation now vanished. "How do you like that? The coffee hasn't even arrived yet and I've already cried and put you to work. Quite the beginning, huh?"

I laughed. The drinks and food soon arrived and our conversation drifted fluidly from topic to topic. We talked about our families. Marcela recalled her limited memories from her seven years living in Queens. And after some playful pleading, I even got her to briefly speak a little English.

Speaking in her non-native tongue, Marcela suddenly became bashful.

She sat forward and lowered her voice. She glanced over her shoulder to see if anyone appeared to be listening. I was pretty sure I noted a subtle blush appear on her olive-colored skin. And what I heard surprised me very much. While I expected a strong Argentine accent, I was instead met with the pure, unbridled cant of a native New Yorker. There was no hint of a foreign accent whatsoever. Her discomfort with the language, however, was apparent in her limited vocabulary and awkward word choice. Many of her sentence constructions were clearly direct translations from Spanish, made comprehensible only by my knowledge of the language. After just a few minutes, she switched back into Spanish. And her confidence immediately returned. Eventually, with each of us having moved on to our second cup of coffee, the conversation again returned to Tupungato.

"So you seem to have become attached to this town," I said. "How much time did you spend there growing up?"

"A lot," she began. "I was very close to my grandparents. Omar and I were their only grandchildren, and we loved to spend time at their home. My grandpa worked as the county treasurer, but his real passion was working his land. They owned 100 acres on the edge of town, complete with its own vineyard, small olive orchard, and a number of different animals. Omar was still pretty young, so I remember my grandpa spending most of his time with me out on the land while Omar stayed inside with our grandma. I have vivid memories of riding horses with my grandpa to check on the vineyard. Every day I was there we had to examine the vines. I remember how excited he would get to teach me, about the soil, the weather, the stages of grape maturity… I think I spent the majority of my last two summers in Tupungato before we moved to New York."

"That must have been hard to leave at that age, to leave your grandparents and other family behind. Do you remember understanding why you had to move?"

"Yes and no. My dad was a government employee as well. When the coup occurred, I understood he'd lost his job and couldn't find work. I was told we needed to move to the United States so that he could get a job. It wasn't until many years later I came to realize that his opposing ideology could have put our family in danger had we stayed."

I again sensed Marcela was on the verge of tears. I saw the pain in her eyes as she looked away to gather herself. She turned back toward me, but kept her eyes down, looking at the table. I sensed she had more to tell. I waited, and she soon found the strength to continue.

"My grandparents stayed behind in Tupungato. I remember there was talk they would go with us, but ultimately we were told grandpa needed to stay behind to care for the farm. I'm sure it was hard on the whole family, but it was devastating for a six-year old girl partially raised by her grandparents. I remember sobbing at the airport as we waved good-bye. I can still picture my grandfather, dressed in his grey suit and black hat, rubbing my cheek and telling me how much he loved me. It was the last time I ever saw him."

She looked away again. But this time she couldn't hold back the tears. She sniffled, clenched her fist, and sighed, trying hard to hide her over-flowing emotions.

This was the last straw. As difficult as it had been previously, it was now impossible to continue as a passive bystander. I instinctively reached out and gently squeezed her arm. She looked back at me and smiled.

I waited for her to compose herself.

"What happened to him?" I said in my most heartfelt voice.

"Still to this day I'm not sure. On my tenth birthday my mother took me aside and told me he'd passed away. I remember how hard she tried not to cry in front of me. And I remember my utter disbelief. I'd talked to him just days earlier on the phone, as we'd done weekly since our move to New York. When I questioned my mother, she told me only that he'd developed sudden health problems. That was as much as we were told. And I was too young to know what else to ask."

She paused again.

"There was talk of trying to return to Argentina for his funeral, but ultimately it was too difficult. Instead we dressed up in our nicest clothes and went to evening mass. It was something we hadn't done together apart from Christmas for years. It was a very tough time for our family."

She stopped and took a drink of her coffee.

"Did you ever find out more about his death?" I asked.

She nodded. "Many years later, back in Argentina, I came home one night and walked in on my mother in tears. It was the anniversary of my grandfather's passing. We cried together, and as she steadied her emotions, she asked me if I wanted to know the truth about his death. When

I nodded, she took my head in her lap, and rocking me, proceeded to tell me he'd been murdered. Killed by the dictatorship for harboring political beliefs in conflict with the regime. I was stunned. While I'd begun to feel over the years that my mother knew more than she'd told me, I never for a minute had considered the possibility he'd been killed. But as it turned out, just before the coup, my grandfather had been on the verge of being elected a state senator for the province. But with the sudden overthrow of the government, his political aspirations were destroyed. And he soon lost his job as county treasurer as well."

"My grandparents were well enough off for my grandpa to have been able to retire to the farm. But as a leader of the local socialist party, he decided to speak out against the military regime. Their initial response was to confiscate half of his property. And when he continued to fight to form a cohesive opposition, he became another victim of their unconscionable brutality."

This time, as the tears again began to well-up, she kept her eyes locked on me. She forced a smile, as if apologizing for her show of emotion. I returned the smile, just now realizing I was still resting my hand on her arm. I withdrew it, rearranging myself in my chair as I looked away, before again allowing my eyes to meet hers.

"I'm sorry if I'm asking too much, but do you know what happened?"

She shook her head. "We don't know the details. Just that he went to work one day and never came back. Two of his colleagues never made it home that day either. My mother didn't even find out about his death until several days later when she called as part of our standard communication. My grandma had been too distraught to call us. Or maybe she'd been in denial. She hadn't even yet reported his disappearance. My mother convinced her to do so, but we never again heard anything."

"That must have been awful for your grandma," I said, shaking my head in disbelief.

"It was," she said nodding. "She was never the same after. When we moved back to Argentina in 1984, the difference was dramatic. It was as if she'd aged 20 years in the seven years we were away. She'd let everything go. The land, the house, her own appearance. The only time she left the house was to buy groceries. My aunt, my mother's sister, had tried to intervene. But she'd moved to Cordoba years before. And my grandma rejected several attempts to get her to move. Her home was in Tupungato, and she was determined to spend the rest of her days there. Upon our return, we tried to go out and take care of the land. My mother actually moved in with her at one point for several months. But ultimately it was too much. Our home was in Mendoza. The restaurant my father had opened was on the peatonal. Our school was here. Eventually my parents made the difficult decision to let the land go and honor my grandma's wishes to stay in her home. We visited as much as we could, but her deterioration continued at a rapid pace. She passed away in 1986."

I couldn't believe what I was hearing. I knew the history well from my class. I knew there were at least 30,000 reported to have disappeared. And I knew that while most of the abhorrent activity occurred in Buenos Aires, interior provinces including Mendoza hadn't been spared. Dr. Martinez had vividly described military planes performing night flights to drop bodies into Lake Carrizal in the desert 30 minutes southeast of Mendoza.

But now it was so much more tangible. The look on Marcela's face, twenty years later, made it that much more difficult to comprehend.

"You've been through so much with your family," I said. "I can't even begin to appreciate how hard it must have been."

Marcela smiled again. "Yeah, not your typical upbringing. But it hasn't been all bad. There've been some benefits to dealing with adversity. First and foremost has been the relationship I have with my mother. We've been through so much together. And since my brother moved to New York, we've become closer than ever. Every time I start feeling sorry for myself, I think about what she's been through. To stay so strong through it all. She's given me so much."

"And I'm sure you've given a lot in return. I can't imagine she could have gotten through all of this without you."

Marcela leaned back in her chair. "I think that's probably true. My friends always give me a hard time for spending so much time with my mom. But she's my best friend. And I don't ever see that changing."

She looked down at her watch. "Wow," she said. "It's already two. It feels like we just got here."

I looked around. There were only a few people left at the tables, and traffic on the peatonal had slowed substantially.

"Yeah, I suppose it's getting late. Should we ask for the bill?"

"I think so," she agreed. "But I hope you're not thinking of trying to escape my company just yet. I have a second stop planned for the evening. You don't have to get up early tomorrow do you?"

I put my hands behind my head and looked up as if contemplating my schedule. "I'm supposed to be at the university by ten a.m. on Monday, but until then I'm pretty wide open."

She laughed. "Good. Because I was hoping to continue your cultural enrichment. And two in Mendoza is still early. Some of my friends probably still haven't left their houses yet."

I shook my head, fully aware by now she was telling the truth. "I don't know how you guys do it. I think that's one Argentine routine to which I'll never acclimate. So where are we headed?"

"If it's okay with you, I think we'll keep it a surprise." She raised her eyebrows twice in mock flirtation. "All I'll say is that it's one of my favorite spots in Mendoza. And I can't wait to show it to you."

She flagged down the waitress, who eventually produced the bill. I volunteered to pay, but Marcela insisted we split it. She then led me back down the peatonal in the direction from which we'd come.

I had no idea where we were going. Not even a guess. But it didn't much matter. The night was still young. And I was feeling high on emotion I hadn't felt for a long time. Maybe ever.

22

With the night having finally grown cool, we walked quickly. Lost in conversation, I paid little attention to our exact route. I knew we'd crossed the main boulevard of San Martin, leading us into the east 4th section. This was an area of the city I'd been told could be seedy at night, 'the red district' as I'd heard it called. But while there were fewer people out on this side of San Martin, I otherwise didn't notice activity that appeared alarming.

After about a mile walk, Marcela turned midblock into the entrance of what appeared to be an outdoor mall, with a narrow walk lined by small shops leading us away from the street deep into the center of the block. I'd been into several such malls downtown before, often inconspicuous amongst the busy commerce lined streets. With no one else in sight, my initial reaction was to question whether the mall was even open at this hour. But as we turned the corner at a small tiled plaza that appeared to mark the center of the mall, I heard distant music. And while it was difficult to make out the style, I was pretty certain someone was singing.

Marcela slowed as we approached the establishment from where the music was emanating. She took my arm in her hand and spun me to a stop.

"Are you ready to see one of the places that makes Mendoza so special?" she said beaming.

"Absolutely," I responded. "Can't say I would've been likely to stumble upon this place myself."

"Come on, follow me."

She took me by the hand and led me into a dark, smoky room. We walked past a small bar set against the wall of the narrow entryway, arriving to a wider part of the room where all the action was occurring. The area was framed with at least 25 small tables, almost all of which were occupied with wine glasses and jackets. Yet only a few people were scattered around the perimeter at the tables. Almost everyone, at least 50 people by quick estimate, were floating and spinning around the center of the room. The famous Argentine Tango. I smiled at Marcela and nodded in appreciation. What a spectacle. And they were dancing to live music. In the back corner of the room, on a small makeshift stage, there were two musicians. An elderly man was seated in a chair sweating profusely as he played the accordion-like bandoneon. I'd seen it played by street musicians on a couple of occasions in Mendoza, but I'd never heard it accompanied. At his side, dressed in a sexy knee-high black dress, a young woman of no more than 25 was lost in song. With her eyes closed and fists clenched, bending forward at the waist, she sang with fervor. The room was alive.

Marcela led me to a back corner, taking a seat at one of the few tables that appeared unoccupied. I sat down next to her, angling my chair toward the dance floor. With the loud music making conversation difficult, I sat back and watched in amazement. The crowd was primarily older, with the majority in their fifties and sixties. But there were a handful of younger dancers as well, with at least a few couples who appeared of college age.

I focused on one of the younger couples, studying their movements. The man was clearly the lead. He stood tall, almost rigid, with his right forearm tight across the woman's mid-back and his fingers curled around her upper flank. Pressed tightly against his torso, she rested her left hand on his shoulder, while her right hand met his in the classic extended arm position. Her eyes were closed, seemingly focused on moving her feet to follow his lead.

I studied their feet to see if I could pick up on a basic step. But it was soon obvious there was no simple pattern to their movements. Unlike other dances of which I had basic knowledge such as swing or salsa, it appeared there was no clear repetition to the dance. Each individual step was clearly marked by the lead, allowing his creativity to result in a great variety of movement patterns and velocities: slow and fast walks, both forward and back, with small steps and bigger ones; intermittent spins, from ninety degrees to 360 degrees, always maintaining torso contact with their partner; and those decisive little kicks, the female rapidly flexing her knee either in front or behind her other leg, or sometimes even dangerously around her partner's leg. As effortless as it appeared, I knew it couldn't come easily.

I allowed my eyes to drift around the room from couple to couple. I noticed the general direction of dancing appeared to be counter-clockwise around the periphery of the floor. I watched as the male leads waited patiently with small steps and twirls for space to open in front, before exploding with larger steps to claim new territory. I observed that older couples seemed to implement a simpler form of the dance, with an emphasis on walking and short twirls, void of the kicks and rapid spins more common amongst younger dancers. And I realized there was no conversation on the dance floor. Torso to torso, with heads positioned above their partner's right shoulder, the dancers displayed an intense commitment to the dance. It was beautiful.

As the song ended, the dancers made their way back to the tables. I noticed many of the dancers either were not there as a couple, or were not dancing with the person whom accompanied them at their respective tables. I sensed a strong feeling of community, as if the majority of dancers were regulars who gathered to share their appreciation of the dance.

"So what do you think?" Marcela asked.

"Spectacular," I said, shaking my head in disbelief. "Can I assume you know how to do this?"

"Sort of. I'm learning. I've been coming here to listen to music for a while now, but just started taking lessons a couple months ago."

"What prompted you to start taking classes?" I inquired.

"I grew up listening to this music. My parents were both music lovers and excellent dancers. We always had music on in the background. In the car, during meals, even as we fell asleep at night. And much of the time it was tango. But as I got older, I got into other types of music. My friends listened to pop. Tango was lost on our generation. Then maybe a year ago a friend of mine brought me here on a whim. And my love for the dance was reborn. Initially I'd come and sit by myself, listening to the music and watching the dancers with envy. I turned down opportunities to dance, fearful I'd make a fool of myself. Then one night I overheard a young couple talking about a new tango group. I inquired about joining and they welcomed me. I've attended maybe ten classes now and I love it. I'm still a beginner, but I'm more determined than ever to learn."

"How about your mother? Have you brought her here yet?"

"She came once. She loved the music, but wasn't interested in dancing.

She has her group of friends with whom she gets together to dance. Mostly folklore. But I don't think she's danced tango since she separated from my father. I'm certain it reminds her of him, their time together. And I'm sure that's hard."

She raised her voice to finish her sentence as the music began again. People stood, invitations were extended, and the dancers returned to the floor. An older male of at least 60 years old, looking dapper in his light gray suit, approached the table and addressed Marcela.

"Un baile por favor señorita Marcela?"

"With pleasure Arturo," she responded, winking at me as she stood to accept his hand. They assumed the starting position and their dance began. True to the style of his generational counterparts, his lead was simple but elegant. Marcela moved smoothly and confidently, her torso still as her feet mirrored each of his steps. While she may have been new to the dance, she was clearly a quick study. In fact I noticed just two small details that distinguished her from more experienced dancers. First, unlike most other women, Marcela's eyes were open. Her facial expression demonstrated a deep concentration, clearly working hard to place each step as guided. Second, her implementation of the little kick, something I'd later learn was called a "gancho", was both less frequent and more subtle than many other dancers. She appeared to lack the confidence to employ the adornment more liberally. But apart from these little details, she was comfortable on the dance floor.

As the second song ended, she came back to the table and pulled me to my feet.

"Ok, now it's your turn," she exclaimed. "A smart guy like you, I'm sure you've picked up the basics by now."

"Easy," I said pulling away slightly. "I've never been much of a dancer. And I'd never even seen tango before tonight. I'm afraid I'll embarrass you."

"Don't worry," Marcela reassured. "I know most of these people by now. They'll get a kick out of seeing a Yankee on the floor."

I followed her across the room to a less crowded area providing more starting space.

"I'll help you lead," Marcela declared. "Just try to keep forward on your toes. I'll talk you through some basic movements."

"I'm game," I announced. "Just be patient with me."

The music began and my tutorial was underway. First there was the basic step. One back with the right foot, two back and opening with the left, three stepping forward with the right in front of the left, four with the left in front of the right, five with the right tucked behind the left. A brief pause. Then six forward with the left with a subtle spin counterclockwise, seven squaring the right up with the left, and eight pulling the left together against the right. We repeated the basic step several times. I kept my steps small, careful to avoid stepping on Marcela's feet. So far so good.

Then there was a variation of the basic step. Skipping one and starting with two, opening with the left foot. Again, not too difficult. My confidence was slowly growing. Marcela used her left hand to pull my right elbow close to her side, allowing me to stretch my forearm further across her mid-back.

"You need to stay tight to keep control," she said. "Use your right arm to guide my weight, to let me know which foot I need to step with. You're in control. I'm just along for the ride."

I smiled, and the dance continued. Next it was basic walking. Forward, forward with a slight curve, backward, then in combination. Shoulders back, head up, marking each step, and always to the beat of the music. Faster parts of the song required quicker steps, slower sections meant more deliberate steps, sometimes allowing for brief pauses. Marcela was a good instructor. While I was never able to fully relax, by the end of three songs I was able to alternate the basic step with different walking patterns, working hard to always remember onto which foot I'd guided her weight.

The song ended and I pulled back and smiled.

"Not too bad for a gringo," I announced proudly.

"Not bad at all. You may be a natural," Marcela quipped.

We walked back to our table. Marcela flagged down the waitress and ordered us a carafe of red wine.

"You can't dance tango without a little red wine," she declared.

"I'm willing to make the cultural sacrifice," I joked.

We moved our chairs closer to allow our conversation to continue despite the loud music. She educated me about the history of tango, about its Buenos Aires roots and its African influences. She identified each song by name, along with either the singer or the orchestra that first performed it. And she explained the different styles of ballroom tango. The classic tango, the faster milonga, and the more rhythmic waltz style. The musicians alternated amongst these different types, playing three songs of one before transitioning to the next. There was always a brief interlude between music types during which dancers drifted away from the floor for a sip of wine and often to find a new partner. Marcela confirmed that few people danced exclusively as a couple; the majority preferred to vary partners both to enjoy different styles of dance as well as to augment their personal skillset. She also pointed out the traditional way in which the man extended an invitation to dance: a tip of the hat, a nod of the head, or a formal extension of his hand, many times without a word exchanged between prospective partners.

Marcela continued with her instruction on the dance floor as well. Sticking to the traditional tango style, we returned to the floor on multiple occasions for one or two songs at a time. She was patient and encouraging, offering just enough information to allow me to maintain my focus while still keeping it fun and relaxed. I was enraptured. The music was great and the dance was beautiful. But it was so much more. The dark bar, the formal dress, the carafes of wine. And more than anything, it was Marcela. Her passion for the music and the dance was contagious. Her confidence and composure were striking. And her touch was seductive. What started early in the evening with an innocent touch of the forearm, progressed throughout the night under the influences of both the wine and the dance. The frequency and duration of our hand and arm contact increased steadily at the table. And the tightness of our embrace grew stronger on the dance floor. By the end of the night I allowed myself to close my eyes on the floor, engrossed by the floral tones of her perfume and the warmth of her body pressed against mine.

Finally at six a.m., with the live music having long been replaced by compact discs, and with only one other couple remaining, we decided to end our evening. We made our way to San Martin St. where a number of taxis were waiting. During the ride to Marcela's apartment, there was silence between us for the first time since our evening had started together eight hours earlier. While there was an element of exhaustion as daylight emerged, I knew there was more to it than that alone. I felt certain that Marcela too recognized that our time together had extended far beyond two friends hanging out. Or for that matter, even two interested parties enjoying a first date. This was something different. I knew the silence stemmed in part from a mutual understanding that this developing relationship, while still yet undefined, was something that needed to continue.

The taxi pulled up in front of Marcela's building. I walked her to the door. There Marcela stopped and turned toward me. She lifted her head gradually until our eyes met. We remained silent, gazing into each other's eyes. I broke the silence.

"Thanks for a great night."

"I'm glad you liked it," she responded. "As I said before it's a special place for me and I'm glad I got to share it with you."

"Me too," I said.

Again there was a pause. I felt myself begin to flush, struggling with the uncertainty on how to end such an amazing night. Possibly sensing my unease, Marcela restarted the conversation.

"So what are doing Sunday afternoon?" she said.

"Nothing that I'm aware of. What were you thinking?"

"How about joining my mother and me for lunch? She's a great cook, and we always have lunch together on Sundays. I've already told you so much about my family, I think you'd enjoy meeting her."

I nodded.

"Yeah, that'd be great. What time should I come over?"

"How about one? Argentine time that is." Again she flashed her smile.

"Sounds good. I'll make sure to arrive a little late."

I thought about leaning in for a kiss. I was pretty sure it would be reciprocated. After a night like this, how could she not be feeling what I was? But ultimately I chose not to. I stepped in close and eschewed the traditional cheek kiss for a hug. I held her close against me, allowing myself to feel her warmth one more time. I took her left hand briefly as I pulled away. Then with my mind still spinning in exhilaration, I walked back to the taxi and made the short trip back to the house.

23

$e$xhausted from the late night, it was after noon by the time I garnered the strength to get started the following day. I lay in bed smiling as I recounted the events of the previous night. It seemed surreal. Two weeks ago I hadn't even met Marcela. And now the following day I was going to her home to meet her mother. How had this all happened so quickly?

I got dressed and walked around the corner to my favorite carryout place. It was an unmarked private home from which the family prepared a handful of traditional Argentine dishes during afternoon hours. I'd stumbled upon it one day on my way home from the university when I happened upon a line of people in the courtyard waiting for their food to be prepared. I inquired as to what they were waiting for and had been delighted to discover the little gem which I'd since visited often. While I'd enjoyed many dishes on the limited menu, I'd developed a particular fondness for their milanesa, a garlicky baked version of a lightly breaded steak best complimented with a heavy squeeze of lemon. I ordered it and then stepped outside to wait on the patio.

The sun was out and the day was already warm. While late September in Mendoza usually meant around 80 degrees, the temperature was well on its way to over 90. I leaned against the railing in the one corner of the patio covered by shade. My thoughts returned to Marcela. But this time the smile was interrupted by a competing emotion. I pictured Sara at home in Chicago. I assumed she'd been on call the previous night, working hard while I'd been out with Marcela. And I knew she would be worried about me now, wondering why she hadn't received a phone call in a week.

I knew well I should have been overcome by guilt. She didn't deserve this. She'd always treated me so well. She'd never for a minute strayed from her commitment to me or to our planned future together. And now I was going to pull something like this? Just two weeks removed from her visit, and only months away from moving in together?

I recognized that the pursuit of a serious relationship with Marcela was impossible. I only had two months left in Argentina before my return. That wasn't sufficient time to build a lasting relationship. And even if it were, my future was in Colorado, while she seemed quite content with her life in Mendoza. I couldn't envision a scenario where these obstacles could be overcome.

Yet to my surprise, rather than feeling dismay for my decision to have gone out with Marcela, I instead felt uncomfortable only with not having called Sara to tell her. I knew this spoke to the potency of the connection I was forming with Marcela. There was a fervor to my attraction I hadn't previously experienced. And I wasn't prepared to let logic and guilt interfere.

I knew Sara and I needed to talk. But what would I tell her? What was this relationship I was developing, and where was it headed? I knew I didn't yet have the answers that she would seek. That she deserved. But I felt they might come soon. As hard as it was, I decided for now my best move was to maintain my silence.

Following an emotional night that provided more tossing and turning than actual sleep, I tried to keep my mind occupied the following morning. After having essentially ignored my university classes for the previous ten days, I pulled out my collection of readings from my history class. I read an article entitled "Challenges for a New Democracy", which outlined the difficulties Argentina faced in 1983 following the end of the dictatorship and the election of Raul Alfonsin.

Like many countries in Latin America, the 1950s and 60s had been decades of strong economic growth in Argentina. The 70s, however, had been inconsistent, with a shift back and forth between free market and protectionist economic policies. The one constant, however, was Argentina's dramatic increase in foreign debt. Throughout much of the decade, Argentina accepted ever-increasing loans from international banks bloated with money from oil-rich nations. Given their history of growth, Argentina, Brazil, and Mexico in particular had been considered a safe investment by international creditors.

Yet with the worldwide recession of the late 1970s, the political strife of a dictatorship, and local factors including a severe drought, Argentina soon found itself unable to make payments on its loans. With a subsequent inability to receive external financial support, the government tried to stabilize the economy by printing more money, increasing wages, and augmenting welfare programs. But this led to hyperinflation. Just months before Alfonsin took office, with inflation over 100% per year, the peso was replaced by the peso argentino at a rate of 10,000 pesos to 1 new peso.

Upon his election, Alfonsin resumed talks with the International Monetary Fund (IMF) in attempt to resuscitate an economy in dire need of capital. But recognizing a number of policy problems, the IMF again rejected Argentina as it had the previous year. Alfonsin instead had to settle for a $300 million loan from other countries in Latin America, and then another of equal magnitude from the United States. But it wasn't nearly enough. The government soon returned to printing more money and expanding welfare, and hyperinflation raged on. By June of 1985, inflation had increased to 30% per month, highest in the world, and the new peso argentino was already in need of replacement. It was a traumatic return to democracy in a country whose economic struggles would continue for the whole of the 1980s.

At 12:30 I went into my bedroom to get ready. I pulled out my nicest pair of khaki slacks and a light blue short sleeved button-down shirt. Unhappy with the multitude of wrinkles, and devoid of both an iron and dryer, I turned on the hot water in the shower, hung the clothes on the towel rack, and closed the door. Fastidious in my preparation, I then shaved, combed my hair, and even applied a local cologne I knew to be popular. With the bathroom steamed, I turned off the shower and meticulously hand-pressed my shirt and pants. Satisfied with their improved appearance, I dressed, took one final look in the mirror, and headed off on foot.

On yet another cloudless day, I forced myself to walk slowly. Having created awkwardness on more than one occasion for showing up on time, I knew I didn't want to arrive before 1:30. I walked through a local plaza with a large grassy area and playground surrounded by a red-tiled walk. I stopped to watch a group of teens involved in an intense game of soccer. On the other side of the plaza I slipped into the corner wine shop to purchase a bottle of wine. The attendant recommended a bottle of Bonarda. He explained that while the Malbec had garnered much acclaim for Mendoza, the Bonarda grape was considered its equal by many locals. He described it as lighter-bodied and less rustic than Malbec, with a more moderate acidity. Far from a wine connoisseur, I wasn't sure I'd appreciate the described characteristics, but I was happy to accept his recommendation.

Walking through the large park adjacent to Marcela's apartment complex, I looked at my watch and saw it was still only 1:20. I forced myself to sit down on a park bench in the shade where I waited impatiently. Finally at twenty to two, I walked across the last section of the park and rang the bell which called up to Marcela's apartment.

"Hello, who is it?" Marcela answered in her best English.

"Someone looking to share a bottle of wine in exchange for an authentic Argentine meal," I responded.

"Wow, what a coincidence. We just so happen to be serving such a meal. I accept."

The buzzer sounded and the door clicked. I pushed the door forward and walked into the lobby. I pushed the button for the elevator labeled 'odd floors', and waited as the rickety elevator made its way down. The elevator stopped abruptly and was silent. I opened the brown wooden door, slid open the black accordion-style gate, and then closed both behind me. I pressed the button for the fifth floor and the elevator jolted upward. It was a noisy and rough ride. I knew there was no chance it would be found up to code in Chicago. I also knew that with earthquakes common in Mendoza, this would be the last place I'd want to be caught during a quake.

The elevator stopped and I opened the doors. I walked down the hall to apartment five and knocked on the door. Marcela opened the door, but before I was able to approach for the customary greeting, I was immediately accosted by two small dogs. They took turns jumping up toward my waist as Marcela laughed and did her best to pull them away. Her mother came to the rescue, apologizing profusely as she pulled them away into another room.

"Quite the welcome, huh?" Marcela said, smiling as she leaned in for her cheek kiss.

"I can't imagine anyone sneaks into your apartment unannounced," I said.

Marcela's mother returned and walked toward me with open arms. She was dressed formally in a red dress, partially covered by her white apron. I felt relieved by my decision to dress up for the occasion.

"It's so nice to meet you Jake," she said, placing her hands on my shoulders as we exchanged kisses.

"You as well Silvia," I responded. "Thank you for the invitation."

I handed her the bottle of wine which she admired before thanking me.

"Welcome to our home. Please have a seat."

She pulled out a chair for me at the small kitchen table which had been neatly set for three. I scanned my surroundings. The door to the apartment opened into an L-shaped kitchen, with the larger part of the room no more than six feet by eight. Off one end of the kitchen was a small pantry which appeared to be crammed full with miscellaneous kitchen and other storage items. Off the other end of the kitchen, leading to the back of the apartment, was a narrow tiled hallway that I presumed offered access to the bedrooms. Although I couldn't see into the rooms, I knew the apartment couldn't be more than 400 square feet.

Marcela sat down at the table across from me as Silvia returned to her food preparation. With both the counter space and stove top filled with a variety of food items, it wasn't overtly clear what Silvia was preparing. But it smelled amazing. I recognized garlic and oregano as prominent contributors to the conglomeration of aromas.

"Ready for a glass of wine?" Marcela inquired.

"Sure," I said. "Let me open it."

I started to stand up, but Silvia stopped me.

"Not in our house Jake. You're our guest today, let me get the wine."

I sat back down, looking across at Marcela who just smiled. Not different from previous Sunday afternoons, I sensed the responsibility of a male guest was to remain seated at the table and enjoy the food.

"Thanks Silvia. Can I ask what you're preparing this afternoon?"

"Of course. Today is the 29th, so per tradition, I'm making gnocchi with tomato sauce and steak."

"Sounds fantastic. I didn't realize 29th was gnocchi day."

"Actually," Marcela said, "its Argentine tradition to eat gnocchi on the 29th of each month. We don't do it every month, but we do it when we can. It's very labor intensive. My mother was rolling out pasta at nine this morning and the tomato sauce has been simmering for hours. She pan sears pieces of strip steak, then finishes them in the tomato sauce. It melts in your mouth. Everything she makes is good, but I think this is my favorite."

"Omar's too," Silvia said. "It's always the first thing I make when he comes to visit."

I could sense from her tone she missed her son greatly.

"Well I can see why," I offered. "It smells fantastic".

Silvia beamed. "You really know the way to a woman's heart. I can already see Marcela was right about you."

I felt my face flush. I glanced at Marcela.

"Mother, behave yourself please," she scolded.

Silvia served the wine, and the meal soon followed. She started us with the small pieces of steak lightly covered in tomato sauce. The steak was indeed tender, making use of the knife optional. The sauce provided an additional richness without overpowering the natural flavor of the beef. She served me a portion twice as big as theirs, and then immediately served me seconds as I was nearing completion. I could see from her demeanor that my input was neither desired nor would be accepted. I happily obliged.

Following the meat, she served bowls of gnocchi, topped with the same tomato sauce in which the meat had been prepared. She topped the dish with a liberal amount of hand grated parmesan cheese, and accompanied it with the simple green salad to which I'd grown accustomed. The gnocchi was brilliant. Its firmness made it unique from others I'd tried. And the tomato sauce, applied more generously than it had been with the meat, was the perfect fit for the pasta. I tasted the prominent oaky flavor of Malbec and enjoyed the heavy hand Silvia had employed with the garlic. I finished my serving and was again rewarded with an unsolicited but much welcomed refill.

Determined in her role as the consummate hostess, Silvia spent little time at the table throughout the meal. Yet her frequent departures did little to detract from the flow of conversation. While Marcela and I had several of our own short exchanges, Marcela served as facilitator during much of the meal allowing Silvia and me to get to know each other better. I answered questions about my family and the set of events that led to my decision to come to Mendoza. Silvia talked about growing up in a large family on the outskirts of Mendoza. She described her reluctance to leave Mendoza for New York, and their difficult but overall positive experience in the United States. She admitted she never allowed herself to become immersed in the New York culture. She offered as proof her very limited English vocabulary despite almost a decade abroad.

After lunch I offered to help with the dishes. But again my request was rejected. Instead Marcela joined her mother at the sink to wash dishes while I was left to my cup of coffee. The phone rang just as they were finishing, and Marcela stepped away to answer. She returned briefly to excuse herself to talk with a parent she'd been trying to talk with for weeks. Seemingly recognizing an opportunity to talk alone, Silvia left the last few dishes, poured herself a cup of coffee, and joined me at the table.

"She's a pretty special young lady, isn't she?" she said with a wry smile.

"Yes she is," I said, nodding in agreement. "I feel very fortunate to have met her."

"I'm so proud of her. She's experienced way too much sadness in her life for a woman not yet 30 years old. But she's always persevered. And now just in the last year or so, she finally seems to be finding the happiness I've always wanted so much for her."

"She's shared some of her past with me, and she's undoubtedly been through a lot. But it's difficult for me to imagine her staying down for any period of time. She's such a positive person. What's changed in the last year to create such beautiful energy?"

"It's been a number of things I think. Some of it is just maturity. Some of it is getting away from unhealthy relationships. But I think the biggest thing is just her recognition of how close she is to realizing her goal. She's worked so hard the last five years, and she can finally see the light at the end of the tunnel."

I looked at Silvia, lifting my eyebrows to convey my lack of understanding.

"I've learned a lot about your daughter in the last couple weeks, but I don't believe she mentioned her goals."

"Oh, I'm sorry," Silvia started. "I guess I just assumed you knew."

She paused, shifted her position in her chair, and glanced over her shoulder toward the hallway where Marcela had disappeared.

"Well I can't imagine she'd be upset if I told you," she said as if trying to convince herself. "She's probably just too humble to have wanted to share it with you. Has Marcela told you about her grandparents?"

"You mean your parents from Tupungato?" I said.

"Yes. Well as you may know, they had a large plot of land outside of town. When my parents passed, that land went to my sister and me. My sister lives in Cordoba and had no interest in the property. She's wanted to sell for years. And it's too remote and too much responsibility for me at this stage of my life. I too had thought it best to sell. But Marcela always loved that land. When we first talked about putting it on the market almost a decade ago, Marcela begged us to hold on to it. She told us she'd save up the money to one day purchase my sister's share. And while it seemed unlikely for a long time, she's recommitted over the last few years and is finally on the verge of making it happen. She's made a tremendous amount of sacrifice to get to where she now is. Has she shared any of this with you?"

"I knew about the land, and what a special place it had been for her. And I remember her saying the government had confiscated property during the dictatorship. But I wasn't aware it still belonged to your family. And while she's mentioned her affinity for Tupungato, she hadn't shared with me her intent to purchase the property and relocate there."

"There's still more than 50 acres. And while the house is pretty run-down after years of abandonment, it's still livable. Marcela has an agreement in place to pay off my sister's interest in the home. So really it's been a matter of saving up enough money for some basic home repairs and to purchase the necessary equipment to make the vineyard operational again."

"The vineyard?" I responded with surprise. "She's planning to start a vineyard?"

I smiled and shook my head in disbelief. While we'd only been out together on two occasions, there had certainly been ample opportunity for her to share this with me.

"Restore the vineyard would be more accurate. My grandparents operated the vineyard for more than 20 years. And while it was let go for years, Marcela tells me there are twenty acres where vines can be salvaged. She's been taking classes through the viticulture institute for more than a year now. She must have told you something about this."

"Actually she hasn't," I said. "I'm kind of surprised it hasn't come up. It sounds amazing."

"Her planning and discipline have been admirable. I was skeptical at first, but I've grown quite confident in her ability to pull it off. I'm excited for her, and extremely proud. I'm guessing you may have detected that in my tone." She smiled and looked away.

I hesitated for a moment, and then redirected the conversation.

"Silvia, can I ask you an unrelated question?"

"Sure Jake, anything."

"Is it okay with you that I'm spending time with your daughter?"

"Of course it is," she said quickly. There was a brief pause. "Why, is there reason for me to be concerned?"

"None at all," I said. "I guess I was just referring to the difficult circumstances, with me just being in Mendoza for another two months."

"Jake, I've always believed that one should surround themselves with as many good people as possible. And through what I've heard about you from Marcela, and what I've seen for myself this afternoon, I have no doubt you are a good person. She's clearly happy when she's around you. And nothing makes me more content than seeing her happy. As long as you two are realistic about what your relationship is, and stay away from promises you can't fulfill, I think you'll be fine."

"Thank you," I said. "That means a lot. And I share your sentiment. Although we haven't discussed it, I sense we're on the same page in our appreciation for what we're developing together and the limitations we face. I'll make sure to remain open and honest if I'm fortunate enough to continue to spend time with your daughter."

As the words came out of my mouth, I thought of Sara. I now knew what I had to do. And I had to do it as soon as possible. Things had now progressed, and remaining silent was no longer an option. Marcela deserved it. And Sara even more. I resigned myself to full disclosure as soon as possible.

Just as I was gathering myself to continue our conversation, Marcela returned from her phone call. She stopped as she saw Silvia seated at the table next to me.

"I'm sorry that took longer than I thought. I hope my mother hasn't embarrassed me too much in my absence."

"Quite the contrary," I said. "She only gave me additional insight to support the conclusions I'd already been forming." I winked at Silvia. "It was nice for the two of us to have a chance to talk."

"Good," Marcela said smiling. "What do you think about taking a walk through the park? My mother is used to taking a siesta after our meal, and that will give her a chance to lie down."

"Sounds like a great idea," I said. "It's a perfect afternoon. Is that alright with you Silvia?"

"Absolutely," Silvia said. "Just make sure to come back for flan. People tell me mine is the best. We can have it with our afternoon Mate."

"Perfect," Marcela said. "We'll be back in an hour."

I stood up, kissed Silvia goodbye, and followed Marcela out the front door. We made our way out of the building and into the park where I'd stopped earlier.

We strolled along the wide, tree-lined tile sidewalk, favoring the side that provided partial shade from the still powerful sun. We touched on a number of different topics including the food and her studies. But upon our arrival to a shaded bench near the end of the walkway, Marcela took me by the hand and pulled me into a seated position at her side. She crossed her right foot on her left knee, allowing her right knee to rest on the bench between us.

"Thanks for coming over this afternoon. I know my mother enjoyed your company. And I found you pretty tolerable as well."

I laughed. "I had a great time. It was fun getting to know your mother. And it proved to be quite educational for me as well."

I smiled and quickly raised and lowered my eyebrows.

"Oh yeah?" she said. "Did my mother tell you about some of my misguided past?"

"Actually she didn't. Apparently she's left that to you. She spent most of the time talking about your future."

I stopped there, studying her eyes, awaiting a reaction.

She displayed a look of uncertainty, but then smiled and nodded her head.

"How much did she tell you?"

"Seemed like quite a lot to me," I said. "Your pending acquisition of your grandparents' property. A restoration of their vineyard. Your viticulture classes. It was quite enlightening. Is there more I'm missing?"

She smiled sheepishly and shook her head.

"No I think that pretty much covers it. That loud mouth. I can't believe she just blurted it all out. I wanted to be the one to tell you. But I was waiting for the right time. I thought I'd take you on a surprise tour when you come out to the school to meet my kids. So much for that idea."

She shook her head and looked away.

"It sounds amazing. Your mother made it sound like it's something you've been working toward for a long time."

"Yeah, I guess you could say that," she said. "It's a dream I first had years ago. And one I thought might be unattainable on several occasions. But I think I've turned the corner. My teaching job has given me the stability I needed to progress. Then I stumbled upon these classes last year and suddenly everything seemed to come into focus."

She paused and gathered herself.

"I mean I still have a ways to go. It's far from a sure thing at this point. I still have more saving to do, and a number of logistical hurdles to overcome. But for the first time I'm starting to look at it as a potential reality rather than a dream. And while it's often quite scary, it's also really exciting."

I kept my eyes locked on hers. I saw tremendous happiness and pride. After years of struggle, she was following her passion and on the verge of achieving her goal. I instinctively squeezed her hand.

As she returned the squeeze, I abruptly released my eye contact, and then sat up and withdrew my hand from her hold.

"Marcela, there is something I need to tell you," I said.

My smile was gone, my demeanor now serious. A look of concern emerged upon her face. I looked away again and then found the courage to continue.

"I have a girlfriend in Chicago," I started. "Someone I have been seeing for more than a year."

I paused and waited for her response. But she remained quiet.

"She's a resident at the hospital where I did my fellowship. She has one year left in her training and is in the process of looking for a job in the area where I'll be working upon my return."

Again I paused. And again Marcela stayed silent.

"I'm sorry for not having told you earlier. I guess I just got caught up in the emotion. I wasn't expecting to meet anyone during my trip. And I could never have fathomed I might meet anyone like you." I looked away again. "And when I did, I thought at first maybe we could just share a friendship. Just hang out like I do with others I've met at the university. But it has quickly become apparent this is much more than that for me."

My mouth was dry and I struggled to get the words out. But I had to tell her how I felt. I had to be honest. And I had to be clear about my intent.

"I apologize if I was out of line. I have no idea what it is that we have together or where it might be headed. But I know I've never before experienced such an intense desire to spend time with anyone."

Marcela reached out and took my left hand. She then placed her left hand on my cheek and gently redirected my face toward hers. She leaned in and I followed her lead. My lips touched against her upper lip, then shifted and found her lower lip. She pulled back, still holding my face to maintain our eye contact.

"You've verbalized my emotions perfectly. I understand the challenges of our relationship. I know your future is in the United States, that your time left in Argentina is finite. And the last thing I want to do is interfere with a relationship you have at home. But I've never before felt the emotions you've stirred up inside me during the last few weeks."

She looked away, then turned back and continued.

"I've always been one to follow my instincts. And every last one of them is telling me to spend as much time with you as possible. I understand the risks, and the hurt that might follow. But I'm willing to accept that. You still have two months left in Argentina, and I'd love to share that time with you. But at the same time you need to feel comfortable. I don't want to hurt you. If you decide that spending time with me is not worth the risk, I'll understand. But if you desire to continue what we've been developing together, I'm willing to forge ahead. But I won't do it behind anyone's back. I know firsthand what that is like, and I refuse to hurt someone else the way I've been hurt before. Can I assume by your forthrightness we're in agreement on this matter?"

She removed her hand from my face and took my other hand in hers.

"Absolutely," I said. "I've wanted to have this conversation with you for over a week now. I guess I just needed confirmation that we shared the same feelings. And it's such a tremendous relief for me to have been honest with you."

I paused and withdrew my hands from hers.

"I need to call home tonight and have a difficult conversation. I owe it her, and I couldn't live with myself if I didn't."

She nodded, and wiped away a tear from her lower lid. She stood up and pulled me to my feet.

"Let's finish our loop through the park and get back for our dessert. I don't want to keep my mother waiting."

"Me neither," I said. "I can't wait to try that flan."

I smiled and we resumed our Sunday stroll. I felt relieved our conversation had gone so well. My perception had been accurate. She felt the same way that I did. And now we could move forward without presumption or uncertainty. But first there was one more obstacle I had to confront. It was a conversation I couldn't have imagined having just weeks before. And yet here I was, on the verge of generating tremendous pain for someone I cared about greatly. On the verge of potentially ruining a relationship I'd felt so blessed to have found. I shivered at the thought of what I was about to do.

24

I arrived home just after eight. The dessert had been executed to the same high standard as the main course, and I was now uncomfortably full. I'd thoroughly enjoyed the afternoon. Yet as day had turned to evening, and my pending phone conversation neared, I'd become distracted. I struggled at times with my Spanish comprehension, often having to seek clarification of details Silvia provided. Seeming to sense my discomfort, Marcela eventually intervened, announcing to her mother that I had to get home to prepare for my classes. She accompanied me downstairs where her farewell was brief, but comforting. As I turned away to start my walk, she grabbed my hand and held me for a few seconds at arm's length. She stayed quiet while looking into my eyes, giving me a look which seemed to acknowledge her recognition of the difficulty that awaited me. I flashed an appreciative smile, then turned and started to walk, not allowing myself to look back.

When I arrived home, I lay down on my bed to rehearse the conversation in my head. I knew there would be emotion on both ends. I couldn't imagine telling her how much she meant to me without breaking down. But I also knew that I had to stay on message. As difficult as it would be, I had to be clear in my explanation of both my feelings and intentions.

At nine p.m., I forced myself out of bed and walked around the corner to the cabina. I dialed her number, breathing deeply as I felt my stomach tighten in apprehension. The phone rang several times before it was answered.

"Hello," Sara said with a tired voice.

"Hi Sara," I responded uncomfortably.

"Jake! Thank goodness! I've been so worried. Why haven't you called?" There was great concern in her tone.

"I'm sorry Sara. Things have been so busy with the university and my teaching. And I tried a couple of times last week and missed you." I provided my first lie.

"Busy, Jake? Really? You're on vacation. I worked eighty hours last week. That's a pretty lame excuse. I went so far as to call Fernando yesterday to make sure he didn't know more than I did. I was worried."

"I know," I said. "I should have kept insisting until I found you. I just have a lot of things going on right now."

There was a pause on the other end. I recognized the vagary of my statement. I sensed her discomfort with the conversation.

"What kind of things? Bring me up to speed on what I've missed over the last two-and-a-half weeks," she said with a frustrated tone.

I hesitated. Here it was. The moment I'd been dreading. It was time to come clean.

But I couldn't get the words out.

"I've just been busy here in Mendoza. I've been reading a lot for my university classes. And my teaching preparation has become more time consuming. It's been fun, but definitely more work."

I shifted in my chair. I wanted desperately to tell her everything. I was fighting against myself.

"Very disciplined of you," she said with a forced laugh. She sounded somewhat reassured. "What else? How about weekends? Have you been back on your skis? Any more hiking trips with your friends?"

"No, actually I haven't," I said. "I'm thinking about trying to ski next weekend before the season is over." I paused. "I did get a chance to go tango dancing this weekend."

I swallowed hard and awaited a response. There was no going back now.

"Oh yeah, tango?" she questioned. Her words were tepid. I closed my eyes and again and took a deep breath.

"Yeah it was quite the cultural experience. Live music, an old-fashioned salon. It felt like a scene from a movie."

There was an awkward silence. I knew what came next. And I was pretty sure Sara knew as well. It was several seconds before Sara forged ahead.

"Do I dare inquire as to whom you went dancing with?"

I remained quiet and Sara's suspicion was confirmed.

"Jake, please tell me this isn't happening." Her voice cracked with emotion. I pictured the tears beginning to well-up in her eyes.

"Sara, I never for a moment thought this even a remote possibility. It's something I can't even explain to myself. I've loved you more than anything in my life. And you don't deserve this."

She was quiet. Her sniffles grew louder. She awaited further explanation.

"I'm confused Sara. I know I still love you. We've shared something very special together. But I've met someone here I feel I have to get to know better. I know it makes no sense, but it's what I'm feeling. And I can't ignore it."

I awaited a response. But she wasn't ready. Or wasn't capable of providing one yet. Surely she was lost in process mode, trying to comprehend my hurtful delivery. I pressed on, doing my best to portray the multitude of emotions that overwhelmed me.

"I honestly can't foresee the possibility of building a sustainable relationship here in Argentina. I'm moving to Denver in two months and I'm excited about building my future there. And I still hope there's a way we can build a future together. I just know that right now I've met someone who is pulling me in another direction. And although it may not work out, I could never do anything behind your back. As hard as this is for me, that would be much worse. You deserve to hear the truth."

"Who is she?" she said quietly.

I hesitated. "Someone I met through the university."

"What's her name?" I'd barely finished my sentence. There was anger in her voice now.

"Marcela."

"And when did you meet her? Were you two already seeing each other when I was there? I've only been back for like three weeks."

I knew this question was coming. I told her the truth about our encounter at the movies. But it wasn't comforting. She remained on the attack.

"I can't believe this." She was sobbing now. "I thought we were perfect for each other. We share the same dream Jake. We've planned a future together. And now in just three weeks you're ready to throw it all away? How is that possible? Was I that far off on my interpretation of our relationship?"

Her words stung me. Now it was my turn to fight back tears.

"Of course not Sara," I said. "I guarantee you I felt everything you did. And while I'd understand if you decided you didn't want anything to do with me, I hope I'm not closing the door on a future together. I still have strong feelings for you. But I just can't now."

Her emotion was pouring out.

"Why not Jake? What is it? I don't get it. If you truly felt the way I do, you wouldn't be giving up this easy. Are you sure you're not just getting caught up in the experience? Or just wanting to get laid? Have you really thought this through?"

"I have Sara. Every minute of the last two weeks. I've considered the experience possibility. But regardless, it's an overwhelming sensation I have." I paused. "I'm sorry Sara."

There was more crying from the other end. But she was out of words.

"I'm sorry Sara," I repeated. "I love you. I always will."

Again she remained silent.

"Good-bye Sara."

I waited a few seconds, and then hung up the phone. I couldn't fight back the tears anymore. Alone in the small telephone booth I sobbed uncontrollably, harder than I could ever remember crying. My clarity was gone. I'd never felt so confused in my entire life. I thought about calling my parents, looking for their reassurance that everything would be alright. I thought about calling Sara back to apologize and beg her forgiveness. But ultimately I just slumped back in my chair and cried some more.

25

The following day, during the interval between my university classes, I went directly to the computer lab. Although we hadn't discussed it the previous day, I felt confident I'd find her there. And after a most difficult night, where I didn't sleep more than an hour, I knew I needed her at my side as soon as possible.

I arrived and was surprised to find all three computers occupied, something I hadn't encountered during my many trips to the lab. And to my disappointment, Marcela was not one of the users. I put down my bag by the door to hold my place, and then walked over to the long bank of windows. I stared out at the mountains, contemplating the turbulent events of the previous 24 hours.

"Amazing view, isn't it?"

I was startled by the voice. I turned and smiled. She'd managed to sneak in to the viewing position adjacent to me without warning of her arrival.

"I'm always surprised there aren't more students up here studying," I said. "I would have loved to have a study room like this when I was in school. I imagine the mountains would have provided a good energy to get work done."

"Yeah I don't know why it's generally empty up here. Maybe it doesn't allow adequate socialization. Or maybe it's because it's a non-smoking area."

She smiled and fixed her gaze upon my eyes. I smiled back and met her look for several seconds. It was a rare but powerful moment of silence between us that seemed to convey everything. My confirmation that I'd carried through with my phone conversation. Her compassion for me for having done so. And our mutual understanding and excitement that we were now free to pursue a proper relationship.

I finally broke the silence.

"So what night do you take your tango classes?"

"Wednesdays. Nine p.m. at the same place I took you Friday. Can you join me this week?"

"For sure," I said. "And what about that trip out to Tupungato to see your school? Think we might be able to squeeze that in later this week?"

"How about Friday?" she suggested. "I'm not sure I'll be able to set up your hospital meeting by then but I'd love to have you meet my students. We can leave together from the university if you don't mind missing your second class."

"I think I can make an exception," I quipped.

She laughed, and again our eyes locked. I took her by the hand. She rotated her wrist, intertwining her fingers with mine.

"I have to go because I have a meeting with a parent before class," she said.

I nodded in understanding.

"But I'm looking forward to Wednesday," she assured. "I think you just might be a natural. We'll see how you respond to some formal training."

I smiled and shook my head.

"I don't think so. But I know I'll have fun learning with you."

We slowly released hands, and as she leaned in for the standard good-bye, I cupped her cheek in my hand and redirected her lips to mine. I used my hand to maintain our kiss for several seconds before pulling away. It was something I never would've felt comfortable doing before in such a setting. She tilted her head slightly and raised her eyebrows to express her surprise. She again took my hand before stepping back slowly.

"See you Wednesday," she said in English.

"I can't wait," I responded.

I watched as she turned and walked away. It was official now. Everything was out on the table. Fear and uncertainty had given way to an overwhelming sense of excitement. I shook my head and stared back out toward the towering mountains. I had no idea how this was all going to play out. No idea what the future held for the two of us. But I was pretty confident of one thing. I was falling in love.

26

While my emotions fluctuated greatly over the subsequent days, and sleep remained a most challenging exercise, I generally felt more excitement than despair. I tried to convince myself I'd done the right thing. I'd been honest with Sara, and honest with myself. And while I'd created a lot of uncertainty about my future, one thing was now clear: I was free to submit to the unrelenting force to which I'd been a prisoner since our night at the trolley stop.

Although it was only 48 hours before I saw Marcela again, it seemed much longer. I knew my return to the United States would arrive quickly, and now that I was committed, I felt it all-together too long to be without communication. But I also wanted to be careful to not come off as suffocating. While we'd gotten to know each other quite well for such a short period of time, we were clearly still in the 'feeling out' stage of our relationship. Unable to imagine things having developed any better, I was hesitant to change the pace of progression.

At nine o'clock Wednesday evening, I wrapped up my second class and made my way out through the busy building. I walked through the Plaza de Independencia to the peatonal, and then retraced our route from the previous weekend. I arrived by quarter after nine and found the outdoor mall was still quite busy. I'd learned before that the nine p.m. closing time for retail shops was often delayed by the presence of customers. And on a warm, pleasant evening, almost all shops remained open.

I arrived to the entrance of the bar and unsuccessfully searched for a name to the establishment. I was surprised to not hear music. I entered with some uncertainty and scanned the room. There were only two customers in the front area adjacent to the bar. And while the larger area at the back offered more activity, it was a far cry from the full house I'd encountered on my first visit.

I acknowledged the bartender and walked toward the back. I looked around and saw Marcela hadn't yet arrived. I took a seat at an open table and inconspicuously observed the action. There were about fifteen people, the majority of whom appeared approximately my age. And while a few sat and talked, most stood around a couple who was demonstrating a tango step. They performed the step several times, pausing to emphasize the more technical parts. Afterwards, they split up into couples to practice. They each performed the step several times, and then rotated to a new partner.

When the group appeared confident with their new maneuver, a new couple stepped forward to demonstrate something different. And following their instruction, other individuals intervened with suggestions regarding possible modifications. It became clear the group didn't have a single instructor. Rather than a formal class, it seemed to be more of a club, with a group of individuals who shared a common interest gathering to teach one another.

I ordered a glass of wine and continued to follow the informal instruction. Although there didn't appear to be fellow novices amongst the group, I didn't find the level of material too intimidating. While I doubted my ability to perform the steps with the same fluidity I saw from most, I felt pretty confident I could execute the different maneuvers.

Ultimately the group determined it was time to start the music. One of the leaders walked over to a portable cd player set up on the stage where the musicians had performed on Friday night. After sampling a few possibilities, he settled on a slower tango and the dancers assumed their positions around the perimeter of the floor. I surrendered any effort to conceal my role as a spectator and squared my chair to the dance floor.

One by one the couples entered into dance, starting with simple walking steps before sprinkling in the more exotic twists and twirls. I watched intently as the couples showed off some of their new material. There was a range of abilities, but the overall skill level appeared moderate. And with the start of the music, there was a dramatic transformation in the mood of the room. The joviality and casualness was now gone, replaced by the focused intensity I saw nights before. I smiled as I admired the beauty of their movements.

The song ended and the dancers dispersed across the floor as the next tango was chosen. Upon the restart, I was approached by one of the female dancers who slightly outnumbered the men. She introduced herself as Adriana.

"Are you dancing with us this evening?" she inquired.

"Hoping to a little later," I said. "I was invited by a friend who dances with the group, but she's running late."

"Oh yeah? Who's that?"

"Marcela," I answered.

"Oh sure, Marce. She's an excellent dancer for being so new. And you? Have you danced before?"

"Last Friday night was my introduction," I said.

"And what was your impression?" she asked.

I nodded in approval. "I thought it was amazing."

"Fantastic. So are you ready to show me what you learned?"

I hesitated. "Are you willing to show patience with a beginner?"

"Of course. I'm still new myself. I remember what it was like at your stage."

She extended her hand to formalize the invitation. I took it and we carefully worked our way around the dancing couples to a free corner of the floor.

"Would you like me to give you advice as we dance, or would you prefer I remain quiet?" Adriana asked.

"I'll take all the help I can get," I responded with a smirk.

I took her right hand with my left and extended the underside of my right forearm across her mid-back. She elevated our hold and pulled back her shoulders as a cue for me to stand up straighter. I listened carefully for the rhythm, focused on matching my steps with the marked beat. Remembering Marcela's advice to keep it simple, I started with several repetitions of the basic step. I concentrated on keeping my steps small, being extra careful to avoid stepping on her feet. And I tried my best to remain well out of the way of the other dancers.

But as the dance progressed, I allowed myself to start to relax. I mixed in some simple walking, and then even added in a gentle spin. Seeming surprised by my ability, Adriana repeatedly offered words of encouragement. And as the music built in intensity, I further impressed with an only minimally awkward effort at leading one of the new steps I'd seen presented earlier. I blushed as Adriana voiced her approval more voluminously.

Despite a failure to anticipate the song's completion leading to an uncomfortable conclusion, I was proud of my initial performance. Adriana smiled as if accusing me of having downplayed my ability. I put up my hands in defense to indicate I might have been the recipient of some beginner's fortune. She asked about my background and I acquiesced with the basics. But before I was able to learn anything about her, the music was back on and the dancing resumed. She confirmed my self-analysis by recommending a repeat dance. I gladly accepted.

And for the most part, with the exception of a few missteps for which I apologized profusely, it was again successful. I even timed my final step perfectly with the last beat of the song. Adriana again nodded in approval. She then spun around to face the center of the floor.

"My friends I present to you our guest this evening, Jake from Chicago!"

There was a boisterous reception with applause and shouting. Many dancers approached and introduced themselves. I thanked them for allowing me to participate. I emphasized my novice status and was met with universal words of encouragement. Then within minutes the music was restarted and the dancing resumed. And I was back out on the floor.

Although I lacked the confidence to ask others to dance, I was happy to accept invitations. They offered helpful suggestions while never showing frustration. I was amazed at how much I was able to pick up in a short time. But after 30 minutes of dancing, I began to struggle with mental fatigue. I became sluggish with my lead and failed to mark the steps with vigor. And with a limited repertoire of maneuvers, I tried to reach beyond my comfort zone with more advanced steps, generating confused looks and forced restarts with increasing frequency. I excused myself from the dance floor and walked to the bar.

As I returned to the table, Marcela arrived.

"So you started drinking without me?" She leaned in for the greeting kiss.

"Dancing too," I responded. "And the group tells me I'm progressing well for a gringo."

She laughed. "Wow, good for you. I can't wait to see what you've learned."

She placed a black nylon bag up on the table in front of me.

"What's this?"

"A little something that might facilitate your skill acquisition," she said emphatically. "Or at least allow you to fake it better."

I tugged at the draw string and opened the bag. In it was a pair of shiny black leather shoes. Tango shoes I presumed. I looked up at Marcela admiringly.

"I wasn't sure about size," she said. "Is 44 ok?"

I paused for a minute as I looked inside for the tag.

"I'm not sure," I responded. "But they look about right."

I leaned in for a kiss.

"Thank you," I said. "This is cool. I can't wait to try them out."

"Just wanted to make sure your experience was authentic."

I walked to the bar and ordered a glass of wine for Marcela. I then went back to the table and laced up my new shoes as she made the rounds greeting her friends. As she returned to the table, I stood up and rotated my feet to show off my new footwear.

"Perfect fit," I declared.

"I'm glad," she responded. "Let me get my shoes on and you can show off your new moves."

I watched as she strapped on her three inch narrow black heels. Dressed in a knee length grey skirt and a low cut black blouse, her proper tango attire was complete. She stood and extended her hand, and our first tango practice together was underway.

The following three hours flew by. During the first part of the night, upon Marcela's recommendation, we alternated partners within the group. She explained that the rotation of partners was part of the club's foundation, and that dancing with others would hasten my development. And while I would have preferred to spend more time in her embrace, I appreciated the theory behind dancing with others and enjoyed the opportunity to get to know other group members. We danced different styles of tango, with the music rotating among the slower tango, the fast-paced milonga, and the more rhythmic waltz-style. And while I initially struggled greatly with the latter two, I slowly began to grasp the basics.

Yet as the night grew later, Marcela and I transitioned away from the group rotation and danced almost exclusively as a couple. And while our initial dances included jovial discussion and Marcela's frequent teaching, later dances took on a different personality. The conversation quieted; the embrace tightened. Her head rested on my left shoulder. My guide forearm pulled her torso more tightly against me. Lost in the ambience of the music and the wine, my focus shifted away from my foot position and preparation for my next step. I smelled the scent of her hair. I felt her breath against my neck. And I allowed my mind to envision what might happen next if we were alone in another setting.

Slowly the members of the group began to disperse for the night. Finally, at 2:00 a.m., Marcela took my hand and walked toward our table. We changed out of our shoes, said goodbye to the remaining dancers, and headed out to the street. With the trolleys done for the evening, we got into the back of a waiting taxi. I looked at Marcela and smiled.

"Is there time for you to come over for a while?"

She hesitated, then smiled and shook her head.

"I wish I could," she said. "But my mother would be worried. Or disappointed. Or maybe both."

"Are you sure?" I insisted with my most inviting smile.

"Yes," she nodded. "I have to play by house rules. It's just the way my mother is." She looked away before turning back. "But she's used to me being out all night on the weekends." She winked.

"I understand," I reassured.

She snuggled up against me as the taxi pulled away in route to Marcela's apartment. As I stroked her hair, I thought back on the night. It had been another unbelievable experience. And the best part was it just kept getting better. Each moment we shared together somehow seemed even better than the last. And with the weekend just days away, I felt confident the pattern would continue.

27

On Friday afternoon, I met Marcela at the library after my morning class. Although I continued to enjoy my Mendoza viticulture class, the decision to sacrifice the class to spend the day with Marcela had been an easy one. We walked hand-in-hand out to the large school parking lot to where Marcela had parked her mid-80s white Fiat 600. She tipped the parking attendant a few coins for having 'guarded' her car and we set off for Tupungato.

Although I'd been to the mountains to hike on several occasions, I hadn't yet traveled in the direction of Tupungato. I knew the city was located about 75 kilometers southwest of Mendoza, and I'd heard the backdrop was even more amazing than in Mendoza. I assumed the drive would be quite scenic.

The first fifteen minutes of the trip was start and stop as we worked our way out of Mendoza city passing through the neighboring communities of Godoy Cruz and Lujan. Although the houses were smaller than in the fifth or sixth section of Mendoza, the neighborhoods were well-maintained and the overall appearance was similar to that of the capital city. But as we entered on to a two-lane highway on the edge of Lujan, the scenery changed abruptly. The small houses with well-groomed yards gave way to an expansive brown desert dotted with sparse shrubs and the occasional adobe house. The vast emptiness was perfectly flat and stretched south and east as far as the eye could see. But as I looked out to my right toward the mountains, the contrast was marked. Brought to life by a grid of brown irrigation ditches, countless plots of healthy vines weaved their way toward the base of the mountains. The resultant color transition was remarkable: blue sky to white mountains to green vines to brown desert. It seemed impossible for such green to emerge from an otherwise desolate land.

As we worked our way closer to Tupungato, the mountains became even more formidable. Part of this steady growth resulted from our westward track that brought us in closer proximity to the mountains. But it was more than that. The tallest peaks south of the city were even more daunting than those immediately west of Mendoza. And the foothills tapered down to a very narrow band yielding an even more striking transition from desert to mountains.

But in spite of the breathtaking views and pleasant conversation, the ride itself was far from comfortable. With a rough surface and frequent potholes, the highway was in desperate need of repairs. And while the road was predominantly straight, there were multiple hairpin turns that necessitated rapid slowdowns. I rolled my window down intermittently to help fight off waves of nausea which recurred throughout the ride.

The road conditions, however, were only part of the problem. Even more disconcerting was the complete lack of traffic control. While I'd experienced this on several occasions within the city, it was much more exaggerated on the rural highway. Despite a speed limit posted at the metric equivalent of 60 mph, the variety of speeds was marked. Tractors and large trucks plodded along at no more than 30 mph, while several cars raced by at speeds that surely exceeded 100 mph. Marcela was forced to brake quickly on several occasions to allow a passing car to dive back in to the right lane and narrowly avoid a collision with oncoming traffic. And along sections of the highway with a more prominent shoulder, some cars even dared to pass on the right, declaring their intent by sounding their horn. Clearly well-conditioned to the chaos, Marcela remained calm and collected through it all. I often resorted to clenching the dashboard and closing my eyes.

After a harrowing thirty minutes for me, Marcela exited off the highway and we entered into Tupungato. It appeared larger than I was expecting. With the city stretching up into the foothills, I estimated the population between 5,000 and 10,000 people. But despite its surprising size, the town maintained a definite rural feel. While the main street was a paved boulevard, many of the cross-streets were gravel. The great majority of the buildings were just a single story. And while driving down the city's principal streets, I saw only two traffic lights. Arriving during the mid-afternoon siesta, the town was quiet.

"What's that white stucco building across from the plaza?" I inquired.

"That's the municipal building," Marcela responded. "It's been rebuilt twice after earthquakes. The last time was back in the mid-80s."

"It's beautiful. I imagine the plaza gets pretty full in the evenings and on the weekends."

"It does," she confirmed. "There's an open-air market every Saturday with various crafts and great food. Some of the best lamb you'll find anywhere. I try to make it here at least once a month when I come out to the vineyard."

"And how often is that?" I asked.

"Lately it's been quite a bit," she said. "More weekends than not. I'm doing my best to have my first real harvest next year."

"Wow, look at you," I said. "You are making progress. I didn't realize how close this was to reality."

"I hope so. Like I said before, the classes have been invaluable. And I have a partner who has been of tremendous help throughout the process. A co-worker's husband who spent a couple of years working at a vineyard back in college. He's an accountant now, but always had an interest in getting back into the wine industry. He wants to be a partner in the business, although I've been hesitant to commit to that. I'd like to do it my way. So I'm trying to convince him to start as a consultant."

"Do you think he'll agree to it?" I asked.

"I'm not sure. He's still thinking about it. I think I have his wife on my side. We've worked together for years and she believes in me. But then there's the 'machismo' issue. I know he'd prefer to be in charge."

"And when might I get the opportunity to tour this operation of yours?" I said with a smile.

"I was hoping this afternoon at about 5:30." She smiled back. "That's if you don't have anything you need to get back for this evening."

I nodded. "Awesome. I can't wait to see it."

At the south edge of town, we turned right and made our way southwest through a sparsely populated area. We continued for several miles until we came to a single brown brick building at a fork in the road. There Marcela turned into the large parking lot and parked in a small shaded area amongst a group of about fifteen cars.

"Welcome to General Heras Primary School," she said.

I got out and stretched my back. I couldn't imagine having to make this drive every day. I looked west at the towering snow-capped peaks. The setting was amazing for its remoteness.

"How many schools are there in Tupungato?" I inquired.

"Three primary schools and one secondary school," she answered. "The other schools are in the city. We get a few from the western edge of the city, but almost all of our students are rural. Some travel from a distance that makes my commute seem short. And I have a few who still come on horseback."

"Unbelievable. This is the end of civilization. What percentage of your students go on to complete high school?"

"About half. Many finish primary school and go back to work on the farms or in the vineyards. Some push on and try to follow a different path. It's one of the things I love about my job. It's much more than teaching. I end up being a guidance counselor and social worker as well."

We walked through the front door of the long narrow building. We turned right and continued to the end of the hallway. There were a handful of students at their lockers but otherwise the school was quiet. We entered a classroom through a door labeled "Miss Marcela's English Classroom" in purple construction paper. Marcela put her bag down by the desk and I walked the room's perimeter. It was a classic classroom, with a large blackboard facing five neat rows of wooden desks. The opposite wall from the entry was almost all windows, providing that beautiful view of the mountains. As I studied the decorations on the wall, it became clear Marcela shared the classroom with a science class. The near wall and half of the back wall were devoted to science themed pictures and student projects. The back corner of the room, however, was adorned with English language decoration.

There was a map of the world with pins highlighting countries where English was the primary language. Encircling the map there were informational cards prepared by students with basic data about each of the countries. Adjacent to the map there were short poems in English that appeared to be original works of the students. And at the edge of the windows, there were pictures and information about "the place of the week", which on the day of my arrival, just so happened to be Chicago. I smiled as I read through the grammatically challenged student paragraphs that described my home city.

"What do you think?" Marcela asked. "Were we accurate in our description?"

"Pretty impressive," I responded. "They may know more about Chicago than I do" I looked back out at the mountains. "But how do you get anything done with that bank of windows? I'd think the students might become distracted by that background."

"Another reason I love my job. I can't imagine many others in the world have a view like mine. But it doesn't interfere with learning. Around here this is just your typical view. The students are accustomed to it." She looked out the window and then turned back. "So are you ready to get involved today? I thought you could talk a little about yourself and about Chicago. I'm certain the kids will have a ton of questions."

"Of course. I'm an experienced English teacher now." I smiled.

"Good," she said. "And let's keep it all in English. If the students realize you speak Spanish, they'll get lazy and revert to Spanish. I want them to use their English. I think you'll be surprised at how well they're doing."

"It's a deal," I said switching into English.

"Perfect," she responded. She walked over to me smiling and took my hand. "Thank you for coming. The students are going to love you."

She erased the board and took out her materials. Slowly the students filed in. Marcela greeted each upon their arrival with a variety of English salutations and the students answered in kind. They sat quiet and orderly, offering only the occasional whisper and smile as they glanced at me. As more students arrived, it became clear the students were of differing ages. I inquired and Marcela explained that the mandatory core curriculum was provided in the morning. The post-lunch session was optional, with a variety of classes including English, music, and physical education. She estimated half the students returned for the afternoon, meaning only about ten students per grade. Marcela taught three fifty minute combined classes: kindergarten/1st grade, 2nd and 3rd grade, and 4th and 5th grade.

Promptly at 2:30, with the kindergarteners and first graders settled in their seats, Marcela walked to the blackboard and began the class. She spoke slowly, annunciating each word to aid with comprehension. She used her hands constantly as she spoke, attempting as much as possible to illustrate many of the more challenging words she employed. She walked around the room, studying their faces to confirm their comprehension. And when she ascertained confusion, she started her sentence over, finding a different way to communicate her idea to avoid speaking in Spanish. I smiled as I watched her. She was amazing.

I looked out at the little faces and saw universal engagement. Their eyes glued to their teacher, I could see their brains spinning to comprehend everything Marcela said. Occasional looks of doubt were quickly replaced by smiles as a repeated hand gesture or different word choice created a sudden understanding. And when she sought student participation with well-spaced questions, she was greeted with a majority of hands, each struggling to stretch higher than the others to be granted the opportunity to speak.

After a short warm-up activity, Marcela introduced me as her 'special friend', and it was my turn to speak. Trying my best to emulate Marcela, I stood up and paced across the room as I began to talk. I tried to speak clearly, but quickly realized the students were struggling with either my accent or word choice. But with an increased use of my hands, and with the assistance of Marcela's intermittent alternative explanations, the students gradually appeared more comfortable. And when I asked questions, I was met with even more hands, anxious to impress with their knowledge.

After a brief introduction of myself and an opportunity for the students to teach me about Tupungato, I asked the students if they had any questions for me about the United States. Again the desire to participate was almost universal.

"Do you know Brad Pitt?" was the first question I received.

"No, I do not," I responded to a disappointed audience.

Many of the hands went down. Apparently it had been a popular question. Marcela explained that Brad Pitt had filmed a movie near Tupungato years before and that some students had seen him during his stay. Many students confirmed their viewing by wriggling their arm in the air.

Other questions emerged from the group. How about George Clooney? Or Julia Roberts? Time and time again I was forced to disappoint by acknowledging I hadn't met their movie heroes. Disappointed, but undeterred, the questions shifted to athletes and musicians. Marcela finally came to my rescue by asking questions to which I could provide more intriguing answers. What was the prettiest place I'd visited in the United

States? What was my favorite movie? How was my childhood school different from theirs? The children sat on the edge of their chairs and listened intently. They had follow-up questions that took us off on tangents. They were enthralled, and I loved every minute of our interaction.

After more than twenty minutes of discussion, Marcela stepped in and announced it was reading time. Upon Marcela's cue, they walked over and sat upon the carpet in the front corner of the room. Marcela took a book from the adjacent bookshelf and asked me if I'd be the reader for the day. I agreed and the students cheered. I moved my chair over and spent the last minutes of class reading to the group of mesmerized students. I couldn't believe how well-behaved and respectful they were. Marcela had been right; they were a special group. I knew it had a lot to do with their very special teacher.

The following two classes were every bit as enjoyable. The students were equally polite and engaged, and their superior English and added maturity created a more fluent and intellectual conversation. By the third class I at one point found myself trying to explain the political system of the United States. I looked over at Marcela who could only muster a shrug and a flash of that magnetic smile.

Following the dismissal of the last group, I helped Marcela put things away and ready the classroom for the following morning. As we finished she walked over and put her arms around my waist.

"I knew they'd adore you," she said, having switched back to Spanish. She leaned in for a kiss.

"Well I was very impressed," I responded, taking her hands in mine. "You clearly have a special bond with your students. They were glued to your every word. And they really do speak amazingly well."

"I'm very proud of them. It makes me feel good to see them progress. I know without a doubt this is what I was meant to do."

I nodded. I knew she was right. Her passion and enthusiasm were obvious. It was yet another addition to the growing list of characteristics I found so attractive in her. I thought for a minute about my own job. While I wasn't unhappy, I was pretty sure I'd never experienced the feelings that teaching seemed to evoke in Marcela. I smiled at her and stretched forward for a longer kiss.

"So are you ready to go to my grandparents' place and see what I've been working on for the last two years?" she asked.

"I can't wait," I said.

I helped her with her things and we walked out to the car. We drove back toward Tupungato, reaching the center of town before turning west and driving up into the foothills. After no more than a fifteen minute drive, Marcela turned off the main road onto a gravel road which disappeared between two adjacent arid hills. We were entering an area of complete isolation, without homes or other cars in sight. We continued up the road for about five hundred yards before pulling into a gravel parking area sheltered by a group of poplar trees. The trees were thick, obscuring the view of the adjacent valley. But as the rays of light from the late afternoon sun penetrated through openings in the cover, I began to sense I was in a truly extraordinary place.

Marcela opened the trunk and took out two large travel bags.

"You get the heavier one," she said with a smile. "Now follow me on the first part of your tour."

I obliged and we headed up a dirt path which wound through the trees along a dry creek bed. The path was in poor condition, and we walked cautiously to avoid stumbling. After no more than 100 yards, we emerged from the grove of trees. I dropped my bag and stared out at the valley in awe. It was without question the single most picturesque background I'd ever seen.

In the foreground there was a relatively steep descent down to a narrow valley that lied hidden behind the single row of foothills that we'd bisected on the gravel road. On the floor of the valley, I saw an extensive vineyard that spanned the entire width of the valley and stretched south around the corner as far as I could see. And in the background, I looked up at the most spectacular row of mountains I'd ever seen. Rugged, snow-capped, and towering above the valley, I shook my head in disbelief.

"Welcome to El Cordon de la Plata," Marcela said.

I was speechless. I sat down on the ground and scanned the panorama, struggling to comprehend the majestic beauty.

Marcela sat down next to me and took my hand.

"I told you it was a special place," she whispered.

"Unbelievable. I never imagined this. Is this all your grandparents land?" I asked.

"Across to the base of the mountains, and then down to the largest irrigation channel," she explained, pointing toward the corner.

I remained silent.

"They also own the land on this side of the hill," she continued. "The home is up the path another fifty meters or so. The view is even more amazing from up there."

"I can't believe this property has been unoccupied for so many years," I said incredulously. "It's so amazing. I'm shocked none of your family has ended up here. And you must have had countless offers to purchase and develop."

"Its beauty is undeniable," Marcela said. "But it's very remote. Definitely a different way of living, one that none of my family members was interested in pursuing. As far as offers go, I know there have been inquiries. But the wine industry was pretty stagnant in Argentina for a long time. It's just been the last couple years where we've started to see growth."

"True," I said. "But even without the vineyard, there must have been interest from someone in buying the land for a country home or for development purposes."

"Maybe," she said. "I don't know the full history. But you don't see a lot of that here. Most of the Buenos Aires and international money gets invested down in Patagonia. And the few people in Mendoza I know who are wealthy enough to afford a second home all have places on the Chilean coast."

She reached into her bag and pulled out a blanket. She stood up and opened it neatly before spreading it out next to me. She then reached back into her bag and pulled out a small grocery bag.

"I thought we might have a glass of wine before continuing with the tour," she said.

"I think that's a great idea," I replied.

I moved over onto the blanket and took the bottle and corkscrew from Marcela. She handed me two plastic cups, and set up a small portable wooden table on the edge of the blanket. She then set the table with plastic plates and napkins, and put out a number of food items on a wooden cutting board including a goat cheese spread, thin slices of Serrano ham, and whole grain crackers. I poured two glasses of wine and handed one to Marcela. I held out my glass and offered a toast.

"To your soon to be new home in the most amazing setting I've ever seen."

"And to the continued development of our special relationship," she added.

I smiled and winked.

"Chin chin," I said per Argentine tradition, touching my glass to hers.

"Chin chin," she echoed.

I took a sip of the rich dark Malbec. I looked at the bottle and saw it was from Tupungato.

"Nice wine," I said. "Is this similar to the flavor these vines will produce?"

She shrugged her shoulders. "I hope so. Should be close. This bottle is from a vineyard less than ten kilometers away."

"Alright," I said. "Now tell me the whole story. My wine class has me fascinated. Tell me what you've done so far and what still needs to be completed before you have bottles on shelves."

She sighed. "Well I'm not sure how much detail you want. It's been quite a process." She paused, appearing to contemplate where to begin. "I guess it started in earnest about four years ago. I'd been out to the land many times over the years, but had spent most of my time up at the house. But one day I decided to walk through the old vineyard. It must have been late February or March. As I began to walk through the rows, I was overcome with sadness. I had vivid memories of having been there with my grandfather two decades before. I remembered the great pride he'd shown as he taught me the appearance of the perfect vine. And now, abandoned for well over a decade, it appeared completely lost. There were weeds everywhere. The scrub brush was so thick that in many areas the trellises weren't even visible. It broke my heart."

"But when I arrived to the end of a row, in an area where the brush wasn't as thick, I caught a glimpse of beautiful color buried deep beneath the brown of the brush. There were grapes. Large, dark purple bunches of grapes. I pulled away multiple armfuls of the dry overgrowth, and was amazed to find many branches appeared to be producing healthy grapes. I broke out in laughter as I stared at my most unexpected discovery. As I walked down the next row back toward the house, I stopped periodically to pull away brush and evaluate the vines. And more times than not, even in areas of heavier cover, I found scattered clusters of grapes. I couldn't believe they could still be growing after so many years of neglect."

"Other than tell my family, who seemed far less fascinated than I was, I didn't act on this revelation for a year. But one day after school, I was introduced to Javier, the partner of whom I spoke earlier. He was picking up his wife Julia and we got to talking. He's from the area and knew of my grandparents. Somehow the topic of the vineyard arose, and I shared with him my discovery of the previous year. His eyes instantly lit up. He told me about his vineyard background and asked if I'd show him around sometime. I was happy to do it, and weeks later I walked part of the property with him and Julia. As we walked, he went into more detail about his experience in the wine industry and shared his vision of again someday being part of a vineyard. He stopped often during the tour, working harder than I had to expose the trunks of the vines. He even brought along a shovel, and at times dug to examine the root system. By the time we returned to the car, his mind was made up. He wanted in. The vines were in surprisingly good condition, without mildew or signs of disease. He thought they could be salvaged without a need to replant. And he was ready to work with me to make it happen."

She paused and took a drink of her wine.

"Wow, so you really hadn't thought about it before his proposal?" I asked.

"Not seriously," she replied. "I mean it had crossed my mind. But it was more of a dream than anything. I just didn't think it feasible, with my limited knowledge and resources."

"Until that day," I said.

"Sort of," she replied. "It got me thinking. But soon after I decided to enroll at the university and quickly got busy with classwork. And after some follow-up conversations with Javier, things cooled. I began to see his desire to take control, and it turned me off. It was my grandparents' land. If it was something that was going to happen I thought it needed to be our family that took it on. So it went on the back burner for a time."

I nodded. "Sounds like the Marcela I know. Passionate, independent, committed to her family." I smiled at her. "So what was the final impetus to get this started?"

"That's a good question," she said, pondering the inquiry. "I think timing more than anything. I was starting my third year at the elementary school at the time, and it was during that year that I grew to love this community. I had an extra special group of kids that year, and got to know their families well. I started spending more of my free time here, and slowly came to understand that Tupungato was where I wanted to live. The sincerity of the people, the serenity of the mountains, the languid pace of life. I realized that living on my grandparent's property was my destiny. And that restoring the vineyard was something I needed to do."

"So you went back to Javier with your epiphany?" I asked.

"Exactly. I told him I'd made the decision to move forward. That I was doing it both for my grandparents and for me. That it was going to be my operation. And that I needed his assistance in making it a reality."

I smiled and shook my head. "I'm guessing his vision was somewhat different?"

"It was," she responded, pausing to take a bite of her cracker and cheese. "At first he was turned off by my declaration. But his passion for the project was sufficient to agree to 'begin the process' with me, with an agreement to work out the details as we moved closer to production. It's something that two years later we're still trying to work out."

"Ok, so now you've made your decision, how do you even begin to make this happen?" I asked.

"Well there were two major projects to tackle. First we had to begin the tedious process of rescuing the vines. And second we had to evaluate what we had to work with in terms of facilities and equipment. Those are stops two and three on our tour. I think we still have an hour or so before sunset. Are you ready for a walk?"

"Definitely," I said, hopping to my feet. I reached over and helped Marcela up. I took the bottle of wine and topped off our glasses as she put away the blanket and food items. Then holding our glasses in opposite hands, we held hands as we carefully made our way down the well-worn path toward the fields below. Reaching the edge of the vines, Marcela led me past several rows of stumps before starting down a row of vines with more substantial growth. At the end of the row, next to an irrigation ditch carrying a moderate current of brown water, she kneeled down next to one of the vines.

"You don't know how much work it took to get to this stage," she began. "First we had to clean up the irrigation ditches. Some were clogged with debris, while many were eroded to the point of complete uselessness. It took months, and a lot of help from other teachers and their husbands, to get them back to looking like this one."

"Most irrigation work was done on weekends with a team. On days when it was just me, or me and Javier, I began the process of preparing the vines. The first step was to clear overgrowth and redefine rows. There were weeds everywhere. Under Javier's direction, we pruned and pruned until we found the main stump of the vines. If the stump appeared healthy, we cut it to a height of no more than one foot. If the stump looked bad, we dug underground to expose the root system and find a shoot that could produce a new vine. I can't even begin to estimate the number of hours we spent exposing the foundation for our vines."

"Is that what I saw in the rows when we first descended?" I asked.

"Yes," Marcela said. "That's phase two. My grandfather had about twenty acres of vines. We started with just two. That's what you see in these rows. Over the last six months we've moved forward clearing another two. That's what we saw on our way in. Ultimately I'd love to incorporate all twenty acres, but that's years away. I'd need several fulltime staff members to run an operation of that size. Four acres is more manageable. I feel confident I can do that with just a part-time staff."

"So those little stumps we saw will produce vines like this in a year?" I asked.

"They'll start to produce shoots," Marcela corrected. "It'll likely be another year before we get substantial vine production bearing fruit. Do you see the several different branches emerging from this stump?" she asked, pointing toward the plant in front of us.

I nodded.

"Over the last month we've been pruning again. We identify three to five branches that appear the healthiest and most evenly dispersed around the trunk, then cut away the rest. We want branches to grow uniformly and circumferentially around the main trunk. We then tie these branches to the trellis to provide them with the structure they need for healthy growth."

She pointed out how the four branches emerging from the trunk had been delicately fastened to a small wooden post attached to the wire of the trellis.

"What about the trellis?" I inquired. "It looks like it's in excellent condition. Is this your work or is it original?"

"A little bit of both. It actually was in decent shape overall. But there was some wind damage. And with some of our pruning, we did additional damage to the wires. I'd say overall we had to replace maybe 25% of the posts and 50% of the wire. It took time, but compared to the pruning and irrigation restoration it was easy."

"What type of grapes are these?"

"All Malbec for now. Ultimately I'd love to grow different varietals, but it was easiest to start with just one."

There was a pause in our conversation. I scanned the area, nodding my head in appreciation of the tremendous work that had been done. I took her in my arms and hugged her tightly. I pulled away and smiled.

"Well I'm impressed," I said. "This is quite an accomplishment."

"Thank you," she said proudly, returning the smile. "We still have a long way to go, but I'm proud of what we've achieved so far. Now follow me and I'll show you our equipment facility and cave."

We walked back down the row of vines and then back toward the hill we'd descended. Once there we picked up a second path which ran adjacent to the hillside. As we stepped through some thick brush, I saw a moderate-sized adobe building 100 yards ahead. We walked over and stopped at the door. Outside the building there was a tractor and forklift, both aged sufficiently to create doubt about their functionality. The building itself also showed obvious wear, with a number of cracks in the wall we could see and a door that clearly needed replacement.

"We still have work left here, although not as much as I'd anticipated when I first arrived," she explained. "The tractor and forklift run perfectly. That's all the heavy equipment we'll need initially. And the building itself has a solid foundation. It needs some touch-up work, like roof maintenance, but overall nothing major."

She took out her keys and opened the padlock on the door. She turned the knob and forced the door open with two firm blows with her shoulder. I followed her into a large rectangular room. I estimated the room was 50 feet long by 30 feet deep. With the light of the day fading, I waited for my eyes to adjust to the semi-darkness.

"The electricity is still out," she said. "There hasn't been a need thus far as almost all of our work has been done in the field."

She stepped to the center of the room to an open area from which she could pivot and point out the various components of the operation.

"Everything you see here upstairs is in working order. It's not the newest technology, but it will allow us to accomplish what needs to be done." She pointed toward the back corner. "The grapes will come in through the large door in the corner. They'll be dumped onto the vibrating belt along the back wall. The belt automatically removes small grapes while workers manually pick out leaves, stems, and grapes that are either unripe or overly ripened. When the grapes reach the end of the belt they are loaded into the destemming machine you see in the opposite corner. From there they are placed on the second shorter belt which runs back to the center of the building. This is the final opportunity to manually remove debris and poor quality grapes."

"That sounds like a lot of work," I said. "I assume bigger vineyards do it automatically?"

"I think some do," she replied. "But my understanding is most around here continue to do it manually. That was one of Javier's roles during his years working at vineyards. He likes to emphasize that manual grape selection is an essential part of producing high quality wine. Green grapes give the wine a bitter taste; overly ripe grapes have a high sugar content and increase alcohol content."

"Okay, so now you have your grapes. Time for fermentation?"

"Exactly," she said. "You've been paying attention in class." She smiled. "So from the end of the belt the grapes will be transported in vats to this front corner."

She walked carefully over and kneeled down on the floor. She twisted a small knob until she was able to lift off a round metal cover exposing a large oval shaped tank built into the floor.

"This is one of our three cement fermentation vats. They're in excellent condition. We have two large 10,000 liter tanks and this smaller one. And the design is great. They're set up off the ground in the wine cave below allowing us to access the tops through this floor. So all we do is bring the grapes over and drop them in. The metal radiator you see emerging from the side of the tank is to control temperature."

She closed the cover, and then led me over to a narrow concrete staircase in the opposite front corner of the building. She picked up a flashlight from a dusty shelf and we started down to the cave.

"Fermentation takes about three weeks. Temperature and sugar content are monitored regularly. When the process is complete, the juice is pressed to remove skins and seeds. And now the wine is ready to go into barrels."

We reached the bottom of the staircase and made our way to the center of the room, which appeared to match the upstairs dimensions. It was cold and dark, and I struggled to make out my surroundings with the partial illumination of the dim flashlight.

"There in the corner you see the vats," she said, using the flashlight as a pointer. "We connect tubing from the vats to the barrels and the aging process is underway."

"Where are the barrels?" I asked.

"Very observant of you," she said smiling. "That's one big outstanding issue. Unfortunately the oak barrels that were down here weren't salvageable. There were at least 40 French oak barrels, but they were in really bad shape. I was able to sell a few of them to a local collector, but the majority had to be burned."

"So where do you get new barrels?"

"Either the United States or France. But almost everyone around here uses French Oak. And unfortunately it's very expensive. It's our greatest start-up cost, and financially I'm not quite ready to make that acquisition."

"How expensive are they?" I asked.

"New barrels are a minimum of $750 each. And I need about 15 to get started. But Javier and I are close to purchasing some lightly used barrels from a large local vineyard. We can get them at a third the price of new barrels, and they can be restored. They used to do it at the vineyard where Javier worked. You shave down the inner layers of the barrel, and then add thin oak stays. He said you can prolong the barrel life by five years."

"That'll reduce cost. But do they still impart the same flavor? I'd think barrel condition would be a pretty important factor in determining wine quality."

"I'm not sure. It makes me nervous too. But Javier promises it won't compromise the wine. And financially it's really my only viable option at this time."

I nodded. I scanned the remainder of the cave. It was empty with the exception of some equipment stacked in a back corner. I inquired and Marcela explained that it was old bottling equipment. They hadn't yet decided whether it made more sense to get it running, or instead to pay to have their bottling done in town where they planned to have their wine labeled.

She led me back upstairs and out the front door. After a couple of forceful pulls to close the door, we started back down the path toward the house. It was getting dark now, and the temperature had fallen dramatically since our arrival just two hours earlier. We walked quickly but cautiously, taking care to avoid a misstep on the rugged trail. I took the lead as we began our climb up the hillside, stopping to take Marcela's hand during the more arduous portion of the ascent. At the top of the hill we picked up Marcela's bag, and then headed away from the car along an even more deteriorated path before arriving at the house.

The night was clear, and the emerging stars and three-quarter moon provided adequate light to view the exterior of the house. It was a single story adobe house built into the hillside. It had a typical Spanish style tiled roof, and similar to most houses in Mendoza, the windows were barred. At the entrance to the home there was a large rectangular tile patio, replete with cracks from years of neglect. There was a fire pit at the front left corner of the patio, and a partially eroded Argentine grill on the right. I slowed and looked back over the valley as we walked toward the front door.

"What a view," I said, shaking my head in amazement.

"It's fantastic. It never gets old. We'll see if we can't get a fire started shortly. Would you like a brief tour of my future home first?"

"I'd love one," I responded.

She unlocked the door and led me into complete darkness. Relying almost solely on feel, she reached into a small drawer and pulled out a flashlight. She clicked it on, with the dim light revealing a moderate sized foyer.

"No electricity here yet either," she said. "That's still down the list of necessities. We'll have to rely on the flashlight and candlelight this evening."

"I think we'll be okay," I said, taking her by the hand.

She led me to the right into a big room, sparsely decorated, with a rectangular wooden dining table in the center of the room. There were two large windows off the front of the room that provided a view of the valley.

"This is the old dining room. I don't think anyone has sat in here for at least a decade. But I have vivid memories of family gatherings here during my childhood. We used to pack fifteen or twenty people around this table during winter months when it was too cold to sit outside."

We exited the room to the left through a narrow doorway into a galley-style kitchen outdated by at least one generation. There was a small breakfast table at the back of the room, and a single window off the right side above the sink.

"Eventually it needs to be redone," she said. "But as long as the appliances are functional when the electricity is restored, I'll be content keeping it how it is for now."

"What about water?" I asked. "Does the plumbing work?"

"Yes, everything seems to work well. I turned the water back on a month ago, and I haven't had issues."

We walked through the rest of the house. There were two small bedrooms and one larger bedroom off a narrow hallway at the back of the house, with a single bathroom in between the smaller rooms. The tile on the bathroom walls was damaged along the back wall. Marcela confirmed my suspicion that a leaky roof was responsible for the wear. From the hallway we turned back toward the front of the house and entered into a large living room, stuffed full of furniture and other miscellaneous household items. We slalomed through the myriad of obstacles until we arrived at a small clearing at the front of the room.

"Not too long after my grandma passed away, my mother and aunt came out to the house to divide up family heirlooms and prepare the house for sale. The living room became a holding area for things with which they couldn't decide what to do. But with uncertainty regarding the decision to sell, the project stalled. The living area has functioned as a storage facility ever since. One of the first things I'd like to do in the house is to make this room habitable again. Some of these things can go to family members. Most of it needs to go to the junkyard. It's a shame because this is the most beautiful room in the house, and right now it's unusable."

I nodded in agreement.

"It would at least be nice to be able to access the fireplace," I said, pointing toward the side wall. "And I can't imagine it would take long. You make a few phone calls to family members acknowledging your intent, and then pick a date where those interested can meet here to pick out what they want. Then we rent a truck for the day and everything else goes."

She smiled at me and took my hands in hers.

"There is some firewood along the back of the house. And there should be matches in the drawer at the entrance. Think you can get a fire started outside while I light a few candles?"

"I can handle that," I answered. "I'll meet you out front in a few minutes."

She gave me the flashlight, and then made her way back through the crowded living room toward the bedrooms. I completed the loop back into the foyer, found the matches, and headed out to the patio.

To my delight, the dry wood started up quickly. When I was confident the flame was strong enough to allow me to step away, I went back into the living room and uncovered a small sofa I'd seen earlier. I pushed it through the front door and positioned it in front of the fire pit. I then went back into the house and carried out a small, dusty wooden table. After centering it in front of the sofa, I pulled out napkins from Marcela's bag and cleaned it off. I refilled our wine glasses, added some wood to the fire, and sat back on the sofa to enjoy the view.

Marcela soon appeared, having reinforced her dress with a wool sweater to ward off the cold of the night. She unfolded a blanket and extended it as she sat down beside me.

"It's going to be a cold night," she said, shivering as she snuggled close.

"The temperature variation here is incredible," I said. "It must have been 80 degrees today, and now it can't be more than fifty."

"It's one of the characteristics that make our grapes so special," she said smiling.

I took a sip of wine. I stared out over the valley, searching unsuccessfully for another house light. I looked up at the countless stars that were emerging exponentially as dusk faded to night.

"I can't believe we're just a few minutes outside of Tupungato," I said. "It feels like we're alone in the middle of the Andes."

"It does," Marcela agreed. "These foothills block out any noise or lights from the city. And all the land you see is private, owned by just a small few. So you hardly ever see other people. It's a very unique feeling, powerful really. I always feel such a closeness to the land when I'm here."

I turned my head toward Marcela and looked into her eyes.

"Can I ask you a question?" I said.

"Of course," she said. "Anything."

"Why do you think we're so good together?"

She hesitated, clearly surprised by the question. "What do you mean?"

I thought for a few seconds, and then tried again.

"I guess I mean, how do two people, with such different upbringings, and seemingly variant and unrelated life paths, seem to be such a perfect fit together?"

She again paused, taking a drink from her glass before finding an answer for my question.

"My single friends, and even some of the married ones, always talk about what they're looking for in a man. It's one of their favorite games to play. Type of personality, career, goals, etc. They all seem to know exactly what type of person they think would be best for them. But when they ask me I always say the same thing: I have no idea. I don't believe in developing blueprints for relationships. I don't look for specific attributes or try to identify a specific style. I look for people that make me feel good. That make me happy. People who are genuine, people who are real. I don't feel what I do for you because of your profession, or your hobbies, or because of where you're from. For me it's the way you make me feel. The way you look me in the eyes. The way you squeeze my hand. The way you listen to me when I talk, and the clarity and honesty you employ in your words. I feel a connection with you that supersedes any superficial differences we may appear to have. I feel a connection with you I've never felt before in my life."

I shook my head in amazement.

"How's that?" she said smiling. "Did I answer your question?"

"I don't even know how to begin to respond," I said, taking a sip of my wine.

"Then don't," she said, reaching her left hand up to my right cheek and pulling me in gently until our lips touched.

I snuck my arm around her waist and pulled her in for a long, soft kiss. She brought her knees up on the couch, leaning in for another kiss before stretching across my lap until she sat straddling me. She placed her hands on my cheeks and smiled seductively.

"Sometimes the best things come to those who wait," she whispered, lowering herself toward me to again engage my lips.

Eventually she pulled back and smiled. She handed me my glass before reaching for her own.

"To a relationship that just keeps getting better," she said, touching her glass to mine.

"Salud," I said smiling.

She raised her glass to her mouth and drank from it until only a small sip was left. I finished my glass as she stood slowly.

"As beautiful as it is out here I think we can find a more comfortable place."

"I'll follow you," I said.

She took me by the hand and led me back through the now candlelit house to the largest bedroom. There she'd lit multiple candles creating both the perfect mood lighting as well as a noticeably warmer room. She took me to the edge of the bed before turning to face me. We resumed our playful kissing until eventually, as our amorous activity became more involved, she gently pulled me onto the bed.

That first day together in Tupungato, a day that I today reflect upon often, was truly ethereal. It was an experience that could only be created by the sum of all of its parts. It was Argentina. It was the vineyard. And it was the woman I'd never expected to meet. The woman that was changing the way I saw the world. The woman with whom I was now fully in love.

28

The following week passed quickly. After spending most of the weekend with Marcela, including helping her with field work at the vineyard Saturday and another Sunday afternoon lunch with Silvia, I settled into what was becoming my new routine: morning classes at the university, afternoon prep work for my evening English classes, and then nightly gatherings with Marcela. One night we met on the peatonal for dinner. Wednesday night was tango night with the dance club. And the other evenings were just spent hanging out with Marcela at her apartment. Sharing dinners with Silvia, taking walks through the park, watching soccer games and movies. It didn't so much matter what we were doing, just as long as we were together. And although my house was more private than her apartment, it just wasn't the right fit on weekday evenings for a variety of reasons, none bigger than this was family time for Marcela and she felt it important to be with her mother.

Following my Friday morning university classes, I again accompanied Marcela to Tupungato. This time, however, it was with additional purpose. Marcela had arranged a meeting for me with the hospital director, and I was excited. As much as I'd enjoyed some time away from radiology, and as much as I was enjoying the challenge of teaching, I'd come to the realization I missed medicine. After dedicating more than a decade of my life to becoming a physician, I looked forward to again being able to implement my skillset. And while I recognized I probably wouldn't be reading MRIs, I looked forward to rediscovering my general medicine education, much of which had gone unused during my final years of training.

Marcela dropped me off at the hospital just before two. She wished me luck, and arranged to pick me up after her class. We planned to again spend the night and the following day at the vineyard.

From the outside, the hospital was about what I'd expected. The majority of the building was just a single story, with its total footprint appearing just slightly larger than Marcela's elementary school. There was a small portion that included a second story, with its different colored brick suggesting it was an addition to the original structure. I walked up a short flight of stairs to the main entrance. There were several employees outside smoking, but otherwise there was little activity.

I entered through the front door into a small, empty lobby. It was clean, but simple. Void of televisions, reading materials, and wall decorations, the room offered a dozen or so simple wooden chairs and a barren wooden reception desk that was unattended. Off the lobby there were doors in both directions. There was a sign on the door leading toward the more extensive hall indicating a patient care area. The opposite more abbreviated hallway was unmarked, but gave the appearance of an administrative area. I walked down this hall until I arrived at the first open door. There I encountered a middle-aged woman logging calculations into a three-ring binder. I introduced myself and explained that I was there for a meeting with the director. She guided me back to the lobby and promised to inform Juan of my arrival.

After a ten minute wait Juan hustled in and apologized for his tardiness. He was tall and thin, and almost completely bald. And while he dressed neatly in a dark blue suit, his mannerisms gave the impression of a person somewhat overwhelmed. He led me to his office back down the administrative hallway. We entered a large and untidy room, with binders and loose papers covering the majority of the surface area including his desk, the chairs, and even a significant portion of the floor.

"Sorry for the mess," he said, moving folders off one of the chairs to provide me with a place to sit. "We're going through a reorganization right now and things are a little crazy."

He sat down at his desk and I sat across from him.

"Thanks for agreeing to meet with me," I said.

"I'm happy to do it," he responded. "Marcela became a friend years ago when she taught our daughter. She's been a wonderful addition to both the school and the community."

"She's a phenomenal person," I replied. "I feel very fortunate to have met her."

"So Marcela told me you're a radiologist, and you might be interested in helping out at our hospital. Do I have it right?"

"Yes," I said. "I finished my training in July, and I go back to start work in December. I wanted to see if I could do some volunteer work before my return home."

"Interesting," he responded. "Yes I think we might be able to find something for you. We don't have a radiologist at the hospital. The medical physicians and surgeon read their own films. If they have questions, we send the films to Tunuyan where there is a part-time radiologist who can overread. It's not the best system, but we've had to make it work. You might be able to read some of these films to limit delays we encounter when they're sent out."

"I'd be happy to do that if it's helpful," I began. "But actually I was thinking I might be able to help in the emergency room. I spent quite a bit of time there during my training, and I heard from Marcela that you may face some staffing challenges."

Juan smiled. "Challenges, huh?" He looked away, appearing perturbed by the suggestion. He turned back slowly. "Yes, I think that's probably an accurate term. I'd consider the ER one of several challenges we face as an institution. I'd be interested to know how she characterized these 'challenges'?"

I squirmed in my chair. "She didn't intend anything derisive by her observations. And I'm not sure how well she understands the inner-workings of the department. But she told me that she's been there on occasion with her students over the years. And her observation was that the ER is staffed by recent medical school graduates serving a mandatory internship. And while she has appreciated their compassion, it was her opinion that a lack of experience and manpower has on occasion created some... difficulties."

Juan sat up in his chair, placing his elbow on his desk with his palm supporting his chin. He looked away again, appearing to choose his words carefully.

"As a rural hospital, we face many of the same challenges that small hospitals across our country face. The same challenges that hospitals all through South America face. Our biggest issue is a lack of resources. I've toured hospitals in Buenos Aires, Santiago, even Mendoza. We simply can't afford to offer many of the technologies offered at large institutions. The second biggest problem we face is a lack of specialty care. Medicine here, as I'm sure you're aware, doesn't reimburse as it does in your country. Many physicians earn little more than the average government employee. The ones who earn better do so by practicing private medicine in the wealthier areas of larger cities, not by working for public hospitals in rural Argentina. That makes physician recruitment difficult for a hospital like ours. We have four full time physicians on staff. Three generalists and one general surgeon. We have one midwife and one part-time obstetrician who support our generalists to provide women's health. Access to other specialists is very limited, generally one-half day per week. Many specialties like orthopedics and neurosurgery aren't offered at all, mandating a trip into Mendoza. It's not what you're used to, but I think overall we do an excellent job of providing care under the circumstances."

Juan paused and took a drink of water. I remained quiet.

"So what did you have in mind in terms of helping in the ER?"

I sat up in my chair and cleared my throat. "I was thinking I might be able to help in a couple of ways. First, I'd like to see patients. I could come out a couple times a week, either giving the other physicians time away, or by helping them during high volume times. Second, and maybe more importantly, I could take a look at some of your protocols. I have friends in the United States who've completed emergency medicine residencies. I know they're involved in designing evidence-based protocols to help assure rapid, consistent, high-level care. While I recognize a lack of resources might make it impossible to implement these same protocols, I suspect we could use these as models to form our own."

Juan nodded.

"Sounds interesting. I do think that's something that could benefit us. One of the issues we have in the ER is that we're not always consistent in our ability to provide definitive care. There is a great variety amongst our rotating physicians in terms of their comfort level in treating more complicated patients. We've always left it up to the individual physicians to determine what they are capable of treating and what needs to be transported to larger centers. I know that has created some frustration within our community, with some patients choosing to bypass our ER and seek emergent care in Tunuyan or Mendoza. The advancement of protocols might diminish these inconsistencies."

He paused.

"Do you have time for a tour? I'd like you to see our hospital and meet one of our ER physicians."

"I have as much time as you do," I said. "I'd appreciate the chance to get input from one of the doctors."

Juan led me back down to the lobby. There we passed through the opposite door and started down a hallway lined by patient rooms. Juan summarized the basics. Two floors of 12 patient rooms, most of them shared. Forty total beds with an average census of 10 patients. Surgical and medical patients were mixed together on each floor, with a small corner of the second floor reserved for obstetrics. Most inpatient stays were for uncomplicated problems like pneumonia, dehydration, or appendicitis. More complicated cases were stabilized in the ER and transferred.

Juan entered one of the empty patient rooms. It was as basic as it could be: two simple hospital beds divided by a white sheet suspended from a rod, with a single wooden chair at the foot of each bed. No televisions or artwork. No closets or private baths. Personal items were kept at the bedside or placed in a common storage area by the nursing station. Patients needing to use the bathroom called nursing on a bedside intercom system and were assisted to one of the two bathrooms on each floor. There was a dramatic difference from the plush hospital rooms I was accustomed to back home.

We stopped by the nursing station where I met some of the nurses. With only three patients on the floor, the friendly staff had ample time to chat. There were three nurses assigned to each floor, meaning a nurse was responsible for anywhere from one to five patients depending on the census. They felt well supported by their physician staff, although admitted a fluctuating census could occasionally make things challenging. And for the most part their interaction with the ER was smooth, however they acknowledged that the annual physician turnover created a tense environment upon arrival of the new physicians. I thanked them for their time and then followed Juan through a set of double doors into the adjacent ER.

The pace of activity there was consistent with that which I'd observed elsewhere. The staff of three was seated at a large semicircular desk in the center of the room, sharing Mate as they discussed the happenings of a telenovela. They acknowledged Juan and me with the customary greeting and Juan briefly summarized my background and desire to volunteer. Both the nurse Cyntia and assistant Karen seemed excited. They asked about my training and the impetus for my travel to Mendoza. I obliged with the brief version of the story I'd told countless times.

Jorge, the young physician, was less welcoming. With his wrinkled scrubs, unshaven face, and messy black hair suggesting he'd spent the night at the hospital, he remained quiet throughout my introduction. He responded with repetitive abbreviated nods, creating an appearance of both apprehension and uncertainty. Following an awkward pause in the conversation, I addressed him directly with what I believed to be a comfortable icebreaker.

"So I understand there are just two of you that staff the ER regularly?"

"That's correct, Dr. Serati and myself."

Silence.

"And how do you divide the shifts?" I persisted.

"It varies. Typically 24 hour shifts, sometimes longer. I'm 40 hours into a 48 hour shift now."

"Wow, that's pretty brutal. Especially with the stress of the ER."

Jorge looked over his shoulders at the empty exam rooms and smiled. "It can be, but there's enough quiet time to make up for the craziness." He seemed to be warming up a little. "And the call room is pretty nice. Not too different from my apartment in town, and I don't have to cook."

Karen and Cyntia laughed.

There was another pause in the conversation until I again broke the silence.

"I haven't worked in an ER in the last year or so, but I enjoyed my work during residency. And while I didn't anticipate practicing medicine here, I find myself missing it. What would you think about me taking on some shiftwork?"

Jorge toggled his head from side-to-side, processing the request. "What did you have in mind?"

Sensing uncertainty, I was careful to not come across as threatening. "I'm pretty open. Whatever you think best. Either taking on some shifts by myself to give you guys a break, or else providing additional coverage during busier times. I was thinking I could come out two or three days a week."

Jorge looked toward Juan who responded with a quick nod. Jorge then turned his body and looked directly at me for the first time.

"I think we might be able to work something out. Obviously I'll want to talk to Dr. Serati first." He paused. "And I guess my inclination would be to have you start with a couple of late afternoon and early evening shifts at our sides so you can see how we run things. I'm sure it'll be different from what you're used to. Then if things go smoothly, I'd think we might be able to cede a few hours here and there as long as chief approves."

He looked over at Juan.

"I think that's a prudent way to proceed. As soon as I get copies of Jake's licensure, it'll take about a week to get him approved. I'd think we might be able to have you ready by the week after next."

"Good," Jorge replied. "I'll talk to Dr. Serati later today and if he's comfortable with the arrangement we'll shoot for two weeks then. We'll do an orientation before your first shift."

"Excellent," I said. "I look forward to it."

I shook hands with Jorge, exchanged good-bye kisses with Cyntia and Karen, and then followed Juan back to his office. There we exchanged contact information and I promised to fax my paperwork within the next few days. Juan would confirm my acceptance by the ER staff, and then work to expedite the attainment of my privileges to allow the earliest possible start date. I thanked him and headed out front to wait for Marcela.

As I sat on the brick wall awaiting her arrival, I was overcome with excitement. When Marcela had first suggested the hospital work, I'd been somewhat reluctant. Practicing emergency medicine in a foreign country after years of the tranquility of reading films was certainly out of my comfort zone. But with time to consider the request, and especially now after seeing the hospital and meeting the staff, I was filled with a nervous energy I hadn't felt in a medical setting in years. Direct interaction with patients, the provision of acute hands on care, and the opportunity to help shape the implementation of medical services in an underserved community. While I knew it would be a formidable challenge, I couldn't wait to get started.

29

F riday night was another beautiful night in Tupungato. Cuddled by the fire late into the night, I enthusiastically recalled my afternoon at the hospital. And after a lazy start to the morning, it was back to work in the vineyard on Saturday. On this occasion we were joined by Javier, providing me with my first opportunity to meet Marcela's prospective business partner. And while I did occasionally note flashes of the authoritativeness that worried Marcela, for the most part I enjoyed our interaction. Javier's knowledge of the wine industry was impressive, and I finished the day with an unwavering confidence that their blossoming operation would achieve success.

After another traditional Sunday with Marcela and her family, this time alongside her more extended family in the neighboring suburb of Godoy Cruz, it was back to school on Monday. But as we entered the last week of October, my routine of morning university classes and evening English instruction was beginning to evolve.

My history class was already wrapping up. Final exams were the first week of December, and the once feared Dr. Martinez was going to be away at an international conference for the latter half of November. In fact this was really the last week of formal lectures. And while my attendance over the previous two weeks had been spotty, I made sure to attend the final two lectures, both in an effort to finish my education of modern day Argentine history, as well as to show my gratitude to Dr. Martinez.

The last two lectures focused on the Carlos Menem era, and the recent transition into the De la Rua presidency. Menem was elected president in 1989 as a representative of the Peronist Party, the party founded by Juan and Eva Peron with a platform built upon the promise to protect the well-being of the common people. However the party had evolved during the previous forty years, creating within it various factions. Carlos Menem was much more centralist than the party's founders, creating a large ideological gap with the leftist Dr. Martinez. Yet despite their differences, the professor highlighted various successes of Menem's presidency. After years of hyperinflation during the Alfonsin administration, Menem's decision to peg the Argentine peso to the dollar at a one-to-one exchange rate brought hyperinflation to a crashing halt. This Convertibility Plan, combined with the privatization of many utilities, created a substantial increase in productivity and a much needed influx of foreign investment. During the first half of the 90s, Argentina's GDP soared more than 35%. Other highlights of his first term included building an improved relationship with Chile following the resolution of multiple longstanding border disputes, and the advancement of various social programs which helped lower the country's poverty rate. His successes enabled him to modify the constitution to allow for a second successful presidential bid in 1995.

But Dr. Martinez's criticism of the administration was greater than his praise. He lashed out at the former president for his decision to pardon the former leaders of the dictatorship as an act of national reconciliation. He was sharp in his criticism of Menem for his handling of the bombings of the Israeli Embassy in 1992 and the Buenos Aires Jewish Community Center in 1994. But he saved his harshest criticism for Menem's economic plan. While his neoliberal policy initially had a stabilization effect, the economy had spiraled downward during his second term. The mass privatization of state-owned utilities increased inequality in income distribution. And ultimately the overvalued peso, strangled by its peg to the dollar, rendered Argentine goods too expensive to compete with those of other countries. Add to that a Brazilian economic crisis in 1999, Argentina's biggest trading partner, and a decrease in world prices for Argentina's primary exports, and the result was a sharp decline in productivity and a spike in unemployment. The economy contracted and Argentina entered into a crisis of its own.

Although lectures for my wine class were scheduled to continue throughout November, my attendance was infrequent during the final month. While my interest in the wine industry continued to blossom through my interaction with Marcela, I was finding the content of the second half of the course less interesting. The viticulture portion of the class had ended and the course became focused on the history of individual wineries that had come to prominence over the previous two centuries. I'd started attending some evening classes at the viticulture institute with Marcela, and I found these classes much more educational. Besides, the decision to skip the later class provided me the freedom to join Marcela at the school in Tupungato.

My English teaching was also in a state of flux. One conversation class ended the last week of October. The other classes, however, were scheduled to continue throughout the month of November. And while I still enjoyed the students, the classes themselves were ever more challenging. I began to struggle to find content for conversation that would engage the entire class. And my lack of understanding of the rules of English grammar was becoming an issue. While my explanation of student errors as "not sounding right" was initially met with laughter, students now occasionally seemed perturbed. I found myself spending time before class reviewing an English grammar book I'd checked out of the library. This was not how I'd envisioned spending my time in Argentina.

While my enjoyment of the conversation classes was waning, two other teaching engagements were only becoming more gratifying. First, I was relishing my opportunities to interact with Marcela's students in Tupungato. I attended classes one or two times per week, contributing where I could while being cautious not to overstep my bounds as a teacher's assistant. I knew a significant part of my contentment came from the chance to work alongside Marcela. But there was more to it than that. I began to realize that much of my enjoyment was rooted in the community of Tupungato itself. Each day I became more convinced Marcela had been right about this place.

The other teaching job I always looked forward to was with the cardiologist Dr. Gordon. Over the previous month I'd continued to spend time with Mariano and his family both as teacher and friend. We met Tuesday and Thursday afternoons in his home studio for a formal class that often evolved into an informal lunch with the family. Unlike some of my institute classes, the conversation between teacher and student was always easy. And while we spoke about many topics, the conversation generally flowed back to medicine. During our first class in November, Mariano was left shaking his head when I announced my intent to volunteer in Tupungato.

"Are you sure you realize what you're getting yourself into?" he asked incredulously.

"I think so," I responded with some hesitation. "I think it'll be rewarding to help provide care for an underserved population."

Mariano smiled and nodded his head slowly as he often did when processing new information and organizing his thoughts.

"Don't get me wrong. I think it's great you're trying to help. But I'm afraid the majority of their problems don't have a viable solution. As beautiful as Tupungato is, poor rural areas will always struggle to attract physicians. And I think you'll find the lack of resources suffocating." He paused. "And how much time do you have left in Mendoza anyways, six weeks? Do you really think you'll be able to make changes in such a short time?"

"Actually I've been giving it some thought, and I think I'm going to extend my trip and stay through December."

I stopped there and waited to see how Mariano would respond.

After an initial stare providing the impression of uncertainty, a wry smile emerged.

"The Latin lover," he said with a snicker, referring to me as he often did since my revelation a few weeks earlier of my relationship with Marcela. "You're really falling for this girl. I thought you needed to be back in December to find a house before you start your job?"

I nodded. "That was the plan with Sara. She wanted to do that together. But those plans are off for now. So I figure I'll just rent initially to provide additional time to figure out where I want to be. The hospital has some temporary housing for physicians. So I think an end of December return should be doable."

"Wow," he replied. "Have you shared this with Marcela yet? Have you two talked at all about the future?

"No and no," I responded. "Actually it was just last night I started thinking about a delayed return. And we both kind of agreed from the beginning we wouldn't focus on the future, just enjoy the time we have together. I think deep down we both know our relationship is not sustainable. Her future is here, with her family, her teaching, and the vineyard. And my career is back in the United States. As wonderful as it's been, a long-term relationship doesn't seem feasible."

"I agree," Mariano said. "So be careful Jake. The longer this lasts, the more difficult your transition will be upon your return. And I can already see its going to be hard on you." He raised his eyebrows. "Don't get me wrong, I'd be happy if you stay an extra month. You might finally get me proficient in this confusing language of yours. But don't let your emotions obstruct your appreciation of your reality."

I nodded. "I'll do my best."

He paused and looked down at his watch. Per usual we were already fifteen minutes past our finish time.

I restarted the conversation. "If I do extend, it gives me more time to accomplish other things I was hoping to do during my stay. One thing I've been wanting to do now that the weather is turning is to travel down to Malargue to fly-fish. Remember I told you about Marco, the fly-fisherman I met when I skied Las Leňas?"

"Yes I remember," Mariano said. "The guy from the fly-shop. Have you two been in touch?"

"We haven't. I've been meaning to call him for a while now, but have gotten a little side-tracked with some other things." I smiled. "But I was thinking I might call today to see if he would be available to fish this weekend. Marcela has something planned with her friends on Saturday night, so I thought I might go down for a couple days. Would you have any interest in joining me if it works for Marco?"

Mariano pondered the invitation. "Fly-fishing, huh? You know I'm not much of a fisherman. And I've never been fly-fishing before. Sure I wouldn't be holding you guys back?"

"Not at all," I reassured. "We'd have a great time. Besides, I don't know Marco that well, and it's not a short trip down there. I'd appreciate the company."

Mariano nodded. "Well I think it could work. I need to run it by my wife, but I don't think we had any plans this weekend. When were you thinking we'd leave?"

"Whatever works best for you," I said. "We could take the overnight bus Friday, and then maybe come back Sunday afternoon?"

"No, no. We don't need to take the bus," Mariano declared. "I'm happy to drive; we'll get there much quicker. What if we left early Saturday, and tried to be back by dinner time Sunday?"

"Works for me," I said. "Let me check with Marco, and I'll let you know."

We wrapped up the class, with Dr. Gordon needing to get back to the hospital. I declined the invitation to join the rest of the family for lunch, planning to surprise Marcela at the university and join her for afternoon class in Tupungato. If I wasn't going to see her for an entire weekend, I couldn't miss an opportunity to see her during the week.

30

Marco was thrilled with my call. He was supposed to work Saturday, but was able to switch out of his shift to free up the weekend. He invited us to stay at his family home and we took him up on his offer. So Mariano and I departed in his Ford Explorer at five a.m. on Saturday. We spent two amazing half-days fishing the Rio Grande with Marco and his father playing both host and guide. With perfect fishing conditions and not another fisherman in sight, the trout haul was tremendous. We caught an even mix of Brown and Rainbow fishing exclusively on the surface with dry-flies, the largest fish approaching twenty inches. Even Mariano, the novice, got in on the act. With a spectacularly remote backdrop, good companionship, and another asado back at Marco's late into the night on Saturday, it was a memorable weekend.

Mariano dropped me off at home at 10:30 Sunday night. We congratulated each other on a successful trip, and made mention of a possible return in December prior to my departure. I went inside to drop off my things, then headed down the block to the cabina to call Marcela. Silvia answered the phone, sounding excited to talk. While I'd worried from the beginning she might be uncomfortable with my relationship with Marcela, Silvia had become a good friend. I'd developed a strong respect for her, based in large part on her unwavering love and support of her daughter.

She demanded a full recap of my trip and I complied. Despite having lived in Mendoza most of her life, she'd never traveled to the southern part of her province. She hung on each word of my description, interjecting only occasionally with questions to aid in her visualization. We spoke for fifteen minutes before the conversation turned to Marcela. As it turned out, convinced I wouldn't return until late, she'd accepted a late invitation from a friend to attend an outdoor tango gathering at a quaint plaza in the city's fifth section. She'd tasked Silvia with convincing me to join them if I were to arrive home at a decent hour.

I pondered the suggestion, but ultimately decided against it. It was just far enough to prevent me from walking, and public transportation at this time on a Sunday night would be difficult. I said goodbye to Silvia, asking her to relay a message that I'd meet Marcela at the university the following morning with plans to join her for the afternoon in Tupungato. I then hung up the phone, and started to walk out to pay for my call. But before reaching the counter, I turned back to my booth. I knew I had other calls I needed to make. Calls I'd been postponing for weeks. I felt my heart begin to race as I sat down at the stool and again dialed the phone.

The first call was to my parents. While I'd checked in once a week during the first months of my travel, it had now been almost a month since our last communication. During this last call home I'd revealed my developing relationship with Marcela. And the result, while disappointing, hadn't been unexpected.

I'd first broken the news to my father. And while he'd not outwardly expressed discontent, he'd cautioned me about becoming too attached to my surroundings. While he wanted me to enjoy the experience, he reminded me that my home and career were back in the United States. I'd worked hard to earn the academic appointment that awaited me. He didn't want me to do anything rash that would interfere with this opportunity.

My mother had taken the news much harder. While she too had expressed concern about the implications on my career, her focus had centered upon Sara. Her emotions had overflowed. First tears, and then anger. She couldn't comprehend how I could be willing to risk the future Sara and I had been planning together. She told me I was making my decision out of loneliness. She pleaded with me to reconsider, to think things through carefully and fully appreciate the ramifications of my decision. I'd been forced to end the conversation hastily with my mother having cycled back into tears.

From the minute I'd hung up, I'd wanted to call back and again try to convince my mother of my decision. But I knew my efforts were in vain. She was very cerebral, and everything she'd told me had made perfect sense. But it was now time to try again.

My mother answered the phone on the second ring.

"Hello?" she said.

"Hello mother," I responded softly. "How are you guys?"

There was a brief silence on the other end.

"We're doing… okay," she said.

"I'm sorry for not having called," I said. "I've been thinking about you guys a lot, but just thought it better to let things settle down a little."

"I understand," she replied. "Our last conversation was pretty hard on everybody." She paused. "I'm sorry I lost control of my emotions."

"Don't be sorry," I said. "I knew it would be difficult on you."

"It was," she said. "It still is. You know, I just want the best for you."

"I know mother."

Again there was silence.

"So, what have you been up to?" she asked with a cautious tone.

"Still busy with teaching and the university," I responded. "And I just got back from a weekend fly-fishing trip. It was amazing."

"I bet it was. I know how much you enjoy fishing."

The small talk continued, with each of us tiptoeing around the eventuality of our conversation. She broke first.

"So are still seeing this girl?"

"Her name is Marcela," I said calmly. "And yes, we are still dating."

The awkward silence returned. This time I restarted the conversation.

"She has a really neat story. Can I tell you about her?"

"Sure," she said reluctantly. "It sounds like I need to learn a little about her."

I started with broad strokes, summarizing her upbringing and her family situation. My mother was quiet at first, but gradually, as the conversation turned to Marcela's teaching, she became more engaged. Seemingly spurred on by a shared profession, she had questions about the Tupungato school and the educational system in Argentina. After a ten minute conversation, we appeared to achieve a small breakthrough.

"Well," she said, "she does sound like a nice girl."

"You'd like her a lot mom."

"Can I ask you a question?" she said.

"Sure," I replied, fearing what might be coming.

"Have you spoken at all with Sara?"

"No. Just a couple of brief emails."

"And how has she responded?"

"She hasn't said much. Our communication has been pretty superficial. Just work stuff." I paused. The doubts again began to creep into my mind. "But I know she's hurting. Still trying to figure this all out the same way I am."

"So you haven't spoken about your future, about what happens when you come home next month?"

I knew now wasn't the time to mention the possibility of me staying an extra month.

"No, not yet. But we'll have that discussion soon. The timing just hasn't been right yet."

"Sure," she said. "I understand."

I sensed she was fighting her emotions.

"Mom, you know how much I love you guys. And everything is going to work out. You just need to trust me for now."

"Alright Jake, I really am trying my best," she said with a labored chuckle.

"I'll call you next Sunday," I replied.

"We'll look forward to it. You take care of yourself."

"Will do. Love you."

I hung up the phone and took a couple of deep breaths. I rubbed my temples with the tips of my fingers. I again reached for the phone, hurrying to dial the number before I had a change in heart.

One ring. Two rings. Three rings. Just as I started to hang up the phone I heard a voice.

"Hello?"

"Hi Sara," I said.

Silence. Clearly she was surprised by the call.

"Hi Jake," she finally responded with a quiet, monotone voice.

"How are you doing?" I asked, bracing for the response I might draw. Unlike with my mother, whose reaction was predictable, I had no idea how Sara would react to my phone call. While she'd been polite enough during a couple of brief email exchanges, a phone conversation promised to reveal much more.

"Not great Jake," she responded, her voice starting to break. "Needless to say it's been a difficult month."

"I know," I responded gently. "I know it has. And I'm sorry I've made you go through this. I never for a minute thought this would happen, and never wanted to hurt to you."

She remained silent, her staccato breathing revealing her emotion. I also stayed quiet. I struggled to find the right words. I realized I didn't know what I wanted to say to her, or even what I could say at this time. I'd called because I'd felt an overwhelming need to call. But what was it? Was I calling out of a desire to try to console her? Or because I felt like I owed it to her after everything we'd been through? Or was I calling for myself? Maybe I feared losing her forever. Maybe I was seeking a way to keep a door open for us in spite of what I was feeling for Marcela.

"How is work going?" I finally offered, trying to provide a path for a less temperamental conversation.

"Work is fine Jake," she responded, her voice laden with frustration.

Again there was silence. I listened to her breathing, waiting for her to say something. But it soon became clear nothing was coming.

I made one additional effort to promote dialogue.

"Have you started interviewing yet?" I said, referring to the hospital positions she was preparing to explore.

"No, not yet. You know that's scheduled for December."

I did. But I didn't know what else to say. I immediately regretted calling. Clearly a civil conversation was still impossible. I searched for the proper words to gracefully end the conversation. But before I could find them, Sara opted for directness.

"Are you still seeing your Argentine friend?" The tone was indignant.

I paused to find the right way to answer. But my hesitation told Sara all she needed to hear.

"I get it Jake," she said forcefully. "You feel sorry for me. And I'm sure that's making it hard on you. But I don't need your pity. I'll be fine. I just need to work through this on my own. And emails and phone calls with you are not part of that solution right now. As long as you are seeing someone else I think it best we break off communication. It's what I need for now, and I hope you can respect that."

I knew she was right. As much as it stung me to hear her words, I understood it was probably necessary for both of us.

"I'm sorry Sara," I said quietly.

"Me too Jake," she said. "But I need to move forward."

"I understand Sara," I said, struggling to get the words out.

"Good luck to you Jake."

"Thanks Sara," I responded, suddenly realizing the finality of the moment. "You too."

She hung up the phone. I sat back in my chair, phone still in hand, processing what had just transpired. Tears welled up in my eyes. She'd made her decision, and had now stated it clearly. She was moving forward without me. Suddenly everything was cloudy again and uncertainty prevailed. I limped back to the house and crawled into bed.

31

I awoke the following morning feeling marginally better. As painful as it had been to hear Sara's words, I tried hard to convince myself that maybe it was something I needed to hear. Maybe residual uncertainty about our relationship had been clouding my judgment. And while I knew I still had a lot to figure out in the coming weeks, our conversation had helped with regard to my plans for the coming months. I was indeed going to extend my trip.

I spent the next three days accompanying Marcela to the school in Tupungato. I waited and broke the news of my decision to lengthen my trip on our way back to Mendoza the first day. And while she voiced excitement, her enthusiasm seemed guarded, not quite what I was expecting. I presumed she was protecting herself against the inevitability of our separation. I was reminded of Dr. Gordon's words of advice.

While I again enjoyed my interaction with the school children each day, I spent much of my time looking forward to Thursday. On Monday Juan had called to inform me that I'd been granted temporary privileges at the hospital. The ER physicians had accepted my request and wanted me to come Thursday for my first shift. They wanted me to arrive by two p.m. during their shift change so they could both be there to provide an orientation. I'd then work until ten p.m. Juan had taken the liberty of checking the bus schedule from Tupungato and had discovered the last bus back to Mendoza left at 10:30. He'd assumed that a two p.m. start would allow Marcela to transport me to the hospital, and that a ten p.m. finish would provide ample time for me to get to the bus terminal. In discussion with the ER physicians, and in trying to adhere to my desired experience, they'd thought I might start out working Tuesdays and Thursdays. We would try it for a few weeks and then re-evaluate. It was exactly what I'd hoped for.

Marcela dropped me off at the hospital Thursday on her way to the school. She was every bit as excited as I was. She'd wanted to wait around after her class to drive me home to allow for an immediate report. But I didn't want to inconvenience her. Ultimately I succeeded in convincing her I'd take the bus with the promise of a phone call upon my return.

I walked into the emergency room and found it much as I had upon my tour: empty. Jorge, Karen, Cyntia, and a man I presumed to be Dr. Serati, were drinking Mate. I greeted the women with the customary kisses, and then shook hands with the two young physicians. Jorge was again somewhat gruff, but Dr. Serati, Matías, was much more amicable. He fetched me a chair, offered me a Mate, and then proceeded with a litany of questions regarding my background and training. Having done a rotation in Miami with a cardiologist during his last year of medical school, Matías understood the US training system and knew what to ask. It was close to three o'clock before the conversation slowed and Jorge proposed we get started.

The 'orientation', from start to finish, lasted less than ten minutes. Karen showed me around one of the four exam rooms, pointing out the equipment and supplies I'd have access to. Cyntia then talked me through the single large storage cabinet in one of the corners of the ER that housed supplies not found in the rooms. Matías and Jorge sat down with me for a few minutes to review basics including a list of phone numbers of local physicians, information about the surrounding hospitals, and other medical resources they'd found helpful. Finally, after giving me an opportunity to ask some simple logistical questions, Jorge took it upon himself to explain their philosophy of practicing emergency medicine in a rural hospital.

"Matías and I have six months left here," he began. "Afterwards we're off in different directions: Matías is pursuing specialty training in cardiology while I've accepted a fellowship in nephrology. While we've enjoyed our time here well enough, we both recognize our future is not in emergency medicine. And as beautiful as the surrounding area is, it didn't take long for us to realize the limitations of the system."

Jorge paused, allowing Matias to build upon this introduction.

"We both started the year trying to treat aggressively. But within weeks we realized the hospital isn't prepared to handle complicated presentations. We each had a patient die early in the year that we knew, under different circumstances, should have experienced a complete recovery. While this was difficult to accept at first, we've come to grips with the reality of our situation. And it has changed the way we treat."

Jorge reassumed control of the conversation from his counterpart.

"We now divide presentations into simple and complicated. Simple presentations are those that can be treated and discharged, or those we think can be treated with a brief hospitalization of just a day or two. Complicated presentations are those that may require a more prolonged hospital stay. We treat the simple cases, and we transport the complicated cases to Tunuyan or Mendoza."

I nodded my head in understanding. I wasn't surprised by anything I'd heard. Their explanation was consistent with what I'd heard from both Marcela and Juan.

"It's hard sometimes," Matías said. "Your first instinct of course is to want to treat everything. And family members often think we're transporting patients due to insufficient training, or even laziness. They don't understand. I've had patients become quite hostile with me."

"Have you shared your frustrations with Juan or with the local physicians?" I inquired.

"Not really," Matías responded shaking his head. "Jorge and I have talked about doing it. But ultimately we decided our lack of experience, and limited time here, really doesn't afford us that opportunity."

"And even if we tried," Jorge said, "I'm not sure it's practical to think things could be different."

"Sure," I said reluctantly. "I understand. I'll follow your lead."

I wanted to challenge this philosophy. I wanted to tell them that one of my goals for working in the ER was to examine shortcomings and see if there was indeed a way to provide better service. But now wasn't the time. It was too early. First I had to observe how the ER functioned, and more importantly I had to earn the respect of my colleagues.

Jorge wished us luck and gathered his things. He was off until the following afternoon and planned to head into Mendoza to meet up with friends. He would see me the following Tuesday for my next scheduled shift.

I thanked him for his time and took a seat alongside Matías. But we didn't have to wait long. Within fifteen minutes of Jorge's departure, we had our first patient. And as Matías had suggested could happen, by four p.m. we had three of our four rooms full.

I started out shadowing Matías. The first patient was an elderly man with chest pain. Matías started the familiar process of ruling out an acute cardiopulmonary disorder. History and physical examination, EKG, chest x-ray, blood tests. While I hadn't myself conducted the work-up in years, such a common evaluation was engrained in me. While a few blood tests varied from those obtained in the United States, the process was otherwise identical to what would have been done back in Chicago.

Patient number two was an elderly woman with dizziness. Every ER physician's least favorite chief complaint. It was a presentation that could be completely benign or life-threatening. The list of possible diagnoses was several pages long. But fortunately this particular patient appeared stable. And as Matias began a thorough work-up, it appeared the issue was a simple one, a recent change in blood pressure medication that had lowered her pressure too much.

I was initially content shadowing Matias. I studied the interaction between the young physician and staff, starting to get a feeling for the all-important flow of the emergency room. And while I had confidence in myself, I recognized I hadn't been in this type of medical setting for years. It was good not to be thrown immediately into the role of independent practitioner.

But when Karen announced that the third patient was an adolescent with a probable wrist fracture, I seized the opportunity. With Matías's blessing, I walked in and introduced myself to the patient and his mother. The patient was a sixteen year-old boy in obvious discomfort, having fallen off his skateboard and landed awkwardly on an outstretched hand. I looked at his wrist and saw it was already quite swollen. I had little doubt it was indeed broken. I stepped out of the room and ordered x-rays, and then reviewed the reassuring results of the first patient while awaiting my pictures.

Ten minutes later the boy was back and the fracture confirmed. It was a non-displaced fracture of the radius bone that was significantly angulated. I knew it was in an unacceptable position and would require reduction. I showed the films to Matías and asked permission to proceed. Matías admitted it was not a procedure he was comfortable with, and recommended splinting and having the patient follow-up with the orthopedist in Tunuyan. But I was uncomfortable with the degree of angulation and gently pushed Matias to allow me to try. Matías acceded and I presented the plan to the patient.

While I hadn't reduced a fracture of this type for years, and had never done so independently, it was something I'd seen my father do countless times during my youth. I stepped out and gathered my supplies, including lidocaine for local anesthesia and the necessary splinting supplies to hold the reduction. Cyntia followed me into the room to assist.

After cleansing the area well, I injected the anesthesia at the fracture site with only modest resistance from the patient. Then after allowing the medicine a few minutes to take effect, I picked up the forearm amidst a rush of adrenaline. Placing my thumbs on the top of the wrist at the site of the fracture, and wrapping my fingers around the mid-forearm, I delivered a rapid and forceful push in the direction I wanted the bone to shift. There was an audible and palpable snap, the boy jumping seemingly more out of surprise than pain. Feeling confident in the reduction by both the sound and improved appearance of the wrist, I had Cyntia wet the plaster splinting material while I supported the wrist in its new position. I covered the arm in padding, and then applied the splint from the palm, down around the elbow, and back up to the knuckles. I held the splint in place as Cyntia wrapped the hardening material in an ace-wrap. Within minutes the splint was dry and I stepped out of the room content with my accomplishment.

The repeat x-rays showed marked improvement. I knew that assuming it held its position the fracture would heal well. Matías produced the information for the orthopedist in Tunuyan and I discharged the patient with instructions to follow-up in seven days. Matías congratulated me on a job well done and requested I get started evaluating a young boy with ear pain that had just been brought back. I smiled knowing I'd passed my first test.

The next several hours produced a steady flow of patients, just enough to keep both Matías and me busy. And while I looked to Matías on occasion for guidance regarding such issues as medication availability and follow-up accessibility, for the most part I functioned independently. I was surprised at how easily things came back to me, especially in a setting and language not native to me. And I was astounded by how the work made me feel; I couldn't remember being this energized in a medical setting in a long time.

At nine p.m. the activity slowed, and we were able to sit down together for the first time since mid-afternoon. We exchanged details about patient interactions, with me still radiating excitement from my first day. By 9:30 all of our patients had been discharged, and I started to tidy things up in preparation for my trip back to Mendoza. I decided that upon my return I was going to surprise Marcela and provide her with the details in person. I asked Karen for directions to the bus terminal, and then walked to the bathroom to change.

But just as I was sitting down to take off my shoes, I heard a sudden commotion from outside. A door slammed open and a woman screamed. I struggled to make out what she was saying. I heard Karen direct them toward a room and then suddenly Matías was yelling, barking out orders with a foreboding urgency. I took a deep breath, tied my shoe back on, and ran out to see how I could help.

I arrived to the work station where I found Cyntia, a look of panic on her face as she scrambled to dial the telephone.

"What is it?" I asked.

"A young boy in respiratory distress. He's going to need to go to Mendoza."

I raced into the room. As I pulled open the curtain, Matías was in front of the patient accommodating him with a non-rebreather mask to maximize oxygen delivery. The boy's mother was in tears, leaning against the wall for support and pleading with Matías to help her boy. At her side was a familiar face, clinging to her mother's leg desperately. I froze for an instant, overwhelmed by the realization that the terrified young girl was Beatriz, one of Marcela's students. Our eyes met briefly as I squeezed through to the other side of the bed to assist Matías.

Now with an improved view of the patient, I immediately saw the urgency. The young boy, who looked no more than five, was gasping for air, his neck and chest muscles exploding outward with each respiratory effort. His lips were blue, and his face was pale. His eyes were shut, seemingly employing every ounce of energy to struggle for air. He was in florid respiratory distress, a chilling sight I'd never before witnessed in a young child. I gulped as I started to organize my thoughts.

"Asthma?" I asked Matías.

"I assume so," he answered, his voice cracking. "Mom says he has a history."

I looked up at the screen to review the vitals. The boy's pulse was racing at 140, and his oxygenation level, despite now being supported by the oxygen mask, was still dangerously low at 75%.

"Oxygen's up all the way?" I asked.

"As high as we can go with the mask," Matias responded. "Cyntia's calling EMS for transport. Karen's preparing an albuterol nebulizer as we wait. I'm going to try to get an IV in him and get him a bolus of Magnesium."

I nodded in agreement, my mind working hard to think of anything else that could be done.

"How about a respiratory therapist?" I blurted out.

"I wish," Matías said. "Only in bigger hospitals."

Karen hooked up the nebulizer and Matías began looking at the boy's arms trying to find a vein. My eyes returned anxiously to the screen. The oxygen saturation level remained in the mid-70s.

I stepped out of the room for a minute to compose myself.

"How long until EMS is here?" I asked Cyntia.

"Five minutes," she answered.

"And then how long to the children's hospital in Mendoza?"

"About 45 minutes by ambulance this time of night," she responded.

I shook my head. An hour was a long time. I knew the boy's respiratory muscles couldn't continue to work this hard for much longer. They would soon fatigue, and his oxygenation level would fall further. I didn't know if he could survive the transport. I paced the floor outside the room. I turned back to Cyntia.

"Does the ventilator in room one work?" I asked.

"I think so," Cyntia said, shrugging her shoulders. "Honestly I haven't seen it used since I've been here. We always mask and transport."

"What about supplies, like endotracheal tubes and attachment equipment? Do we have everything in the supply cabinet?"

"I'm pretty sure it's all on the top shelf. Not sure about tube sizes, but some stuff is there."

"Pull it out," I ordered. "Find the smallest tube we have, and find the appropriate attachment tubing. Make sure the ventilator is ready to go."

I walked back into the room to get an update.

Unsuccessful with the first arm, Matías had switched to the other and appeared to have found success. Karen was adjusting the mask to make certain it was as snug as possible. But there was no improvement in the boy's condition. His respiratory effort was still at an unsustainable intensity. And the oxygenation level had decreased into the upper 60s. I looked at the boy's mother, now slumped over the bed, rendered too weak by emotion to stand. And I again made eye contact with Beatriz, sweet little Beatriz, the girl that had asked me questions about Disney World during my initial school visit. She now stood alone against the wall, fear and incomprehension rendering her frozen in place.

"I'm giving him a dose of Magnesium, then we'll go ahead and transfer," Matías announced.

"His sats are dropping Matías," I responded. "I think he's starting to tire. I don't think he can make it to Mendoza. I think we need to intubate him here."

Matías stood up and looked at the screen, processing the suggestion, and then looked back at me.

"And if we do? Then how do we transport him? We can attach a bag and valve but I don't think we have a reservoir for supplemental oxygen. He'll be worse off than with the mask."

I shook my head. "Then we'll have to keep him on the ventilator here until he's stable enough for transfer. I assume the children's hospital can send someone out with a portable ventilator or at least with a bag and mask with a reservoir. Look at him Matías, he's not going to make it. It's our only chance."

Matías put his hands on his head, closed his eyes, and lowered his chin. He sighed deeply. He looked back up.

"Alright, I think we have to try."

I raced out of the room and found Cyntia. She'd laid out everything she could find in room one and was now at the desk updating the EMS team that had just arrived. I walked up to the two men and introduced myself quickly.

"Do you have a reservoir to add oxygen to a bag and valve?"

"No, we don't," one of the men responded, shaking his head.

"Then we're going to have to treat him here for now. He's too unstable for transfer."

I hurried back to room one and looked at the ventilator. It seemed similar to the machines I remembered using during my early training. Matías walked into the room.

"Have you used this machine before?" I asked.

"No. And I've never intubated a child. Have you?"

"No," I answered. "But it can't be that different from an adult. We can do this. We have to do this." I said it as much for myself as for Matías.

I reached down and grabbed the package with the smallest diameter tube. I then surveyed the tubing Cyntia had pulled out.

"It looks like everything's here. You and Karen bring him in. I'm not sure he's conscious enough for it to make a difference, but I think some sedation would be good. Get some lorazepam, and some morphine so he's comfortable when we get him intubated. We'll have to figure out the proper vent settings later."

Matías ran out to get everything ready. I stepped out after him and addressed the mother. I was empathetic, yet succinct. Her son was experiencing a severe asthma attack. He was in acute respiratory distress. He was too sick to be transported. The only option we had to try to save her son was to sedate and intubate him. The machine could assume the work of his rapidly fatiguing respiratory muscles. And we could deliver a higher content of oxygen to his starving lungs. We had to act immediately. There was no other option.

The mother again burst into tears. She nodded her head in understanding.

"Just save my son," she cried. "Please, I beg you, save my son."

Karen moved past us wheeling the bed into room one. I turned to follow, and Matías joined us with the necessary medications.

"Give him a dose of lorazepam now," I told Matías. "Karen, recline the bed and see if you can extend his neck for me. I'll tell you when to remove the mask. If I can't get it right away I'll have you replace his mask."

I reached down and opened the endotracheal tube. While it appeared to be a pediatric tube, I thought it was probably larger than the ideal size for a five year-old. But it was what we had. I picked up the laryngoscope and looked at it. It too appeared too large for the small mouth of the boy. I flipped it into the correct position and the light turned on.

"Ok Karen, remove the mask please," I ordered, taking a deep breath as I steadied myself.

Karen took off the mask and tipped the boy's head back. I inserted the laryngoscope along the edge of his tongue, and then rotated it to pull the tongue forward to expose the vocal cords. I placed my elbow on the table in an attempt to stabilize my shaking hand. The boy remained still. But I saw nothing. I applied more pressure forward with the scope. I had Karen increase the boy's neck extension. But still no sign of the cords. I looked up at the boy's face. Absent the support of the mask for just a minute and now even the skin of his face was becoming blue. I swore as I pulled out the scope and Karen quickly replaced the mask.

"Do you want me to try some cricoid pressure?" Matías asked, his voice trembling as he spoke.

"Yes, please," I responded, frustrated with myself for not remembering that pressure on the neck cartilage could aid with cord visualization.

Karen removed the mask and again positioned the head. I inserted the scope as Matías varied his pressure on the front of the boy's neck. Initially it did nothing. My hand continued shaking as I tried desperately to change my angle. Then suddenly I saw them. A brief glimpse of the glistening cords.

"There!" I shouted.

Matías held firm pressure as I steadied my hand and confirmed adequate visualization. With my right hand I eased the tube down to the cords, watching it pass through. I knew I wanted it a few centimeters past the cords, but not too deep to prevent the tube from entering a single bronchi and ventilating only one lung. With the boy's face again turning blue, I gave it my best guess, held the tube in place, and hooked up the bag. I had Matías listen to the lungs while I squeezed air from the bag. Matias gave me the thumbs up: good breath sounds in both lungs. The tube was in. I inflated the cuff around the tube to secure its placement, and then taped it in position. Karen handed me the attachment tubing and I secured the endotracheal tube. I stepped back and wiped the profuse sweat off my forehead.

"Okay, I'll start him on some initial settings," I said. "Matías go see if you can look up how to calculate tidal volumes for a pediatric patient. Karen please restart the albuterol nebulizer."

They nodded in confirmation. I set the rate at 20 and estimated the volume at 200 ml. I set the oxygen at 90%. I dialed in the settings and watched hopefully as the machine began to do its work.

At first the labored breathing continued, the boy's own respiratory drive fighting against the work of the machine. I shook my head and called in Matías to give the boy a small dose of morphine. But gradually, the boy's respiratory rate started to slow, and his accessory respiratory muscles began to relax. I looked up at the screen and saw the oxygen saturation climbing back into the 90s. I smiled, sighed, and shook my head in relief. It was working.

I stepped out to update Matías and Karen, and then turned my attention to the boy's family. By now the mother and sister had been joined by the father and both sets of grandparents. I introduced myself and explained the continued severity of the boy's condition. While he was more stable now, he was still very ill. We would do our best to treat him here for now with the goal of transporting him to Mendoza as soon as possible. The mother hugged me. I squatted down and took Beatriz by the hands.

"We're going to make your brother better," I whispered.

I squeezed her hands and then excused myself to return to the bedside. I wanted them to remain outside for now, but promised to allow them to see their boy as soon as possible.

I entered the room and found Matías. He'd lowered the tidal volume per his calculation, and had been able to turn the oxygen down to 80%. The boy was now breathing just slightly above the rate of the machine.

"I ordered a portable chest x-ray and some blood work. We'll get a blood gas and see if we need to adjust vent settings. Looks like we might have to keep him for a while. Cyntia got ahold of the children's hospital and they can't send a transport team yet."

"What? Why not?" I asked in frustration.

"They only have two teams, and they're both in the field. And there's still one more patient in front of us. My guess is he may end up being here most of the night."

I shook my head nervously. "Not what I wanted to here. Let's hope the worst is behind us."

"I think it might be," Matías said. "I'm giving him a dose of IV steroids, to repeat every 6 hours for the first 24. We'll do nebulizer treatments every 2 hours. And I have IV fluids going at 100 ml per hour."

"Sounds good," I replied, "and let's titrate the lorazepam hourly to make sure he's comfortable."

"I can do that," Matías said.

I walked back to the work station and slumped down in my chair next to Karen. I looked at the clock on the wall and saw it was 11:30 p.m.

"Looks like I'm not getting back to Mendoza tonight," I said, finally able to muster a smile.

"No, you're not," she said. "So you might as well stick around and see some patients."

"Is there anyone else here?" I asked, suddenly realizing I was oblivious to all other activity in the ER.

"Rooms two and three are full. An OB patient in two and abdominal pain in three. Take your pick." She handed me two charts from which to choose. I stood up, smiled, and grabbed the top chart. Karen stood up and looked at me, a tear welling in her left eye.

"Thank you Jake," she said, extending her arms for a hug.

"Thank *you* Karen," I answered.

She nodded and remained quiet, wiping away the tear. I smiled and walked toward room three.

The rest of the night went smoothly. Matias and I discharged the two additional patients quickly, allowing us to dedicate our attention to the boy. It wasn't until I received the first set of blood test results before I ever learned his name. It was Erick. I smiled when I saw the name, thinking of my father more than 5000 miles away. How proud he would have been to see his son in action this evening.

We were excited by the initial test results. No indication of infection, and a pretty good blood gas. We again lowered the oxygen concentration on the ventilator. We took turns checking on Erick every 15 minutes, recording vitals, listening to his lungs, and studying his respiratory effort. By three a.m., following another albuterol treatment, we agreed he was stable enough to bring in the family.

As Matías had predicted, it wasn't until seven a.m. before the transport team finally arrived. By that time Erick had received his second dose of steroids and was continuing to demonstrate rapid improvement. In fact he was looking so comfortable we even briefly considered a short trial off the ventilator to see if he might be ready for extubation. But ultimately we thought better of it. The team was here and was ready to transport to a facility much better equipped to deal with complications that might arise off the ventilator.

The team transferred him to the portable ventilator and loaded him into the ambulance. I walked outside to say goodbye to the family. This time there were hugs and kisses from each of the family members. I walked back to the station and joined the rest for a celebratory Mate. Exhausted from both a lack of sleep and the emotional intensity of the night, we remained mostly quiet, sipping our tea and enjoying the much welcomed silence.

Finally at eight a.m., ten hours after my shift was scheduled to end, I gathered my things and prepared to depart. I told the staff I planned to stop by the children's hospital later in the day to follow-up on Erick. I promised an update upon my return Tuesday. Matías thanked me for my help, and we agreed to have a formal debriefing with Jorge as soon as we could. As ecstatic as we were with the outcome, we recognized how close we'd come to tragedy.

I said my goodbyes and headed out the front door to find the first bus back to Mendoza. I knew there was one person who would be anxiously awaiting my arrival.

32

The next three weeks passed quickly. Erick recovered fully and was discharged home within 48 hours of his transfer. The family showed their gratitude by dropping off gifts for the staff including a leg of lamb for each of us who had cared for Erick in the ER. And following my memorable first night, I quickly gained acceptance from the hospital staff. Word spread of Erick's care, and I was approached by many to welcome me to their hospital.

Jorge too was complimentary. Apologizing for his initial cold reception, he now expressed an interest in working together in the ER. Following our debriefing with Matías during my second week of work, the three of us agreed to work together on quality improvement projects at the rural hospital. Jorge reached out to staff physicians to compile a formal list of diagnoses that would be treated in house. And together with Juan, he began the process of putting together a continuing medical education program for hospital employees to assure the staff remained up-to-date. Matías took the lead in an effort to begin tracking outcomes. The hospital needed objective data to determine its areas of greatest deficiency.

For my part, I was determined to expand services the ER was able to offer for life-threatening emergencies. After multiple discussions with Jorge and Matías, I decided to focus my efforts on the treatment of strokes and heart attacks. Previously these patients were triaged and transferred to tertiary care hospitals in Mendoza. But I knew the prolonged transfer time undoubtedly resulted in poorer outcomes. The successful treatment of both diagnoses revolved around the prompt resolution of the obstructing clot. The longer the patient went without adequate blood supply, the higher the likelihood of morbidity and mortality. Many patients weren't receiving definitive treatment for 120 minutes after their presentation to the hospital. This was unacceptable.

Both conditions could be treated with a clot-busting drug that could be administered in the ER. This was the gold standard treatment for patients presenting early with stroke symptoms. And while it wasn't quite as good as immediate cardiac surgery for heart attack patients, it would undoubtedly yield better results than the current delayed treatment being provided. While the medication was widely available across Argentina, it hadn't been employed in the Tupungato hospital due to concerns about dealing with rare complications from medication administration. That needed to change.

I exchanged emails with a former medical school classmate turned ER physician to obtain their protocols for administering the medication. I organized hospital wide-training for staff regarding use of the medication. And I even got Juan to organize community talks educating the public about the availability of the medication and the importance of early presentation to the ER. We hoped to be ready to offer the treatment by the first of the year.

Outside of the hospital, I was now spending almost all of my time in three different endeavors: helping at the school in Tupungato, working the fields at the vineyard, and enjoying time with Marcela. I continued to spend frequent afternoons in the classroom with Marcela's students. The Friday afternoon class became a standing appointment, allowing me to stay over at the Tupungato house with Marcela.

Unlike my conversation classes, which by the end of the semester I'd come to see as work, time with the kids in Tupungato was pure fun. Having never really spent time working or playing with young children, I was surprised to find my interaction with the students was effortless. I made up stories about my favorite childhood personalities. I led them on scavenger hunts outside on the playground. And I worked hard to help them with their English. As Marcela gave the lessons, I made rounds providing individual support, correcting spelling and helping with pronunciation. The students seemed to enjoy it, and I couldn't get enough.

Saturdays were dedicated to work at the vineyard. Javier stopped by to provide direction and help where he could, but Marcela and I did most of the work ourselves. Most of our labor focused on pruning the second year vines. Blessed with favorable weather, the vines were thick, and the work was exhausting.

The last Saturday of November, however, was devoted to a unique project. Marcela had announced during our midweek tango that we were going to begin our work day by planting rosebushes at the end of each row of vines. She'd learned in one of her viticulture classes that this was common practice in California. She informed me that common vine pests, including insects and fungi, were attracted by the sweet smell of roses. She wanted to make certain that if pestilence were to arrive at the vineyard, it would make its presence known early by its effect on the rosebushes. This would then in theory allow time to treat the vines before they were damaged. While Marcela hoped to maintain an organic vineyard, she thought we needed to be alerted if the vines were threatened.

My initial reaction was that the project didn't seem an efficient use of time with so much other work still requiring our attention. I gently suggested our time might be better spent continuing our pruning or working on equipment facility maintenance.

"We can do those things afterwards," she replied. "I don't think the rosebushes will consume the whole day."

"What about other vineyards in Tupungato?" I asked. "Do any plant rosebushes or employ a similar technique for pest detection?"

"None I'm aware of. I think we'd be the first," she answered proudly.

I nodded. "Isn't pestilence pretty rare here with the dry climate and altitude?"

"True," she responded. "Fortunately. But not impossible. I've heard of vineyards occasionally having to spray."

I nodded again, this time with a smile emerging. "So are we taking on this little project for vine preservation, or might you call this more of a cosmetic undertaking?"

She smiled and shrugged her shoulders. "I don't want to be just another vineyard in the valley. I want it to be a reflection of who I am, of my family. I think the roses will be a nice personal touch, one that will help make it truly special." She smiled, took my hands, and leaned in for a kiss.

Conversation over. I stood no chance on this one. We spent seven hours that Saturday pinching our fingers on thorns as we planted small bushes on each end of all of our rows. The equipment facility was left for another day.

Much of the remainder of my free time was spent at Marcela's side. While I tried to be respectful of her need to study for finals in early December, I found myself spending more and more time with her each week. And while we never discussed my departure, we pursued our relationship with an urgency that spoke to the imminence of its arrival. During the last two weeks of November, I had lunch or dinner with her every day but one. We continued to dance tango every Wednesday with the tango group, and became regulars at the Sunday night outdoor milongas as well. And we spent countless hours sitting around Marcela's kitchen table sipping Mate. Although I still wasn't sold on its bitter taste, I was now fully indoctrinated, and had come to appreciate it for its tranquility and socialization.

On the Friday following Marcela's last exam, she and I took a twelve hour overnight bus to Buenos Aires. Since the first night we danced tango together, Marcela had often voiced her desire to dance in the nation's capital. She explained that while the tango scene was rebuilding in Mendoza, it was still a far cry from Buenos Aires, the world's premiere tango destination. She'd been there once as a teenager on a school trip, but that was years before she'd started dancing. Current tango group members carpooled across the country frequently for long weekends, but Marcela, determined to save every last dollar for her pending purchase, had declined previous invitations.

After an early morning stop at a roadside restaurant for pastries and coffee, we arrived at the Buenos Aires bus terminal at 10 a.m. Stepping off the bus I was immediately reintroduced to the familiar discomfort of high humidity, a condition non-existent in Mendoza. But in the sprawling coastal city in early summer, it was suffocating. By the time we reached the front of the terminal to hail a cab, I was already dripping with sweat.

Following a travel agent's recommendation, I'd booked a hotel located just a block off Florida Street in the heart of the city. The agent had promised a boutique hotel ideally located to provide easy access to the city's multitude of tango dance clubs. When we walked into the lobby and saw beautiful hand painted murals of tango dancers on the walls, I knew we were in the right spot.

We found our room and unpacked our things. We showered and changed, then set out to explore. With Marcela guiding, we started by weaving our way through the commercial area around Florida street. The streets were lined with small shops and restaurants, and were packed with people. Clearly the heat was not proving a deterrent. Many of the cafes and restaurants offered outdoor seating, and just about every seat was taken. And when we entered some of the local stores, including a store sought out by Marcela dedicated solely to tango shoes, there was scarcely a place to stand amongst the masses.

In fact the only pockets of open space along the street were those claimed by street performers. On almost every block there was at least one performer entertaining an interactive crowd circled around them. And while we saw a little of everything, the majority of performers were couples dancing tango. With each opportunity Marcela nudged through the crowds until we had an unobstructed view of the presentation. And despite occasional repetition amongst the shows, we never left disappointed.

The couples were all dressed in traditional garb: the male in a bright suit with matching tango shoes, the woman in a sexy knee length dress with high heels. Some of the men wore stylish hats, while others left their slicked back hair fully exposed. Each couple had a small portable stereo set up next to a donation hat. The performances all started with a brief introduction, many of which included an increasingly familiar account of the origin of tango. According to most versions, the dance was born in the mid-to-late 1800s in the working class neighborhoods of Buenos Aires, inspired from African rhythms. The dance then evolved and took on its modern day form in the early 1900s following the arrival from Germany of the bandoneon, the accordion-like instrument which carried the melody in most tango music.

But it was the dance portion of the presentations that was most spectacular. Unfazed by the heat, the dancers performed with a striking intensity, eyes glaring and faces maintaining a slight scowl. Many of the dances were set to the same popular tango songs I now recognized from my time at milongas. Most started slowly with simple walking and delicate spins, before eventually exploding with a flurry of kicks and twists that left the appreciative crowd cheering and whistling. Each dance was followed by chants for an encore, with the dancers always complying before taking a break to encourage donations and allow their body temperatures to cool.

After lunch we rode the subway to the nearby Recoleta neighborhood. Walking through this affluent area, and again later in the afternoon while in the adjacent area of Palermo, the city took on a different feel. With many older ornate buildings, both residential and commercial, the city felt much more European. The small shops, bright colors, and crowded streets were replaced by high rises, wide boulevards, and large shopping malls. I was impressed by how clean this part of the city seemed, and enjoyed the contrast of its relative tranquility. The afternoon was highlighted by a visit to Eva Peron's elaborate tomb in the Recoleta cemetery.

By seven p.m., with our energy level waning, Marcela took me to the famous Café Tortoni for a late afternoon coffee. The popular Café had been one of the most memorable experiences from her first trip to Buenos Aires. Like many Argentines, and quite different from my upbringing in Wisconsin, Marcela had an affinity for style and elegance. With its marble tables, beautiful tile work, and opulent mirrors, Café Tortoni offered plenty of each. Served by waiters in vests and bowties, we sipped our coffee and soaked in the atmosphere.

From there it was back to the hotel to change into our more formal dress. It was time for the main event. In true Argentine fashion we started our evening at 11 p.m. with dinner around the corner from the hotel. Our conversation was pleasant as always, but as the evening progressed, I noticed Marcela showing more affection than she often did. She stared into my eyes, massaging my hand with hers. And there were several brief moments where she remained quiet, appearing to be fighting back emotion. I knew what it was, because I too was feeling it. But I fought the urge to address it. Instead I held her gaze, squeezed her hand, and smiled.

Just after one a.m., we paid our bill and walked out to find a cab. Marcela had done exhaustive research, and had put together a plan for the evening. She wanted to visit three different clubs, and it needed to be done in a particular order. The first stop was known for its live music, the second had the city's best dance floor, and the third was the largest milonga in all of Buenos Aires. And these were just the Saturday night destinations. She had two different spots lined up for Sunday. She trembled in excitement as we rode to our first stop. I steadied her hand with a squeeze. I knew in my heart that there was no place I'd rather be.

The first location was as promised. We sat at the club for over an hour, amazed by the vigor of the bandoneonista that belied his advanced age. I watched as dancers made their way around the floor. I was pleasantly surprised to see the majority of dancers in attendance were of a beginner or intermediate level. While I'd been excited to see the different clubs, I'd feared the level of dance might prove intimidating. But I soon realized I'd be able to blend in. When the band announced a brief break and the stereo music began, I took Marcela's hand and led her out on the floor. We didn't sit down again until the band finished their second set.

The only disappointment with the first club was that they didn't serve wine. But this was remedied upon our arrival to our second destination. I ordered a half bottle of the house red and we toasted to our night of tango in Buenos Aires. Again the emotions surged, and again we both remained silent. But this time the feelings were too powerful for Marcela. With a tear visible in each eye, she excused herself to the bathroom. It was fifteen minutes before she returned.

Ultimately there was dance at the second location as well, although we both agreed the atmosphere was nothing special. While Marcela confirmed the dance surface was of the highest quality, the choice of music was not her favorite. Instead of the more traditional orchestral tango, many selections were new age tangos, devoid of the marked beats of the classic style. This promoted a more contemporary style of dance, recognizable for its many spins and prolonged pauses. With Marcela disappointed with the song choice, and me struggling with the unfamiliar style, we finished our wine and headed for our final destination.

We arrived to La Viruta at 3:30 a.m. After waiting in a short line, we paid our admission and followed the crowd down a dark staircase. Having now danced at two Buenos Aires milongas, I was beginning to feel comfortable with the scene. But as I rounded the corner and entered into the massive dance hall, things were suddenly different.

First, the crowd was enormous. Whereas the number of dancers at the first two clubs combined hadn't been much more than 100, I estimated there were four or five hundred dancers packed into the dimly lit basement club. And while the large rectangular room was substantially larger than the previous locations, there was still very little room to maneuver both on and off the dance floor. Second, as we stood against a sidewall trying to get our bearings, I quickly realized the average skill level amongst dancers was several notches higher. I watched in awe as the dancers floated through tight quarters, somehow finding just enough space to complete very advanced twirls and kicks. And finally, it soon became evident this was an old school traditional tango hall. Unlike our previous stops where groups of friends sat around tables on the perimeter of the floor laughing and telling stories, those in attendance here had clearly come for the sole purpose of dance. The ratio of dancers to spectators was at least 4:1. And those who weren't dancing sat quietly, the women awaiting an invitation and the men trying to decide whom to invite.

Marcela soon coaxed me to the dance floor, where I struggled to get going. I'd never danced in such tight quarters before. I moved anxiously, trying to avoid bumping into other couples. But slowly, with Marcela's encouragement, I began to find my rhythm. Sticking to much smaller steps than I was accustomed, I led Marcela around the perimeter of the floor. I kept my steps simple, only occasionally adding small spins when confident space allowed. After two small collisions with adjacent couples during the first song, I managed to make it through the next two songs cleanly. When the third song ended I smiled at Marcela and sighed. She hugged me again and pulled me in for a kiss.

The rest of the night got gradually better. As the crowds thinned, the dancing became easier. During our brief breaks from dancing, as we sat at the table holding hands, and watching the dancing, I couldn't help thinking about the totality of my journey. I'd left Chicago four months earlier in search of adventure, a break from routine. But here in Buenos Aires, at five a.m. in a basement tango club with Marcela, I knew I'd found so much more.

With daylight breaking, we made our way to the door and took a taxi back to the hotel. Following an amorous climax to our beautiful evening, we lay together, remaining quiet and gazing into each other's eyes. Marcela broke first and began to give in to fatigue. Her eyes closed for progressively longer periods of time. But I lay wide awake. My thoughts returned to my journey. I was not the same person I'd been four months ago, not even close. Argentina had changed me. Marcela had changed me. And I was certain I'd never been happier than I was now. I lifted the back of my hand to my eyes to dot away the tears. I placed the pads of my fingers on Marcela's shoulder and caressed her arm. Her eyes opened slowly in response to my touch.

"I'm not ready to go home yet," I whispered.

She took my hand in hers.

"Me neither," she answered. "But we still have one more night tomorrow."

"No," I said, "I mean I'm not ready to leave Argentina yet. I want to stay." I paused and squeezed her hand in mine. "I love you Marcela."

She smiled and opened her eyes. "I love you too Jake."

I hugged her tightly and we lay together in silence. No others words were needed. I'd finally expressed what I knew we both had been feeling for some time now. I felt both relief and pride. I'd finally done it. Something I could have never done just months before. I'd allowed my mind to relinquish control to my feelings. I was in love, and I was not prepared to give it up, regardless of the consequences of my decision. I kissed her shoulder gently, then her neck, and then pulled her in for a passionate kiss.

33

Our second day in Buenos Aires was an extension of our first. Giddy from my declaration that I wasn't leaving at month's end, we packed in another full day of activities. Despite a late start, we found time to walk through the open market in San Telmo, tour La Boca, and even take in a late afternoon Boca Juniors soccer game amongst a raucous crowd. And following an extended evening nap, it was back out on the town for another night of dancing.

Monday was a short day. Struggling to get out of the hotel by check-out time, we had only enough time for a late breakfast before hustling to the bus station to catch our bus back to Mendoza. While Marcela had been able to find a sub for her Monday class, she needed to be back Tuesday to finish her last week of class. And although my schedule was more flexible, I was supposed to be back to work an ER shift Tuesday afternoon.

We arrived in Mendoza early Tuesday morning and shared a cab back to Marcela's apartment. After not sleeping well on the bus, Marcela went up to try to sleep, promising to pick me up later to drive out to Tupungato together. I had the taxi take me home where I lay down to rest. But having myself slept decently on the bus, and still riding the adrenaline from our whirlwind weekend, I couldn't sleep. Finally after an hour, I got up, took a shower, and walked down the block to the cabina. Having made my big decision, I now had calls I needed to make.

My first call was to Dr. Smith in Denver. My only communication with the radiology program director during the previous six weeks had been two brief email exchanges, both instigated by Dr. Smith. The first email had just been to check-in and make sure I was enjoying my travels. The second email had been more substantive. And it had helped mitigate some of my nerves regarding the call I was about to make. Dr. Smith had informed me they'd succeeded in hiring not one, but two musculoskeletal radiologists to replace the departed Bill Minter. Three different physicians had responded to the posting, and two were such strong applicants that the program had decided to bring both aboard. One of the physicians, a name I didn't recognize, had been able to start immediately. This had allowed the program to continue its plan to accept its first fellow in July. The second, a radiologist I'd met briefly while interviewing for fellowships, was planning to start with me in January. Initially I'd been taken aback by the decision, questioning whether it might take away from my ability to focus on musculoskeletal films. But months later I was starting to look at the decision as a sign.

Not expecting to find Dr. Smith in his office, I was surprised when he answered on the second ring.

"Hello?"

"Dan, its Jake Schmidt calling."

"Hey Jake, how are you? It's been a long time. Are you in town yet?"

I gulped. "No, not yet, I'm still down in Argentina. I've had an amazing experience."

"Glad to hear it," he responded warmly. "I imagine your Spanish is pretty good by now."

"It is," I confirmed. "Just about speaking like the locals." I forced an uncomfortable laugh.

"So when do you get to Denver?" he asked. "We're having our residency holiday party on the 17th, and I'd love for you to be there. And I still need to put together the call schedule for next month. I wanted your input before I do it."

I took a deep breath.

"Actually that's the reason for my call," I began. "I've decided to prolong my trip for a few months, so I'd like to delay my start date."

Silence.

"Okay," he said finally, his tone conveying obvious disappointment. "But we were hoping to have you here in January to begin preparation for the fellowship. There's a lot of work that still needs to be done. Can I ask the reason for the change?"

"It's complicated," I said. "Really a number of things. I have a project

I've undertaken in the ER of a rural hospital, and I haven't yet accomplished my goals. There are other things as well that remain unfinished."

"So what are you thinking then Jake, maybe a March 1st start date?" he suggested.

"I was thinking April 1st," I responded quickly. "That would give me three months to acclimate before the fellow arrives."

I kept my answers short, being cautious not to elaborate too much. Again my words were met with silence.

Finally Dr. Smith spoke. "Well I guess that could still work Jake. But I have to tell you I'm disappointed. Especially this late in the game. I mean we're what, three weeks away from your original start date? We've already delayed fellowship items awaiting your arrival. And it's going to create extra work for your new associates. You're not getting off to the dream start."

"I know," I said. "And I apologize. I certainly never anticipated this. But it's just something I need to do at this time."

"Okay then," he responded. "I'll alert the staff and we'll make some changes. Might I suggest you email your new colleagues offering an apology and an explanation for your decision?"

"Yes," I replied. "I'd like to do that. Please send me their email addresses when you have a chance."

Dr. Smith cleared his throat. "Jake, just one more thing. Are you still fully committed to this program?"

I chose my words carefully. "You have a tremendous program Dan. There's no place I'd rather practice radiology."

"Alright," he responded, seeming satisfied with my answer. "But let's stay in closer contact over the next few months. And please let me know as soon as you have your return date so we can start to plan."

"Will do Dan, we'll talk soon."

I hung up and exhaled forcefully. I felt bad for not being fully transparent, but I needed to protect my own interests. The truth was I had no idea when I was going home. Maybe it would be before April, maybe after. I'd picked April 1st because I felt like it was a short enough delay that it would likely be accepted. And it had, with about the expected amount of resistance. Now I was ready for call number two. But this one I was excited to make.

The phone rang three times before it was answered.

"Hello?"

"Good morning Mary, its Jake."

"Jake! Where are you? Are you back from your trip?"

"Nope. Still in Argentina. I'm finding it hard to leave summer, it's beautiful."

"I'm sure it is. Were you hoping to find Steve?"

"I was. Is he still around this morning, or has he already gone in to the office?"

"No, he's here," Mary said laughing. "He's just getting out of the shower. It snowed a foot last night so he's playing hooky and going skiing. Let me get him."

"Thanks Mary."

I smiled and shook my head as I waited for my uncle to take the phone.

"Hey buddy," Steve said. "It's been too long. Wish you were here to join me for some skiing today."

"I heard. Wish I were too."

"So what's going on down there, I talked to your dad last week and he told me you were staying through December. He mentioned you met a girl?"

"I have. She's pretty amazing. In fact the whole trip has been amazing. So much so I've decided to stay down here for another couple of months."

"Really," Steve replied with a surprised voice. "Denver okay with your decision?"

"For now they are. They ended up hiring two new radiologists which gives the program some flexibility."

"Wow," Steve said, still clearly trying to process it all. "Have you told your folks yet?"

"Not yet. I actually just made the decision this weekend."

"Wow," he repeated again. "What are you going to do with your time?"

"A lot of things," I responded. "I've done some shifts at a local ER and I want to do more work there. I'm also going to help with a summer school English class at an elementary school. And I'd like to take a fly-fishing trip south to Patagonia. What do you think? Any availability to join me?"

He laughed. "Seriously? What'd you have in mind?"

"Five to seven days. Mid-to-late January. You'd fly to Buenos Aires, then on to Bariloche. I'd meet you down there. I have a buddy who might be able to join us. Great fisherman. If he can't make it he can put together an itinerary for us." I paused. "So what do you think? Can you make it happen?"

"That's a tough invitation to pass up. Obviously I have to run it by Mary, and I may have to tweak a few things at work, but I'd say at this point I'm probable. That's a trip I've wanted to take for years. And it sounds like we've got a lot to discuss."

"We do," I confirmed. "Give it some thought and shoot me an email. I'm pretty flexible so I'll let you pick the exact dates, then I'll go ahead and put something together. It would be pretty sweet."

"Alright," Steve said. "I'm going to head out to the mountain. You'll hear from me soon."

"Perfect. I can't wait."

I hung up the phone and started back to the house. I had other calls to make, but I'd find time later. Things were falling in to place. And I was feeling too good to have anyone try to dampen my mood.

34

The school year finished in mid-December, creating even more time for Marcela and I to spend together. And with Silvia's blessing, we spent more and more of that time at the house in Tupungato. December and January marked the heart of the growing season, and there was lots of work to be done.

In addition to vine maintenance, we began the task of preparing the equipment facility and wine cave. With perfect weather over the previous months, the vines were maturing beautifully. It was beginning to look like the second year vines might produce limited grapes yet this season, affording us the opportunity to trial a test product. So we spent long hours scrubbing the equipment, walls, and floors. We replaced the front door, and did our best to patch the roof. We hired an electrician to restore the electricity. And with Javier's assistance, we completed the purchase of ten lightly used oak barrels, ready to be whittled down by Javier himself to maximize their ability to impart a natural oak flavor. The once abandoned property was taking on the feel of a fully operational vineyard.

We found time to work on the house as well. The electrician replaced eroded wires and installed a new oven. We cleaned out the majority of the storage items from the living room finally rendering it a functional space. We even made a few simple decorative purchases to begin the transformation from a deteriorated old house into Marcela's new home.

And regardless of how long we worked, or how tired we were, we found time every night to finish our day with a glass of wine on the cracked tile patio watching the lasts rays of light disappear behind the mountains. It was the perfect end to every day we spent together.

I spent Christmas with Marcela's extended family at her aunt's house in a suburb of Mendoza. And although it didn't feel quite right celebrating

the holiday in 90 degree heat, I discovered in their celebration more sim-
ilarities than differences. While the schedule was notably different with a
ten p.m. gathering time and a one a.m. meal, the essence of the day was the
same: Good food, good conversation, and quality time spent with family.

New Year's, however, was quite different than any I'd previously experienced. We again gathered with family late in the evening. But at midnight
everyone flowed out into the streets to watch the home fireworks shows.
While Marcela's family hadn't purchased any themselves, the majority of
their neighbors had bought substantial fireworks, many commercial grade,
and took great pride in shooting them off from their sidewalks. I watched
nervously as fireworks ricocheted off overhanging tress and power lines.
Not quite how things were done back in Chicago.

After the show, the family returned inside for a dinner, which ended
with dessert and coffee sometime after two. At that time, the party split
in two. Those older than forty remained in the house to continue their
conversation early into the following morning. Those of us younger than
forty were off to the clubs to dance. Marcela and I joined her cousin at a
packed dance club in the hills outside of Mendoza. We danced until the
sun came up, then went out for breakfast at one of many busy cafes on the
peatonal. I didn't crawl into bed until after noon.

Work at the hospital continued to go well. My announcement that I'd
be extending my stay was met with enthusiasm. Having by now gained
the full confidence of my associates, I began the new year by taking individual shifts on Tuesdays, giving Matias and Jorge one opportunity per
week where they could both be off. I then alternated shifts alongside Jorge
and Matías on Thursdays, enjoying the opportunity to both learn from
my colleagues and build together on the protocols we were starting to put
together. And our efforts were already proving successful.

During the second week of January, following extensive hospital-wide
training, Matías became the first physician in Tupungato to treat a heart
attack with the clot-busting medication tpa. Two days later, Jorge administered the same medication to treat an elderly female stroke patient. She
had dramatic improvement within hours of her treatment. Both the staff
and administration were thrilled with our improving outcomes, but none
more than Juan. After years of dealing with criticism from the community
regarding the quality of care at his hospital, change was in the air. Patient

volume was already ticking up, and individuals consistently left the hospital complimentary of the care they'd received. In fact the only complaints Juan heard during the first weeks of January were those from staff members bemoaning their decreased opportunities for Mate consumption.

On January 16th, Marcela drove me to the airport to catch my flight to Bariloche. She accompanied me inside and waited until the last call forced me to pass through security. I squeezed her tightly and whispered those three little words we'd been exchanging with increasing frequency over the previous weeks. I worked my way through the security area, before finally having to turn a corner and enter the gate area. I looked back toward the entrance one final time and saw Marcela was still there, standing alone, smiling and waving.

The flight to Bariloche was easy. I arrived mid-afternoon, and took a shuttle downtown to find a hotel for the night. With Steve's flight scheduled to arrive the following morning, I'd wanted to arrive early to rent a car and arrange for lodging. While Marco had been able to give me the names of rivers to fish, he'd camped on each of his trips and couldn't provide information regarding lodging options.

Although it took several attempts, I eventually found a hotel room for the night just one block off the central plaza in Bariloche. As it turned out the city was at capacity. Groups of recent high school graduates from across the country had descended upon the city for their graduation trips. I discovered it was Argentine custom to take a graduation trip, and Bariloche was the most popular destination in the country. The students took day trips to surrounding attractions, and then returned to the city to party all night long.

Up against the close of shops for siesta, I hurried from the hotel to a local travel agency. Having become worried I might not find a vacancy in one of the areas Marco had recommended, I was soon put at ease. While the city of Bariloche was full, surrounding communities offered plenty of options. I secured a three bedroom cabin that was part of a lodging complex just outside of Junin de Los Andes. About 2.5 hours north of Bariloche, it was the area that Marco had thought most centrally located for the rivers he'd wanted us to fish. The agency also helped me reserve a car from the airport for the following day.

That evening I wandered through downtown aimlessly. The city, situated on a gentle slope adjacent to the majestic dark blue Nahuel Huapi Lake, was surrounded by mountains. And while there were a handful of the barren, jagged peaks similar to Mendoza, the majority of the mountains in the immediate vicinity were tree covered. I found the scenery more reminiscent of the Rockies. The architecture was also quite different from what I'd seen elsewhere in Argentina. Many of the buildings were constructed in a chalet style, similar to that of a Swiss village. And on this particular midsummer weekend, the city was vibrant. Circling back to the main plaza, I found a single unoccupied bench to sit down, eat an ice-cream, and people watch. Groups of adolescents came and went, laughing and chasing, lost in full celebration mode.

I slept in the following morning before making my way to the lobby for a leisurely breakfast. From there I gathered my things and walked around the corner to the plaza to catch the shuttle back out to the tiny airport. Arriving early, I procured my rental car, parked in front, and walked back into the small airport lobby to await Steve's arrival.

At 10:30 a.m. I greeted Steve in the lobby with a big hug.

"So glad you could make it," I said. "It really means a lot to me."

"Thanks for having me," Steve responded with a big smile. "It's great to see you."

We gathered his bags, made our way out to the car, and started the drive north along the edge of the foothills.

"So where are you taking me?" Steve inquired.

"Junin de Los Andes," I responded. "My friend Marco told me that if we wanted to wade and dry-fly fish, this would be the best area."

"Marco couldn't make it?"

"No, unfortunately not. It's high season for him now and he couldn't get away. And I couldn't get John either. Apparently three weeks' notice wasn't sufficient."

Steve laughed. "Well as nice as it would have been to fish with someone who knows the water, or to spend time with your brother, I'm really looking forward to our chance to catch up. You've got a lot to tell me about."

"I do," I said nodding. "I never imagined six months ago I could end up in the situation I'm in. And as happy as I am, it's still a little overwhelming. I'm still trying to process everything."

"Well you know I'm always happy to give my two cents. I can't promise it'll help, but you know I'll always be honest with you Jake." He paused. "So can I hear about her now? I've been dying to get the full story since your invitation a few weeks ago."

"Sure," I responded. "I've been excited to talk to you about her." I took a deep breath. "It's hard to even know where to start."

"How about the beginning?" Steve suggested. "How'd you two meet?"

I smiled, and started into our story. I began by describing our first night together, alone at the trolley stop, awaiting a trolley we both knew likely wasn't coming. I talked about how comfortable it had been between us from this initial interaction. But from there, as much as I tried to focus my story on Marcela and the evolution of our relationship, I inevitably drifted tangentially to the activities that had come to dominate my life over the last several months. First there were interludes about tango and the Tupungato school. I circled back to Marcela and her family, only to again transition away. Next it was my work at the hospital including a description of my memorable first shift. Steve steered the conversation back to Marcela, but before long our conversation had wandered off again. The vineyard. Mate and asados. My neighborhood in Mendoza. With each shift to a new topic, I spoke with a renewed enthusiasm. With Steve craving details and listening intently, I did almost all of the talking. After two plus hours of driving, nearing our destination, there was finally a short lull in the conversation.

I broke the silence. "So what do you think?" I asked nervously.

"I think she sounds like a pretty amazing girl," he said, nodding his head in confirmation. "And she's clearly had quite an influence on you. It sounds like she's been the inspiration behind just about everything you've become involved with here in Argentina."

I measured my uncle's words, having not previously made this realization on my own.

He continued. "I guess what's most striking to me as I listen to you talk, is how much your trip has evolved since its inception. It was my understanding you were coming to Mendoza for the adventure, for the skiing, and the fishing. But you've now talked for two hours about your experiences here, and you haven't yet made mention of any of those things. It's pretty clear this trip has been life changing for you."

I nodded in agreement. "It's true. And the most amazing thing is I haven't even really felt the desire. I never could have predicted that. Things here are just different."

Steve smiled. "You clearly have some difficult decisions to make. Do you know what you're going to do?"

"Not really," I said. "The only thing I'm sure about currently is that I'm not prepared to leave yet. I'm too invested right now in everything I'm involved with. I'm just not ready to give it all up. I've kind of adopted a 'wait and see' strategy, taking a couple of months at a time, hoping at some point there will be clarity."

"How long do you think the fellowship program will give you to reach a decision?"

"I'm not sure. Much beyond April might prove difficult. We'll see."

"And your parents? How did that phone conversation go?"

"About as you'd expect. Dad was pretty quiet. Seemed confused. He wants to be supportive, but he's uncomfortable with the whole thing. Mom was ready to get on the next plane down here to get me. It's just not the way she was raised. It's going to be a struggle for her. I feel bad, but I need to do this for me."

I glanced at my uncle anxiously.

"You do," he replied. "I spoke with your father last week, and they're definitely nervous. But I think it's important you remain patient." He paused. "You've worked hard Jake, achieved a lot, and I'm confident you'll always have career opportunities. But at the end of the day it's important to maintain your perspective. While I admit the Denver position sounds attractive, it's just a job. And it seems to me your time here has taught you there are more important things in life."

I smiled and nodded. Uncle Steve. It was exactly what I needed to hear in that moment. We hadn't even yet arrived to our fishing destination, and already it had been a successful trip. A sense of tranquility slowly descended upon me.

We arrived to our cabin shortly after two and were more than satisfied with our accommodations. Clearly new construction, it had everything we could have hoped for. The highlights of the wooden cabin were a beautiful stone fireplace in the center of a large open living area, and a tiled patio adorned with oversized cushioned chairs and a large Argentine grill. I knew it would be put to use during our stay.

We put our things away, and then turned our attention to fishing. We put together our fly-rods, put on our gear, and headed directly to the river. Our initial destination, and the area where we would spend the majority of our time during the week, was the Malleo River. Marco had raved about the river during our telephone conversation weeks earlier, calling it one of the best dry-fly fishing rivers in all of Argentina.

Accessibility to the river proved a non-issue, with much of the river located on state-owned land. But the early fishing report was not favorable. To my great surprise, we encountered two separate groups of American fishermen on our first afternoon. And as a result of the relatively crowded waters, or maybe the unseasonably cool temperatures, the dry-fly fishing was slow. I caught one medium sized Rainbow, and Steve caught a couple of smaller Brown. But that was it. While the river itself was beautiful, with frequent bends and a steady rolling current, the fish were disinterested. As evening arrived, I was forced to make the always disappointing switch to wet-fly. And while the fishing improved slightly, it still paled in comparison to what I'd been anticipating.

Yet after a long night of good conversation on the patio, we put aside our mild disappointment and set out the following morning with renewed excitement. And with bright sunshine and warmer temperatures, our results improved immediately. Having finished the previous evening with a wet-fly, I began the morning fishing below the surface. But after watching Steve pull three good Rainbow out of the first pocket he fished, I converted back to dry-fly. And I never went back. I caught six trout fishing the far edge of a long center run just above where Steve started, two of which I measured at 18 inches. Steve, who worked his way up to fish the near side of the run, caught five more. The fish had been turned on, and they didn't stop during the following four days.

While the fishing was consistently strong, the peak of our success came during our second evening of fishing. After an equally satisfying afternoon away on the Alumine River, we were back on the Malleo for our evening fish. Opting for a new section of the river upstream from where we'd previously fished, we were delighted to find the river divided into braids creating a multitude of smaller pockets filled with fish. And as the sun became low in the sky, and the temperatures cooled, we were greeted with an always exhilarating sight: feeding fish. Despite the strong fishing of previous days, I'd only seen a handful of fish feed. But what started out as some intermittent dimpling on the surface, soon blossomed into a full-fledged feeding frenzy, with fish zealously attacking the small hatching flies settling on the surface of the water. Looking up at the setting sun, I saw that the air had become saturated with bugs. I reached into my fly-box and pulled out a small Adams fly I thought best mimicked the hatch. I tied it on, and what followed was the single best session of fishing I'd ever experienced.

My first cast, a practice cast into a foot of water to make sure I could see my fly, was immediately inhaled by a 12 inch jumping Rainbow. I released the fish, took several steps up river to reach the bottom part of a moderately deep run against a grassy bank, and casted again. Within a second of hitting the water the fly was again devoured. This time a 14 inch Rainbow. I shouted in excitement as I played the hard-charging fish until it tired. By the time I released my second fish, Steve had joined me at my side, tying on a small Adams of his own. For the next hour we fished together in the larger channel of the river. With almost every cast being met by a hungry fish, we initially took turns pulling in fish of all different sizes, playing each fish until it was ready to surrender. But after at least 10 fish between us, maybe 15, the fishing was so unbelievable that we found ourselves purposefully leaving slack in our line after hooking smaller fish, hoping the fish would get off to allow a faster opportunity for another cast and the potential of a bigger fish. As darkness approached we fished simultaneously, side-by-side, our flies sometimes landing within feet of the other's fly. On multiple occasions we fought fish concurrently, taking caution to guide the fish away from each other to prevent tangling of our lines. It was after 10 p.m. when we finally yielded to darkness. And in our estimate, in the last hour alone, we'd caught more than 30 fish.

The last three days of fishing, while never as spectacular as that second night, were very good. While we explored other smaller rivers in the area during some fishing sessions, we always returned to the Malleo. And after spending much of the first two days fishing apart, with one fisherman fishing two or three runs and then leap-frogging above the other to provide him with a similar section of river, we spent the last three days fishing almost exclusively together. While small pockets were often only amenable to one fisherman, we divided larger runs or bends in half, with one fisherman fishing up the nearside and the other across the river on the far side. And while this method of fishing was not as efficient in terms of yielding the greatest number of fish, it allowed us to maintain a constant running dialogue as we fished.

By the fourth day, under brilliant sunshine and warm temperatures, with our covetousness of more trout beginning to wane, we took an extended lunch break along the bank of a small stream that emptied into the Malleo. As it had for days, our conversation meandered seamlessly from one topic to the next. But as Steve had done many times before, including our initial conversation in the car, he ultimately led the conversation back to Marcela. He was clearly fascinated by both her personal story and our relationship, and I'd spent many hours talking about her during our trip. But on this occasion, unlike most of our talk, the conversation assumed a more serious tone.

"Marcela sounds like a really wonderful girl. It's a shame I won't get the opportunity to meet her," Steve said.

"Yeah, it is. In retrospect it would have been fun to have you come into Mendoza for a few days first. You could have seen the city and had a chance to get to know her. We could have then flown down here together."

"It sounds like a place I need to visit at some point."

He paused, and then started up again.

"Jake, I'd understand if you don't want to discuss it, but how about Sara? How's she doing with all of this?"

"We really haven't spoken," I responded comfortably. "But I assume she's focusing on her work and trying to move forward. She's a pretty strong person."

Steve nodded. "Do you ever think about her, about your relationship, and why you think you ended up making the decision you did? I mean don't get me wrong, Marcela sounds wonderful, but it always seemed like you and Sara had something pretty special as well."

"We did," I said. "And I do think about her sometimes. Especially after a good shift in the ER. I've often wanted to share stories with her. But I really haven't analyzed my decision much. As lame as it sounds, as much as Sara and I had in common, I guess this just felt right. I mean from that first night at the trolley stop with Marcela, nothing has ever been so easy, so natural. I'm so comfortable with her, and I'm always happy. The last four months are unequivocally the happiest of my life."

I looked over at Steve and saw he was smiling.

"What?" I said. "Was it that corny?"

"No," Steve said, his tone serious again. "It's just the way you expressed yourself."

"I know," I replied, shaking my head. "I've never been very good at explaining my feelings."

"No," he corrected. "I thought your answer was excellent. It struck a chord with me."

He looked away.

"Oh yeah?" I said. "How so?"

He sighed. "Did your father ever tell you how Mary and I met?"

I thought for a minute. "I don't think so. I guess I assumed you met during your time in the forest service."

Steve shook his head. "No. Actually I never knew Mary during that time."

I was surprised by his disclosure. "Really? So when did you meet?"

"Actually it wasn't until years later," he began. "I finished my time with the forest service in 1971, and started law school in Missoula. During the first semester of my second year, I met someone. Her name was Ann. She was a classmate of mine, from a small town near Helena. And over the next year-and-a half, we fell in love. I thought she was everything I was looking for. She was smart, motivated, and beautiful. Everything. And we had a ton in common, both in terms of career interests and hobbies. We graduated together in 1974. And we were married later that summer."

My eyes got big. "Married? Seriously? I had no idea."

"Yes. And everybody immediately loved her. My parents, your father, all of my closest friends. Everyone was convinced I'd found my soulmate. And so was I."

"Okay," I said slowly, still in disbelief of what I was hearing.

"Following graduation we bought a house together and starting practicing law in the same firm. We worked hard during the week, and then did fun stuff together on the weekends. We both loved the outdoors, so we hiked, biked, and skied all over western Montana. It was a really fun time."

"Really?" I said, still trying to process this most surprising revelation. "So what happened between you two?"

"So one weekend, during our second summer together, Ann decided to go home to visit her family. I'd planned to go along, but at the last minute I had things come up at work. I remember being disappointed because I'd always enjoyed spending time with her family. I finished my work up by Saturday afternoon, and considered driving up and surprising her. But it was a long drive, and ultimately I opted instead for a short overnight hiking trip on my own. It was a perfect summer day and I decided I needed to be outdoors. So I drove down the Bitterroot valley to an area I'd always wanted to explore. I put together a route and hiked in to a beautiful lake. It was a picturesque setting, and I had the place all to myself. I set up camp right on the water, caught a few trout for dinner, and started a fire. Then just as it was getting dark, with my fish still on the grill pan, I heard a voice. I turned and looked, and there she was."

"Mary?" I asked.

"Mary," he confirmed, nodding his head. "She was working with the forest service and was stationed in a small cabin I hadn't seen on the other side of the lake. And she'd come over to scold me for setting up my camp outside of a designated camping area."

I laughed. "So what happened?"

"I pleaded ignorance, told her about my history in the forest service, and fortunately she was lenient on me. We got to talking, and before we were finished with our introductions, the fish was done. So I invited her to stay for dinner, and she accepted. We ended up sitting out by the fire that night until three a.m., just talking."

"Just talking?" I said smiling.

"Just talking," he said raising his hands up in his defense. "Now I'd be lying if I told you I wasn't attracted to her. But I honestly never had any amorous intent, and I don't think she did either. I remember talking quite a bit about Ann and our relationship. However almost immediately, I remember being overcome by a feeling I'd never experienced before alone in the presence of a woman. It was a feeling of complete and total relaxation, almost a Zen-like experience. I remember sharing with Mary that night, within hours of meeting her, things that I still hadn't felt comfortable telling Ann after more than a year of marriage. The whole thing was surreal. Finally Mary announced she had to get back to her cabin. I made no physical advances, but I asked for her contact information. And she requested mine. She left the campsite and I lay wide awake the rest of night. Didn't sleep for a minute, trying to find an explanation for what had happened. I got up at dawn, packed up my things, and hiked out to the car."

"Wow," I said. "I can't believe it. So what did you do next?"

"Well I tried as hard as I could to forget her, to forget that night ever happened. Ann got home and we resumed our routine. But as content as I was with Ann, my feelings for Mary didn't lessen with time. So after more than a month of resisting reaching out to her, I decided I needed to contact her. I had to see if that sensation that had overcome me during our first encounter would be repeated. I called her up one morning from work and asked her if she wanted to get a cup of coffee. And she said yes." He paused to take a drink of his water. "So I met her at a small restaurant midmorning on a Saturday, and I immediately felt just as I had that night in the mountains. We talked for three hours before I had to force myself to leave. That's when I knew I had a problem."

"When did you tell Ann?" I asked.

"Ann went home to visit her family again about a month later, and this time I made up an excuse not to join her. Instead I met Mary at the forest service cabin on the lake where we'd first met. We spent 24 hours together, and my mind was made up. I knew what I had to do. Ann was great. She was beautiful and smart, and we had a ton in common. But she wasn't Mary. Although we were a good fit in many ways, together we just never had that inexplicable connection I'd immediately shared with Mary. And still share to this day. I told Ann on Sunday night upon her return, and I moved out of our house that night. Mary and I were married less than a year later."

"Wow," I said again, my mind racing in many different directions. "I assume the decision was not well received by all?"

"Ah, yes, that's a fair statement. Although maybe not well received by anyone would be more accurate. My friends couldn't figure it out. They used to make fun of Ann and me for wanting to do everything together. Your grandparents really struggled with it. They flew out to Missoula and pleaded with me to reconsider. But ultimately they worked through it. They met Mary, fell in love with her like I did, and were ready to move on. But it was your dad who had the hardest time. He'd always looked out for me, as big brothers are inclined to do I guess. And he'd loved Ann from the first day he met her, so much so he actually cried during our wedding. True story. He was furious with me when I called and told him about Mary. It's probably just been the last ten years or so that I think he's finally gotten over it and accepted Mary. It took a long time."

"Wow," I said again, just now realizing the frequency of my repetition. "Thanks for sharing your story. Means a lot to me, especially with what I'm going through."

"Obviously our situations are not the same. And I certainly don't want to tell you what to do. This decision is for you and you alone to make. But I guess my advice for you would be twofold. First, always make the decision you feel in your heart is best for you. Don't let opinions of others, even those who are close to you, prevent you from making the decision you feel is right. While it may take some time, ultimately those who love you will accept you for who you are. And second, the easiest decision and the best decision are not always the same. Don't let perceived obstacles stand in the way of making what you believe to be the best decision."

I nodded. It felt good to hear Steve's words, to get confirmation of the conclusions I myself had been forming over the previous weeks. I stood up and hugged him.

"Thanks Steve. I appreciate it. I still have some stuff to figure out but your counsel means a lot."

"No problem. I just want the best for you Jake. Now let's get out on the river. We're running low on fishing time, and it might be a while before I get back down this way."

35

e fished one last session the morning of our fifth day before driving back to Bariloche. We had lunch in town and then headed to the airport to say our goodbyes. Steve had a late afternoon flight into Buenos Aires in advance of an overnight connection back to the States. And I took an evening flight back to Mendoza where Marcela was waiting for me at the airport.

I quickly settled back into my summer routine. I helped Marcela teach summer school two afternoons a week. I worked my ER shifts two days a week. And the majority of the rest of the time was dedicated to the vineyard. After all, the first week of March was fast approaching, and in Mendoza that meant one thing: the Vendimia.

The Vendimia was the annual grape harvest festival in Mendoza, and while I'd never before experienced the event, I'd heard so much about it over previous weeks that I almost felt as if I had. The event was a week-long celebration of wine and its importance to the province of Mendoza. I'd been told that both national and international tourists flocked to the city to enjoy exhibitions, tastings, extravagant meals, and much more. The highlights of the week occurred during its final two days. First, the city hosted a provincial beauty contest of great prestige which crowned the queen of the Vendimia. And then, on the final day, the city's amphitheater played host to a day-long extravaganza filled with musical acts and dance performances representative of both local tradition as well as that of greater Argentina. In fact this year many of our tango friends were set to perform as part of the grand finale.

And while the festival was important to the people of the province as a whole, it was essential to those in the wine industry. Although we wouldn't have a finished product to exhibit, Marcela was looking forward to the week as an opportunity to introduce both the public and the industry to her emerging business. So we worked harder than ever to finish preparing our equipment building and wine cave to be ready to offer our first tours of the property. Marcela contracted with a local Tupungato cafe to host a dinner on the grounds of the vineyard featuring different wines from the Uco valley where the vineyard was located. And with the cooperating weather ready to deliver us a limited grape crop of our own, Marcela arranged a mid-week grape stomp which included both live music from a local guitar player as well as the property's first scheduled outdoor milonga on the patio outside of her grandparent's home.

While we found the work satisfying, we also found it exhausting. On days when I didn't teach or work in the ER, we often spent 12 hour days working to ensure everything would be ready. During a stretch from the last week in January through mid-February, we spent all but one night at the house in Tupungato. On more than one occasion we questioned aloud whether we'd bitten off more than we could chew.

However by mid-February, with still two weeks to spare, we surprised ourselves by finishing the bulk of the preparations. By mid-week we reached a point where we actually ran out of things to do. The only remaining items on our list were last minute things to be set-up during the final 48 hours before Vendimia week.

So with some unexpected free time to fill, I suggested to Marcela that we escape for a few days to celebrate our accomplishments. She agreed and knew exactly what she wanted to do. She'd often spoken to me about her summer trips across the mountains to the Chilean beaches. While she'd not traveled the last three summers as a cost-saving measure, she'd taken the trip almost every other year since her return to Mendoza from New York. She was excited to introduce me to one of her favorite places.

We spent Wednesday evening in Mendoza with Silvia. We'd seen her very little during previous weeks, and knew we wouldn't be spending much time in Mendoza around the Vendimia. Silvia prepared dinner, and we sat around the table talking late into the night. Following a short night of sleep, Marcela was outside my house at seven a.m. We made a brief stop in town for breakfast, and then headed west for the mountains.

The trip up to the Chilean border at the top of the pass went smoothly. While we had to slow on several occasions to wait for the proper time to pass slow moving semi-trucks on the steep winding road, the highway was relatively empty. Although the pass could get extremely crowded in the summer due to heavy travel from Argentina to the Chilean beaches, it was now late in the beach season, and most Argentines were either already in Chile or back in Mendoza.

With Marcela driving, I was able to once again admire the immensity of my surroundings. Towering jagged peaks, scant vegetation, and long stretches of road without a sign of civilization dominated the landscape. I realized it had been almost six months to the day of when I'd last made this trip across the Andes from Santiago into Mendoza. As I stared out the window, I couldn't help but think about how much had changed since that time.

The customs process was slow, but easy. I'd been somewhat nervous as I'd outstayed my three month tourist visa by several months. I'd heard from others I needed to be prepared to pay a fine. But when I made it to the front of the 20 minute line, the agent instead stamped my passport nonchalantly without even looking for my entry stamp.

From there we passed by an empty Portillo ski area, navigated the series of 180 degree switchbacks, and made our way down the steep pass into Santiago. There we stopped for gas and a quick lunch, before finishing the last 90 minutes of our drive. We pulled into Viña del Mar just after two p.m.

Marcela had several friends who owned condominiums along the coast. And while many of the properties were filled during the popular month of February, she'd found one vacant during the dates of our trip. She'd never stayed at the property before, but knew its location well. After stopping at a small grocery store, we made our way through the crowded city and then turned north along the coast for a few miles until we arrived at the building. It was a ten story high rise set directly on the beach. The building itself was somewhat outdated in appearance, but the quieter location at the outskirts of the city and the spectacular views of the water were exactly what we'd been seeking.

Our unit, on the ninth floor, was a small one bedroom condo that was sparsely furnished. But it made no difference to us. It had a functional kitchen which provided us the opportunity to prepare our own meals. It offered beautiful views of the water from both the living room and the bedroom. And it had a small deck where we could start our days with a cup of coffee and finish them with a bottle of wine.

Apart from a delicious seafood dinner in town on night two, and a short hike a few miles further north up the coast on day three, we spent the rest of our trip either in the condo or out on the beach. We took walks along the miles and miles of crowded beaches. We lied out in the warm sun, only occasionally venturing into the cold Pacific waters. But more than anything, we enjoyed our time together, just the two of us, an escape from our busy days at the school and the vineyard.

Our conversation touched on all topics except one: our future together. After my declaration in Buenos Aires two months earlier that I wasn't ready to leave Mendoza, we'd again returned to our previous strategy of living in the present, avoiding any discussion of my return to the United States. And while it had been surprisingly easy for the most part, I found it more and more difficult during our four days in Viña. Finally on the last night of our trip, inspired by my conversation with my uncle weeks before, and disinhibited by the wine, I broke our unspoken pact and carried the conversation to our future.

"Have you spoken with Javier recently about his investment in the vineyard?" I asked.

"No, I haven't," she responded. "I've been putting it off as long as I can. But now that I'm close to being in a position to purchase the property, and with us potentially only a year away from our first full harvest, it's something that needs to be figured out soon."

"What kind of an arrangement are you hoping for?"

"It depends on our projected budget." She paused for a second, looking away. "I mean I'd love to be in a financial position to employ him, for me to be sole owner. But I know he's looking for more. And realistically I don't think that model is viable. I'm pretty sure I'm going to need him as an investor. But I guess as long as I'm majority owner, we should be able to work something out."

I nodded. "Well I've been impressed with him. His knowledge and experience have been invaluable, and he hasn't led us astray with any recommendations thus far. And more than that he just seems like a good guy. I think you could do a lot worse in a business partner."

"Yeah, you're right. He's been great. But you know my concerns, you know what this property means to me. Maybe I'm being a little selfish, but I want it to be done on my terms."

I looked away, sighed, and turned back toward Marcela. "Would I be offending you if I asked about the financial details of your buyout of your aunt?"

She smiled. "I think it would be pretty hard for you to offend me at all."

She leaned forward and kissed me.

"It's really pretty simple. The property was reassessed for tax purposes three or four years ago. And with the dilapidated building and abandoned vineyard, the assessment value was 250,000 US dollars. Half belongs to my mother, so that got us to 125. And for a variety of reasons, including a slumping housing market and an understanding that it would take a substantial financial commitment to ready the property for sale, we ultimately agreed on 100,000 dollars. With some start-up money from my repenting father, and a lot of personal sacrifice over the last four years, I have about 85 set aside. With another year of being frugal, I'm hoping to complete the transaction by the end of the year. While my aunt has been great about supporting my vision and allowing me to stay at the home and work the property rent-free, it's important to me that I make the full payment before we begin to turn out a product."

I took Marcela by the hand. Even under the effects of the wine I felt my heart rate quicken.

"What would you say if I told you I wanted to make an investment?" I asked.

She sat up straight and smiled, her facial expression caught half-way between surprise and excitement.

"What did you have in mind?" she responded cautiously.

I looked down, before returning my eyes to hers. I shook my head, and then started to laugh.

"I don't know," I said. "I really have no idea. I could help with the 15,000 you still need. Or I could pay a percentage of the operational budget. Or really help in any way you best see fit."

Again I looked away.

"I guess the bottom line is that it doesn't much matter to me. All I know is that after the five best months of my life, I'm ready to invest in us. I want to be here with you in Tupungato. I want to be at your side, working to help make this dream of yours become a reality any way I can. I love you Marcela."

Tears welled up in her eyes. She smiled and shook her head slowly, clearly struggling to find the words to express her feelings.

I continued to explain my proposition.

"I want to be clear I have no intent of interfering. It would be your business, your decision-making. I'd function purely in a support role. I think it's pretty obvious I'm not qualified to do much more anyway. But this is where I want to be, this is where I need to be. I've been struggling internally for the last couple of months, but now things have never been so clear. I have an irrefutable desire to stay here in Argentina and continue to build on everything my life has become since I met you."

The tears now streamed down her face. She squeezed my hand. Her expression turned serious.

"But what about your career Jake? You can't just walk away from everything you've worked so hard to accomplish."

I shook my head. "But that's just it Marcela. I wouldn't be, not at all. I've found more satisfaction working in the ER here than I've had in medicine for a long time. And I know there's an opportunity for me to assume a bigger role. And even if it doesn't work out, or I have a change of heart, I'm confident there'd be opportunity to do musculoskeletal radiology in Mendoza. It doesn't exist right now, but its coming. And if we were to come to the conclusion at some point that things aren't working between us, and I need to go home, it's not like my medical training is erased. I might need to go back and repeat some training, but I don't think it would take much. It would be a small price to pay for the chance to continue to experience everything you've helped me find."

She leaned in and hugged me tightly. She wiped away her tears and slowly pulled away. She took my hands in hers.

"The last months have been amazing for me Jake. I never dreamed I'd meet someone like you. And when I did, I just assumed it was too good to be true, too good to continue indefinitely. I'd pretty much accepted this would be a temporary relationship. But I love you more than anything. And if you're certain this is what you want, and that you're not sacrificing your degree, I'd love to have you stay here with me."

She paused and smiled.

"And honestly it doesn't matter to me either how we set it up," she continued. "I've accomplished more in the last few months than I had in the previous year. There's no way we are where we are today without you. You believed in me and the vineyard from the beginning, and your support has been inspirational. It's pretty clear to me we make a great team."

I leaned back in my chair and pulled her against me. We held each other tightly, both remaining silent. This was it. This was the moment that everything had been building toward over the last several months. This was the feeling I'd been seeking for so many years without ever fully realizing exactly what I was looking for. Sitting out on the small deck on the Chilean coast, overlooking the setting sun on the Pacific Ocean, things were suddenly fully transparent. My life was here. My future was here. I'd never before been more certain of anything.

36

The trip back to Mendoza the following day was slow. It was a Sunday in late February, and with the Vendimia now only a week away, many Argentines were finishing their vacations and making their way back to Mendoza. And many Chileans were heading east to Mendoza for the festival as well. But neither the slow travel nor the interminable line at customs could dampen our spirits.

Marcela spent the following day in Tupungato teaching a summer school class. I began the arduous task of comparing an ER inventory list a colleague from Boston had emailed me with a similar list from Tupungato hospital. I wanted to determine which additional supplies we might obtain to improve our care. We then met up at the Spanish Plaza for a packed pre-Vendimia milonga with live music. It was a beautiful late summer evening and we danced late into the night.

The following day was Tuesday February 22nd. It began as a routine summer Tuesday for both of us. I had a solo ER shift scheduled from two to ten, while Marcela had her last summer school class of the year from 2:30 to 5:30. We drove together to Tupungato. She dropped me off at the hospital, and then continued on to the school. Knowing that on her last day of class she would be there later than normal, she offered to stick around and pick me up at the end of my shift. But I convinced her not to wait. With ten o'clock often a busy time in the ER, and with a recently added 11:30 p.m. bus from Tupungato back to Mendoza, I sometimes elected to stay late to help until things quieted down. And I knew Silvia would be expecting Marcela for dinner. So we instead made plans to have lunch at Marcela's house the following afternoon.

I kissed her goodbye and headed into a busy ER. The staff reminded me it was a full moon, often the indicator of a crazy night in emergency rooms everywhere. But following a steady first several hours, which included another stroke patient, the seventh such patient to be treated at the hospital, the second half of the shift was eerily quiet. Between seven and ten p.m., generally the busiest time of day in the ER, I treated just a single patient. For the first time in over a month during one of my shifts, we actually had time for Mate.

Jorge arrived at 9:45 and needled me for my slow shift, convinced a quiet start on a full moon had sealed his fate for a chaotic night. I wished him luck, said my goodbyes to the staff, and hurried off to catch my bus.

I arrived in time for the 10:30 bus, which meant that if everything went smoothly I'd be home by midnight. The bus was often empty this time of night, and this night was no different. I settled in to my own seat half way back in the bus, clicked on my reading light, and pulled out a medical journal to pass the time. The bus made its way out of the terminal and weaved through the small town toward the entrance to the rural highway.

I felt the bus accelerate as we made our last turn onto the main route. I was reading an article which summarized different private insurance plans available in Argentina, and I was struggling with its complexities. With my eyes beginning to feel heavy, I reclined my chair and fought to finish my page. But just as I reached the last paragraph, I felt the bus begin to slow. Initially the velocity dropped to around twenty miles per hour. I glanced out the side window, but everything was dark. I assumed we were caught behind a semi-truck or tractor and were waiting our opportunity to pass.

But within a minute, the bus slowed even more. And as I put my journal down and sat up in my seat, the bus came to a complete stop. The driver mumbled something unintelligible. I leaned out to the aisle to look out the front window. I saw several sets of taillights in front, but an approaching sharp right curve prevented me from visualizing the full extent of the situation. I weighed the possibilities. I thought first of an accident, but there had been little volume on the road and it was still likely too early for alcohol to play a factor. Road construction was another possibility, but I hadn't noticed work being done on my way out earlier. A police checkpoint also crossed my mind. But I'd never seen police checks conducted on this stretch of remote highway before. The bus lurched forward.

With the bus now barely moving, the music played by the driver had become quite loud. One of the passengers seated in front of me asked the driver to lower the volume. As soon as he complied, I heard a faint sound in the distance. At first it sounded like a high pitch whistle, a noise I didn't immediately recognize. But as I focused in harder, the sound suddenly became clear: an ambulance siren.

My thoughts turned to Jorge. We couldn't have been more than ten minutes from Tupungato, and while the most severe trauma was sometimes diverted to a trauma center in Mendoza, this accident was so close to Tupungato that I thought it would likely end up there. Jorge's prophecy might have been right after all.

Stopping and starting every few seconds, the bus gradually made its way around the curve. I again leaned out into the aisle to try to locate the accident. This time I could see everything. The bus was now at the crest of a hill which gave way to a long straight flat section of highway. With the bright sky above the city of Mendoza as a backdrop, I saw a line of taillights that appeared to stretch for approximately a half-mile. There, at the front of the line, I saw the flashing lights of several rescue vehicles, including an ambulance that just now appeared to be starting back toward Tupungato in the adjacent lane. While I couldn't see flames, there appeared to be smoke billowing up from the area. I moved up several seats to acquire a better view out the front. The ambulance siren amplified as it raced toward the bus with lights flashing. The bus driver eased the bus over to the shoulder and the ambulance raced by. Mate social hour in the ER was about to come to an end.

I wished I could be there to help. I thought for a minute about trying to get off the bus to hitch a ride back to the ER. But there were no cars traveling in the oncoming lane. I suspected they'd closed the highway to westward travel. I thought about asking my fellow passengers if anyone had a cellphone I could borrow. I could call Jorge and let him know what was in route. But surely the ambulance had already radioed ahead. And they would have had more helpful information than I could offer. I realized there was nothing I could do. I sat back in my chair, folded my arms across my chest, and waited impatiently.

The bus continued its slow, intermittent travel. It took more than ten minutes to make it to the bottom of the hill, and we were still a ways away from the accident. So much for my midnight arrival. The police lights continued to flash. And the smoke drifted higher into the air. The closer we got to the scene, the more convinced I became that the outcome would not be good. I again thought about Jorge. I was pretty sure Matias was in town and could be called in to assist. And the general surgeon lived only 20 minutes away if there were a need for emergent surgical intervention. I tried to put myself in Jorge's shoes, reviewing my algorithms for severe trauma. While I'd seen a lot over the previous months, I hadn't yet treated a patient involved in a major motor vehicle accident. I felt my heart rate accelerate.

More than 30 minutes after the accident had first come into sight, the bus slowly approached the scene. The accident appeared to be on the right shoulder, extending off the highway onto adjacent open land. Traffic was being directed onto the opposite shoulder away from the accident. We eased past two empty police cars blocking the right lane. We approached the fire truck, with several firefighters behind the truck talking and pointing, their work appearing complete. I shifted closer to the window and cupped my hands against the glass to get a glimpse of the damage. But with the darkness, the bright flashing lights, and the thick smoke-filled air, it was difficult to see much of anything.

We came upon the last police car and its flashing lights, and suddenly the air cleared. I saw two policemen standing in the road talking. Further in front there was a group of men with shovels that appeared to be trying to clean something from the road. I squinted hard to see what they were doing. Then suddenly it was clear. Painfully and agonizingly clear. I pulled away from the glass in horror, trying to erase the images from my head. The scene was gory. The road was bloodstained. Two large horses lay dead at the margin of the shoulder. I shivered, closing my eyes and clenching my fists. I took a deep breath and covered my face with my hands. I heard the groans from my fellow travelers.

The bus crept forward past the final part of the scene. I didn't want to look again. I'd seen plenty already. Enough to know what had happened. Enough to have a pretty good idea as to the outcome. And definitely enough to interfere with any chance of a reasonable night's sleep. But I couldn't stop myself. I thought about Jorge in the ER. I thought about the single ambulance I'd seen race by. I turned back toward the window, suddenly feeling the overwhelming need to know the final piece of story. I cupped my hands to the window one more time. And my heart stopped.

I screamed out in terror. I pushed against the window to get to the aisle. I raced up to the front of the bus.

"Let me off the bus!" I screamed.

"Sit down please," the driver replied angrily.

"Let me off this fucking bus now!" I shouted even louder.

"Sir, please sit down, I can't leave you here in the middle of nowhere!" he shot back, raising his voice to meet my volume.

"Let me off this bus right now!" I screamed uncontrollably. "I'm a doctor. I can help. I need to go to the hospital!"

The driver braked. The doors opened. I raced down the stairs and off the bus. I ran toward the car. I heard voices in the distance, but was oblivious to what they were saying. The white fiat was on its side, the windows smashed. I raced around the car desperately, looking for any way possible to see inside. I squatted and tried looking through the back passenger side window, but everything was dark.

The voices were suddenly very close. "Get away from that car!" someone yelled.

Ignoring the orders, I arrived at the front of the automobile and crouched down on the ground surrounded by glass. I looked through the large hole in the driver's side windshield. I frantically pulled away chards of glass in attempt to get a better view inside. It was dark and difficult to see anything. I felt a burn on my right hand and looked down to see I was bleeding. I saw what appeared to be sheets of paper littered around the passenger seat. I reached inside, grasping a single sheet between my index and long fingers. I rolled back and sat up in a single motion, fighting to read the words in the darkness: Milonga Dinner Party in Celebration of Tupungato's Newest Vineyard. I fell back and screamed again just as two men arrived at my side.

"What the hell are you doing!" a man shouted. "This car was just on fire! You need to get away!"

I lay on my back, tears emerging from my eyes. "It can't be!" I shouted.

The policeman pulled me up to a seated position.

"What? What is it?" the man shouted.

I sat still for a few seconds, unable to find the words to attempt a response. Then I jumped to my feet.

"I'm a doctor. I need to get to the Tupungato hospital now!" I screamed.

"What?" asked the policeman again. "What are you talking about?"

"I know this woman. I need to help her now. I need to go to the hospital," I said, forcing myself to slow my rapid breathing.

The first policeman looked back at the other and shrugged. He put his arm on my shoulder to help steady me.

"Ok, if that's what you want. Santi, can you take him to Tupungato? I think that's where the ambulance was headed. And get him a towel for his hand. Looks like a pretty good cut."

"Sure," the second officer replied, raising his eyebrows in uncertainty. "Sir, why don't you come with me."

I raced ahead, the policeman struggling to keep up.

"Let's go!" I pleaded. "We need to go now!"

We jumped in the first vehicle and the policeman accelerated ahead on the right shoulder around oncoming traffic. I buried my head in my hands. My mind was racing in all different directions. The damage had been substantial. But did the ambulance's decision to go to Tupungato imply the trauma wasn't too severe? And what would Jorge do? Would he try to stabilize her there, redirect the ambulance to the larger center in Tunuyan, or arrange for a medflight to Mendoza? And why was Marcela returning to Mendoza so late at night? Her class had ended at 5:30. She'd told me she was planning to stay after to finish her work for the summer session, but I'd assumed she would've been home hours earlier. Was there any possibility at all it wasn't her? I turned to the officer.

"Was it a young woman in the car?" I asked.

"That's what I was told," the officer answered quietly.

"What, you didn't see her?"

"No, I arrived late. The paramedics were already involved in the extrication."

I swallowed hard upon hearing the description. "Did you get a report on how severe the injuries were?"

The officer shook his head. "I didn't hear anything formal. I was just told it was bad."

I clenched my fists and closed my eyes tightly. Why hadn't I agreed to let her pick me up? With things having been so slow in the ER, I'd thought about calling her to see if she was still at school. Why hadn't I called? I looked over at the odometer.

"Can't we go faster?" I pleaded.

"Sir, the turn-off is just around this corner. We'll be there is less than five minutes."

I again forced myself to take deep breaths. I thought about the road. I'd never felt comfortable with the drive to Tupungato. The narrow lanes. The sharp curves. And the complete lack of traffic law enforcement. Cars speeding at over 100 miles per hour. Unsafe passes of several cars at a time, ducking back into the proper lane at the last possible second. But I'd never seen animals on the road before. It was such a desolate, arid area. Why were there horses on the highway?

The police car turned off the highway into the small town. Sounding his siren, the officer raced through stop signs. I sat up in my chair and thought about what came next. What was I going to do? How would I react to seeing her? Would I even be able to think clearly enough to help make proper decisions?

The car pulled up in front of the ER entrance. The ambulance was still there, parked in front, its lights still flashing. They hadn't been redirected. I jumped out of the car without acknowledging the officer. I raced to the door, grabbed the handle, and then stopped briefly. I tapped my foot on the ground, closed my eyes, and took two deep breaths. I pulled the door open forcefully and hurried inside.

The front desk was unattended. I walked through the second set of doors into the work station. Karen was standing against the counter with her back to me. She turned upon hearing my entrance and looked at me, her face expressionless.

"Karen," I said, fighting back my emotions.

"Jake," she responded, stepping forward into my path. Her eyes were red.

"Where are they?" I said desperately, scanning the small ER and seeing all of the room curtains pulled shut.

"No Jake," she said calmly, shaking her head and putting her hands on my shoulders.

"Karen where are they!" I shouted, trying to step past her.

But she held on to me tightly. "No Jake, please no!" she pleaded.

I put my hand on her right shoulder and pushed her out of the way. I stepped past her forcefully as she spun around behind me, trying with all her strength to stop me with her arms around my waist. I fought forward toward the first exam room, but just as I was arriving, I looked up and saw Jorge emerge from room two. I froze. Jorge looked at me with a blank stare.

"Is it her?" I asked.

Jorge nodded, his expression grim.

"And?" I said, now stepping in the direction of the room.

Jorge shook his head slowly.

"No!" I screamed. "No!"

I pulled Karen's hands off of my waist frantically and started to run toward the room. But Jorge jumped in my path and locked his arms around my chest.

"Jake you can't go in!" Jorge screamed.

I tried with all my strength to push by, but Jorge brought me down to the floor. I rolled to the side, trying desperately to free myself from his grip.

"No!" I screamed again. "It can't be! It can't be!"

Karen lied down on the floor next to me and put her arms around my shoulders to help Jorge restrain me. I gave one last unsuccessful effort to free myself before collapsing back on the floor in defeat. I lay on the floor trembling uncontrollably. Tears streamed down my face. Karen hugged me tightly. My whole body was numb. Marcela was gone. The single most amazing person I'd ever met. The woman who had gifted me a degree of happiness I'd never imagined even existed. The woman with whom I was planning my future. And now in an instant it was over. The clarity gone. My shoulders slowly relaxed. I brought my hands to my face. And darkness descended upon me.

37

The first several weeks after Marcela's death were without question the most painful of my life. Much of this time remains nebulous to me today, likely in part because of my transient incoherence from the severe trauma, and in part because of my efforts, both conscious and subconscious, to block out this time of unparalleled agony.

While the first week was difficult, I was so busy running around that I somehow managed to remain semi-functional, even in spite of a complete inability to sleep. I first had to cancel all planned Vendimia festivities at the vineyard. I then had to help with Marcela's funeral arrangements. And finally I spent as much time as I could with Silvia, who was an emotional wreck.

On the morning of the funeral, I received an unexpected visit from Fernando. I'd felt the need to talk to someone back home in the United States about Marcela's accident. I'd gone to the cabina the day after her crash with plans to call both my parents and Steve. But instead at the last moment I'd changed my mind and called Fernando, with whom I hadn't spoken in over a month. I knew my family would just insist I fly home, and I wasn't ready to have that conversation yet. But I knew Fernando would provide the emotional support I so desperately needed without grilling me about my future plans.

As it turned out, Fernando provided that support, and much more. Upon hearing the news, he immediately voiced his desire to fly down to be with me. And when I insisted I'd be alright, he'd flown anyway, leaving the next day to arrive in Mendoza the day of the funeral. I broke down and cried in my friend's arms upon seeing him, really the first good cry I'd allowed myself since the night of the accident. I spent much of the next 48 hours with Fernando and his family, all of whom offered the utmost support. But Fernando had to fly home two days after the funeral to get back to his work, and while his family continued to reach out to me, I slowly withdrew.

The three weeks after the funeral were agonizing. My mood alternated between disbelief, anger, and the most difficult emotion of all, a powerful sensation of guilt. Why hadn't I agreed to have her pick me up after my hospital shift the night of the accident? Why hadn't I called to check on her at the school given the slow pace of the ER that night? And most painfully, why hadn't I insisted she not drive at night given the obvious perils of the rural highway? All of this could have been avoided with a single change in my decision-making.

Overwhelmed with sadness, I drifted into a state of dysfunctional despair. I immediately gave up my hospital shifts. I canceled my classes with Dr. Gordon, as well as those with a second physician I'd recently acquired as a student. I couldn't bring myself to attend any Vendimia events. And with Marcela's brother and father now in town, I spent progressively less time with Silvia. I spent more and more time alone, many days leaving my house only to get something to eat, or not leaving at all. I was completely devastated. Both mentally and physically defeated. I felt more alone than I had in my entire life.

It took me until the end of the third week to finally gather the strength to call home to talk with my family. And when I did, the response was as expected. My parents took turns, pleading with me to come home to Wisconsin where they could help me recover. I could spend a couple of months with my family, and then still get out to Colorado by the beginning of the fellowship. Or if I preferred to stay closer to home, my father was certain he could find a job for me at his hospital.

I'd been somewhat less certain about how Steve would react. And while he wasn't as adamant as my parents, he too recommended I return home. He did it, however, with different perspective. Rather than focusing on my long term plans, he focused solely on my short term well-being. He told me he couldn't imagine the sorrow I was suffering. But in the midst of such tragedy, he felt I needed to be surrounded by the people who loved me most. He knew I'd need to lean heavily on my family and friends to help me begin the healing process.

And whether my family was successful in convincing me to return, or whether I'd finally made the calls because I'd already subconsciously made up my mind, I couldn't be sure. But within 24 hours of talking with my family, I'd purchased my ticket back to Chicago. I picked a return date of April 1ˢᵗ, which gave me two weeks in Mendoza to say my goodbyes.

So over the next week I began the most difficult process. While I reached out to many by phone, I forced myself out of the house to make face-to-face visits with those I'd become closest to. I spent an afternoon with Dr. Gordon and his family. I spent several hours one afternoon in the ER in Tupungato with Jorge and Matias. And I had one final reunion with Fernando's family. While tears were shed at every gathering, overall my announcement was met with universal support and understanding. Everyone offered their most heartfelt condolences, and promised to open their doors should I choose to return one day. And while each farewell seemed more difficult than the last, I became increasingly convinced I was making the right decision.

But there was one goodbye I dreaded more than the rest. One I knew would be agonizing for each of us. One I both wanted and needed to save for last: Silvia. During the four months since our initial encounter, our relationship had blossomed. By the last month before Marcela's passing, I'd begun to feel almost a mother-son connection. And I was pretty confident she felt the same. Undoubtedly much of it stemmed from my relationship with her daughter. But I also sensed some of it was rooted in the fact that her only son, who she loved immensely, was thousands of miles away in New York. I thought that in some ways I was filling a void left behind with his departure. And now, with the loss of her daughter, and my decision to leave, I worried tremendously about her well-being.

On my last Sunday in Mendoza, one week before my scheduled departure, and days before my dinner with Silvia when I planned to tell her of my decision, I received an unexpected visit. Without a phone of my own, I'd always given my landlord Nestor's phone number as an emergency contact. While eating dinner alone in my house that night, I responded to a knock at the side door. It was Nestor, relaying a message from the principal of the Tupungato School to have me call her as soon as possible. I took the number and thanked him. I thought for a minute about the unusual message. This was a woman I'd met only two or three times. What could she be reaching out to me for, especially with the fall semester not yet even having started?

I finished my dinner and then walked down the block to the cabina. I found an empty booth and dialed the number.

"Hello?"

"Julia? It's Jake Schmidt returning your call."

"Jake," she said in a sorrowful voice. "We were all heartbroken by Marcela's passing. I'm so sorry for your loss; she was such a special person."

"Thank you Julia," I responded.

"Jake, I'm sorry to bother you during such a difficult time," she began. "And please forgive me if you feel it inappropriate to ask." She paused. "But I was calling to ask a favor. I know you spent a lot of time helping Marcela at the school over the last several months. I've heard so many wonderful things from parents about your interaction with our students. Well as you may or may not know, tomorrow is the first day of school. And with Marcela's tragic passing, we haven't been able to find a new English teacher for our children. Would you have any interest in helping us out until we can hire someone fulltime?"

I remained quiet, pondering the request. I knew it would be extremely challenging for me to set foot in that classroom without Marcela. I had no idea if I'd be able to keep my emotions in check. And even if I could, with my mind still enveloped by the fog, I didn't know if I'd be capable of functioning in the role of teacher.

But at the same time I also knew it would be great to see the children one last time, many of whom I'd gotten to know well. And I'd been planning to return to the school later in the week to say goodbye to the teachers I'd befriended. And most importantly, I knew how much it would mean to Marcela for me to be there.

"Julia, you know I want to help you and the children anyway I can. But I'm leaving to go back to the United States April 1st. I'd only be able to teach one week. Is that something you would still have interest in?"

There was a brief pause. "I'm sorry you've decided to leave Jake, although I certainly understand. You'll be missed by many here in our community. I'm sure you have a lot to do during your last week here, and I don't want to inconvenience you. So don't worry. We'll postpone the

English classes for now and fill the time with other activities. We'll add some extra English later once we find our new teacher."

"Actually, I don't have much this week," I responded quickly. "And I'd enjoy the opportunity to see the children one more time. Plus I know Marcela wouldn't want the children to go without English. If you don't mind the brevity of my commitment, I'd be happy to teach for the week."

"Are you sure Jake? I don't want to burden you during your little remaining time here."

"I'm sure," I replied. "It'll be a nice way to finish my stay here."

"Okay then. That'd be great. I know the kids will be ecstatic."

"So 2:30 tomorrow?" I asked.

"Yes, 2:30 until 5:30 if that works for you. Are you able to arrange transportation?"

"Yes, no problem," I confirmed. "I'll take the bus into Tupungato and catch a taxi from there."

"Would you like me to arrange for someone to pick you up at the bus terminal? I'm sure someone in my family would be able to get you."

"No, don't worry," I reassured. "It's an easy cab ride. And I'm sure I can hook a ride back to the terminal after class with one of the other teachers."

"Thanks again Jake. I look forward to seeing you tomorrow then."

"See you tomorrow."

I hung up the phone and walked home. I was nervous about being able to control my emotions in front of the children. But at the same time I was excited. I knew it would be good for me to get out of the house. And it definitely was the right thing to do for Marcela.

The following afternoon I made the trek out to Tupungato. I trolleyed downtown, walked the six blocks to the bus terminal, took the hour long bus-ride to Tupungato, and then found a cab to the school. It was a long trip, and the bus component was dreadful. Approaching the scene of the accident, I sunk down in my seat and covered my face with my hands. I breathed deeply and tried hard to focus my thoughts on the school children. But my body trembled. And the tears returned. I had to remain seated alone on the bus to compose myself for several minutes upon our arrival.

As I walked into the school, I immediately regretted my decision to come. My legs were wobbly. I felt lightheaded. I looked around at the children at their lockers. Many made brief eye contact before quickly looking away. I put my head down and hurried toward the classroom. As I arrived to the door I was approached by Julia. She gave me a warm smile and extended her arms for a hug.

"Thank you again Jake," she said softly. "I know this is hard for you but it means a lot to these kids. I think it will help many with their mourning."

"I hope it helps me as well," I said, my voice cracking.

She smiled compassionately. "If there is anything I can do to help, please come and get me. I'm available all afternoon."

"Thanks Julia."

I walked into the classroom and looked around. The lessons and projects from the summer school session had all been removed from the walls. New English posters and decorations covered the walls welcoming the kids back to school. I thought back to Marcela's last night at the school.

I walked to her desk and took a seat. I tapped my leg. I rubbed the maturing scar on the top of my left hand. Slowly the children filed into the classroom and found their seats. They sat still and remained quiet.

There had been a change in scheduling and the first class this school year was the 4th and 5th graders. I knew all the students except one. I started the class by speaking about the accident.

"I know that most of you are aware of the tragic accident that took the life of Miss Marcela during the summer."

I paused and took a deep breath.

"It's been a very difficult time for all of us that had the honor of knowing her. She was a great teacher and a wonderful human-being. And she loved her job more than anything."

I paused again. I felt the tears emerging. I dabbed my eyes with the tissues I'd placed at my side before class.

"I know how much you cared about Marcela. I saw the special bond you shared with her." Another pause. "I'll be here to help out for the remainder of the week. I know this is what she would have wanted."

The tears were coming faster now and I again reached for the tissues.

"This is going to be very hard for me given how close I was to Miss Marcela. I ask only that you respect me in the same way you did her. I'll do my best to control my emotions, but it won't be easy."

I scanned the room and saw tears on many of the faces. I forced a reassuring smile. I walked around the room, providing tissues to those in need, briefly touching the top of many of the children's hands or shoulders. Apart from the sniffling, there was complete silence.

Then I transitioned into my teaching. I'd decided on the bus that they'd spend the afternoon talking about their summer vacations. I split the children into groups of two and had them interview each other in English about what they'd done over the summer. I then had them write a single paragraph summarizing what they'd learned from their partner. And I ended the class by having the students read their work in front of the class. It had been one of Marcela's favorite exercises.

I walked around the classroom while the students worked, listening and providing assistance wherever possible. The students remained focused on their task, committed to doing their best to speak only in English as Marcela had always insisted. And as I walked around the room, I realized to my surprise, that for the first time in weeks I was able to think more clearly. I was overcome by a feeling of tranquility. For the first time since Marcela's death, I found myself smiling.

The second class was similar to the first. Again I began the class with a brief discussion of the accident. And again there was an outward display of emotion. For my part, I found it easier to talk about Marcela. There were fewer breaks in my sentences, and I felt better able to comfort the students with brief smiles and reassuring words. I repeated the same activity and they responded equally well. The hour passed quickly.

The last class of the day, the combined kindergarten/1st grade class, presented a unique challenge. I didn't feel this group of young students was prepared for a discussion about Marcela's death, so I chose instead to avoid the topic all together. But it was obvious from the beginning that some students were uncomfortable with this approach. Some first graders I knew well from the previous year, students I knew to be outgoing, remained silent. They kept their heads down, seemingly afraid to look up and make eye contact with me. The hour dragged on and I found myself doing much of the talking, often forced to switch into Spanish in attempt to comfort the students. When the bell finally rang, I excused the children and sat back in my chair, exhausted from an emotional afternoon.

The students filed out quickly. But one girl remained behind. Her name was Maria, and she was one of the first-graders I'd worked with extensively during the previous year. She had two older siblings in the school, and Marcela had known the family well. The mother had sometimes volunteered in the classroom. I looked up at Maria and smiled. She stood up cautiously and slowly approached my desk.

"Mr. Schmidt?" she said.

"Yes Maria?" I responded, sitting forward in my chair. "What is it dear?"

"I'm sorry Miss Marcela had the accident," she said.

I looked at her and smiled.

"Me too honey."

She looked down at her feet, and then slowly lifted her chin.

"My mom said Miss Marcela was an angel, sent down to help us be better people. My mom said now she has gone back to her home in heaven."

I kept my eyes on the little girl. I felt a tear well in my left eye. I nodded my head.

"I think your mom is right, Maria."

"My mom told me that if you were here today I should give you a hug," she said. "Is that okay?"

I stood up from my seat.

"I'd like that very much Maria," I said.

I kneeled down to her level and gave her a long hug.

"Thank you Maria," I whispered into her ear. "Thank you very much."

She walked out the door, stopping once to look back and wave. I returned the wave, and then collapsed back in my chair. I turned and stared out the window at the mountains. I'd never myself been a spiritual person. I'd been to mass twice with Marcela and her mother during my time in Argentina, but before that it had been years since I'd stepped foot inside a church. But suddenly, inspired by the words of a six year-old, I considered the possibility that maybe Maria and her mother were right.

Maybe she had been an angel. She'd come into my life during a time where I'd felt unfulfilled. I'd been lost, without knowing what I was looking for. And slowly, during our time together, she'd helped transform my life. She'd been responsible for introducing me to everything that had grown important to me during my stay: the school, the hospital, the vineyard, the tango, and the community of Tupungato. She'd made me a better person. And in the process she'd helped me find true happiness. I closed my eyes and rested my chin on my chest.

I spent most of the next two days replaying Maria's words over and over in my head. And each time I did, I became more convinced by them. If I required any additional persuasion, I needed only recognize how I was feeling during my time at the school. As good as my first day had been, the following two days seemed even better. The younger children gradually became more comfortable in my presence, and returned to the talkative group I remembered from the previous year. The older kids continued to honor Marcela with a work-ethic that would have made her proud. And I felt increasingly comfortable in the classroom, the fog lifting, my vitality slowly returning.

Following class on Wednesday I walked down the hall to find Clara, Javier's wife. We hadn't yet spoken since Marcela's death. She was just packing her bag for the day when I knocked and entered.

"Jake," she said with solace. "I tried to catch you last night but you were gone by the time I arrived. I'm so sorry."

She walked over and gave me a hug.

"Thanks Clara. It's been difficult." I paused and pulled back slowly. "Clara, can I ask a favor?"

"Sure Jake, anything, what is it?"

"Would you be able to drive me up to the vineyard on your way home?"

"Of course," she replied. "Just give me a minute to gather my things. Is there anything in particular you need to get? Do you still have things there?"

"No," I said, shaking my head. "Nothing really. I just feel like I'm ready to see the property again. I'm going back to Chicago Monday, and I'd like to see it one more time."

"I understand," she said nodding.

She finished preparing her bag and we walked out to the car together. During the short drive we talked about Marcela's family and my future plans. We pulled into the small gravel parking area.

"Do you want me to go up to the house with you Jake, or would you prefer I wait here?"

"Actually Clara, you don't need to wait. I'm not sure how long I'll be."

"Really Jake, it's no problem. I can wait as long as you need me. Otherwise how will you get back to the bus terminal?"

"Yeah, no, it's fine Clara. Thanks for the offer. But I can just walk down to the main road and hitch a ride back to town. It won't be a problem."

"Are you sure Jake?" she asked.

"Yes, thanks Clara. I'll see you at school tomorrow." I smiled assuredly.

"Ok then, I'll see you tomorrow." She reached across for a departure cheek kiss.

I got out of the car and walked slowly up the path to the area where Marcela and I had sat together during my initial visit. I sat down and then lay back on the ground looking out over the valley in its entirety. It was a perfect evening. Now just after six p.m., the sun was beginning its descent behind the mountains. I closed my eyes and focused on my breathing. I felt the warm sun against my skin. The valley was silent. It was celestial.

I lay there for an unknown amount of time. I opened my eyes slowly, uncertain as to whether or not I'd briefly dozed off. I stood up and stretched my back, again scanning the winding rows of green in the valley below. I looked up the path toward the house, but couldn't get my body started in that direction. Instead, without a clear understanding of why, I was drawn down the steep hill toward the vineyard. I walked cautiously but quickly, making it to the bottom before turning left to walk the edge of the vineyard.

I walked past the first year vines which appeared similar to when I'd last seen them more than a month prior. I then turned right and walked another 100 yards until I arrived at the second year vines. My pace slowed as I strolled up and down several rows. I studied the vines as I walked, looking for the purple clusters of grapes we'd been on the verge of harvesting during the Vendimia week.

Some clusters were still bright in color. I picked and sampled several grapes, my mouth puckering from the bitter taste. But as I continued my walk, I began to notice many clusters were starting to lose their purple color, instead taking on an almost greyish appearance. I stopped to further examine. I saw many grapes were now smaller and wilted, clearly over ripened from neglect during the previous month. I looked down at the ground and saw many older grapes had already fallen from the vines.

I looked up and down the row of vines before resuming my slow walk through each row of second year vines. But things now felt different. In sharp contrast to every other time I'd walked the vineyard, rather than appreciating it for its unparalleled beauty, all I could focus upon were early signs of neglect. Subtle shrub brush latching on to vine posts. Scattered wind damage to the trellis system. And more and more grapes littering the ground. It was undoubtedly the first stage of a slow deterioration toward what the property had looked like years before.

My thoughts turned to Marcela. To her bond with her grandparents. To her dreams of restoring vitality to a property that meant everything to her. And to her years of sacrifice and commitment. She'd come so close to completing her goal. To fulfilling her dream. And now just one month later, everything seemed lost. I wiped away tears from my eyes.

I arrived to the end of the last row. I looked back down the valley one final time before starting my retreat toward the hillside. But as I turned back around, out of the corner of my eye, I noticed a red color several rows down from where I'd emerged from the vines. I walked back down to get a better look. And as I approached the color, I was stunned by what I saw.

At the end of one of the center rows of the second year vines, amidst an otherwise immature rosebush, those which Marcela had insisted we plant together several months prior, was a single large, spectacular red rose. I moved in closer for further inspection. The surrounding branches were dry and brittle, without any sign of another viable bud. And the bushes at the ends of the adjacent rows were equally barren. But the solitary rose was brilliant. Neatly centered within the bush, and fully opened in response to the day's last rays of sunlight, it was shaped perfectly. Thick, velvety petals flowing outwardly in circumferential layers from the flower's center. I leaned in and smelled the sweetness. I stepped back and shook my head in amazement.

I looked back down the rows of vines. The dry, wilted grapes. The shrub brush. The damaged vine posts. Then my eyes returned to the rosebush. The single, perfect red rose staring at me. Defiant. Healthy. Flourishing. I closed my eyes and pictured Marcela at work in the vineyard. Her ragged gloves, baggy gaucho pants, and dusty tank top. Her hair pulled back behind her blue bandana. Her Carmel-colored skin brilliant under the potent sun. And that smile. That insuppressible smile that had enamored me from our first encounter. I opened my eyes. I felt a rush of energy surge through my body. My arms and legs tingled. And suddenly everything was clear again. I was overcome by a sensation of absolute peacefulness. And as I turned to start my way back toward the road, I couldn't suppress a smile of my own.

The following afternoon I was back out in Tupungato for my classes. As soon as the last children exited the room, I closed the door and hurried down the hallway to Julia's office. I wanted to make sure to catch her before she left for the evening. I knocked on the door and entered. She was seated at her desk.

"Julia, can I have a word with you please?" I asked.

"Of course Jake," she said pointing to the chair. "Please have a seat."

I sat down and looked across the desk at Julia.

"How are things going Jake?" she asked sympathetically. "I wanted to catch you after class the last two days, but I got hung up both times. I'm sorry for not having reached out. How are you and the children doing?"

I nodded. "Really good actually. The children have been wonderful. I've enjoyed working with them immensely. These have been the first happy moments I've had in many weeks."

Julia smiled again. "That makes me feel good to hear that. I had a feeling this might be good for everybody."

"Julia, I've been doing a lot of thinking the last couple of days. Being here in Tupungato, here with these kids, has been powerful for me. It's provided me with insight I was lacking. And it's given me hope for the future that had been absent just a week ago." I looked down briefly, and then looked back across the desk. "I have a proposition for you."

"Okay," she said cautiously. "What is it?"

"I'd like to stay on for the year as your English teacher," I said nervously.

She lifted her eyebrows and sat up on the edge of her seat. "Are you sure Jake?" she said. "I thought you were planning to leave next week?"

I shrugged my shoulders. "So did I. But until the last three days with these children, I didn't know what I wanted." I paused and breathed deeply, fighting back a wave of emotion. "Julia I was going back to the United States because it was the easy decision. It was what my family told me to do. But being here again, back in a state of mind where I can again think clearly, I now know different. I know this is where I belong now. This is where I want to spend my future."

Julia nodded slowly. She leaned across the desk. She touched the top of my hand with hers. "Jake if you're sure this is what you want, we would be honored to have you here as our teacher. I know I'd be speaking for all students and parents when I say that." She smiled. "Now I'll need to work out a few details regarding a work visa, but given our history of having difficulty filling this position, I don't anticipate having any issues."

I nodded, wiping away tears from both eyes.

"I'm sure," I said. "And it would be my honor. My honor to be part of such a special community. And my honor to follow in the footsteps of such a wonderful person."

Julia smiled and nodded her head. I stood up and thanked her. She gave me a long hug. I then excused myself and began the process of getting back to Mendoza. I suddenly had a lot of planning to do.

The following day, following my first good night's sleep in a month, I left the house early and was at the terminal in time to catch the nine a.m. bus back to Tupungato. I arrived at Juan's office at the hospital just before 10:30.

"Good morning Juan, how are you?" I said walking in and taking a seat amidst the piles of paperwork.

Juan sat up in his chair, clearly startled by my entrance.

"Hey Jake," he said, his face assuming a perplexed look. "What are you doing here?"

"I've made the decision to stay," I announced matter-of-factly.

"What?" Juan said. "What happened? Why the change?"

I paused. "It's kind of a long story. But essentially I just came to the realization that this is where I'm supposed to be. And now that I've made my decision, I'd like to discuss a more permanent role here at the hospital."

Juan leaned back in his chair. "Alright," he replied tentatively. "What'd you have in mind?"

"I'd like to become director of ER services, overseeing the provision of care in the ER."

Juan nodded. "And what were you thinking that would entail?"

"I'd continue to work one or two hospital shifts per week, similar to what I've been doing, although my hours will need to change. But I'd additionally like to assume the role of hiring, orienting, and overseeing the interns who spend their year here. I want to provide the leadership and support I think they need to optimize care. And I want to provide the continuity that has been desperately lacking."

Juan remained silent.

"I want the best for this hospital," I said. "I have a vision of what I think we could grow to be. And I'm determined to get it done for the community, for Marcela, and for myself."

Juan smiled.

"I don't doubt that for a minute," he said. He sighed. "Well I'm definitely intrigued. But you'd have to understand we wouldn't be able to pay you much. By now you're quite familiar with our limited resources."

"That's fine," I said. "That's the least of my worries Juan. We'll work something out. I just want to be here."

"Alright," he said smiling. "I'll need a little more time on this one. I want to get some input from the other physicians. But I think we just might be able to put something together."

"Good. I'd appreciate it greatly. In the meantime, with your permission, I think I'm ready to resume my ER shifts."

"Absolutely. Whenever you feel you are able. I know Jorge and Matias will be thrilled to have you back."

I excused myself and headed to the ER to share my news. From there I found lunch at Marcela's favorite café in Tupungato before heading off to the school for afternoon classes. Things were starting to take shape again. Slowly I was beginning to realign the pieces that had been abruptly broken apart. But there was still one important piece that was missing. One big uncertainty I planned to discuss the following night over dinner. I knew it would be the most challenging component of the life I was now trying to reinvent. But I was ready with a heartfelt proposal.

I met Silvia out on Saturday night at La Marcigianna, one of the nicest restaurants in Mendoza. While she'd wanted to see me, it had been a struggle to convince her to leave her home. She'd tried instead to have me over to her apartment for dinner, but I'd been persistent, and ultimately she'd agreed.

I arrived first and was seated at a table by the window. I ordered a glass of wine and waited anxiously. Ten minutes later Silvia hurried in and joined me at the table. She looked exhausted.

"I'm sorry Jake," she said as we exchanged greeting kisses. "I got started late trying to get myself together. Sometimes I feel like I'm moving in slow motion."

"Don't worry Silvia," I said compassionately. "I know how you're feeling. I'm just glad you could join me."

"Me too." She forced a smile. "It's good for me to get out of the building, and even better to see you. I feel like I haven't seen you in weeks. How are you holding up Jake?"

"I'd say I'm doing fair. Some days are better than others. The last few weeks were extremely difficult. I had a lot of trouble mustering the strength to even get out of the house. But the last couple of days have been a little easier." I looked down briefly. "Is Omar still in town?"

"No," she said, shaking her head. "He had to go back last Tuesday. He couldn't afford any more time away from his job. It was very difficult to see him go. Very difficult. He wanted me to say goodbye to you for him."

I nodded and thanked her. The waiter arrived and took Silvia's drink order. Afterwards we resumed our conversation, focusing primarily on our families. Emotions ran high for each of us. Eventually it was Silvia that broached the subject I'd been waiting to address.

"So have you made any plans yet regarding your future?" she inquired delicately.

I nodded.

"Actually I have. Just in the last few days." I paused. "I've made the decision to stay in Argentina."

I stopped and awaited Silvia's reaction. She sat expressionless for several seconds, but then slowly produced a smile. She reached across the table and gently squeezed my hand.

"I'm so happy Jake," she said, her voice cracking. She looked away and dabbed her eyes with her napkin.

"I've been teaching Marcela's classes at the school this week in Tupungato," I said. "It has been very special for me. It's not official yet, but its looks like they're going to offer me a teaching position."

Silvia again nodded. "Marcela would be very happy to know that."

"I think she would too," I said. "Those children meant so much to her."

"They did," Silvia agreed.

"And I've spoken to the hospital, and they're going to see if they can create a more permanent position for me in the emergency room."

"Really Jake? Similar to what you've been doing?"

"Yes, for the most part. Along with some administrative duties I hope."

She again wiped away tears. She looked up at me.

"Well I may be acting selfishly, but I'm very happy with your decision to stay," she said. "I thought for sure you'd decide to go back home."

"I thought about it," I said. "I actually have a plane ticket for next week I still have to cancel. But I've been doing a lot of thinking this past week. And I know now this is where I'm meant to be."

Silvia smiled again, still battling her emotions. I took a deep breath and pushed forward.

"I have something else I wanted to discuss with you Silvia," I said.

"Sure Jake," she said. "What is it?"

"With both the school and hospital in Tupungato, it makes more sense for me to live out there." I paused. "I was wondering if you and your sister would consider selling me your family's house and property."

Silvia sat back in her chair and brought her hand to her chin pensively. She remained silent for what seemed an eternity. She sat up in her chair and looked across at me.

"Well I don't see why not," she said, lifting her eyebrows. "I'll need to talk with my sister. But I can't imagine she'll have a problem. As you know she's wanted to sell for a long time. I'd think it might mean something for her to sell to you. And I know it would be special for me."

I smiled.

"That would make me happy," I said. "It's become a very blissful place for me over the last several months. Almost divine. Both the home itself and the vineyard. And I've learned so much from your daughter. I'd like to try to operate the vineyard as Marcela had wanted. I want to see her dream out, to make sure it's realized. I think I can do it. And I'd like you to consider entering into a partnership with me."

I stopped there, knowing it was a lot for Silvia to process. I didn't want to get caught up in the details, in part because the details weren't that important to me, and in part because I hadn't yet really thought them through. But I felt confident it could all be worked out in the future.

The tears continued to flow. "I think that would be great," she said sniffling. "Great for you to do something you enjoy. Great for me to maintain a relationship with you. And more importantly, great for Marcela, to celebrate her by fulfilling her vision."

She reached across the table and took my hands in hers.

"Thank you Jake," she said. "Thank you my son."

The next several months were challenging, but slowly things came together. With Silvia's blessing, her sister was willing to work something out. And two months later, the deal was complete. Mostly via my own savings, and with a little help from Uncle Steve, I was able to secure the money to pay Silvia's sister the amount she and Marcela had agreed upon. Silvia and I became equal partners in the vineyard, with Javier acquiring a smaller share and the role as director of operations. On July 1st, amidst a whirlwind of emotion, I moved into my new home in Tupungato.

By the beginning of August, almost one year to the date of the beginning of my trip to Argentina, everything was a full go. My new interns had arrived weeks earlier, and after two grueling weeks where I logged long hours at the hospital, the orientation process was complete. And so far things were going well. Working out a deal with Juan, I covered the ER on Tuesday and Thursday mornings alongside the interns, giving me the opportunity to both supervise and collaborate. I then took one solo shift per week on either Saturday or Sunday night. And I was available to the interns for emergency back-up during much of the remainder of the week. ER volume continued to trend up, so much so that Juan was in preliminary discussions with the city to obtain funding for a limited ER expansion.

My hours at the school continued to be some of my most satisfying each week. While there were still many difficult moments, where I'd suddenly be overcome by emotion triggered by something a child did or said to remind me of Marcela, most of my time spent with the children was joyful. After a three week winter break where I found myself missing the kids tremendously, school was back in session. Now committed to a career in education, I ordered textbooks on teaching techniques and often spent hours in the evening out on my patio, reading and prepping, determined to honor Marcela by becoming the best teacher I could be.

And things were increasingly busy at the vineyard. My perception of Javier had been accurate, and under his leadership the vineyard was beginning to thrive. The month before we'd produced our first product, a limited quantity of Malbec following a three-month aging process. And with several successful tastings, we were already discussing our first contracts with distributors. With an initial positive response, we were now hoping to plant an additional acre of vines, and were looking to hire our first part-time employee. With Javier in charge of the day-to-day operations, I took it upon myself to provide vineyard tours and organize special events. And with the encouragement of my friends from the tango club, I was organizing our first outdoor milonga. It was scheduled for October 3rd, Marcela's birthday.

The most difficult and debated decision we faced during the first several months of operating the vineyard was what to name it. Somehow, during the many long hours of conversation about the vineyard I'd spent with Marcela, the subject of what she planned to call it had never come up. I initially proposed we name it after Marcela, but it was decided that her name was too common. Different derivations of her name, her last name, and various nicknames were also deemed improper fits. And the more I thought about it, the more I thought she wouldn't have wanted the vineyard named after her anyway. She was far too humble. The more thought I gave it, the more I felt she would have wanted to name it after her grandparents. After all it was her relationship with them that had brought her back to Tupungato and inspired her to take on the vineyard restoration in the first place.

In the end it was Silvia that provided me with the idea for the name. During one of our almost weekly dinners together, a gathering which became an essential part of the healing process for each of us, she incidentally mentioned that Marcela's childhood nickname for her grandfather had been Nonino. This was the diminutive form of nono, the Italian word for grandfather. It also just so happened to be part of the title of Marcela's favorite tango, *Adios Nonino*, Astor Piazzolla's most famous piece that Marcela had requested each time she was in the presence of a bandoneon player. I knew immediately it was the perfect fit. So ultimately, with Silvia and Javier's blessing, I named the vineyard Nonino.

I picked up my work bag and walked out the back door of the hospital. It was September, and it was an unusually cool evening. I opened my car door, started the car, and quickly turned on the heat. I sat back in my seat and sighed. It had been an exhausting day at work, and I was both hungry and exhausted. I thought about stopping somewhere on my way home to get food, but ultimately decided against prolonging my arrival. I turned out of the parking lot and made the fifteen minute drive home.

I parked my car and hurried into the house. I went to my bedroom and changed into my down pajama bottoms and a hooded sweatshirt. I then walked into the kitchen and opened the refrigerator, hoping I might find something I'd forgotten about. But I didn't. I went to the cupboard and pulled out some spaghetti. I started the stovetop, poured myself a glass of wine, and waited for the water to boil. Alone in the quiet house, I fought to keep the tears away.

When the noodles were done, I strained off the water and poured them into a bowl. I added butter, a few cloves of garlic, oregano, and a handful of diced tomatoes. I stirred it gently and then covered the pasta with parmesan cheese. I topped off my glass of wine, put on my hat and jacket, and walked outside. It was a cold night, but I knew I'd feel better sitting out on the patio. I always did. Save a couple of nights where I'd worked late, I'd spent time on the patio every night since I'd moved in two months prior.

I sat on the edge of my chair and inhaled the noodles. After months of blandness, food was beginning to offer flavor again. I sat back in my chair with my glass of wine balancing on my chest. I looked out at the outline of the mountains against the dark sky. I let my line of sight wander up to the stars. It was another spectacular show. I scanned the sky meticulously, finding comfort in the sameness of the stars. And then I closed my eyes and did something I was just starting to do again with more frequency. I smiled.

I opened my eyes slowly and looked back out over the vineyard. The moonlight illuminated the long neat rows of trellises. I placed my wine glass down on the patio tile. I shivered and pulled the blanket up tight against my neck. I thought back on my long and difficult journey. What had started out as an adventure, had ultimately been revealed for what it really was: a self-discovery. And after a year filled with both incomparable joy and tragedy, I'd finally found the answers I'd sought. While I still had many difficult days, and knew there would be more ahead, things were becoming easier. For the first time in my life I knew with certainty that this was where I was supposed to be. And as I allowed my eyes to drift back up to the star filled sky, I felt confident of one other thing. Marcela was looking down on me. And she was smiling too.

End